FIRES

OF

GREENWOOD

A Novel Based on the Tulsa Riot of
1921

FIRES

OF

GREENWOOD

CHRONICLING THE EVENTS THAT LED TO ONE OF THE MOST
HORRENDOUS SLAUGHTERS OF AMERICAN CITIZENS IN
THIS COUNTRY'S TROUBLED RACIAL PAST AND THE DEBATE
BETWEEN BOOKER T. WASHINGTON'S ACCOMMODATIONIST
APPROACH TO SEGREGATION AND DR. W.E.B. DU BOIS'
ADVOCACY FOR A MORE RADICAL PROTEST.

by
Frederick Williams

Prosperity Publications

San Antonio

Texas

PROSPERITY PUBLICATIONS

510 Ramsey Road

Suite #3

San Antonio, Texas 78216

@Copyright January 2014

Prosperity Publications

ISBN: 978-0-9709957-6-6

Cover Art: Dr. Melissa Duvall

Inside text design: Mark Blizard

Printed in the United States of America

This novel is dedicated to
the thousands of Black Americans
who decided on that evening of
May 31, 1921,
in Tulsa, Oklahoma,
that they would be free.

Acknowledgments

Before all others, my deference and respect is to God my eternal father and Jesus Christ my savior. It is because of God's love for those very people who stood up for their rights and liberties in Tulsa, Oklahoma in 1921, that I had the courage to write about this tragedy almost one hundred years later. I must acknowledge the many authors who have investigated and written on the Tulsa Riot of 1921 and whose material was quite useful in my research. I also acknowledge Attorney Cynthia Blanche for reading my manuscript and providing me with very useful comments on how to make this a better story. Former Texas State Assemblyman Lane Denton, also provided me with useful recommendations that helped make for a better finished story. It is with great pride, that I thank my mother, Willa Mae Williams who is ninety-three years old and read the manuscript and provided me with advice and recommendations. I must thank the four individuals who perfected this work into a final product, and that is Dr. Sharon Shelton-Colangelo who did my final edit, Dr. Melissa Duvall who designed my cover and Mark Blizard who did the text design and put the finishing touches on it. I want to thank the partners and owners of Prosperity Publications LLC who deemed my work worthy of publication and therefore met the high standards of quality that they demand in all their publications. My most heartfelt thanks are extended to the Terrie Williams Agency for accepting the challenge to assist me in reaching readers, and share with them the tragedy in Greenwood. Finally, I must thank my wife, Venetta Williams for her patience and tolerance with me during the long days, nights and months it took to complete this work.

Prologue

Vanita, Oklahoma, 1908

———————

Damie Rowland stared at the young boy as he crept along the far side of the small one room grocery store in the front end of her home. The skinny kid with baggy overalls and an oversized shirt, and sleeves that came down over the top of his hands obviously wanted to appear inconspicuous, hoping that she would not pay any attention to him. She knew he planned to work his way to the back of the store, snatch a few pieces of freshly cooked corn bread and then make his way back out into the street.

Often the street children would sneak into the store and try to steal something to eat. She knew most of them, but not this particular boy. He had to be a new arrival among the young orphans who lived on the streets of Vinita, stealing and begging for food. His oversized shirt and baggy pants made it difficult for Damie to guess his age, but he couldn't be any more than six. That meant he'd arrived in the city with some older boys or girls and was sent into the store to steal food for all of them.

Ever since she'd dropped out of school, Damie had worked in Mr. Grimes' small store that specifically sold canned goods, some vegetables, a few chickens and fresh cooked corn bread to the Negro community. Now at twenty, she watched these young thieves come in and out with no money. They would stuff food in their pockets, and she'd snatch them before they got out the door. Because this fellow was new in town evidently he didn't know her reputation for catching thieves.

The young boy finally stopped at the back of the store, reached his hand across the counter to the shelf with the corn bread and grabbed a handful of pieces. He stuffed them in his pocket, turned and ran toward the door.

Damie sprang from behind the counter and placed her body in

front of the door with legs and arms spread eagle.

"Stop," she shouted.

The young boy tried to maneuver around her body. She grabbed him by his arms and lifted him in the air.

"I told you to stop."

"Let me go, leave me alone," the boy shrieked.

Damie took her right hand and dug into the boy's pocket, pulling out three pieces of corn bread. "Why you stealing from me?"

"'Cause we ain't got nothing to eat."

"Who is we?"

"Me and my sisters, now let me go." The boy struggled to break loose from Damie's firm grip on his arm.

"You little thief, I should turn you over to the police," Damie scowled.

"They ain't gonna do nothing to me."

"I ought to whip you myself."

"You do, and my sisters will beat you up."

"Where you from, anyway?" Damie released the boy from her tight grip. He had relaxed and no longer fought her. "How long you been in Vinita?"

"We come down from Norman and been living in the woods 'bout four months, least through the summer."

The boy reminded Damie of her little brother who had died of consumption at about the same age of this child years ago in Tulsa. That was in 1901 during one of the worst winters she had experienced. Back then she was too young to help save her brother, and her momma was helpless too. Damie never knew her daddy. She'd heard rumors that he'd left and gone to Kansas City where he took up with some other woman. It broke her momma's heart when her brother died. She took to the streets drinking, gambling and some said prostituting. That's when Damie left Tulsa and moved to Vinita. Now as she stared into the eyes of this skinny desperate child, he might serve to make up for the failure she felt about not helping her brother.

"What's your name? she asked in a softer tone.

"Why?"

"'Cause I might want to help you."

"What I got to do?"

"Nothing. But first tell me your name."

"They call me Jimmy," the boy said relaxing for the first time. "But I don't like that name."

"Who named you?"

"I don't know. Guess one of my sisters did since I ain't never had no mamma or daddy."

"Why you go around stealing from people?" Damie asked. But she knew the answer. The boy stole because of the hunger pains.

"'Cause I'm hungry and my sisters are hungry too." Jimmy took his right hand and harshly rubbed tears from his eyes.

"How long you been living in the streets?"

"Don't know for sure. I ain't ever lived in no house. Ain't nobody but me and my sisters. Sometimes we make friends with some of the other kids on the street. But you can't trust none of them 'cause they'll steal whatever you got."

"Where are your sisters now?"

"Outside waiting for me to bring them some food." The boy nodded his head in the direction of the door. "You gonna let me go?"

This is not a bad boy, Damie thought. She should give him the corn bread and let him feed his sisters, who were probably very hungry also. But if she did and word spread the store would be overflowing with street beggars. And if Mr. Grimes got wind of what she'd done, he'd fire her.

She could practically hear Mr. Grimes calling out to her to put the corn bread back on the shelf, just as if it had never been touched by this boy's dirty hands and stuffed into his filthy pockets. If she gave the pieces to the young boy, at some point she'd have to account for it missing. Mr. Grimes counted all the items for sale in the store and at the end of the day, there had better be enough money in the drawer to match all the missing items.

But she had to help this boy and his sisters. She felt compelled to do so because he affected her in a way more than the other beggars on the street did. God was providing her with a second chance to help save someone in a way that she failed to do with her brother. She had no choice.

Damie held her arms outstretched and thrust the corn bread into Jimmy's hands. "Take it but don't you dare tell any street people I let you get away with this. Do you hear me?" she asked in a stern tone.

Jimmy gripped the corn bread in his hands and sprang for the door. "Can I go now?" he asked.

"Yes, you can go, but don't you dare tell anyone what happened and don't you ever try stealing from me again. You understand?"

"Yes ma'am. But can I come and visit you, maybe do a little work to pay for this?"

"You can do that and maybe we'll see what I can do for you and your sisters in the meantime."

The boy nodded his head and shot out the door.

ONE

Tulsa, Oklahoma, March 1921

The old man strolled, in his majestic manner, the same five blocks from his home on Cincinnati Avenue up to Archer and then over to Greenwood Avenue to his son's medical office. Captain Townsend Jackson had just turned sixty-seven and was in the twilight years of his life that stretched from his childhood as a young slave on a Georgia plantation. While making his daily walk, he would often think of his many accomplishments over the years as well as the enormous changes he had witnessed and experienced in his beloved country. Coming out of slavery as a free man, he had served as a lawman in Memphis, Tennessee, and Guthrie, Oklahoma, before he finally ended up in Tulsa in 1912 and took up the trade as a barber.

On these evening strolls his mind also reflected back on his wife Sophorina. It just didn't seem that fifty-two years had passed since he married the only woman he'd ever loved. They had their ups and downs trying to survive during the years right after slavery when racism was at its worst. But nothing was quite as bad as when he lost her to the dreaded consumption in 1914. He recalled that depressing trip by train to take her body back to Guthrie to be buried.

Captain Townsend reached the corner of Cincinnati and Archer, and headed up Archer toward Greenwood. Again, his mind drifted back to the morning at the Frisco Railroad Station when his youngest son boarded the train taking him east to Nashville, Tennessee, where he'd been accepted into Meharry Medical School. He was now one of the finest Negro surgeons in the country. In fact, it had been written up in one of those fine white medical magazines that Andrew C. Jackson was one of the very best surgeons of any color in the country. That would make any father awfully proud and also serve as proof that this country isn't what it used to be. Anytime an ex-slave's son can become a surgeon praised by the white doctors, well, that was a sure sign of progress.

On this particular evening, Captain Townsend wouldn't meet his son but instead would attend a meeting at the office of the *Tulsa Star*. The Captain hadn't been invited to attend the meeting because he had a strong difference of opinion with Andrew Smitherman, publisher of the newspaper, and John Stradford, owner of the plush Stradford Hotel located right up the street on Greenwood. It was said that Stradford was the richest Black man in Tulsa. But like Smitherman, he was a radical. The two men didn't feel things in Tulsa were changing fast enough and they were always ready to confront the white folks about any little thing that smacked of racism. They were the new generation of Negroes who always gave Captain the proper respect but he knew they felt his way of thinking had past. The young publisher kept writing editorials in his newspaper about the day of the New Negro. This new breed of Black men were described as more inclined to reject the separation of the races, which led to a subservient place in society for the Negro and forced deference to the white man.

The Captain never felt he was subservient to anyone, only cautious as to how much could be achieved for the race at any one given time. Both Stradford and Smitherman believed equality was achievable overnight. However the old man accepted the undeniable fact that white folks had more men and guns.

Captain Townsend finally reached the corner of Archer and Greenwood and turned up Greenwood passing by the Williams Confectionery and Dreamland Theater, both owned by John and Loula Williams. A crowd lined the street waiting for the movie theater to open its doors.

2

"Captain Townsend, how you doing this evening?" Loula stuck her head outside the door to the theater and greeted the Captain as he walked by.

"Fine, Loula," Captain Townsend answered. "Looks like you going to have a large crowd this evening."

"Yes sir, business been real good here and next door at the confectionery," she said. "You on your way to that big meeting this evening at the Star."

"Sure am, and even though I wasn't officially invited, I'm going anyway."

"Good, John's already there," she said ignoring the last part of his answer. "I understand they're going to discuss bringing some big name Negro leader to Tulsa to talk about race relations."

"That's what I heard and that's why I'm going, even though I wasn't invited."

"That don't matter, Captain Jackson, you know your opinion is always welcome when big decisions got to be made about our community."

"That's exactly why I'm going to be there."

"If you need a hot drink after the meeting come on by the confectionery and the treats on me," she said.

"Thank you, I just might do that."

Loula ducked her head back into the theater, and Captain Townsend continued up Greenwood to the office of the *Tulsa Star*.

The front office of the newspaper was packed with men when the Captain walked through the front door. A well-dressed younger man looked hard at him. "Come on in Captain Jackson," Andrew Smitherman shouted from the front of the office. "The meeting just got started. I'm glad you're here."

The Captain strolled up to the front of the room and found a space next to a man he recognized as a war veteran. Even though he didn't receive an invitation to attend the meeting, he took Smitherman's comments as being genuine. Looking around the room, he noticed that most of the men were from the younger generation, as such they were the group of men determined to change the relationship of the Negro community in North Tulsa, with the whites living downtown and on the south side of the city. That is, with the exception of O.W. Gurley, who stood up front just to the right of Smitherman. Whatever business had transpired, Jackson knew his friend Gurley was not pleased. Over the years, he'd come to know his friend as a man of moderate views when it came to racial issues. Gurley was one of the very few Negroes who'd lived in Tulsa longer than he had. He'd accumulated some wealth and did not want his financial security jeopardized by these

3

hot heads determined to force change. Jackson turned his attention back to the front of the room and Smitherman.

"As I mentioned earlier, I've been in touch with the National Office of the NAACP, as to the availability of Dr. Du Bois visiting our city in April," Smitherman said. "They are very much interested in him coming here with the goal of eventually writing a story in *Crisis* Magazine about our success here in Tulsa."

"My God, that's a great opportunity for our community," John Stradford spoke up from his position to the left of Smitherman. "A story in the *Crisis* would put us on the map. The entire country would know just how successful the Greenwood community has been."

"Not so fast," Gurley said as he stepped forward. "Dr. Du Bois is a wonderful scholar, but I been reading some of his editorials in the *Crisis*. I don't believe his views are compatible with the majority of the Negroes here in Greenwood."

"That's right," a man from the back of the room, shouted.

"Yeah, I heard he's some kind of socialist and don't believe in our capitalist system," another man standing close to the Captain added.

"Hold up brothers," Smitherman held his hand high in the air, signaling for order. It was his meeting and he had a right to do so. "Dr. Du Bois is a well recognized scholar and leader of the Negro race. We should consider it an honor that he wants to visit our city and actually write a story about our many successes."

"Don't get me wrong," Gurley said. "I have the utmost respect for Dr. Du Bois and all his accomplishments, but I just think we got to be awfully careful about who we bring to our city. We got a pretty good working relationship with our white folks here in Tulsa and don't need to do anything to upset them."

"What the hell you talking about, Gurley?" O. B. Mann, the large brown skinned veteran standing next to the Captain, spoke up. "We ain't got no good relationship with no white folks in this city or in the state of Oklahoma.

"You got no complaints coming your way, O.B.," Gurley shot back at the ex-soldier who had fire in his green eyes. "You and

4

your brother's doing pretty well over there on Lansing Street with your grocery store."

"My business don't have nothing to do with the matter at hand here this evening," O.B. scowled. "We don't have no relationship with them folks. They got a relationship with us defined on their terms and to their satisfaction only."

"Let's all calm down," Smitherman intervened. Confrontation between O. B. and Gurley was a common occurrence at these meetings. Smitherman had to make sure it didn't get totally outside his control. "Are you all suggesting some kind of censorship?" Smitherman continued. "I recall a few years ago when Dr. Washington passed through our city before he died, and those of us who didn't agree with his philosophy welcomed him with open arms."

"Booker T. Washington was the greatest leader this race has had since Frederick Douglass," Captain Townsend jumped into the fray. "You certainly aren't comparing a visit from Du Bois to that of Washington?" The Captain had remained quiet as long as he possibly could. But any mention of the late Dr. Washington would generate a response from him.

"I do believe Dr. Du Bois can also be considered one of our great leaders," Stradford said still standing to the left of Smitherman. "Keep in mind he is one of the original founders of the NAACP. I believe we should welcome such a distinguished man to our city just as we did for Dr. Washington."

"He'll come in here, fire up the people and then leave the next day," Gurley said. "What you gonna do then?"

"What you mean what we going to do?" O.B. asked. "We'll take care of business if necessary."   5

Gurley glared at O.B. "Racial tensions been high for the last year when that bunch of ruffians took that Belton boy out the jail and lynched him. And he was white," he bellowed. "Those white folks across the tracks just looking for a reason for another lynching. They eat and sleep lynching. The last one they got was white so you know they just aching to lynch a Negro. Is that going to be one of you in this room 'cause a race radical comes through here and going to fire you up?"

"Hold up Gurley," O. B. stepped forward. "Ain't no lynching going to take place here in Tulsa ever again, I don't care who it is, white, Negro or Indian."

"Boy, you crazy," Gurley's voice rose. "You young boys went over there and killed them Germans, and now you come back here and think you going to kill these white folks. You way out numbered, young fellow."

"Mr. Gurley, it's not about being outnumbered," Smitherman intervened. "It's about pride and dignity. We're no longer feet shuffling, hat tipping, head bowing Negroes to white folks. Those days are over."

"Captain Townsend, what you think about all this?" Gurley asked. Being older and more conservative like him, Gurley figured he had an ally in the Captain.

Captain Townsend stepped forward from his position, turned and faced the group. Years ago he'd spoken to this same group of men, only a much larger gathering at First Baptist Church on the same subject. That particular Sunday he echoed the words and teachings of Dr. Washington. With hard work and dedication to temperance and strong Christian morals, all things were possible in this country for the Negro. That was eight years ago, and they were still having the same discussions. This time the community was much more divided on the proper course of action to be on an equal footing with white folks. And the rhetoric was much more harsh, coming from these young warriors like the Mann boy. Even though he disagreed with Smitherman and his group, he still believed a man of Du Bois's stature and age deserved their respect.

"I don't often agree with Dr. Du Bois because I am a firm believer in the late Dr. Washington's approach to our problems. But I do believe we owe the man the respect to welcome him to our community, whenever he decides to come."

While speaking, the Captain gazed at the men gathered around the room. They all were successful and represented the best the race had to offer, living right there in an area of the city designated by Dr. Washington as the Black Wall Street. They were all businessmen who recognized the importance of maintaining a high level of decorum between the races. Still, they were a part of a struggle being played out all over the country, especially in

6

the South. The Captain knew they were being naïve if they didn't acknowledge whatever happens in the Deep South, places like Mississippi, Alabama and Arkansas, also plays out in Tulsa. The Captain himself had just barely escaped a lynch mob in Memphis back in 1889.

"Then you believe we should move forward with the plan for Dr. Du Bois to visit us real soon?" Smitherman's words brought the Captain out of his musing.

He noticed that Gurley had backed off and remained silent. No doubt because he didn't get the response he expected from the Captain.

"Let me add, however, that I do believe Mr. Gurley has a valid concern. We must be assured that Dr. Du Bois does not stir up trouble while he is here." He felt compelled to throw some support Gurley's way.

"No one wants trouble, Captain," Smitherman said.

"Let's hope not," Captain Townsend retorted and then returned to his place next to O. B.

"All right, then it's agreed," Smitherman said. "I will contact the NAACP and let them know we'd be honored to host a visit from Dr. Du Bois."

"One more important point," Stradford spoke up just as the men turned and started toward the door. They stopped and looked back at him. "It's important that we keep this quiet and only among ourselves until it is confirmed that he'll visit our city."

The men replied in the affirmative and continued out the door.

Captain Townsend watched his friend Gurley hurry out of the building. He could understand that man's cautious nature. He had a great deal to lose if trouble came to Greenwood. The man was heavy laden with rental property all over the north side and owned one of the two Black hotels. But it was just possible that he was too cautious and at some point the Negroes might turn against him and refuse to support his endeavors. Negroes in the Greenwood community did have options, and Gurley needed to keep that in mind.

The old man finally strolled out the front door into the cool spring evening. He needed to get home before his bones got too chilled, and he wouldn't be able to get up in the morning. But first he needed to stop by his son's office and give him the news that Dr. Du Bois might visit the city. No doubt the great scholar would want to meet with Andrew. Dr. Du Bois had been the speaker at Andrew's graduation from Meharry Medical School. They both had something in common. They were part of the Talented Tenth that Dr. Du Bois predicted would lead the race out of darkness of oppression into the light of equality.

TWO

So much anger had built up in O. B. when he left the meeting he felt his body would explode. He ran to the back alley behind Greenwood and quickly mounted his white stallion he'd left there in the care of a young fellow who lived in one of the shanties. He tossed the boy a nickel and took off riding back out to Greenwood and right down the middle of the cobblestone road. The few cars on the street and the many pedestrians had to get out of his way as he steered his stallion north toward Standpipe Hill. What he witnessed back there couldn't be what he put his life on the line for over in France for an entire year. Negroes were still talking like they're afraid of white folks. Gurley was living proof that the old dependent Negro, the ones still holding on to the slave mentality, still existed. No doubt the fight was going to come and the old Negro better get ready for it. They'd better buy more guns and less Bibles. What he'd experienced overseas in the killing fields of Argonne, France, proved that power and force wins out over love and prayer. There was no getting around it, war was coming to America and only the strong would survive. As he pulled up in front of Mann Brothers Grocery on Lansing Road, an unpaved dirt road a couple miles from the hustle of Deep Greenwood, he knew soon men like Gurley would have to get out of the way.

McKinley Mann, O. B's older brother and partner, and four other men who had fought overseas in the 92nd Infantry Regiment waited inside the store for him. They were anxious to know what had been so important to make O. B. leave the store for a meeting at the *Star*. O. B. charged into the store and tossed his pistol down on the counter.

"These Oklahoma Negroes are the scaredest bunch in the entire country," he growled. "You'd think this was 1901 instead of 1921."

"What happened?" McKinley asked.

"You all know something about a Dr. Du Bois who works for the NAACP in New York?" O. B. asked.

"O. B., you don't know who Dr. Du Bois is?" One of the men missing his left leg spoke up.

"I ain't much of an educated man, Peg Leg," O. B. shot back.

"Dr. Du Bois is the new leader of the Negro race ever since Dr. Washington died a few years back," another one of his war buddies spoke up.

"No he ain't," McKinley said. "The new Negro leader is that man from Jamaica, Marcus Garvey. He done got all the Black folks wanting to go back to Africa."

"What? I ain't going back to no Africa," O. B. exhaled. "What does a Negro know about Africa?" He took a seat right next to the cash register.

"I know that's right," Peg Leg Taylor said. "It's hot enough right here in Tulsa. I sure know I can't take the sun in Africa. And anyway, I didn't leave nobody in Africa that I want to look up," he continued.

"What about Du Bois?" McKinley brought the conversation back around to the subject at hand.

"Seems as though Andrew Smitherman and John Stradford want to bring him here to Tulsa. Something about doing a story in the *Crisis* magazine about Black Wall Street."

"A story? What kind of story?" McKinley asked.

"I guess about how successful we've been," O. B. answered.

"Hell no, that's all we need is a bunch of Negroes reading about what we're doing down here and the next thing we know, they'll all be moving here," McKinley scowled.

"What? You trying to keep a good thing to yourself?" Peg Leg Taylor asked.

"That's not it at all," McKinley quickly replied. "We ain't doing as good as a lot of people think we are. We got a four-block area of Greenwood, but right in the back alley you got ten blocks of people living like animals in shanties with no running water and no electricity. Unless they coming in here with some money, we don't need no more people out of the South."

O. B. rose up out of his chair, walked over to an icebox just installed in the store, grabbed a soda and returned to where he was sitting. He snapped the cap and turned the bottle up to his mouth. After gulping down half the contents, he placed the bottle on the counter.

"Looks like Dr. Du Bois coming no matter what we think," he said. "They all agree it'd be a good thing, but then turned around and also agreed not to spread the word about his coming."

"Why's that?" Peg Leg Taylor asked.

"They worried it might upset the white folks across the tracks."

"Hell, they going to be upset no matter what we do," McKinley quipped.

"Talking about upsetting white folks, what we gonna do about Memorial Day this year?" O. B. asked.

"I think we should march," one of the men who hadn't spoken up got into the conversation. "We're veterans just like them and we got a right to march."

"Them white folks ain't never let a Negro veteran march in that parade and they ain't going to start this year," Peg Leg Taylor said.

O. B. lifted the drink to his mouth, finished off the contents and slammed it down on the counter.

"Ain't this about the dumbest thing you ever heard?" he shouted. "We good enough to give our life over in France but ain't good enough to march in the damn parade celebrating that sacrifice. Hell, Black boys died just like white boys did. If I'd known this is how we'd be treated when we came back home, ain't no way I'd have joined the army."

11

"You didn't join O. B. You was drafted," McKinley said.

"Don't matter, ain't no way I'd fought that man's war against people ain't ever done nothing to me if I'd known I couldn't be honored for my service."

"You all going to break the law and go to jail," McKinley said.

"We'll ask them one more time to let us march in the parade, and if they say no, then I'll put my uniform back on and march anyway." A big wide smile spread across O. B's fat round face. He again rose to his feet, stuck his thick chest out and strutted his six foot four frame down the aisle. "Yes sir, this year Negro soldiers going to march just like we did when we marched out this town to training camp in Missouri four years ago."

The other three war veterans got up and joined in behind O. B.

"Then we just marched out that training camp right over to France with the 92nd Infantry Regiment and fought better than any white group over there," the veteran right behind O. B. said.

"We marched and we died," O. B's voice trailed off. "Yes, we marched and we died for all the wrong damn reasons."

"Your generation weren't the only one to fight this white man's wars," Peg Leg Taylor said but remained sitting on a bar stool in front of the counter. "Bunch of us Black boys fought with Roosevelt in Cuba. If you boys gonna march, then I'll be right there with you."

"How many of us veterans you think live in Tulsa?" One of the veterans asked.

"Ain't no telling 'bout that. Probably a whole heap," Peg Leg Taylor answered.

"Think we could get them all together, you know, organize between now and Memorial Day?" The same veteran continued to ask.

"You can get some of them to join in, but if a lot of them know you doing this against the wishes of the folks across the tracks, I don't believe they gonna join," McKinley said. "Lot of 'em work across the tracks and if the white folks they work for know they making trouble, they gonna get fired."

O. B. took his big fist up in the air and then brought it crashing down on the counter. "That's the damn problem. We too damn dependent on these bastards for our livelihood. They use our jobs with them like a gun pointed right at our head. How we ever gonna get ahead if we got to always be depending on them? Might as well be back in slavery."

"It ain't quite that bad," McKinley chimed in. "But the only way it's gonna change is when we get economic independence."

"Like Marcus Garvey talking 'bout doing," Peg Leg Taylor said.

"No, no, I ain't talking 'bout going back to Africa," McKinley shot back. "A few years back that man with some group called African Blood Brotherhood came through here talking 'bout going back to Africa, you remember that man, O. B.?"

"His name was Alfred Sam from up around Muskogee," O. B. replied. "Ain't nobody 'bout to go back to Africa. But ain't nobody 'bout to keep taking this bull shit from no white man. Yeah, we gonna march on Memorial Day right up Main Street and let 'em try and stop us. I'm gonna march and my guns gonna be loaded."

"And so will ours," the other veterans chimed in.

"And so will mine," Peg Leg Taylor said.

"'Bout time we took pride in who we are. Yes sir, 'bout time we be the men we were born to be. Ain't no white man no more man than me," O. B. was practically shouting. "And I'm willing to fight and die to prove that point."

The men held their fists high in the air. "Here's to victory and here's to being a man," they shouted in unison.

***

Gurley sat at the kitchen table of his home located on the top floor of the Gurley Hotel. He stared at the steam coming off the top of the hot coffee Emma had prepared for him when he finally got home from the meeting in Smitherman's office. Images of O. B. on top of his stallion galloping down the middle of the street danced in his mind. That hothead was typical of the new breed of Negro determined to lead the race right down a path of certain destruction. O. B. had no reason to be full of so much rage. He and his brother were doing quite well selling groceries to the Negroes living in Greenwood. The young man was doing so well, he could afford to buy an automobile but instead chose to ride that horse right down the middle of the street and across the tracks into the white part of town to deposit his money in the white bank.

Gurley blew on the top of his coffee to cool it off, then lifted the cup to his mouth and took a sip. The primary question confronting successful businessmen like the group at that meeting earlier was how much sacrifice would be sufficient for a Black man to fulfill his obligation to the race? Gurley looked at the entire racial issue from the standpoint of how he could turn the white man's bigotry to his advantage as a businessman. He had pretty much figured that out when he first moved to Tulsa a month after the discovery of oil at Glenpool. He didn't move there thinking he would directly capitalize on the oil strike. Searching for and benefitting from oil was a white man's game, and the few Negroes who came to Tulsa thinking they could play in that game soon learned differently. Yes, Gurley knew the role Negroes would play, and that was as servants to the white folks. But those same people would not be able to buy from white stores or rent from white rooming houses. That gave him the opening he needed to make his money. He opened the first supply store, and from his profits bought up property and built rental units for the ever-increasing number of Negroes migrating from the South to the city billed as the best place to prosper. As the Negroes continued to come to Tulsa, he continued to build more units and soon after built the hotel.

Gurley took another sip from his coffee and smiled. What he had accomplished over a sixteen-year period wasn't bad for an old country boy who had been born to former slaves on Christmas day three years after the end of the Civil War. At fifty-three, he was on top of the world and wouldn't sit by while all these radicals destroyed that ride.

A knock on the front door brought him out of his musing. He glanced at the wall clock. Ten-thirty and a half hour late, Gurley thought as he got up, strolled over to the door and opened it.

"Sorry I'm a little late. Had a disturbance down on Archer in one of the juke joints," a tall brown skinned man, dressed in a sheriff's uniform, said.

14

Gurley waved the man inside and closed the door. "Come on in the kitchen Deputy," he said to Deputy Sheriff Barney Cleaver. "Like some coffee? Emma just brewed a fresh pot."

Cleaver plopped down in one of the four chairs around the kitchen table. "No sir, I'm off in a couple hours and don't want nothing to keep me awake when I get home."

Gurley took a chair across the table from Cleaver. "They met over at the *Star*," he said. "Decided they're going to sponsor Dr. Du Bois visiting our city either at the end of this month or sometime in April."

Cleaver placed both hands folded on top of the table and leaned forward. "That could be bad news; I hope you know that."

"Certainly I know that. I opposed the visit but was pretty much outnumbered. Smitherman had the place loaded with his people. Only person who came close to agreeing with me was Captain Townsend. But in the end, he sided with them."

"We've been getting more and more reports about Du Bois speaking out against the government. Last week he spoke in Philadelphia and accused the government of failing to live up to its promise to take a more active role for Negro equality."

Gurley took another sip from his cup of coffee. "I don't know what'll happen if he comes in here riling up these hot heads, especially O. B. Mann."

"Sheriff McCullough got his sights set on Mann," Cleaver said. "He knows if trouble going to come out of Greenwood, it's going to start right over there on Lansing Street with the veterans that hang out at his grocery store."

"Can the sheriff get an ordinance barring the man from speaking?" Gurley asked. "We just can't afford for him to come in here and stir up the crowd."

15

"That'd have to come from the police chief and not the sheriff. And I don't think you'd have any trouble getting Gustafson to support that idea. Might as well say he's a member of the Ku Klux Klan here in the city.

"I understand his chief detective is a high ranking member in the Klan," Gurley added.

"Problem is getting the mayor to go along with it," Cleaver said. "They're very reluctant to trample on someone's freedom of speech rights, even our people. They would consider that a little drastic."

"Not as drastic as if we have a race war that we can't win." Gurley walked back over to the stove and poured more coffee into his cup, then returned to his chair at the table. "Don't get me wrong, I respect Dr. Du Bois a great deal with all his education and helping establish the NAACP. I don't believe he'd come here deliberately with the intent to start trouble. It's not him I don't trust, it's the others like that Mann boy."

"How do you think I feel?" Cleaver leaned further across the table. "If there's trouble, I got to be on the side of law and order—"

"Yeah, even when you know the law and order you're enforcing ain't fair to your people." Gurley interrupted Cleaver.

Cleaver picked up on the point he was making. "I don't mind arresting that riffraff back in the alley at the juke joints. They ain't nothing but trouble for everybody. But the worst is when I know the Negro ain't doing nothing wrong, but white folks want him arrested anyway. That bothers me."

Now it was Gurley's turn to lean forward. "How can you do that job?" he asked but didn't wait for an answer. "You know those white folks hired you and stuck you down here for a reason."

"Yeah, I know, to do their dirty work. But I figure it's better if you have a Black man keeping law and order in a Black community. And it does show some progress. In the Deep South, you ain't got no Black policemen at all."

"You getting along with Sheriff McCullough okay?"

16

"He leaves me pretty much alone and lets me handle this area. He's determined there will not be another lynching in Tulsa County. He got elected right after that Belton boy was lynched last summer and pledged right away there would be no lynching on his watch. I believe he's serious about that."

Gurley finally leaned back in his chair. "He needs to know that Negroes are also determined that there'll be no lynching in Tulsa," he said.

"Tomorrow's Thursday, and you know what that means," Cleaver said, changing the subject.

"Yeah, Greenwood Avenue's going to be packed with people. It's maid's night off, and they gonna be strutting their stuff up and down the avenue.

"And the back streets gonna be full of gambling and Negroes drinking that Choc beer and smoking their dope. I'm gonna be awfully busy."

Both men rose from their chairs and walked toward the front door.

"I'm worried about what Jones is going to write in the *Tribune* when he finds out Du Bois is coming to Tulsa," Gurley said. "He'll have editorials denouncing the man right up to the day that he comes."

"He's gonna editorialize about it. But just like Du Bois can speak out, so can Jones write about his speaking out. Guess it's the American way," Cleaver said as he grabbed the door handle and swung the door open. The two men shook hands. Then Cleaver walked out into the hall and started toward the stairwell.

Gurley strolled back into the kitchen and put his cup in the sink. He turned off the kitchen light and walked down the hall to his bedroom. The lamp on the bed stand next to Emma was on. She probably wasn't asleep yet. He sat down on the side of the bed and allowed his head to droop. He often would sit there and think about the events of the day before he finally got undressed and into the bed.

How had he ever gotten himself in this position as mediator between the white power structure and the Negro masses? It was a position he wasn't exactly happy with. Sometimes he felt like he was spying on his people and reporting back to white folks about what they were doing. At that moment he felt that way. But communication was key between the races. Nobody else in the community wanted that role or even knew it existed. Did that make him a traitor? He preferred to view his position as a mediator or better still, the man who would ultimately keep the peace between the races.

Suddenly he felt Emma's hands massaging his back.

17

"I can always tell when you're not happy with the outcome of one those meetings you always going to," she said.

Gurley reached his hand back and rested it on top of hers. "There's trouble coming, Emma. I don't know when, but soon Tulsa will not be safe for the Negro."

Emma brought her body around and sat on the side of the bed next to him. She was a petite woman who seemed to have gotten even smaller with age. In his eyes she was still the most beautiful woman in all of Tulsa, and the entire world for that matter.

"All of a sudden, why are you so worried?" she asked.

"Since Lloyd Jones bought the *Tribune* last year, he hasn't done nothing but editorialize on how evil and wicked Negroes are."

"That'll pass soon as he finds out he can't compete with the *World*. He'll move on to some other town and some other adventure."

"But he'll have done such a job at destroying race relations, I don't know if we'll be able to recover." He turned to directly face his wife. "And then you got those crazy Negroes who are drinking, gambling and killing over on First Street and parts of Archer, feeding his fuel for his fire."

"I don't think the good white people of Tulsa going to pay him no attention."

"What are you talking about? Word is that the Ku Klux Klan done set up operation in Oklahoma City and are reaching their tentacles over here to Tulsa. His paper can become the official mouthpiece for the Klan."

18

"But that won't affect us. White folks don't have no problems with hard working, good Negroes like you and Captain Townsend, and especially Dr. Jackson. Besides, God ain't going to let nothing happen to us." She kissed her husband on the cheek, crawled back on her side of the bed and turned out the light on the nightstand. "Come on to bed. Tomorrow's maid's day off and you going to be awfully busy at the hotel."

THREE

_____

Dick Rowland jumped off the jitney bus at the corner of Third and Main and ran across the street to the shoeshine stand where his friend Robert Fairchild was already shining a white businessman's shoes.

"Boy, you already fifteen minutes late and had two customers angry 'cause you weren't here when they showed up this morning," Robert said as he snapped the shine rag across the shoe of the man who was busy reading the *Tulsa World* while resting in the shine chair.

Dick grabbed his white gabardine apron from across the chair and wrapped it around his body. He set up his brush, shine rag and polishes in an orderly fashion so that when he began moving quickly shining shoes, he could methodically reach to a certain spot and get what he needed. He'd been shining shoes for the past two years after he dropped out of Booker T. Washington High School, and considered himself to be quite proficient.

Robert put the final touches on the shoes, rolled down his customer's pant leg and tapped him lightly on his leg.

"Now sir, if that ain't just the finest shine you going to get here in Tulsa," he said to the man as he climbed down from the chair.

The man looked down at his shoes and smiled. "That's pretty damn good, boy," he said. He went in his pocket and pulled out a dollar bill. "Keep the change. You did a damn good job. My shoes are as shiny black as your face." He laughed and walked away.

"You set yourself up for that, Robert," Dick said as they both watched the man head across the street toward the Drexel Building.

"What do I care about what that son of a bitch says? Just

words coming out his mouth, and they don't hurt me at all." Robert smiled and held the dollar bill high in the air. "Besides, I got a damn big tip. I'll take all their stupid comments as long as they line my pockets with dollar bills." He stuck the money in his pocket, climbed up in the customer chair and reared back. "Why you so late anyway?" he asked.

"Stayed up a little later than I should've last night," Dick said as he looked down the street for a possible customer. The next one was his. But the next customer needed to come on soon because he needed to get over to the Drexel Building and talk to Sarah about tonight.

"Mr. Simons gonna fire your ass you keep getting in here late," Robert admonished.

"I ain't worried 'bout that ofaye. He ain't going to do nothing. Customers like me too much for him to fire me."

"Where you get that word from?"

"What word?"

"Ofaye."

"That's what Black folks call white people up in Harlem, New York."

"How you know that?" Robert adjusted his body in the chair to look more directly at Dick.

"The railroad porter who rents a room from Aunt Damie when he has a layover in Tulsa, told me that's what they call 'em up there in New York."

"Damn, he goes all the way to New York?"

"Hell yes, he goes to Chicago too. Always brings back copies of the *Chicago Defender*. According to that paper, Negroes up in Chicago and in New York is doing all right. They taking care of business and ain't taking no shit from the nobody. They openly date ofaye women up there with no hassle. White folks better not talk about lynching no Black man. They'll get lynched."

"That's where you need to be living much as you like white girls," Robert said chuckling.

"Ain't that I like white girls all that much as they like me.

They can't get enough of this fine chocolate thing I got for 'em."

Robert laughed instead of just chuckling. "That fine chocolate thing going to get you lynched down here with that fine chocolate thing stuffed in your fine chocolate mouth."

"I ain't worried none. They ain't gonna find out. Last thing a white woman want the white man to know is that she been sleeping with one of us. They safe because they gonna make sure they don't get caught." Dick finished just as a man dressed in a business suit got out of a cab and headed toward the stand.

"Welcome, sir," Dick greeted him. "Let me give you one of the best shines at the best shine stand in Tulsa."

Without smiling the man climbed up in the chair, put both shoes on the shoe rest and opened his newspaper. Dick glanced over at Robert, nodded his head and went to work on the man's shoes.

Dick took big stride steps into the Drexel building just down the street from his shoeshine stand. He'd finished the man's shoes and then took off down the street, anxious to take care of his pending business. Once inside the building, he strolled down the corridor toward the elevator located way in the back. He looked over to his left into Renberg's Fashionable Men's Clothing Store. Silk suits, cotton trousers and flashy shirts were showcased in the window. Every time he passed Renberg's, he felt the anger building inside of him. He'd love to be able to go inside and try on one of the suits or a sport jacket. Even try on a hat. But he couldn't because the store had a very large sign right outside the door that read, "WE PREFER WHITE BUSINESS ONLY," which was a polite way to say, "Don't bring your black ass inside this store unless it's to clean it up." 21

Dick reached the elevator just as it arrived back on the first floor and the door swung open. A broad smile crossed his face as he stared right into the brown eyes of an attractive brunette who operated the elevator. He stepped inside.

"Third floor, please," he said.

The young girl didn't look over at him or say anything. She closed the elevator door and pushed the handle to go up, causing the elevator to jerk as it lifted. While the elevator was in motion, Dick quickly moved in close to Sarah and placed his arms around her waist.

She tried to break loose from his embrace. "Stop, boy, what you think you doing, anyway?"

"Hugging my favorite girl, that's all," Dick whispered.

"Not here. You want to get both of us killed?" Sarah adjusted the handle as the elevator reached the third floor.

Dick moved back to his original position as the elevator came to a stop and Sarah opened the door. He sauntered out into the corridor, then turned and glanced back at her.

"I'll walk back down," he said. He again looked down the hall. It was empty, so he moved in close to Sarah and kissed her on the forehead. "See you tonight." He turned and started down the hall to the small cubicle with a toilet, washbasin and a sign that read "FOR COLOREDS ONLY."

Dick finished with his last customer a little past five o'clock, jumped on the five-thirty jitney bus that went north on Main and made a right at Archer Street. After passing Greenwood, he got off in front of Aunt Damie's boarding house. He hopped up the five steps to the porch and then hurried inside. He could hear her in the kitchen cooking. The smell of fried chicken filled the foyer. His room was on the second floor. It was the same room he'd occupied since Aunt Damie bought the place when he was still in junior high school. There were four other bedrooms upstairs that she rented out on a monthly basis. Aunt Damie refused to rent on a daily or weekly basis because she always argued that those rates attracted riff-raff from the joints in the alley, right up the street from her place.

She had two renters, one a man in his late thirties who worked for the Baltimore and Ohio Railroad, and Jake, who was in his forties and did clean up work out at the oil wells. One of the rooms

22

was empty. Dick had the fourth one. The renters paid their rent on time and were pretty quiet most of the time. Every once in a while, Jake would sneak the prostitute Georgia upstairs and into his bedroom. Aunt Damies' bedroom was downstairs at the end of the house away from the front door. She didn't know what was going on, and Dick didn't bother to tell her. But if she knew Jake was carrying on with one of the prostitutes right above her and in her house, she'd probably have a heart attack.

A couple times Dick had snuck Sarah into his room late at night when all the cheap rooms at the overnight motel over on First Street had "no occupancy" signs out front. He definitely couldn't go to her place over on South Boston. It was an all-white neighborhood and didn't rent to Negroes and would never allow a Negro into a room with a white girl. So on occasion they ended up at his place.

Instead of going straight upstairs to his room, Dick strolled into the kitchen and over to where Aunt Damie stood frying chicken.

"I'm home," he said as he kissed her on the cheek. "Sure smells good, Aunt Damie."

"I had to fry an extra chicken 'cause Earl will be in this evening from his Chicago run," she said without looking up. "And you know Jake can eat a whole chicken by himself and that's not even counting what you gonna eat."

Dick reached in his pocket and peeled off a five dollar-bill from a large roll of bills. He stuck it in Aunt Damie's apron pocket. "Got a little something for you," he said. "I had a real good day. Made over ten dollars in tips alone."

"Thank you, son. I never imagined that shining shoes could bring in so much money. You sure the only thing you doing is shining shoes?"

"Yes ma'am, I swear on my Daddy's grave."

"That sure don't mean nothing since you never know'd your daddy and don't even know if he's dead." Aunt Damie paused, turned and looked at the boy she'd brought into her home almost fourteen years ago when he tried to steal corn bread from the grocery store in Vinita. Now he was a tall, muscular, good-looking

23

man loved by the women, especially the prostitutes down on First and Greenwood. She just hated that he'd quit school before he graduated from Booker T. Washington. But he seemed to be doing pretty good shining shoes, and it seemed to be what he liked doing. She'd preferred that he finished school, but realized not everybody was cut out to graduate.

"You need to buy you something new," Dick said. "Something real nice and can't be shared by no one else."

"I'll use it to buy groceries and pay bills."

"I know you will, but just thought I'd try." Dick ambled over next to Aunt Damie and hugged her. "Got to get upstairs and get cleaned up. Thursday night, and everybody going to be out on the street tonight. Can't miss any of the action."

"Please tell me you ain't going to mess around with that white girl tonight," Aunt Damie said before he disappeared out of the room.

"Can't make that promise, Aunt Damie," he called out from the other room. "But if I do, I promise I'll be real careful." He finished and started up the stairs.

Despite Aunt Damie's request that he not see Sarah that night, Dick knew he would. He liked that white girl a whole lot and didn't' care what the rest of Tulsa, black or white, thought or felt about it. She didn't see him as a Negro or shoeshine boy, and worst as a nigger. She saw him as her man, and that's exactly what he planned be later that night after they partied at Pretty Belle's over on First Street and finally made it to Georgia's Rooms For Pleasure.

After he'd showered, put his finest light green suit with a matching tie and shirt, applied a sufficient amount of cologne and climbed into his green alligator shoes, he was ready for a night of acting up. Finally dressed and ready to go, he took one last look at himself in the full-length mirror in his room. He knew he looked good, nothing like that skinny struggling boy who Aunt Damie caught stealing from her. She'd literally saved his life when she took him in and treated him like her son. And he felt she was the mother he never had. He only wished that she could have taken in his sisters also, but knew she just didn't have the room. He lost

24

track of them after they moved up to Tulsa when he was only eight years old. He wasn't sure he'd ever see them again, but when he jettisoned his name, changing it to Dick Rowland, he abandoned that part of his life at a very young age, forever.

Aunt Damie didn't talk to him for over a week when he dropped out of high school, but he had no regrets about that decision. He was making good money, dating a fine white woman, dressing in the best threads and had saved up enough money to buy the diamond ring he had his eyes on over at Anderson's Jewelry Store on Greenwood.

He strolled back over to his bed, lifted the mattress and grabbed a large roll of bills. He peeled off nothing but fives, tens and twenties and stuffed them in his pants pocket. His first stop this evening would be at Anderson's to buy that ring and then over to Pretty Belle's where he'd meet Sarah at nine o'clock.

Dick bounced down the steps two at a time, hurried into the kitchen where Aunt Damie and Jake were sitting at the table eating dinner.

"Your plate's in the oven, still hot," Aunt Damie said.

"How you doing Jake?" Dick said, walked over to the stove and grabbed a chicken leg. "I can't eat a full dinner. I got to be somewhere before eight o'clock." He hurried over to the kitchen table and kissed Aunt Damie on the cheek, then shook hands with Jake. "I'll be in real late this evening. Don't worry about me."
He finished and headed out of the kitchen to the front door onto busy Archer Street on his way to Greenwood Avenue. His new diamond ring, some good Choc beer and dancing, and finally his fine woman were all waiting for him. What a hell of a night it was going to be on Thursday night, maids' night out in North Tulsa. 25

FOUR

"The number one problem here in Tulsa is out of control niggers," Robert Lloyd Jones said to two businessmen from the Kiwanis club, John Sherman and Hank Swanson, who'd gathered in his office at the *Tulsa Tribune*. The members of the Club had made it known their number one concern was to improve on the reputation of Tulsa nationwide. They read Jones' scathing attacks on crime and the loss of moral decency that seemed to have taken over what was once a very clean and decent city.

It was a Friday morning, and Jones had invited the men who he knew shared his concern for law and order, as opposed to the crime coming out of Little Africa in the Greenwood section of the city, to his office.

"Over on First and Archer anything goes," Jones continued as he sat behind his large oak desk in his spacious office that had book cases filled with books on one side of the room and pictures with important people he'd met over the years on the other side. A big picture window looking down on Archer Street was right behind. "They got drugs, alcohol, this new music called jazz, and you even got nigger men dating white women. This cannot continue to go on in our city. We are recognized as one of the best and most progressive cities in the country. But we also have this cesspool filled with a bunch of savages, jeopardizing our good standing."

"This is not only a problem here in Tulsa, but throughout the South and for that matter in the northern cities, also," Sherman, the President of the local Kiwanis, spoke up. "But our national organization is behind the move to clean up the filth that is polluting our country, and we plan to do our part right here in Tulsa."

"I'm very much aware of the Kiwanis commitment," Jones said. "But we need our city officials on board also."

"I do believe Mayor Evans is on board," Sherman said. "Our problem is with Police Chief Gustafson and all the corruption in the police department. How can he ever be of any help if all his men are on the make for a payoff?"

"You're right, and he's got his hand in everybody's pockets over there," Jones said. He had a strong dislike for the Police Chief and laid a lot of the blame for the city's crime right on his shoulders.

"It really is a shame that all that good property in North Tulsa is being wasted on niggers," Swanson finally spoke up, changing the tone of the conversation. Swanson had made a fortune selling land to outsiders moving to Tulsa to make their fortune. He resented Gurley's success on the north side and believed that Negroes should not profit from the oil business but remain only as servants and workers, not businessmen. He saw great potential for him and the Kiwanis Club siding with Jones to clean up niggertown. To him, cleaning it up meant running the niggers out and taking their land. That was a lucrative business in other southern states like Mississippi and Alabama and could pay off for him in Tulsa. "I believe we all could make a lot of money if we could turn niggertown into a boom town."

"I believe most of the citizens of this city agree that niggers should not even exist in this country. They definitely should not be allowed to own property," Jones said.

"The only good nigger is a dead one," Sherman added to the conversation.

28   "He may not have to be dead, but he damn sure shouldn't occupy some of prime land," Swanson said.

"Question is what do we do about it?" Jones asked.

"We take back our land," Swanson scowled. "We take our land back, and we make sure something like this never happens again. Have you been over there and seen what they've done?"

Jones strolled from behind his desk and over to the large window that looked down on Deep Greenwood. "I don't have to go over there. I can see it from this office window. They've built up Greenwood, and some of them have done quite well. Hell, they even got two first class hotels over there."

"O. W. Gurley and John Stradford both need to be run out of Oklahoma," Swanson's voice rose slightly. "How in the hell two niggers going to have two hotels within a block of each other, and both doing a lucrative business?"

Jones spoke up. "There are going to be some changes made here in Tulsa from top on down to Little Africa." He walked back over and stood by the side of his desk. "This is a good beginning, and I'm going to begin a series of editorials addressing these problems. In the meantime, I have to address the Tulsa Men's Club as their luncheon speaker today."

"Yeah, we know. We'll both be there." Swanson said as the two men got up and followed Jones to the door. He opened it to let them out. "Keep up the good work and you have the Kiwanis support to help clean up the city." The men shook hands, and Jones closed the door and returned to his desk with a very large smile across his face. Soon he would replace the *Tulsa World* as the leading newspaper in the city, and that was his goal.

With five reporters, a linotype operator and a great distribution arrangement with a local trucking organization, Jones figured he was doing pretty well considering he had set up the *Tulsa Tribune* less than two years ago. Again, he sauntered over to the large window and looked down. His office building was located on the south side of Archer Street near the Frisco Railroad tracks and the train depot. From where he stood, he had a great view of Greenwood where all the prosperous Negro businesses were located. He was so close he could read the marquee on the Dreamland Theater. John and Loula Williams were a couple of smart Negroes who had built up a small empire with the theater, confectionery and the automobile repair shop around the corner on Archer.

29

There were a number of other successful business on that side of town, but for the most part, everything around Archer and First was a cesspool. Jones had stayed up in his office many a late night and watched the activities up and down the street. On any given night, it was like a jungle down there with the natives running wild. The white citizens resented their presence; they resented the successful ones because they had more wealth and material possessions than the majority of whites, and they resented the uncouth majority because they were like a blemish on the city's good reputation.

He smiled as he returned to his desk, sat down and reared back in his chair. Those lost souls down there in Greenwood were the answer to his problem. In order to make the *Tulsa Tribune* the number newspaper in the city he had to make the niggers the primary concern. *The World* was still number one because it was a morning publication and been around since the turn of the century, and enjoying a stranglehold on the advertisers. His only hope was to create an interest in an afternoon paper. To do that, he needed stories that would capture the attention of the readers. Those stories could focus on the problem with the niggers in Greenwood, be it the successful ones or the wild ones. And sometimes he could possibly help to create the story. Exaggeration and sensationalism were key components to capture a reading audience.

Jones glanced at his watch. It was eleven o'clock, and the luncheon was set for noon. He had to stop by the bootblack stand across from Hotel Tulsa and get a shine. Hopefully, no one would be in his boy's chair when he got over there. It was important that he get a shine before addressing the Tulsa Men's Group. Shoes reflect the personality of the man. Unshined shoes meant a sloppy demeanor, and shined shoes spoke highly of the individual's character, and character as well as image meant everything to him.

After packing his speech into his briefcase and checking on the progress of that afternoon's edition of the *Tribune,* Jones walked the four blocks over to Third and Main.

It was a cold and windy day, but cold never bothered him. He just threw his overcoat over his shoulder and walked briskly up Main Street. Jones had been raised in the state of Minnesota and had worked in Madison, Wisconsin, as editor of a local newspaper for years. While his friends always complained about the cold, he welcomed it because the chill invigorated him and that's how he felt as he approached the bootblack stand on his way to the Hotel Tulsa. His boy's shine chair was empty, and that worked to his benefit. He could get in and out in only a few minutes.

"Hey, boy, I need a shine, and I need you to make it fast," he snarled at Dick as he climbed into the chair.

"Yes sir, no problem, Mr. Jones," Dick said with a smile. "I'll get you out of here in less than ten minutes." He grabbed the polish, brush and shine rag and applied the polish to both shoes. "You must have a busy afternoon sir; you ain't got no newspaper or nothing to read."

"I have to give an important speech this afternoon, and you know I have to look good, and especially the shoes."

"I can understand that, sir. Can't make no good speech without good looking shoes." Dick brushed the polish in and then grabbed the rag and began the shine, popping the rag every other time for emphasis.

"Boy, you sure know how to make that rag pop, don't you?" Jones said as he watched every move Dick made.

"Yes, sir. Learned it real well, sir."

While watching Dick make his moves with the shine rag and brush, Jones couldn't help notice the sparkle from the ring on the boy's right finger. It couldn't possibly be a diamond. There was no way a bootblack could make enough money to buy a diamond ring.

"That's a hell of a ring you got on your finger, boy," Jones said with some sarcasm. "Can't possibly be a real diamond."

"Oh, no sir. Ain't no way no poor bootblack could ever afford a real diamond. Don't make enough money for nothin' like that."

"I didn't think so, but you sure could've fooled me with the way it's glistening."

Dick popped the shine rag for a final time across the right shoe and then pulled Jones's pant leg down. "There you go, sir, all first class and top of the line shine," he said smiling. 31

Jones climbed down from the chair, pulled out a couple dollar bills and handed them to Dick. "Good job, boy," he said.

"My pleasure, sir, anytime," Dick tucked the bills into his pocket.

Jones started down the street to the Hotel Tulsa. He turned and looked back at Dick who was laughing and talking to the other

Black boy who also shined shoes. There was something about that boy's attitude he didn't like when he asked him about the ring. Almost like he was mocking him. If that damn ring was a real diamond, the fool had better stop wearing it during working hours. Ain't no way white men were going to tolerate having a nigger shine his shoes with a diamond ring on his black ass finger. If he had it on next time he got a shine, he was sure going to tell him that.

FIVE

Smitherman smiled as he read the teletypewriter inside the *Tulsa Star* office. "Dr. W.E.B. Du Bois, editor of the *Crisis* magazine at the NAACP will arrive in Tulsa, Oklahoma, on the Baltimore and Ohio Railroad train on April 20 at 12:00 p.m. for one-day stay and then will continue on to Dallas, Texas. According to the agenda agreed upon with the *Tulsa Star*, he will deliver a speech on April 20 at the Dreamland Theater. He will leave the next morning."

It was settled. The greatest Negro leader of the day would visit Tulsa in just a few weeks. And just as important, he would probably write an article for publication in the *Crisis* about his visit to Tulsa, featuring many of the progressive businesses. His visit would definitely create a stir in both the white and Black community. Smitherman needed to share this good news with Stradford.

He grabbed his coat and practically ran out of his office. Stradford was somewhat like a hero to him. The man feared nothing and no one, especially not white folks. As Smitherman exited his building, located right across the street from the Stradford Hotel, he recalled the hot summer day in 1920 when that bulldog of a man beat a white man right in front of the Dreamland Theater. Stradford had been standing near the curb to the street when a white man riding in an ice wagon made a remark that he considered offensive. Stradford pulled the man down from the wagon and pounded him until he fell to the ground. He then began kicking him until John Williams ran out of the Dreamland Theater and pulled him off the man. The white fellow ran off pledging there would be a lynching that night in Tulsa. Williams volunteered to drive Stradford to Muskogee until this all passed over. But Stradford, a stubborn man, refused to go. Nothing happened that night, and his friend dodged a bullet. In fact, all Greenwood dodged a bullet because there was no way Black Tulsans would allow a white mob to invade their community and take one of their most outstanding citizens away to be lynched.

No one saw that man on the ice truck after that. After beating him so badly, Stradford became a hero in the community. The folks respected him because of his dogged defense of his integrity as a Black man and also because he was the richest Negro in the city.

Stradford was ten years Smitherman's senior, having been born in Versailles, Kentucky, in 1861. His daddy escaped slavery with help from conductors of the Underground Railroad, just before the war. The man made it to Canada. Evidently, Stradford was just like his father and refused to be subservient to any other man. That deliveryman learned that the hard way.

Smitherman strode through the front entrance into the Stradford Hotel. He spotted his friend standing at the registration counter, talking with a man who undoubtedly was a guest at the hotel. He didn't want to be rude and interrupt their conversation, but the news was too important to wait. Just as he approached, the two men shook hands, and the guest walked past him on his way out of the hotel. Smitherman felt relieved.

"We got him," Smitherman said as he stopped right in front of his friend. "I just got confirmation that Dr. Du Bois will arrive on April 20 and leave the next morning."

"Confirmation," Stradford repeated in his deep bulldog voice. "That's great news, and my hat's off to you." He patted Smitherman on his shoulder. "Are you up for a cup of coffee?"

"Sounds good to me."

Stradford stopped one of the maids. "Bring us some coffee to my office," he said. "You want cream and sugar?" he asked Smitherman.

"A dash of sugar, no cream."

"I'll bring it right away," the maid said.

"Come on man, let's talk," Stradford said, turned and strolled toward his office. Smitherman followed close behind.

The two men sat in leather high back chairs in front of Stradford's large oak desk.

"No doubt he'll stay here," Smitherman said.

"Let's think about that for a minute." Stradford adjusted his body in the chair and crossed his legs. "We need O. W. aboard on this visit. He wasn't too happy the other night with our decision to bring Dr. Du Bois here."

"O. W's never happy with anything that might cause some kind of controversy with the white power structure in this city."

"We still need him on our side. We don't want to show any signs of dissension among our ranks to the white folks when they find about this. If they can crack our solidarity, they will use that to disrupt Dr. Du Bois's visit. And most important, he must leave here with the very distinct impression that we are a community in one accord about our future in Tulsa."

"What's that got to do with where he stays?"

Stradford hesitated in answering the question as the maid carried the tray with two cups of coffee into the office.

"This cup is for you, sir," the maid said and handed Stradford the cup.

Smitherman took his off the tray. "Thank you," he said. The maid turned and hurried out of the office.

"What that has to do with where he stays is that we can make O. W. feel good if we ask him to allow our guest to stay at his hotel during this visit."

"What?" Smitherman bellowed. "Yours is one of the finest hotels in Tulsa, and the biggest owned by a Negro in the United States, according to that story in the *Chicago Defender* last year."

35

"That's kind of you to say, but believe me this has nothing to do with the biggest and the best. It simply has to do with appeasing a man who we need as an ally and not an enemy."

"What makes you think O. W. will want him to stay there? Especially if his visit is going to anger the white folks?"

"His ego, my friend." Stradford took a sip from his cup. "What is happening here in Greenwood has been my dream for over twenty years," he continued. "I came here back in 1899, and I think O. W. got here around 1904 or 1905 right after oil was found at Glenpool. The two of us, along with Captain Townsend, set our sights on building a Black community that we all could be proud of. We now have that community. But of the three of us, O. W. allowed it all to go to his head. For some reason, he viewed me as his competition, especially after I built this hotel to be bigger and better than his, just to teach him a lesson."

"You did it for that reason?" Smitherman interrupted.

"No, not really. But the thought did cross my mind during construction. But my point is that O. W. would never turn down the opportunity to have the greatest leader of the Negro race stay at his hotel. But in order to have that honor, he knows he has to go along and agree to the visit."

"I don't like it, but if you think that's best, it's fine with me."

"Believe me, it's best, and I think you should make the offer. He knows how close we are, and it will give him a great deal of satisfaction that you picked his hotel over mine."

"You're a little devious." Smitherman smiled.

"In a good way." Stradford also smiled. "We need to now consider who should have a special meeting at dinner time with Dr. Du Bois."

"We also need to consider security. Nothing could be worst than if harm came to him in our city."

"O. B. Mann and his war friends are perfect for that job if we need them."

"Do you think he'll do it?"

"No doubt. If it's something that's going to rattle the white folks, he'll be all for it." Stradford finished off the remainder of his coffee in his cup. "When do you plan to let the city know?" he asked.

"Right away, in fact soon as I talk with O. W., I'll write an article for this Friday's paper. I still have time."

"Thought you wanted to keep it quiet."

"That's before we knew he'd accept. Now that we're going

36

to have the honor of a visit from him, I want the entire state to know."

"Remember now, that includes Jones over at the *Tribune*."

"There's nothing he can do but rail against his visit in his usual racist acrimonious way." Smitherman finished off his coffee and stood up. "I need to get across the street and see if we can tie up that loose end with O. W."

Stradford also got up. "He'll be on board," he said. "He may not like it but he'll be with us."

"Looks like we're about to put the Greenwood community of North Tulsa on the map." Smitherman smiled.

"It looks that way. Let's make sure it's a positive experience for all of us."

The two strolled back out to the lobby. A number of visitors to the city stood in line at the registration desk, waiting to check in.

"Let me get over here and greet the visitors to our city," Stradford said as he patted Smitherman on his back.

"If we get the kind of publicity we think is possible, that registration desk will soon be overflowing with visitors to our city." Smitherman finished, then turned and headed toward the front door.

***

"Niggers with a lot of ambition are dangerous to the future growth and stability of our city," Jones said as he stood and spoke before a full house of businessmen who had just finished lunch and were listening to their guest speaker for the day. He had been invited to speak on his efforts to make Abraham Lincoln's birthplace in Kentucky a national monument. Once he finished his formal speech, he soon discovered that the crowd was not interested in Lincoln, but in their growing concerns with North Tulsa. "Soon they'll be fighting to overthrow segregation of the races, and we do know that their ultimate goal is assimilation and marriage with our most precious commodity, our women." He finished his comment, and a number of hands shot into the air. He pointed to a tall well-dressed man with sun-scorched skin. "Yes, sir, you have a question?"

"I understand Congress is going to introduce another bill to move lynching from a state matter to the federal level. You think they have a chance of getting that done?"

"Over the dead bodies of the entire Democratic Caucus from the South and just as many Republicans from the North," Jones answered. He loved it when the locals asked his opinion about national political issues. It meant they were depending on him for guidance, and that's what he was striving to accomplish. And it meant more of the local people would buy and read the *Tribune*. "Even if through some miracle, such a bill passed through Congress, President Harding would veto it. He is a solid defender of states' rights. He is rock solid on our side when it comes to the question of the Negro."

Another businessman waved his hand vigorously. Jones pointed to him.

"I heard that he also recently took the blood oath to be a member of the Ku Klux Klan"

"And if it's good enough for the President of the United States, then it's good enough for every decent, law abiding white man to join and support the organization's effort to keep this country white," Jones said.

Another man sitting right up front shouted, "Why the hell haven't we run those damn niggers out of town, yet?"

"When they eventually make that one final error of defiance, then the entire population of white men in this city will load their rifles with plenty of ammunition and run every last one out of town," Jones said, raising his voice for emphasis.

"Hold up now Mr. Jones. We can't run all of them out of town 'cause my wife would be totally lost without Edna, our maid," another business man immaculately dressed shouted from the back of the room.

"In that case, we'll have to make some concessions. The good niggers working in white folks homes can stay," Jones replied.

"That's a very good point," a man Jones knew had very close ties to the Klan rose in his seat and turned to face the men. "When we finally begin to cleanse our culture of these diseased people, we must make sure that we separate the good ones from the bad ones. We must identify those that we know would prefer to still be our servants from those who preach equality. Have you ever heard of such a thing, a coon being equal to a white? Not in this lifetime will that happen." The man finished and sat down.

"But I believe our niggers are essentially happy for the most part. It's only when outside agitators come to town that trouble starts," Jones said, continuing to lead the discussion. "When those uppity folks from up in New York and Chicago poison the minds of our good people, then trouble starts."

"Is there anything we can do to ban those trouble makers from our city?" A man sitting up front spoke up.

" No, afraid we can't," Jones replied. "That's a constitutional right guaranteed under the First Amendment to all American citizens."

"They're not American citizens. Their descendants of slaves who were not given any rights 'cause they were our property," the same man shouted. "Now you mean to tell us that they got the same rights as a white man?"

"I'm afraid so, my friend." Jones embraced the acrimony flowing freely throughout the room. The more he could convince these men that something needed to be done with the savages populating a segment of their city, the more papers he could sell. "But as white men join together, follow good leadership, then eventually we can turn this situation around. If we can't figure a way to get them out of town, then we must use tactics to make sure they stay in their place. They must be made to acknowledge their natural inferiority as human beings to the white race. That's what our great founding fathers believed. It was true then, and it's still true today."

39

"We have to continue meeting like this and show unity of cause," an additional man also immaculately dressed spoke up. "We need your leadership, Mr. Jones. You are more worldly than the rest of us."

"Yeah, that's what we need is wise leadership from Mr. Jones," another man spoke up, and in unison they all agreed.

"So it's settled," the businessman who organized the luncheon took control. "Through your newspaper, we will follow your advice on the Negro issue. Our luncheon and discussion is now over, and we will let our guest go. But we'll all be following your advice through your editorials and stories in the *Tulsa Tribune.*"

"I want to thank you all for your confidence in my leadership. I can assure you that I will not let you down." Jones folded up his notes and prepared to leave. "Before this crusade is over we will have the entire city of Tulsa supporting our cause." He finished, shook hands with the men in the room and left again with a broad smile across his face.

SIX

Smitherman sat at a table by the window in the Little Bell Café, looking out onto Greenwood Avenue. He planned to order Little's famous smothered chicken with rice and gravy for lunch. That was a luncheon delight, and even the whites put aside their animosity toward Negroes in order to eat at Little's.

After leaving Stradford, he'd rushed across the street to Gurley Hotel in an attempt to talk with O.W. about Dr. Du Bois staying there. After waiting for a half hour, Gurley agreed to meet with him for lunch at the café. That bothered him. He didn't like the idea of appeasing this man in order to get his support for Du Bois' visit. But he respected Stradford a great deal and because he thought this was the best approach, Smitherman agreed to the plan. With Gurley's support, chances are white folks might be willing to back off.

Smitherman always wondered about Negroes like Gurley. The man simply couldn't believe that white folks liked him any more than all the other Negroes in Tulsa. He misinterpreted being used for being liked. As far as Smitherman was concerned, white folks weren't capable of having real and sincere feelings about Negroes. Even though he had some influence with them as their pawn, they really did place Gurley in the same category of the poor Negroes living in the shanties in the alley behind Greenwood. As Smitherman watched the man walk into the restaurant and head toward the table, he had to conjure up all the restraint he had not to just tell him what he really thought about him.

"Have you ordered yet?" Gurley asked as he took off his overcoat, sat down and vigorously rubbed his hands.

"No." Smitherman sat up in his chair. "Thought I'd wait for you."

"Sorry I'm a little late and I couldn't meet with you earlier this morning, but I had an entire church congregation here from Norman, checking in. They're the special guests of First Baptist."

"That so?" Smitherman signaled the waitress over to their table. "You getting the special today?"

"No doubt. Don't think I've ever had as good a lunch as this restaurant serves."

"May I take your order?" the waitress asked.

"Yes, we'll both take the smothered chicken," Smitherman answered.

"And a couple Pepsi Colas," Gurley added. "And please rush it through. I'm already late for another meeting."

"Yes, sir." The young waitress turned and walked toward the kitchen.

"What is it you want me to do?" Gurley asked once the girl was out of range.

With Gurley being so blunt and right to the point, this shouldn't take long, Smitherman thought. "Wanted to let you know that Dr. Du Bois has accepted our invitation to visit our city. He'll be here in April."

"Do you think that is a wise decision? One thing these white folks hate is when Northern Negroes come down here and criticize their way of life."

"He's not coming to criticize but to study our success as a community of which you are an important part." Smiitherman had to compliment him. He noticed a slight smile on Gurley's face and felt encouraged. "We felt that the Gurley Hotel would be the best place for him to stay during his visit."

"Who are we?" The smile suddenly disappeared from Gurley's face.

"You know, our committee." Smitherman stumbled with his response.

"Stradford, that ole sly dog of a man," Gurley said and again smiled. "For the past twenty years he ain't found any better pleasure than to try to figure me out."

Smitherman was relieved to see him smile again. "It was more my idea than his," he said.

"Yeah, I bet it was. You and I both know that his hotel is one of the finest and biggest of any owned by a Negro in this country. Makes sense to put a man of Dr. Du Bois's stature up in the very best. So the only reason you're making this offer to me is because you want my support for this visit. Am I right?"

Smitherman remained silent choosing not to answer. He knew his silence would be his confirmation.

"I'm right." Gurley leaned forward with his arms resting on the table. "I have nothing but the utmost respect for Dr. Du Bois, but I still believe it is a mistake bringing him to Tulsa. I'm sure he doesn't mean to do it, but he stirs up Negroes when he speaks to them about their rights under the constitution and about equality."

"What's wrong with talking about equality?" Smitherman asked as he also leaned forward.

"Negroes don't need equality; they need jobs. And most of them wouldn't know what to do if they were treated equal to the white man. First thing they would do is to abuse it."

Smitherman found it difficult to just sit there and say nothing. How could this man who'd made so much money off the backs of his own people say such terrible things about them?

"Don't misunderstand what I'm saying," Gurley continued. "We're just a little over half a century out of slavery. I was born three years after slavery ended. What my mamma and daddy needed most was money and land and a means to survive. They were content with their freedom, but they weren't content with practically starving to death. So, yes, they would've given up equality for economic survival."

43

This was a discussion Smitherman didn't need to have with Gurley, although he adamantly disagreed with him. How was it possible to have economic security without equality?

"When I was a young man," Gurley continued. "We all followed the lead of Dr. Washington, and his concern was not social and political equality, but financial stability for the Negro race." Gurley paused while the young waitress placed their plates on the table in front of them.

Smitherman tossed a fork full of smothered chicken and rice into his mouth as Gurley continued.

"Dr. Du Bois was one of Dr. Washington's staunchest critics, claiming that his approach would keep Black people in the dark for another hundred years. Well, I don't believe that's the case at all. I believe we've made great progress as a race." He stopped long enough to take in a fork full of food.

That gave Smitherman the opportunity to speak in defense of Du Bois. "I believe a more accurate description of Dr. Du Bois's position is that we needed to also fight for equality along with economic security."

"Being from up North in liberal New York, it was easy for him to make that argument. There are very few repercussions for speaking out about equality up there. In the South, and for the most part right here in Tulsa, if a Black man talks like that, all his sources for an income would dry up. What's the average Negro suppose to do, speak up for equality or feed his family?"

"We seem to do both pretty well here in Greenwood," Smitherman retorted.

"We do well because of white people's oil money," Gurley shot back at him. "We've done pretty good in building up a strong business community, but remember we make our money by providing services our people can't get from the white community. And the money our people make in order to sustain our businesses comes from working across the tracks as maids, chauffeurs and all kinds of servant jobs to white folks. So no way are we an independent community, free from the white man's influence." He paused to take another fork full of chicken and rice. "I will support your decision to bring Dr. Du Bois to town and will gladly house him in the Gurley Hotel," he continued with a mouth full of food. "But once it's all said and done, and he's gone back to New York, I will pray that our community is not harmed by his visit."

"We appreciate your support." Smitherman needed say no more. He had accomplished his mission. The two men sat quietly eating one of the most delicious lunches served anywhere in Tulsa.

44

***

Captain Townsend hurried over to his son's house on Detroit Avenue. It was Wednesday, and that was the day he always had dinner with Dr. Jackson and his wife, Julia. They had made that a practice ever since Sophorina died over seven years ago. Often the Captain's daughter, Minnie Mae and oldest son Townsend Jr., along with their families, would join them. Lately, Townsend Jr. was spending a lot of time up in Chicago. He felt more comfortable out of what he considered the strangulation of racial bigotry in Oklahoma.

This evening the Captain figured if any other family members would be there, it would be Minnie Mae and her lawyer husband, H. A. Guess. Of course Julia would be there, fixing one of her special meals for him. A man couldn't ask for a more beautiful daughter-in-law than Julia. He was especially happy this evening because earlier in the day, Smitherman had stopped by his barbershop in the basement of his home and informed him that Dr. Du Bois would visit their city next month. No doubt their guest would want to meet with Andrew since he spoke at his son's graduation from Meharry Medical School.

Whenever Captain Townsend made that walk down Detroit Avenue, he was amazed at the large, beautiful homes the prosperous Negroes owned on that street. All-brick two-story homes lined the street for one long block. His son's house was located between Smitherman's and the popular principal at Booker T. Washington High School, Z. W. Woods. Detroit Avenue was the racial divide with the west side of the street occupied by prominent whites. Naturally, Captain Townsend was proud of all his children, but he was especially proud of Andrew, who had been recognized by the distinguished Mayo Brothers of Cleveland, Ohio, as the most outstanding Negro surgeon in the entire country. His son dispelled the myth of Negro inferiority. Dr. Jackson and eight other physicians as well as all the educators and businessmen residing in the Greenwood area represented that Talented Tenth of the Negro population, designated by Dr. Du Bois as the leaders who would pave the way for racial equality. As that number continued to increase over the years, the white race would have no other

45

option but to recognize that the Negro race was indeed equal to all other races.

The Captain climbed the five steps to the verandah and opened the front door to his son's home. He removed his coat and placed it on the large coat rack by the door in the foyer.

"It's me. I'm here," he called out and strolled into the parlor to the left of the foyer. The kitchen was all the way in the back, and they probably didn't hear him come in. He continued through the dining room and a small nook, and opened the kitchen door.

Julia immediately looked up. "Poppa, I didn't hear you come in," she said. "I was just about to put the corn bread in the oven." She stopped, walked over to the old man and hugged him. "Andrew is upstairs."

"I'll go up there and get him," Captain said. "Probably in his study."

"You know that." Julia returned to mixing the ingredients for her corn bread. "We got baked chicken, sweet potatoes, greens and corn this evening."

"Young lady, you're determined to put weight on my already overweight body," Captain said as he walked through the kitchen to the door that lead up the stairs.

"Wait until you get a piece of rhubarb pie," Julia replied.

"Can't wait." Captain started up the stairs to the second floor. It was a narrow stairwell, and at his age, he held onto the banister.

"Hey young fellow, you up here," he called out as he reached the top of the stairs and lumbered down the hallway past the master bedroom and the four guest rooms.

"I'm in here, Father," Dr. Jackson replied. "Come on in. I'm just closing out my report on today's surgeries at the hospital."

Captain took a seat in a chair next to Dr. Jackson's desk where he sat in a large leather high back swivel chair. His oak desk was covered with medical books and financial papers. He put his pen down and looked directly at his father.

"You forgot tonight was my night to get a free meal off my son?" Townsend asked with a smile.

"Not at all," Dr. Jackson said. "I was trying to get these reports finished before you got here. It was an extremely busy day at the hospital. An unusual number of consumption cases, and most of the patients are from the back alley shanties."

"I'm surprised that more people from those disease-infested shacks don't get the consumption. How they can live like that is beyond my understanding."

"Not everyone is blessed like we are," Dr. Jackson said as he folded the worksheet and placed it in the far right side corner of the desk.

"If they'd stop doing all them illicit drugs and liquor they might be able to find a job."

"If everyone of those folks living in the back alleys of Greenwood stopped what they're doing and tried to find a job, there wouldn't be enough for them. White folks going to make sure of that."

The Captain adjusted his body in the chair. Sometimes his son irritated him because the boy always found excuses for people who didn't seem to have enough sense to help themselves. When things went wrong down there, they always blamed the white man. Hell, whites couldn't be the reason for all their misery.

"At least they can try to better themselves," Captain said.

"When segregation ends, and all jobs throughout the city are open to everybody, then you might see some changes."

Captain leaned forward. "Ain't worth arguing with you about."

"We weren't arguing Father, just a friendly discussion."

"Anyway, Smitherman came by late this afternoon to tell me that Dr. Du Bois has agreed to visit Greenwood in April."

"Amazing, that's outstanding. Finally our small community is going to get the recognition it deserves."

"And you, son, are going to get the recognition you deserve as one of the finest surgeons in the country."

"I don't quite see how his visit is going to affect me one way or another."

47

"Because he's going to be so impressed with our community that he'll probably write a story for the *Crisis* about us. And of all the success stories, yours is the best of them all."

"I think it's more appropriate for him to interview Dr. Bridgewater since he was the first Negro physician in the city and does run Frissel Hospital."

"But, my dear boy, Dr. Bridgewater does not have as good a reputation as an outstanding surgeon as you do."

"Thanks for the vote of confidence, but I do believe that you are a little prejudiced on this particular subject. However, I'll be more than happy to meet and talk with such an outstanding scholar."

"Andrew, you need to come downstairs right now," Julia called from the foot of the stairs. "Hurry please."

For a moment, the Captain and his son stared at each other and then Dr. Jackson jumped to his feet, rushed out of the room and down the stairs. Captain was right behind him.

Halfway down the stairs, Captain saw a white man standing at the front door. Dr. Jackson stood right in front of him. What possibly could his son have done to bring a white man to his house? As he reached the last stair, it became clear to him that the man knew his son, and the conversation appeared tense but not confrontational.

"Dr. Jackson, please you got to help us 'cause we don't know what to do," the man said in a pleading voice.

Captain Townsend reached the bottom of the stairs and stood next to Julia as they both watched and listened.

48

"You say he's running a temperature?" Dr. Jackson asked the man.

"Yeah, we're pretty sure he is. When my wife touched his forehead, his neck and his arms, they all were burning up."

Dr. Jackson looked hard over at Captain and Julia, then turned back to face the white man.

"Does your son have any visible rashes anywhere on his body, and has he been vomiting?"

"He's got a bright red rash on his face and his neck. He can't keep nothing down."

"Why did you come to see me and not a doctor on your side of town?" Dr. Jackson asked.

"'Cause a man I work with out at Glenpool told me you is one of the best doctors in town, even though you is colored."

Again, Dr. Jackson looked at his father and wife.

"It sounds to me like your son is a very sick boy. The symptoms you describe would lead me to believe that he may have scarlet fever."

"Oh Lord, help me," the man shrieked. "My boy's going to die."

"Hold on," Dr. Jackson said. "That's only a preliminary diagnosis. I won't know for sure until I can examine him. Where do you live?"

"I live off East Archer in the white area."

"How'd you get way over here?" Dr. Jackson asked.

"I ran all the way," the man answered with no hesitation. "You got to help us Dr. Jackson. I don't know what will happen to my wife if she loses her only child."

Captain Townsend was tempted to rush over there and ask the man to leave. He felt sorry for him, but there was no way his son could go into white Shantytown and treat a white child. Instead, he relaxed, knowing that his son would tell the man that he couldn't help him and that he should find a doctor in his section of town.

"Come on into the parlor and have a seat while I get my medical bag."

49

"Andrew, what are you doing?" Julia spoke up.

"I'm going to help this man's son," Dr. Jackson said as he escorted the man into the parlor.

"Son, we need to talk to you in the kitchen, now," Captain said as he and Julia followed Dr. Jackson and the man into the parlor.

"No time to talk, Father. Got to help this man's son."

"You owe it to Julia and me to give us a few minutes in the kitchen before you go off and do something you might regret," Captain shot back. "Five minutes is not going to make that big a difference." He grabbed his son by the arm and escorted him through the kitchen door followed closely by Julia. Once inside, they closed the door.

"What do you think you're doing?" Captain Townsend scowled. "You're going into a district where we are not welcome. Those people over in Shantytown going to be full of that Choc beer. They going to be drunk, and you know when white folks get drunk they can't restrain their hatred for us."

"Andrew, please listen to Poppa," Julia chimed in. "Most of them folks over there are nothing but white trash. They're jealous of successful Black men like you. If they find out you over there treating a white child, you just might not get out."

"What if the boy dies?" Captain added. "You going to have a lynch mob over here and if that happens, this whole town will explode. And they going to have to kill me, too."

Dr. Jackson stepped back to get some breathing room between the two of them and him. "Don't you think I'm aware of all that?" he said. "But I got no choice. I'm a doctor. It's my job to take care of anyone who comes to me with a sickness that I have the ability to cure, and especially a child."

Dr. Jackson hugged his wife and kissed her on the cheek. "I'll be all right. If I'm not back in an hour and a half, call Sheriff McCullough and let him know where I've gone." He turned to face the Captain. "I have to do this. How can I let my fears interfere with my responsibility? I'll stop by your house when I leave so you'll know nothing went wrong."

"No you won't, 'cause I'm going with you," Captain shot back. "I ain't gonna sit around at home and worry if my son's being pummeled by a bunch of hooligans."

"Sweetheart, keep that dinner warm because you going to have two hungry men on your hands in just a couple of hours." Dr. Jackson again kissed his wife, then turned and headed toward the kitchen door. "Come on old man; I'll drive."

"Oh, now that's just great. Not only are we going into enemy territory, but we're gonna do it in a brand new Ford, giving those folks even more reason to hate us."

Captain Townsend sat up front with Dr. Jackson while Luther rode in the backseat. The seating arrangement made the Captain feel a little more relaxed. If jealous white folks did see them, at least the white man was sitting in the backseat, and they could rationalize that the Negroes were chauffeuring him.

Dr. Jackson drove up Detroit Avenue and made a left turn at Archer. He then headed east across Greenwood onto a dirt road. The first two blocks east of Greenwood were lined with businesses on both sides of the street. After that, the streets were unpaved and both sides filled with shanties, some constructed with tin and others from crate boxes. The Captain breathed in the distinct odor from the outhouses situated right behind the shanties. These folks were just as bad off as Negroes who lived under those same deplorable condition, only on the western side of Greenwood.

As they drove further into the poor white district, Captain Townsend could only shake his head. How could these people possibly believe the myth of white superiority, given their living conditions? They were superior to no one and worse off than many Negroes in the city. It was a wonder that every child living in these conditions was not sick.

"Dr. Jackson, make a right into this alley coming up on the right," Luther said breaking Captain's musing on living conditions, racism and notions of superiority.

Once the paved roads ended, so had the streetlights, and when Dr. Jackson made the right turn into the alley, it was completely black outside. Captain stared over at his son as if to say are we really doing this. His son briefly shot a glance at him as if to answer, yes, we are.

51

"My house is the third one on the right," Luther said, leaning forward from the back seat. "You can park in front."

"If I park in front, I'll block the alley, and no one will be able to get by," Dr. Jackson said.

"Don't worry, Dr. Jackson, don't nobody ever drive no automobile down this alley, only horses. Yours is the first one ever to be down here. It'll be all right 'cause I'll be outside watching it while you're inside. Everybody knows not to mess with it parked in front of my place 'cause they know I'm an expert shot with my rifle. I fought over in France during the Great, War and was a sharp shooter." He opened the back door and jumped out of the Ford. "Come on, follow me."

Dr. Jackson and Captain got out of the car and walked directly behind Luther as he opened the front door. They followed him inside. The stench and the heat inside was so strong that Captain thought he might have to go back outside. It was cramped inside with a living room, kitchen, and two small bedrooms.

"If you want to have a seat in this room," Luther said looking at Captain Townsend, "then I'll take the doctor to the back bedroom where my boy is."

Just as he finished talking, a woman wearing a loosely fitting full length cotton dress and an apron strolled to the entrance of the bedroom.

"Helen, this here is Dr. Jackson, and he's going to make our boy well," Luther said.

"How you do?" Dr. Jackson said as he and Luther walked past her and into the dark bedroom with the only light from a flickering candle, struggling to stay lit, sitting on the night stand next to the boy's bed.

Luther turned and walked back into the living room, and Captain watched as he went back outside to protect the car. Captain got up, strolled over to the entrance to the bedroom in order to observe his son perform his skills to make a young boy well.

Dr. Jackson leaned over the young boy who was sweating profusely and having trouble breathing. He placed the back of his hand on the boy's forehead.

"How you doing, son?" he asked.

"I don't feel good," the young boy whispered. "It's so hot in here."

"We'll see if we can cool it off for you and have you feeling much better real soon," Dr. Jackson said in a very low whisper. He reached in his medicine bag, pulled out a container and poured its milky contents into a small glass. "Here, drink this," he said.

He held the boy's head up and helped him to drink the solution.

"Aahh, terrible," the boy scowled.

"Terrible to taste, but good to make you well," Dr. Jackson explained.

He placed the rest of the container on the nightstand and then stood up. "Give him a small cup of this every four hours. It will help to break the fever, and then we can begin the healing process," he said to Helen. "I'll be back in couple of days to check on him and also bring some more medicine. By all means, don't let him go outside to use the outhouse. Get some bedpans for him."

"Yes, Doctor, we already have them," Helen said.

"Make sure he takes all that medicine. It's absolutely necessary if he wants to get better," he said walking back out into the living room. Captain followed him out the door.

"Is he going to be all right?" Luther asked as the two men approached him.

"If you make sure he takes his medicine and gets plenty of rest, he should be all right," Dr. Jackson said.

"We will," Luther said as he snatched the crankshaft. "Doctor, I'm kind of broke right now on account there ain't been a lot of work over at Glenpool. But soon as work picks up, I'll make sure I pay you."

"Let's worry about getting this young fellow feeling better first, and then we'll deal with the other." Dr. Jackson climbed into the driver seat. Captain had already sat down in the passenger seat.

"Don't worry about your car when you're down here," Luther shouted from the front of the car as he prepared to crank it up. "When these folks find out what you're doing for my boy, they ain't going to let nobody mess with your car or with you."

"I'll hold you to that," Dr. Jackson said. "Crank her up."

Luther rotated the crankshaft and Dr. Jackson started the car. "See you tomorrow, and make sure he stays inside and takes that medicine."

"Will do, Doctor, and God bless you," Luther shouted as they started to drive up the alley.

"Now, that wasn't too bad, was it?" Dr. Jackson glanced over at his father.

"You're right," Captain glared out the window at a number of whites sill outside lined up in front of the shanties and staring at them as the drove by. "But I'll feel much better when we cross over Greenwood to our side of town."

SEVEN

Mabel Little had the first chair closest to the entrance to the Little Rose Beauty Shop. Four other chairs lined up in a row with sufficient space between each one so the other beauticians had plenty of room to work their wonders on the customers that came all day long to get their hair pressed, curled or waved.

The shop was right next door to the Little Café. Mabel's husband worked at the café all day while she managed the four beauticians besides doing hair herself. Loula Williams had a standing appointment every Thursday morning with Mabel to get her hair washed and then straightened. Loula was always right on time at nine in the morning. In fact, some Thursdays she would be walking outside before the shop opened and waiting when Mabel arrived usually fifteen minutes early. Both of them were successful businesswomen married to men who were also very successful. Loula and John owned the Dreamland Theater and Williams Confectionery right on the corner of Archer and Greenwood. John also owned an automobile repair shop around the corner on East Archer. Mabel and Pressley owned the café and the beauty shop. They also had rental property on Hempstead Street. Besides being two of the most successful businesswomen in Greenwood, Mabel and Loula also were members of Mount Zion Baptist Church.

Loula was Mabel's favorite customer because they shared so much in common and often spent the two hours it took to do Loula's hair talking about church matters. This was an important subject since they were in the process of building a new church at the corner of Elgin and Easton. That's why on this particular Thursday morning she was rushing to finish Loula's hair. She had to get over to the *Tulsa Star* and meet with Smitherman.

"Girl, why you in such a hurry?" Loula asked sitting in the

chair with a full-length apron covering her body.

"First off, I ain't rushing," Mabel replied as she finished setting her friend's hair so that in a half hour it would be full of waves. "But, yes, I am in a hurry. Got to get over to the *Tulsa Star* before noon to place an ad for tomorrow's paper. Smitherman's gonna run a story on the progress the church is making toward completion.

"Just don't mess up my hair being in such a hurry," Loula said.

"Told you I ain't in no rush," Mabel shot back. She slightly tapped her friend on the shoulder in a playful gesture. Quickly her attention turned from her friend to the customers coming in.

Four young ladies strolled into the salon and found empty seats along the wall across from the beauticians' chairs. All of them were obviously ladies of the night and usually worked the north side of Archer Street two blocks east of Greenwood Avenue. They were regular Thursday customers preparing for Thursday activities in North Tulsa. Mabel didn't do their hair. She left that to the other girls.

Three more young ladies strolled into the shop right behind the four. They grabbed the last three chairs available along the wall. Mabel knew these girls were not ladies of the night, but maids who earned their living, cleaning and cooking for white folks across the Frisco tracks.

"Girl, look at the business coming in here this morning," Loula said.

"My busiest days are Thursdays and Saturdays," Mabel said with a big smile. "All day Thursdays the girls come in to get ready for Thursday night at the clubs. Then on Saturday is my older customers getting ready for church on Sunday morning. The clubs on Thursday and church on Sunday do the same thing. They make us happy." She again patted her friend on the shoulder.

Loula chuckled and said, "Guess they all got to do the same thing and that's to escape what they got to put up with, having to clean spoiled white women's homes and appease their bratty kids."

"And beat off their sex-crazed husbands always trying to feel on 'em when they alone in the same room."

"Girl, I guess we blessed having escaped that life."

Mabel walked around to the front of Loula in order to make her point. "You may have escaped it, but I sure didn't when I first came to Tulsa." Momentarily her thoughts slipped back to when she left home for Tulsa and her mother predicted that she'd be walking the streets within a year. That prediction and her own moral convictions gave her the strength to escape such a fate. But she didn't escape the feeling of abject uselessness having to demean herself by cleaning up after white folks. They would leave the rooms in disgusting condition after checking out of the Hotel Tulsa, where she worked as a maid for over a year. "I had to hold my nose when I went into those rooms after those folks checked out. Sometimes blood would be all over the sheets, which was just nasty, them having sex while in the monthly condition."

"But you kept your eyes on the prize," Loula interjected. "And look what you got now."

"Yeah, a whole lot of bills that got to be paid every month and whole lot of customers that want me to make them look like Cleopatra after two hours in the chair," Mabel said smiling.

"I know one thing for sure," Loula continued. "We sure been blessed with some good men in our lives."

"I wouldn't have it any other way." Mabel finally clipped the last strands of Loula's hair. "Now in just a half hour you going to look so good John going to be chasing you all around upstairs in that confectionery."

"He better be busy working on somebody's car right about now, 'cause like you, we got bills that have to be paid." 57

"Ain't nothing wrong with a little playing in the afternoon. Keeps the spunk in your relationship," Mabel said.

"Humph, I wish that's all it took to get some spunk out my man," a gray haired lady sitting in the next chair interjected. "Sometimes I got to make sure Louis is still breathing he lay there so still, not hardly moving at all."

"I sure don't have that problem," another older lady waiting her turn for Mabel's chair chimed in.

"Lillie, I can't believe Jordan got any spunk in him the way he just kind of lumbers along when you see him walking down Greenwood," Mabel said.

"That's 'cause he saving all his energy for later on in the bed," Lillie retorted. "I don't think that man's ever gonna slow down. Some nights I got to act like I'm asleep."

"You mean with all his gray hair, he can still perform?" Mabel asked and started laughing.

"Girl, there may be snow above but let me assure you, there's fire down below." Her comment brought an array of laughter from all the women and especially the four ladies of the night.

"You go ahead and get it girl while you can," another woman in the last chair spoke up.

"I know I got to give him what he wants or one of these little hussies over here will." Lillie pointed at the four ladies who were known prostitutes.

"Who you calling a hussy?" A tall shapely, dark-skinned and very attractive girl, said from her seat almost directly across from Lillie.

"Alright ladies…alright you know I don't allow none of that in here," Mabel scowled. "And Lillie, don't make no comments about my customers, you understand?"

"But you know, Mabel—"

"Do you understand?" Mabel put more emphasis on her words. "We can tease, laugh and joke in here, but we don't do it against each other," she continued. "God knows we got enough of them peckerwoods across the tracks doing it. We don't need to do it to each other also."

58

Lillie remained tensed up in the chair, but the prostitute had relaxed back where she sat.

Momentarily, a quiet presence took over the shop. They all waited to see who would make the next move in the exchange of words. The chatter then picked up again with private conversations among two or three people at a time.

Mabel felt relieved. She knew that many of her older customers did not like that she offered service to prostitutes. But no one would dictate who could come to her shop. Prostitutes always had to look good and came in once and sometimes twice a week. She sure wasn't going to turn down that kind of business. Their money could be spent just like anyone else's and as she had told Loula, she had bills to pay.

"You know, April ain't far away," Loula spoke up, changing the topic of conversation. "Have you been by to see the progress they've made on the church?"

"I sure have, and it's looking awfully good," Mabel replied in a much more softer tone. She leaned over and whispered, "I believe Lillie's just angry 'cause everybody know what happened with her husband."

"Just leave it alone, girl, just leave it alone," Loula also whispered.

Mabel stood straight up. "Reverend Whittaker is certainly excited," she said in a normal tone. "April fourth is the day the doors will open to the finest looking church in all of Tulsa," she said, having taken Loula's advice to leave it alone.

"It's a shame they can't get it finished a week earlier so we could have our first service on Easter Sunday."

"Reverend Whittaker pushed them hard to get it done by then, but the bad winter has set us back. We had a bunch of days they just couldn't get anything done."

"We better pray that we don't have any more winter days to push it back further."

"I mention that in this little article I wrote to go in tomorrow's 59 paper. Reverend Whittaker actually wrote most of it, and he put a sentence in it, asking the community to pray that we don't have anymore snow, ice or freezing days this winter." Mabel began to take the clips out of Loula's hair. As she removed a clip, her friend tried to feel her hair.

"Girl, stop," Mabel scolded and popped her hand, this time not so gently. "You can't even wait for me to get all the clips out. It looks good, and you going to look beautiful as usual."

Loula folded her hands in her lap. "It better not rain before I get back to the theater."

"You didn't bring a scarf?"

"Sure didn't because it was nice out when I came over here."

"I got a scarf for you," Mabel said as she finished. "You know Tulsa weather changes on the hour. But you'll be all right."

"You and Pressley coming by the confectionery tonight?" Loula asked.

"No girl, I'll be too tired after today, and there'll be too many people out, and those folks that don't drink will all be in your place."

"Or in the theater. We're showing Oscar Micheaux's new movie, *Within Our Gates*, tonight."

"Who's that?" Mabel asked.

"You don't know Oscar Micheaux?" Loula didn't answer her right away.

"No, I don't. I do know who Madam C. J. Walker was because I buy her products. I'm in the beauty business, not the movie business. So is this man a Negro?"

"Yes indeed, he is a Negro, and he is a movie producer."

"What you telling me? A Black movie producer in Hollywood?" Mabel shrieked.

"You got it, and we're showing his movie because the white theaters won't."

"What's the movie about?"

"You have to come and see it. He's an amazing man. His movies are about Black folks who are middle class and educated. He believes it is his job to produce movies to counter the terrible images of our people in white movies."

"Like *Birth of A Nation*? That was a terrible movie."

"Absolutely, right on time. You got it. This movie was produced by him to dispel all the myths of Negroes in *Birth of A Nation*."

"He did that and he's still alive?"

"Some of us aren't afraid. Since he was willing to produce it, the least we can do is show it at our theater."

"We might come out, according to how Pressley feels this evening." Mabel finished, unsnapped the apron from around Loula. She then handed her a mirror.

Loula inspected her entire head moving the mirror from side to side and sometimes tilting her head for a better look.

"It does look pretty good. That's why I keep coming to you." She handed Mabel a dollar bill, walked over to the coat rack and grabbed her coat.

"Wait," Mabel said. She opened a counter drawer behind her, pulled out the scarf and handed it to her friend. "I don't think you'll need this, but just in case, take it." She strolled over to where her friend stood and handed the scarf to her.

"Thank you." Loula said and the two friends hugged. "Hope to see you tonight." She turned and walked out the door.

Just a little before noon, Mabel rushed through the door in Smitherman's office at the *Star.* As she came bursting into his office, he looked up from a number of papers in front of him on the desk.

"Morning, Mabel," he said.

"Did I make it on time?" Mabel asked as she sat in one of the chairs in front of his desk.

61

"Given that it still has to be edited, I'll see what I can do."

Mabel slid the typed paper across the desk to Smitherman. "Don't see what you can do; you got to get it done. I told everybody I know to buy the *Star* on Saturday 'cause there'll be a story on the church in there."

"You telling me I have to do it because you're helping me to sell papers," he said smiling.

"And don't forget that both Pressley and I take out ads in your paper."

"Now you're really laying it on thick. Even pulled Pressley into this."

"You know a lady's got to do what she's got to do to get her way. And I need this ad in your newspaper on Saturday."

Smitherman finally picked up the paper and opened it. "Mabel, you want me to print all this?" He exclaimed. "This is a full length story."

"What's wrong with that?"

"That wasn't our agreement. I agreed to do a short three liner about the church's targeted day for completion."

"Come on now, where's your community and church spirit?"

"We had everything laid out and ready to go to print. I'd left a little room to squeeze in your piece. Now you don't need a little room, you need a whole lot."

"You're doing the Lord's work, and He will reward you abundantly."

"Don't go Reverend on me. It doesn't fit your personality." Smitherman laid the paper back down on his desk. "You know we got Dr. Du Bois for April?" He changed the subject.

"That's what Pressley told me. You're looking for a real fight aren't you?"

"The man's just coming to speak and talk with some of our successful business people, not to start a war."

"White folks are afraid of him, and when they're afraid of someone you know what that means?"

"Trouble, big trouble." Smitherman thought for a moment, then added. "You know the motto for my paper, don't you Mabel?"

"Don't everybody know it?" Mabel shot back. 'You Push Me and I Push You.' You put it all over the paper all the time."

"But not only should that be the motto for my paper, but for every Negro in Tulsa, in Oklahoma and all over this country," Smitherman said as his voice rose.

Mabel and everyone else in Greenwood who knew the feisty newspaperman and trained lawyer expected his temperature to rise as well as the tone of his voice when talking about the injustice against his people.

"Smitherman continued. "You mean to tell me that because white folks fear him that we shouldn't welcome him to our community?" he asked rhetorically.

"You know that's not what I said, and that's not what I mean. This is our community, and we should feel free to invite anyone we want to. I just wanted to make sure you know there can be some trouble."

"Bring 'em on," Smitherman gasped. "Mabel, you know we built this community from the ground up because you and Pressley been a part of that building."

"I know that's right," Mabel replied.

"So Dr. Du Bois is going to come to Greenwood, and you're going to be part of a committee that has a special dinner with him."

"All right, you've made your point. Now can we get back to how much my article on the progress of Mount Zion are you going to cut out?'

"Because it's you, I'll find room for the entire article," Smitherman said.

"God will bless you." Mabel pulled out two dollars from her small purse. "Here is for my ad for this week's paper."

"You're not doing one for the restaurant this week?"

"No, Pressley didn't think we needed to. Anyway, you're getting enough of our money every week."

63

"Just remember, it's for a great cause. Not only do you get to advertise your services to all eight thousand Negroes in Greenwood, you make it possible for us to have a voice that can't be snuffed out by white money."

"That's fine. Just make sure you place the church article in a prime spot."

Smitherman got up and moved to the other side of his desk.

"Anywhere in the *Tulsa Star* is a prime spot."

Mabel also got up. When you plan to put a notice in the paper about Dr. Du Bois coming to Tulsa?" She asked.

"It'll be in this Saturday's edition. We want the entire city to know that the Negroes of Greenwood are pleased to have such a fine scholar and outstanding leader to visit out city."

Mabel sighed. "Okay, Mr. Pleased. We all better pray hard."

"And we better make sure our guns are loaded at all times."

"You and the wife going out tonight?"

"As a matter of fact, we plan to catch the Oscar Micheaux movie this evening at the Dreamland."

Mabel strolled over and opened the front door. A cool breeze shot in and caused her to pull her coat tightly around her body. As she stepped out the door, she turned back and looked at Smitherman.

"You know who this Micheaux man is also?"

"I sure do," Smitherman answered as he walked over next to her at the door. "He's our hope for the race in fighting these terrible images being portrayed in white movies. The one tonight is supposed to be a counter to *Birth of A Nation*, and I have to see it."

"We might see you there. Loula already told me something about this man, and it seems maybe all Black folks should see his movies." She finished, walked out and closed the door behind her.

EIGHT

Dick knew he was pretty much a nobody among all the rich high society Negroes who worked and owned businesses up and down Greenwood Avenue and also owned homes over on Detroit Avenue. But on Thursday night, he definitely became a somebody, and this Thursday was no different. Being someone important was based on the fact that he had a white girlfriend, and all the Black folks in Greenwood knew it. He also had a number of Black girls that liked him a whole lot. Add to the women, his new diamond ring and he knew he was the man.

Those were his thoughts as he left his house and walked over to First Street to Pretty Belle's Place. The cold wind blowing in his face invigorated him, increased his energy level and made him want to dance all night, drink some good liquor and end up in bed with a new woman. Tonight his goal was to sleep with someone who hadn't yet enjoyed the pleasure of his company. As he walked the last block to Pretty Belle's, he knew a new adventure awaited him.

He hurried up to the door and tapped on the peephole. A man from inside smiled at him and opened the door.

"Hey young fellow, how you doing?" A muscular man, who stood at least six feet five, greeted him.

"I'm doing fine as I can right now, Jethroe," he answered as the two men shook hands and proceeded to another door that Jethroe unlocked and opened wide.

Dick stepped into a darkened room with the only light coming from burning candles sitting on at least twenty round wooden tables with no tablecloths. Men and women relaxed in chairs around the tables. Some of the chairs were empty because the occupants were dancing in an open area space near the bar. A combination of smoke and perfume filled the limited amount of air because there were no windows to open to get fresh air inside. The melodious sounds from a record on the Victrola also filled the room. Dick picked up the beat and felt the rhythm running throughout his body. That was dancing music being played, and he was ready to dance. But first he wanted to check out any new blood that might be in the club for the first time. One of those many maids that liked to come out and party on Thursday night might be in there just waiting for him to show up.

Dick strode along the side of the dance floor to the back end of the room where the bar was set up. He reached out and shook hands with a number of men as he walked along the side of the dance floor. He swung his arm in a circular motion making sure the person he greeted saw the shiny diamond ring on his finger. The ring would increase the level of admiration for him.

As he approached the bar, he spotted an old friend he'd known when he first moved up to Tulsa. He hadn't seen him since he dropped out of Booker T. Washington High School two years ago. A wide smile spread across his face and he went through his wide circular motion of extending his hand to the man.

"Jimmy Cleveland, man, how you been?" He asked

Jimmy acknowledged his gesture by grabbing Dick's hand and briskly shaking it.

"Dick Rowland, shit man, how long has it been?"

"Years, but I thought you'd left Tulsa for Chicago?"

The two men finally released their handgrip. Dick made sure he turned his hand with the palm down with the ring exposed. It worked.

"Damn man, look at that ring," Jimmy said.

"Ain't nothing, just a little something I picked up over at William Anderson Jewelry Store."

"Shit, if that ain't nothing, I sure the hell want to see what you call something."

"I guess hard work can pay off," Dick said as he watched Grady Johnson, one of his only friends, walk up to the bar.

"I figured I'd see you in here tonight," Grady said as he positioned himself at the bar. "I didn't think you'd be alone. Where's ofaye girl tonight?"

"Needed a break from her, and anyway she had to go up to Kansas City. Something to do with her divorce being final."

"So you down here slumming with the field Negroes?" Grady said smiling. "Who's your friend?" he asked while looking at Jimmy.

"Hey Grady, this is Jimmy. Jimmy and I went to school together until I dropped out"

The two men nodded at each other and then shook hands. Jimmy turned his attention back to Dick and his ring.

"Damn man, you must be doing something right or that ofaye girl must be taking good care of you. Look at that diamond on your finger. You got to be called Diamond Dick."

The name fit him well, and he liked it a lot. He was a diamond, and it just made sense to refer to him that way. "I can handle that," he said. "Diamond Dick, that's who I am," he shouted to the party folks just as the music stopped and the dancers started back to their seats.

He strode out to the middle of the dance floor, held his right hand high in the air so everyone could see the ring. "Diamond Dick, that's who I am from now on."

"All right, Diamond Dick," someone shouted. A number of women got up and walked over to where he was standing to get a better look at the ring.

"Where's your little white girl?" A short light skinned woman who was dressed to show off her benefits asked.

67

"Sometime she got her own business to take care of, and sometimes I got mine," Dick answered.

"So you decided to come home tonight. You sharing what you got on this side of the railroad tracks."

"You might say that." This young girl wasn't new to the set but he'd never lain with her. This might be his new score for the night. "Let's dance," he said just as the music started up again.

He took her by the hand, glided to the middle of the dance floor and the two of them moved their bodies to the rhythm of Fletcher Henderson's band.

"Why you so quick at the mouth?" Dick said as he took her hand and spun her around. They came close, then away from each other. He took her hand and brought her close to him, all the time sticking to the beat of the music.

"Us girls on this side of the tracks don't like it when our best looking men mess with women outside the race."."

"Ain't nothing but something to do in my spare time. You know I like my chocolate best of all."

"We'll see."

"What's your name, anyway?" Dick asked just as the music ended.

"Ethel, and I ain't a prostitute."

"Didn't say you was." Dick pulled her in close to his body as the melodic slow sounds of Bessie Smith filled the room:

"Gee, but it's hard to love someone

When that someone don't love you

I'm so disgusted and heart broken too

I've got those down hearted blues."

The mood was being set by the slow sounds of Bessie Smith, and Dick pulled Ethel in even closer and tighter to his body.

"Look like you wants more than just a dance," Ethel whispered.

68   "What you think a man gonna want all close and snuggled next to your fine body?"

"You might get what you want if you act right, buy me a few drinks then find a nice place where we can be alone."

"You know I'm gonna make that happen. I'm your man for the rest of the night," he also whispered and a broad smile covered his face.

***

When the lights in the Dreamland Theater came back on, Mabel sat there next to Pressley awe struck over the movie they had just watched. The theater was packed and she imagined everyone else was just as awestruck as she. Earlier she'd seen Smitherman and Stradford with their families sitting up closer to the front. She could only wonder if they were as impressed as she was with the new Negro producer, Oscar Micheaux. She also wondered how many movies this man had produced and were they all as bold as this one. Pressley got up, stretched and started up the aisle. Mabel was right behind him. He hadn't spoken a word about the movie. She wasn't surprised. Her husband was the kind of man who refused to get involved in these racial issues.

They made it to the lobby of the theater and were about to go outside after putting on their coats when Loula called out.

"Mabel, over here. You got a minute come on over?"

The lobby was jammed with people walking and chattering about the movie. She grabbed Pressley's hand and pulled him in the direction of Loula.

"Girl, what a movie," Mabel exclaimed as they approached Loula. "I'm surprised that man ain't been killed."

"Good evening, Pressley, " Loula greeted Pressley then turned her attention to Mabel. "He don't live in the South, otherwise he might be dead."

"How'd you find out about him?"

Loula was dodging the crowd of people still exiting the theater. "Why don't you all come next door?" she asked. "I'll treat you to a coffee or hot chocolate. Both Smitherman and Stradford are going to join us. We're going to discuss what Oscar Micheaux is doing across this country."

Mabel looked at Pressley who nodded his head in approval. "Just for a little while, let's go," she said and the three of them fought through the crowd and out the door.

They briskly walked next door to the confectionery, found an empty table large enough to accommodate twelve people and sat down. The confectionery was packed with couples out enjoying the evening, but Loula had instructed her waitresses to reserve her table since she knew there would be a serious discussion about the movie. Just as soon as they sat down, both Smitherman and Stradford came in the front door. Loula stood up and waived to them. They hurried over to the table and found chairs. Loula told the waitress to bring a pot of coffee and hot chocolate for the children. That being done, she then initiated the discussion.

"What did you all think?" she asked

"The lynch scene was disgusting," Stradford spoke up first.

"I'm trying to figure out how he got that scene and the one of the white man raping the Black woman by the censors," Smitherman said.

"He didn't in some states," Loula advised. "In the Deep South, they censored the lynch scene and the rape scene also."

"You said he produces his own movies," Pressley spoke up.

"Everyone of them, and right now I believe he has four," Loula said. "Wouldn't it be wonderful if we could get him to come down here and speak in Tulsa."

The waitress walked back to the table with a large pot of coffee and cups, placed them on table and also placed cream and sugar with sufficient spoons to go around. She then poured cocoa in the cups for the three children.

"There's going to be enough trouble when Du Bois shows up," Pressley said. "We sure don't need anymore."

"I wonder have the folks across the tracks seen this movie or even heard about it?" Smitherman asked.

"If most of these country folks saw it," Stradford said, "they'd probably enjoy it simply because they'd cheer on the lynching and tell themselves that the white man wasn't trying to rape that woman, she was just playing hard to get."

"You got a point there," Mabel said.

"On a serious note, every Negro in Tulsa should see this movie. If they did, they'd definitely pledge that nothing like that will ever happen in our community," Stradford said as he took a sip from his coffee cup. "Awfully good cup of coffee," he added.

"Did you see the theater was packed?" Loula chimed in.

"What'd you expect on Thursday night?" Mabel asked

"How long are you going to let it run?" Stradford asked as he took another drink from his coffee cup.

"It's here for a week," Loula answered. "Maybe by that time every Negro in Tulsa will have seen it."

"I'm more determined than ever before that there will never be a lynching in Tulsa of a Black man or white man as long as I'm around," Smitherman proclaimed. "Roy Belton's lynching last year will be the last one."

"I'm with you on that," Stradford added.

Mabel finally pushed her cup to the middle of the table. "This conversation is all well and good but I got to open early in the morning. Friday may not be as busy as Thursday, but it'll still be busy. You ready Pressley?"

"Ready, I am." He also pushed his cup to the center of the table, as he and Mabel rose up to leave.

The rest of the party stayed seated.

"Make sure my story runs on Saturday," Mabel said as she looked at Smitherman.

"Already edited and ready for the press," Smitherman said.

Mabel and Pressley walked to the front door and left the confectionery.

"Pressley, there's going to be trouble in this city someday just like it was in that movie," Mabel exclaimed.

71

"If it does happen, it won't be lopsided. Negroes in this city ready to fight just like the men in that movie. And these men are good when it comes to fighting, especially that O. B. Mann fellow."

Mabel tucked her arm inside Pressley's as they walked toward their Model T. Ford. "Remember numbers, Pressley. They may be good but I just don't know if we got the numbers."

NINE

O. B. had just opened the store and began to sweep the inside when Damie Rowland walked through the door.

"How you doing, Miss Damie?" He asked as he continued sweeping.

"Doing real fine, O. B., but I need a couple nice size hens for today. You got some good ones?"

"Sure do," O. B. said and put the broom down. "Come on out back and pick the two you want."

Damie slowly followed behind as if reluctant to go outside. "How you going to kill them?" she asked.

"Same as I always do," O.B. said as he started toward the back door that led to the back area where they kept the chickens.

"Let me pick the ones I want and then go on back inside," she said. "I don't want to watch while you do that thing to kill them."

"You mean wring their necks?" O. B. asked. "How you going to get 'em dead if you don't wring their neck? Cutting off their heads would be worse. Too much blood that way." He opened the main door and swung open the screen door while Damie went out. "How's that boy of yours?"

"Dick's doing fine," she said nervously, walking by O. B. and out into the yard.

O. B. followed, finally caught up and passed her. "Come on over here and pick the two you want."

They ambled up to the chicken coop with over fifty chickens inside. The birds were busy pecking seeds on the ground inside the pen. Damie stood back a few steps as if she were apprehensive about this undertaking.

O. B. looked back at her and gestured for her to step forward. "Come on up here Miss Damie and pick out your hens unless you want me to do it."

Damie crept up to the fence. She spent a couple minutes looking over all the chickens still busy eating. "Oh, I don't know, O. B.," she gasped. "Why don't you go on and do it."

"All right." He opened the door to the chicken coop and stepped inside. The chickens scattered in all directions just as if they detected trouble. O. B. chased one plump chicken until he cornered it, reached down and snatched it by its neck and pulled it close to him.

"No, no, O. B., don't do that thing until I'm back inside the store." Damie started backing up, finally turned and ran inside the store.

A smile covered O. B's face as he walked over to an area in the yard with a large circle imbedded in the ground. Standing right outside the circle, O. B. got a firm grip on the chicken's head and with a couple strong twists, the chicken made a sound and went still. He tossed it in the middle of the circle where it lay motionless. O. B. glared down at the lifeless chicken. He was a superstitious man and believed if somehow that chicken jerked its way out of the circle it wasn't fit for eating. He performed that same act many times and not one of the chickens made it out of the circle. The same was true with this one. Convinced that it would not move, O. B. went back into the chicken coop, spotted another plump hen and grabbed it by the neck. He carried it back over to the identical spot and repeated the same exercise. Convinced they both were dead, he picked them up and took them back into the store.

Damie anxiously waited at the counter. O. B. noticed she seemed to be a little upset.

"No need to fret about these chickens. They good and dead," he said as he walked behind the counter.

"That ain't it, O. B. When I walked back in, some man had a bag and was filling it with groceries. He didn't pay me no mind, so I didn't bother with him. But just when he saw you coming up

74

the steps from out back, he ran out the store."

O. B. instantly dropped the chickens. "Which way did he go?" he asked.

"He went to the left when he got outside."

"How long ago?"

"Less than two minutes, just as you were coming up the steps."

"Watch the store," he said and shot out the door, turned left and ran down the street.

O. B. reached the corner and looked both ways. When he looked to his right, he spotted a man with a sack walking fast up the street. He took off running after him. He was a big man but swift of feet.

"Stop, you son of a bitch," he shouted.

The man stopped and looked back. That was his mistake. Before he could turn and run, O. B's momentum drove him right into the man, knocking him to the ground. The bag flew at least ten feet. O. B. smashed the thief's head against the ground, turned him around and had him in a choke hold.

"You little bastard, why'd you try stealing from me?" he shouted. "I ought to tear your head right off your pathetic little body."

O. B. wasn't aware that he had attracted a crowd. A couple of men, who knew him, grabbed him by the arms.

"O. B., cool down, you're going to kill him," the man who had hold of his right arm shouted. "Come on, you got 'em. Let 'em up."

The two men were not strong enough to break the muscular O. B's grip on the thief's neck. They had to convince him to let the man get up.

"O. B., you don't want to kill 'em for stealing some groceries. You'll go to jail for sure. Let him up."

The man's words finally registered. O. B. loosened his grip on the thief's neck.

"Get the hell out of here," O. B. shouted. "If I ever catch you around my store again, I'll kill you with my bare hands."

The thief had apparently urinated in his pants and looked frightened out of his mind. He turned and took off running toward Archer Avenue.

"Thanks," O. B. said to the two men who had tried to pull him off the thief. He hurried over to pick up the bag full of groceries, then stormed back to where the two men still stood. He thrust the bag into the hands of one of the men. "Here take it," he said.

"But you just ran this man down and almost killed him," the one holding the bag said. "Now you going to give it to me."

"It wasn't 'bout the food," O. B. retorted. "It's about principle. We as a race shouldn't be stealing from each other. God knows we have a hard enough time as it is without making it hard on each other." He finished, turned and walked back to the store.

Damie was in the very same spot inside the store where he had left her. The dead chickens still lay on the floor.

"Thank you, Miss Damie," O. B. said as he reached the counter and stood next to her.

"Did you catch him?"

"You darn right I did, and gave him a good pummeling so he won't be doing that again."

"I need to get on home," Damie said. "How much do I owe you?"

"This time it's on the house," O. B. replied. "If it hadn't been for you, the little thief would've gotten away."

"I really didn't do anything. Just happened to walk back in the store when he didn't expect anyone to be there."

O. B. picked up the two chickens and put them in a brown bag. "Tell that boy of yours there's just too much talking around here 'bout that white girl and that he'd better be careful. Don't want that talk to get across the tracks."

Damie took the bags and gazed at O. B. for a moment. She then headed out of the store, saying nothing about O. B's comment.

***

The loud thumps on the bedroom door caused Dick to shoot straight up in the bed. The brightness of the sun shining through the crack in the venetian blinds made him squint and rub his eyes.

"Dick, aren't you going to work today?" Aunt Damie called out to him.

"Oh shit, what time is it?" He glanced over at the small clock on his dresser. "Nine thirty," he whispered. "Yes ma'am, I'm going to work," he shouted. "Be down in less than twenty minutes."

Dick swung his legs over the side of the bed and jumped to his feet. Instantly, the sharp pain shot through his head. He put his hand across the front of his head as if that would make the pain go away.

"Hurry on down here," Aunt Damie shouted. "I'll have your breakfast ready for you."

"Thanks, Aunt Damie, but I don't think I'm gonna have time for no breakfast."

"You got to eat something. I'll be downstairs."

The mention of food made him nauseous. To eat would send him flying to the bathroom to throw up all that Choc beer mixed with bacon and eggs. He couldn't handle that. There would be no breakfast this morning, only a very little coffee and maybe a piece of dry toast. Just how much did he drink? Suddenly the light came on. Oh yeah, Ethel. What a hell of a night. That's the main reason he overslept. Shit, she wore his ass out. That girl definitely has skills. Now he had to face the day and pay for all that pleasure from last night.

77

He slipped back into his underwear lying on the floor next to the bed where he had taken them off last night when he got home. He grabbed his washcloth, toothbrush and paste, along with a comb and wrapped them in a towel, opened the door and stumbled down the hall to the bathroom. Thank God they had plumbing in this place. At least he didn't have to go outside to relieve himself like he had to do when they lived over on Kenosha and Independence.

What he needed most to do was literally scrub his teeth to get that terrible taste of Choc beer lingering long after he'd taken his final drink last night. He'd told Aunt Damie he'd be downstairs in about twenty minutes, but this morning he was operating in slow motion. It would be more like forty-five minutes, which meant he'd be a couple hours late getting to work. Hopefully, Robert could handle the morning traffic. He'd be pissed off, but so what. Dick had covered for him many times when he came straggling in there late.

It was ten thirty when Dick scrambled into the kitchen practically a new man. The headache had subsided, and his stomach felt much better. But, still, he couldn't sit down to a full breakfast because of the time. Aunt Damie was sitting at the kitchen table when he walked in. She got up and went over to the stove.

"No, Aunt Damie, please, I don't have time for a full breakfast. Just a piece of dry toast and a cup of coffee."

"I don't know why you got to do the same thing every Thursday night," she scolded. "You know darn well you ain't going to want to get up in the morning." Damie grabbed two pieces of bread and stuck them in the oven, then grabbed a cup and poured coffee into it. "You out there with all them nasty girls doing heaven knows what and then can't get up for work." She placed the cup on the table in front of Dick.

Dick grabbed the cup and took a drink of the hot substance. "Just what I need, something real hot."

"What you need is a new brain. Were you out half the night with that white girl?" Damie walked back over to the oven to check on the toast.

78

"No, Aunt Damie, I wasn't out with Sarah. She was out of town."

"Whoever it was sure wore you out," Aunt Damie said and laughed. "You look like something from a week ago trying to get caught up with today." She pulled the toast out of the oven, put the two pieces in front of Dick and sat back down.

Dick grabbed the first piece and devoured it. He followed it with a large gulp of coffee and grabbed the other piece of toast.

"Some of the men worried about your relationship with that white girl. Everybody in town talking about it, and soon it might get back to the white folks what's happening between the two of you."

Dick finished the second piece of toast and again gulped more coffee. He got up from the table ready to leave. "Last thing I worry about, Aunt Damie, is what other people are saying about my business, which is none of their business." He finished, jumped up and headed for the door. "See you this evening."

"Boy, you just better watch what you're doing out in those streets."

He heard Aunt Damie's warning words, opened the front door and stepped out into the brisk March cold. The chill would do him well so instead of flagging down a jitney; he decided to walk the mile to work. He figured that by the time he got there, the hangover from last night would be gone. The way he felt, all-sluggish like, he didn't care if he shined any shoes at all. He just wasn't in the mood for all the smiling and jiving he had to do with some of those rednecks who were rich only because they were white. He often wondered, while bending over shining their shoes, did they really think that he enjoyed kissing their pale white asses six days a week.

Dick reached Main and briskly walked the final three blocks to the shoeshine stand. He felt energized. Recently, over the past three months, he had seriously considered leaving Tulsa, maybe moving up to Chicago. Ever since Ben started renting a room from Aunt Damie and brought copies of the *Chicago Defender* home with him, he'd been reading and really enjoyed how the writers up there encouraged Negroes to move from the segregated South to the North. There were plenty of job opportunities up there for the Black man, and most importantly, a Black man didn't have to take a bunch of shit off white folks.

With only a half block left to walk Dick now was ready to shine shoes and take bullshit from white folks. Hopefully, this afternoon they'd be in good moods and tip well.

79

TEN

Veneice Dunn hurried down the crowded hall on the second floor of Booker T. Washington High School on her way to Julia Jackson's American literature class. Out of all her classes, literature was the one she enjoyed the most and out of all her teachers, Mrs. Julia Jackson was her favorite. Veneice really admired Mrs. Jackson because she was beautiful, made the subject interesting and was married to the most famous doctor in Tulsa. Someday the young woman hoped to be just as successful as her teacher.

"Veneice, you going over to the confectionery on Saturday morning?" a female student asked her from the other side of the hall.

"Don't think so," she replied. "Poppa claims too many boys and too much music is not a good environment for a young girl."

The young girl strolled across the hall and stopped right in front of Veneice.

"I feel sorry for you," the girl said. "Your Poppa don't let you do nothing. Sure am glad my Poppa ain't that strict on me."

"It's not that bad," Veneice replied. She knew Poppa was that bad, but he provided them with a good life and she owed him respect despite his old fashioned and outdated ways of thinking about music, dancing and boys.

"You know this year we can go to the prom as juniors. You think he going to let you go?"

"I don't know that for sure," Veneice answered as she became a little irritated with all the questions. "Only thing I'm concerned about right now is Mrs. Jackson's American literature class and getting there on time. Excuse me," she finished and walked right around the girl who was holding her up from getting to class on time. She never wanted to do anything that was not pleasing to her favorite teacher. Being late would not be pleasing to her.

Veneice made it to the classroom, walked in and sat at her desk in the front row close to Mrs. Jackson. A few other students had also taken their seats, but there were still a couple minutes before the bell rang and Mrs. Jackson had her back turned to the students. Veneice followed her closely as she wrote on the chalkboard, "TODAY WE WILL DISCUSS *UNCLE TOM'S CABIN*."

Veneice smiled, knowing that she'd finished reading the book cover to cover in the month's time given to finish it and was now prepared for the discussion. Suddenly Veneice began to blush as Verby Ellison walked into the room and took a seat right behind her. She liked him a whole lot, but dare not show it. Poppa always warned her about boys. He'd been raised in a family of five boys and was an expert on what they always had on their mind about girls. He never went into a lot of detail but told her and her sister that liking and talking to boys could only get you in trouble.

So why did she get this strange feeling whenever Verby came into the classroom or when she passed him in the halls? It did not make her feel bad, but to the contrary, she felt pretty good, and that's why she always blushed when she was around him. Finally the bell rang. A few stragglers rushed into the classroom just in time so they didn't have to go down to Principal Woods' office, something no student wanted to do.

"You sure looking pretty today," Verby said while tapping Veneice on the shoulder.

She wanted to smile but knew she dare not do so because Poppa warned that boys would say complimentary things to girls just to get close to them, but really didn't mean it.

82

"Why you can't talk to me?" Verby continued. "You could at least say thank you for the compliment."

"Thank you," Veneice said without turning to look back at him.

"Good afternoon, class," Julia said, facing the class.

"Good afternoon, Mrs. Jackson," the entire class replied in unison.

"How are you all this afternoon?" she continued.

"We're fine," again the entire class answered.

"That's good." Julia walked over and stood directly behind her desk. "Today we're going to discuss the classic novel written as far back as 1852."

"Wow, that's a long time ago," a student from the back of the room spoke up.

"George," Julia's tone was stern. "If you speak out like that again, then you'll have earned yourself a trip to Principal Woods' office.

"Yes, ma'am."

"As I was saying, we are going to discuss the novel written by Harriet Beecher Stowe, *Uncle Tom's Cabin*. How many of you have read the entire novel?"

Veneice shot her hand straight up in the air and looked around to see how many other students had also read the novel. Every hand was raised, even Verby's. She glared at him as if she questioned his honesty. He smiled back at her.

"That's good to know," Julia said. "Does anyone care to tell me your favorite character in the story?"

"Veneice got her hand in the air before anyone else.

"Yes, Veneice, who was your favorite character?" Julia asked. "Please stand when you address the class."

Veneice lifted her body out of the chair, turned and faced the class. "My favorite character was Eliza."

"Why Eliza?" Julia continued.

83

"Because she was so brave that she didn't fear the slave hunters or what would happen to her if she were caught once she decided to run for freedom. She wasn't even afraid of drowning when she jumped from one block of ice to another. If she had slipped and went underwater, there is no way she would have lived. That took courage."

"Very good," Julia complimented her. "Why is that an important quality in an individual?"

"Because if you're not afraid, no one can mistreat you. If all our ancestors would have been like Eliza, they never could have kept us as slaves for so long."

"Thank you, Veneice." Julia motioned for her to sit back down. "Someone else care to tell me who their least favorite person was in the story?"

Verby was the first one to raise his hand.

"Yes Verby, please stand and tell us who your least favorite person was."

As he got up from his desk, he looked directly at Veneice and smiled. "Simon Legree," he said loudly.

"And why was he your least favorite?" Julia asked.

"Because he had Tom beat to death," Verby answered.

"I think that's a very good reason to dislike him," Julia said.

"But I got a question I'd like to ask you, Mrs. Jackson," Verby said.

"Yes, what is it?"

"How could men as mean and nasty as Simon Legree ever think they could be someone's master? At Sunday school, we've always been taught that Jesus was our master and savior. If that's the case, why do we put evil men in the same place with Jesus?"

Again, Veneice was surprised and also pleased as she listened to this boy she liked but had to keep her feelings at abeyance. She was shocked that he could come up with such a question and pleased because maybe he wasn't like the other boys Poppa was talking about.

84

"That's a very good question, Verby," Julia replied. "You're right, these were men who should have never been put in the same category as Jesus. But our grandparents and great grandparents were forced to call them master, although I am sure they never felt that way about them."

Verby sat down as a couple more students raised their hands.

"Esther, did you have something you'd like to add to the discussion?" Julia asked a student sitting near the back.

"Yes, Mrs. Jackson. Why do white people think that we have to call them mister or sir or ma'am when they don't show us the same kind of respect? Who do they think they are anyway?" Esther smiled as the entire class applauded her.

"All right, class, settle down," Julia scolded. After they stopped clapping, she continued. "Sometimes we are forced to do and say things we don't like just to survive. Your parents, for example, have to provide you all with a place to live, with food and clothes. To do this they must work for people who have all the jobs to offer, and they make it a requirement that they be referred to in those terms."

Veneice could tell Mrs. Jackson struggled with her answer. She also knew this subject could touch off a long discussion because young people resented the fact that their parents allowed white people of all ages to talk down to them. She'd been with Poppa one time at his work repairing city buses when a white supervisor called him a boy. Poppa's entire body tensed up, but he didn't strike back because to do so would have gotten him fired. But she knew it hurt Poppa, especially since the man did it right in front of her.

"Times are getting better for our people," Julia continued with her explanation. "I know whites are far from perfect, but they are better than when our grandparents were freed. When you all are adults we can only pray they will have changed. Now let's get back to our discussion of today's topic. Can someone tell me another person in the story you didn't like?"

Another young girl sitting in the back next to Esther vigorously waved her hand.

"Yes, Ruth, you seem quite anxious, so tell us who you didn't like?"

Ruth jumped to her feet and without hesitating practically shouted, "I couldn't stand Topsy."

Again, a number of students clapped in agreement.

"Class, I told you about that," Julia scowled. "I love your energy and excitement, but please do not clap or talk out of turn. Continue on Ruth. Tell us why you couldn't stand Topsy."

"Because she is an embarrassment to our race," Ruth said, with plenty of confidence now that she knew the entire class supported her.

"Why do you think she's an embarrassment to our race?" Julia continued.

"Lookit how she's described. My daddy and momma tell me I'd better straighten my hair, wear clean clothes and talk proper less I be an embarrassment to the Negro race. We already got white people talking bad about us, we don't have to prove they're right."

"But she was a slave," Julia commented.

"I don't care; that lady who wrote the book didn't have to make her so ugly. My daddy told me that my grandparents were slaves, but they were beautiful people forced over here from Africa. And the ugly people were the white ones. Why we always have to read about ugly blacks and never ugly whites?"

"Yeah, 'cause Veneice is prettier than any white girl you ever can see," Verby shouted out, and the entire class broke out in laughter.

"That just earned you a trip to Principal Woods' office." Julia pointed to the door.

"Yes ma'am," Verby said apologetically.

"Tell him you spoke out of turn, and that's why I sent you there for the remainder of the class period."

Verby got up and walked toward the door. "Yes ma'am," he muttered and then disappeared out of the classroom.

Veneice followed his movement out the door. She felt a little embarrassed because he'd called out her name, and then somewhat sorry that he'd been sent to the principal's office. But that was sufficient proof to her that he really did like her and that Poppa might be wrong when it came to Verby. She would make it a point to be kinder and nicer to him for the rest of the semester.

"Hey girl, Verby really likes you," Esther said as she walked up Elgin Street with Veneice and Ruth.

"I guess he's nice enough," Veneice said blushing as they crossed over Greenwood on their way to Kenosha Street where all three of them lived a block apart.

"You guys going to be boyfriend and girlfriend?" Ruth asked.

"You know I can't have no boyfriend. My Poppa would kill me."

"Your Poppa doesn't have to know about it. Just something you all can do at school," Ruth suggested.

"Yeah, isn't like he's going to be coming to your house taking you out on a date," Esther added.

Veneice did like the idea of having a boyfriend, and Verby had demonstrated his interest in her. "I don't know, he hasn't asked me to be his girlfriend," she said.

"If he did, what would you say?" Ruth asked.

"I don't know. I'd have to think about it."

"You know the prom's coming up in a couple months and you going to need a date," Esther reminded Veneice.

"Right now, I'm not even thinking about a prom," Veneice sighed. "It's going to take a whole lot of work on Poppa to get him to even let me go to the prom if they got dancing. Then I have to convince him to let me have a date. That's asking a whole lot."

Esther put her arm around her friend and said, "You sure carrying a load. Can't your momma convince him to let you go?"

"I don't know, Poppa got his own mind and don't hardly ever listen to nobody else, especially a woman."

"My daddy's the same way," Ruth chimed in. "If mama trying to give him some advice, he don't hardly listen. He'll say this is men's business and not suited for a woman."

"When I get married, my husband's going to listen to me or else we going to have big problems," Esther said.

"Yeah, my daddy tells us that it's part of the natural family structure from Africa. He said in Africa the man makes all the decisions for his family, and only men attend business or government meetings for the tribe," Ruth added.

87

"I guess Poppa still got a lot of African in him 'cause he sure don't listen to Momma when it comes to making decisions about what we can and can't do," Veneice said.

"Whatcha gonna do girl?" Esther asked as they sauntered down Kenosha toward Veneice's home.

"One thing, I can't decide before I get home," Veneice said.

"Want me to talk to Verby for you, let him know that you're interested in being his girlfriend?" Esther volunteered.

"You got enough nerve to do that?" Veneice asked, as they now stood in front of her yard.

"For one of my favorite friends, yes, I do?"

"Don't say too much, just kind of ask him does he like me."

"I'll be with you when you do it," Ruth said.

"I got to get on inside. Mama doesn't allow us to stand in front of the house and talk. She thinks it looks bad. I'll see you all in the morning," Veneice said.

"And then we'll talk about it some more," Esther said. "This is exciting. Veneice going to have herself a boyfriend."

"Ssh, before Mama hears you."

"She isn't going to hear us," Ruth said.

"See you tomorrow," Esther said as she hugged Veneice.

"Until tomorrow," Veneice ran up the steps to the verandah and into the house.

ELEVEN

"What the hell is going on over there in Niggertown?" Jones screamed as he threw a copy of Saturday's *Tulsa Star* on the floor. Calvin Hendricks, a local member of the recently established Knights of the Ku Klux Klan sat in a chair in front of Jones's desk. Jones had called him once he read the article in the Smitherman paper about Dr. Du Bois coming to Tulsa. He'd never deliberately reached out to the Klan because of their reputation but now felt the time was right for them to begin a relationship.

"They got the nerve to bring that rabble rouser Du Bois to our city and announce it right in our face in this rag of a newspaper. Smitherman's gone too far this time. There is no way the decent white people of this city are going to let that socialist pig speak anywhere in our city."

"I'm not sure I know who this man is," Cal said.

"All you need to know is that he is an uppity arrogant son of a bitch who goes around the country trying to convince Negroes that they are the equal to white folks. He's caused more riots and killings in this country than any other one person."

"Where's he from?" Cal asked

"New York, where else? He travels to other peaceful towns and makes speeches that stir up the local Negroes then he takes off back to New York and hides while all hell breaks out.

"Why don't the government arrest him as a traitor?"

"Because the fucking Harding Administration is afraid it might cause more problems by doing that." Jones got up from his chair, walked over to the window and looked out. "The FBI just doesn't seem to know that an organized effort among all the Negroes in this country could be a real problem. And this Du Bois man is just the man that could get them together to fight whites."

"We ain't going to have that here in Tulsa," Cal exclaimed. "The Klan now has enough members right here in Tulsa to stop that man from speaking. And if we don't have enough good white men here we can sure bring some down from Oklahoma City."

"Where are the reasonable thinking niggers over there?" Jones continued looking down on Greenwood and Archer Streets, ignoring Cal. "What are men like O. W. Gurley thinking about? Don't he know that he and the other leaders don't need to be rocking the boat this way?" Jones walked back over to his chair, reached down and picked up the copy of the *Star*. "And that arrogant Black bastard Smitherman got the nerve to splatter the words, 'The Motto of Every Negro Should be You Push Me and I Push You,' all over the front page of this disgraceful paper. Isn't that like throwing some shit right in our face? That chocolate-covered coon wouldn't get away with this in Mississippi or Alabama and definitely not in Texas."

"Like I said before, we're ready to act," Cal reiterated his position.

"No, I don't think we're ready to call in the muscle yet," Jones replied. "I think we can still take the legal approach. I believe we might be able to get a court order banning him from speaking anywhere in Tulsa."

"What if that don't work?" Cal asked.

"Then we'll talk about the muscle."

"Hell, why don't we just kill him and any of those coons down there that say anything?" Cal scowled.

90

"You just can't go around killing these nigger leaders," Jones shot back. "The country has a certain image it has to maintain throughout the world."

"Yeah, looks like it's a nigger loving image if you're afraid to kill 'em."

"I'm sure that day will come, but we're not quite there yet." Jones leaned across his desk. "I think I need some time to think about this. Hold off on bringing your men down from Oklahoma City. I'll call the mayor, and I know just the right judge to talk to.

If nothing works, then we'll have to consider your way."

"Let me know when and my men will be here," Cal said.

Jones came from behind his desk and placed his arm around Cal. "We'll get this taken care of. Somehow we got to make sure niggertown stays just that, niggertown."

"I'll wait to hear from you," Cal said as he opened the door to Jones' office. "And remember I can muster up a hundred men overnight if need be." He finished and walked out of the office and down the hall.

Jones closed his office door and hurried back into the reception area. He approached his secretary. "Margaret, come in my office and bring your writing pad. I got to dictate an editorial right now for tomorrow's paper."

***

Saturday afternoons were usually Dr. Jackson's rest time. If possible, he tried not to see patients after twelve o'clock and on Sunday, which was the day for prayer and worship. But he had taken a scarlet fever case and his commitment to his practice dictated that he go and check on the little boy. Luther hadn't been back to the house, so that was a good sign. If the boy's parents followed his instructions, then the fever should have broken by now. But he had to go and check for himself.

He got up from his desk, grabbed his medical bag and started downstairs. He knew Julia would not be happy but she had to understand that he had no choice. He could hear music from the Victrola in the parlor. He reached the bottom of the stairs and walked into the parlor. Julia was stretched out on the divan with eyes closed, enjoying the music. If she was asleep, he hated to wake her but didn't want to leave without letting her know he was gone.

Dr. Jackson leaned over her. "Darling, I have to step out for a little while."

Julia jumped. "Oh, you startled me."

91

"I'm sorry. I didn't want to wake you, but didn't want to leave without letting you know I was gone."

"Andrew, where are you going? You have your bag, and I thought you were not going to see patients on Saturday afternoon?"

"I know but I have to check on that little boy, you know the one whose father came by here the other night."

"You mean the white man?'

"Yes, darling, the white man."

"You going down to Shantytown in the middle of the afternoon on a Saturday?"

"I have to. I have a patient down there."

Julia jumped up from the divan. "Well, I'm going with you," she said quite emphatically. "I'm like your father. I'm not going to sit around and wait for someone to knock on my door and tell me something happened to you."

Dr. Jackson stopped, a little surprised by his wife's sudden outburst. "What?"

"You heard me. I'm going with you." She rushed past him. "I'll only be a minute," she said and disappeared out of the parlor.

After the couple passed East Lansing on Archer Street, Dr. Jackson slowed down trying to remember what alley he had turned into the other night. It wasn't quite as cold and people were out. He passed by what he knew as a speakeasy, and men were hanging out in front. They gave him a hard stare as he drove by. It was known by black and white alike that white folks hated to see a Negro driving an automobile. That probably angered them more than anything else. And his was a brand new shiny Ford. He needed to hurry up and find that alley. Once he reached Luther's house, he could relax. The man had told him not to worry while he was at his house. No one would dare bother him.

92

He passed a couple more Choc joints, and again all he saw were hard looking white men who would probably hang him and Julia and think nothing of it.

"You all right?" he asked.

"I'm fine." Julia was also staring out the window. "But I still don't understand why you'd come down here among these people when they could find a white doctor to treat their child."

"I don't expect you to understand," Dr. Jackson said almost in a whisper. "I do hope you will accept what I have to do, no matter the color of the patient's skin. Sickness and disease doesn't discriminate, and neither should doctors."

"White doctors do, Andrew. If I was sick in dire need, you think those white doctors would help me or the white hospital on the southside would admit me?"

"No, I don't think they would," Dr. Jackson finally spotted the alley and made his right turn. He pulled in front of Luther's house and cut off the engine. "But the last people on earth we want to measure our humanity by are white people in Oklahoma. Wait while I check."

"Andrew, don't you dare leave me in this car alone," she shrieked.

"I'm only going to the door." He couldn't help but to smile as he walked up to the front door. He found Julia's apprehension refreshing. Made him feel good that in a crisis she would call on him. He knocked on the door and in moments, Luther opened it.

"Dr. Jackson, you did come back," Luther said.

"I told you I would," Dr. Jackson said. "My wife is with me, and she would never forgive me if I left her in the car."

"Let me slip on my shoes, and I'll go out and watch your car while you all are inside." Luther left the door open and went inside. "Helen, Dr. Jackson is here. And he got his wife with him," he said from inside the house.

Dr. Jackson signaled for Julia to get out of the car. She did and joined him at the door. "Is everything okay?" she asked.

"Just fine, dear. Luther went to put on some shoes. He's going to watch the car while we're inside."

Luther appeared back at the door. "Ma'am," he muttered and slightly tipped his head. "Y'all can go on in now. Don't worry,

93

ain't nobody going to mess with your car."

"Thank you, Luther," Julia said.

As they walked into the house, the same stench and suffocating heat hit Dr. Jackson, and from his wife's response hit her also. She turned from him with a frown.

Helen stood waiting at the entrance to the bedroom. "Thank you Doctor, for coming back," she said as Dr. Jackson walked into the bedroom and over to the bed. Julia stopped right in the doorway next to Helen.

"Ma'am," Helen muttered, and just as Luther did, she tipped her head slightly.

"My name's Julia; how you holding up, dear?"

"How's the boy been doing?" Dr. Jackson called out before Helen could answer his wife.

Helen turned away from Julia and looked toward Dr. Jackson. "I believe the fever's gone and looks like some of the red spots done gone away too," she said.

"Has he been taking his medicine regularly and on time?" he asked while placing the back of his hand on the boy's forehead.

"Yes sir, just like you told us to do." Helen moved a little closer in the room. "Thank you, Doctor. I don't know what we'd done without you."

"We're not quite out of the woods yet," Dr. Jackson said as he lifted the boy's pajama top to check the red spots on his chest. The young boy stared at the doctor.

"How you doing, young man?" Dr. Jackson asked.

94

"Fine," the boy whispered. "Mama said I'm getting better."

"Yes, you're doing just fine. You'll be up and running around in no time." Dr. Jackson rose up from over the boy. "Now I'm going to give your mother some more medicine. I want you to take it just like a big boy."

"Yes sir," the boy said.

Dr. Jackson opened his bag and took out another bottle. He handed it to Helen. "Here, this a little different medication than I gave you the first time. But the dosage should remain the same. I do believe your son is going to make it. The fever has broken, and that's always a good sign." He looked over at Julia who smiled at him. It was a smile that said now I understand.

The doctor closed his bag, and they all walked back into the living room.

"Remember, do not miss giving him the medicine. That is crucial in fighting this disease. And plenty of water and most important, rest," Dr. Jackson instructed.

"Without fail, Doctor, I'll follow your instructions," Helen said.

"Good, and I'll be back in a few days to check on him." Dr. Jackson walked over to the front door and opened it. Julia stood next to him.

The cold felt good after suffering through the stifling heat inside the house.

"God bless you," Julia said as she hugged Helen, and then they walked back to the car.

Luther jumped out of the passenger seat and held the door for Julia. She got in and he closed it shut. He then ran around the other side to open the driver's side door.

Dr. Jackson held his hand up. "That's not necessary," he said and opened his door. "I told your wife that I'd be back in a few days," he said and closed the door.

He waited as Luther cranked the car and he started it. Luther waved as they drove off. The two remained silent until they got back on Archer. As they passed over Lansing and into their side of town, Julia reached over, placed her hand on Andrew's leg, turned and smiled at him.

TWELVE

April 1921

Mabel arrived at the church early just to make sure all the food was ready to be prepared. The other ladies would be there by seven o'clock to do the cooking. Dressed in a blue cotton suit with a blue hat and heels to match, she climbed out of the Ford and watched as Pressley drove off to go home and get ready for the big day at Mount Zion Baptist Church. It had taken eight years to raise the money and finally hire an architect and construction company to build the most magnificent religious edifice in the city. During these long eight years, the congregation had met in a converted dance hall during the winter when it was cold and often outside in an empty lot when it was warm. Outside in the lot, the sun would shine down on them delivering rays of warmth sent directly from God. Now Mount Zion, right across the street from the high school, stood complete and ready for the initial service that morning at eleven o'clock.

After Pressley drove off, Mabel stood right out front and smiled. Every day during the construction she'd walked the two blocks from their home to watch as they laid red bricks, put in the stained glass windows, the large double door and the crowning piece, the belfry that reached out toward the sky and received blessings from God. The congregation knew He was pleased because all one hundred and fifty members had sacrificed for years, always paying their ten percent tithes and finding extra money to go into a building fund. They had sacrificed for the Lord, and Mabel knew that's exactly how it should be done. You make sacrifices, and you will receive rewards. She and Pressley certainly had been blessed with God's rewards, owning two successful businesses, a beautiful two story brick home and of course the recently purchased houseful of new furniture all the way from Europe.

Mabel strode up the five cement steps, through the double doors and into the foyer. She stood there for a moment feeling the newness of the building. She made her way into the sanctuary and stared up at the large cross behind the pulpit and choir stand. Both would be occupied in a few hours, and the choir would fill the church with praise and glory through music to the Lord and his son Jesus Christ. She could feel goose bumps all up and down her arms. Suddenly she choked up with joy, and the tears blurred her sight. She really did love her church and her minister, Reverend R. A. Whittaker, who had kept the congregation together over the years, though there were many times when many different members had wanted to give up. He tolerated no notions of quitting.

As Mabel stood there staring at the pulpit, she could see him always saying God won't tolerate quitters when you have been instructed by Him to build His tabernacle. Sometimes he would fuss, and on other occasions he persuaded and cajoled the members to remain strong.

Mabel walked back out of the sanctuary into the foyer and finally down the stairs to the basement and the kitchen. She silently prayed that this day would be a grand one as more than a thousand residents of Greenwood were expected to fill the church to capacity. They would come from all other denominations in order to help the members of this brand new house of worship praise and thank the Lord for what He had done for them at Mount Zion and all over Greenwood.

A smile crossed Mabel's face when she walked into the kitchen and saw one of the oldest members of Mount Zion, Lucinda Daniels, a short, stocky, gray haired woman who had been with the church since it broke with First Baptist back in 1909. Lucinda was standing over a large steaming pot of hot water, pulling feathers from one of the many chickens on the counter. Mabel was surprised that someone had arrived before her. But on second thought, she knew the one person who would be there on that special day very early in the morning would be Lucinda. That woman loved Mount Zion. Mabel could only wonder what this fine lady, born a slave and still in many ways working much like a slave as a maid in South Tulsa, must feel.

98

"Good morning, Lucinda," Mabel said as she hugged the elderly woman.

"Good morning back to you." Lucinda kept plucking the feathers from the chicken. "I didn't expect nobody here till about nine this morning."

"I was so wired up I just couldn't sit still. So I got dressed and had Pressley drive me on over here. I thought I'd be the first one in the church this morning, but I should've known better than that. I should've known you'd be here."

Lucinda did not look over at Mabel. Instead she kept her concentration on the plucking. "We been waiting a long time for this day," she said, still not looking up. "It's been eight long years." She turned and smiled. "And you played a big role in making this happen once you joined Mount Zion. You got such a good business head, you just made this happen."

"No, Lucinda, it wasn't me. It was a faith in our God that all we had to do was make the effort, and He'd do the rest." Mabel couldn't stand there and watch her friend work with those chickens without doing something herself. She moved over to the icebox, opened it and pulled out several bunches of collard greens.

"What you think you doing?" Lucinda scowled. "Don't you dare get yourself all dirty. You all dressed up for church. We got plenty help on the way, and we'll finish this meal before Reverend Whittaker's halfway through the service."

Mabel dropped the greens on the counter near where Lucinda was cleaning the chickens. She held her arms out away from her dress and rubbed her hands together, knocking off the water and dirt from the greens.

99

"And anyways, this ain't your kinda work," Lucinda railed on. "You're a business lady that got her own business and doing real fine. This kinda work is for us that works as maids."

"What you mean, I want you to know that I have to cook every night for Pressley. And what Negro woman you know that don't know how to cook?"

"That's neither here nor there. Your job this morning ain't to cook. Any minute now this kitchen going to fill up with women who want to cook and are quite good at it. Don't believe me, then go ask those white folks cross the railroad tracks."

Mabel moved back away from counter. "Think we're going to have a good turnout today?" she asked changing the subject.

"Girl, this place gonna be overflowing with Black bodies." Lucinda finished plucking the chicken, grabbed another and dropped it in the hot water. "Every Negro in Greenwood going to be here. Rest of these churches around here going to be missing a lot of their people 'cause they gonna be sitting right upstairs and lot of 'em gonna be standing."

"I guess you're right. This is something the whole community been waiting for," Mabel said. "All the articles in the *Star* done created a whole lot of interest in this church."

"Remember what Reverend Whittaker told us last year when we had our doubts 'bout getting the fifty thousand dollars to finish the construction," Lucinda said.

"Sure do, it still rings in my ears."

Lucinda dropped the chicken back in the water and turned to have direct eye contact with Mabel. "Yes Lord, I remember those words so clearly." She paused for a second, and Mabel saw tears fill her friend's eyes. "God may not be there when you want Him, but He is always right on time," Lucinda continued. "It's when you think you need Him and He's not there that your faith is tested. Last year when the money ran out our faith was being tested."

"You're right. Reverend Whittaker took us right into prayer, helped restore our faith and now look at us."

100   "The rest of those girls should be getting here real soon." Lucinda turned back and grabbed the chicken for plucking.

"I told you I can help."

"And I told you not with your church clothes on. Don't worry, those girls will be here. Ain't no way on God's earth they'd miss participating in this."

Mabel stood watching her friend tackle removing feathers from the chickens. She felt a little guilty for not helping when she heard stirring above them.

"That's them now," Lucinda said.

Instantly, a small army of women bounded down the stairs and marched to the kitchen. Mabel thought maybe every maid in Tulsa had decided to come to the church and help prepare the best meal anywhere in the city. Mabel smiled and she felt warm inside. Young, middle aged, and a few older women were wearing beautiful dresses, some even in heels. Today they were not in their white maid dresses with the white shoes, those demeaning clothes they were forced to wear as badges of inferiority, identifying them as servants lined up ready to work. Their smiles, their chatter and their joy exuded their determination to make this particular church celebration a very special one. Tomorrow morning when they made their way back across the Frisco tracks they would once again put on that veil for the protection of their dignity. But this day they could take it off and be themselves. Mabel felt all choked up as she watched them work their magic.

Four of the younger girls surrounded Lucinda, gently took her by the arm and moved her away from the sink.

"Miss Lucinda, we'll get these chickens plucked, gutted, cut and ready to fry," one of the girls said.

Lucinda looked at her watch. "It's seven thirty and knowing Reverend Whittaker, he going to have a very long church service this morning. They won't be ready to serve dinner until after two o'clock so we got until one-thirty to prepare this meal." She paused and waved her arms. "We got twenty of us here, and we'll have dinner ready by that time. I'm getting ready to divide responsibility right now."

Mabel saw the tears well up in Lucinda's eyes again.   101

"Yeah, Miss Lucinda go get ready for something you been waiting to happen for over eight years," one of the other girls said. "For once we cooking for our folks instead of them, and it feel awfully good."

"Amen," they all said in unison.

The official first morning worship service in the new Mount Zion Baptist Church was scheduled for eleven o'clock. By ten thirty all seven hundred seats in the sanctuary were filled. Visiting worshippers stood in the foyer.

Mabel had met Pressley in the sanctuary just before the crowd arrived. They sat in the second row of pews as VIP's, and right behind the deacons. Mabel would have preferred to sit further back so she could have had a bird's eye view of the visitors. However, since she had been on the building committee for the past four years and worked the business deal with the bank for a fifty thousand dollar loan to complete construction, Reverend Whittaker had insisted that she sit up front.

Mabel couldn't help herself. She kept turning around and looking to the back of the sanctuary as the crowd made its way inside. She saw Smitherman and his family, the Stradfords and Captain Townsend Jackson with his family including Dr. Jackson and Julia, his oldest daughter Minnie Mae and oldest son Townsend Jr. Their family practically took up one entire row. Further back behind them, O. B. Mann and his wife sat with their two children. Just a few minutes before eleven, O. W. Gurley rushed into the sanctuary, spotted Emma, who had saved him room next to her, and made his way to her. John and Loula Williams with their son Billy sat at the far end of the same pew as the Gurley's. It made Mabel feel good knowing that the entire business community, all the leaders of the Negro community, had turned out to celebrate with her church.

Finally, right at eleven o'clock, Reverend Whittaker, two of the senior deacons, Lucinda Porter as the eldest member of the congregation and the choir strolled down the center aisle singing, "I got a song, you got a song. All God's children got a song. When I get to Heaven gonna sing my song. Gonna sing all over God's Heaven."

102

The choir took their place behind Reverend Whittaker who stood at the pulpit and waited for them to finish the opening song. Once the choir was positioned, the singing stopped .

"Praise the Lord, what a glorious day," Reverend Whittaker said. "Isn't it a blessing to know God our Father and Jesus our Savior are by our side at all times, and even though He may not answer when you call, He is always right on time. Praise be to the Lord."

"Praise the Lord," the congregation responded.

"Who has watch over this service?" Reverend Whittaker called out.

"Jesus Christ," again the congregation also called out loudly.

"Who we gonna dedicate this place to this morning?"

"Jesus Christ our Savior."

"Do you love Him? Do you love Him?" Reverend Whittaker's voice reverberated throughout the sanctuary.

"Yes we love Him," the congregation shouted.

The level of excitement was high and could be felt by the congregation. Mabel wasn't sure she could contain her emotions. Reverend Whittaker needed to bring it down a couple levels before she passed out. But the spirit had control of him, and no one or anything could get in the way.

"I want the entire congregation to stand on your feet, raise your arms high in the air, wave them side to side and repeat after me. I love you, Lord. I praise you, Lord. I'm here to serve you, Lord. Bless this new house of worship, Lord bless the members, bless all our visitors sharing this wonderful occasion with us today, bless those who wanted to be here and couldn't make it and bless this church so that it will have a long and prosperous existence right here in the Greenwood community." Reverend Whittaker finished and returned to his pastor's chair.

The energy level in Mount Zion stayed at a crescendo as the Reverend navigated the first service through a series of spirituals rendered by the choir, a number of testimonials by members from the oldest to the youngest, a dozen visitors' comments and an inspiring sermon built around the importance of faith in the individual's life. The first service at the new Mount Zion Baptist Church ended right at two o'clock. The special guests and members who cared to stay headed to the basement where the wonderful aromas of fried chicken, greens and sweet potatoes, tickled their senses and invited them to sit down and enjoy fellowship and an outstanding meal prepared with love from the cooks.

103

The ladies had decorated the thirty round tables with bright tablecloths and a flower arrangement in the middle. Mabel and

Pressley sat a table with Smitherman, his wife, Gurley and Emma, and the Stradford's. After they made it through the buffet lines, they sat, ate and talked.

"This church has to be one of the finest built churches in all Tulsa," Smitherman said.

"It's sure to make some people in this town very unhappy," Stradford added.

"What's new?" Pressley said as he tossed a forkful of greens into his mouth.

"Reverend Whittaker must be very careful," Gurley joined in the conversation.

"Why?" Smitherman asked.

"You remember what happened to Reverend White back in 1913?"

"No one knows why the white folks forced Mount Zion off the property," Stradford said. "But I guess your point is that Reverend White was an outspoken critic of segregation, which was on the rise in Oklahoma back then."

"Our situation here is much different," Mabel said.

"How you figure it's so different?" Gurley asked.

"The congregation owns both the land and the building," she answered. "Only way they can get this from us is to burn it down. And you got to be a pretty godless devil-driven people to destroy a house of worship."

"Remember who you're talking about," Smitherman said.

104

"White people, and that says it all."

"May I get your attention, please?" Reverend Whittaker called out to the guests. He stood at the end of the buffet table, and all the young ladies who prepared the feast stood next to him. The talking stopped.

"These lovely young ladies spent hours this morning preparing this delicious buffet dinner for us, and I just want to thank you all for the magnificent meal and if any of you are in search of a church home, we welcome you here at Mount Zion."

The young lady who had insisted that Lucinda do no more work that morning stepped forward. "We ladies have prepared many meals for those people across the tracks, and tomorrow we will make that long trip over there to do it all week. But today will sustain us and give us the strength to make it through another week. And we want to thank Miss Lucinda for giving us a chance to participate in God's work in a very small way. And thank you, Reverend Whittaker, for being such a man of God." She finished and stepped back to stand with the others.

"This is a most magnificent day and it is just the beginning of many great things we plan to do in the name of the Lord in the days, months and years to come right here at Mount Zion. Enjoy your dinners, and you all are invited to attend Tuesday's prayer meeting and Wednesday's Bible study class here at the church." Reverend Whittaker finished, shook hands with some of the guests and disappeared out of the room.

"When the pastor leaves the room, I think that's a good sign for all of us to do the same," Mabel said.

"I guess the next time this many Greenwood residents will be together under one roof will be when Dr. Du Bois speaks," Smitherman exclaimed.

"Let's hope it goes just as smoothly as today has gone," Gurley added.

"You worry too much, O. W.," Stradford said.

As others around them began to get up and head for the stairs, the entire table did the same.

"Mount Zion is now one of the finest looking churches in the city, we have two wonderful hotels and many other successful businesses and the most important Negro in America will pay a visit to our community in a week," Smitherman said. "I'd say we're doing quite well as a community." 105

"That's because we are blessed, and let's work to keep those beautiful blessings flowing." Mabel ended the conversation as they followed the crowd to the stairs and out of the church.

THIRTEEN

The extremely heavy April rain slowed down traffic at the shoeshine stand on Monday morning, which usually was a busy time. The lack of business caused Dick feelings of anxiety. No customers meant no money, and that was not a good thing. He'd gotten used to having twenty-five to thirty dollars in his pocket or buying himself something new, as well as slipping a ten dollar bill to Aunt Damie every once in a while.

Sitting in the shine chair with the outside door closed tight because of the rain, Dick racked his brain trying to figure out new ways to make money. He'd lowered his standards shining shoes and would do nothing less than that insulting profession. If white, he could do like the white boys and stake a claim to some land, and maybe it would produce oil. It just wasn't fair that peckerwoods had all the opportunities to get rich for no other reason than they were white.

Dick stared out the window at the rain and the people rushing up and down Main Street trying to find shelter. He needed to find a way to make their money without having to practically kiss their butts. Roscoe Wright had found a way, even though it was illegal. White folks loved to play the numbers hoping their lucky number would come in, and Roscoe made lots of dollar bills controlling the outcome of who won or lost. In fact, it also worked with Black people but the real money came from the south side of the railroad tracks.

Dick perked up from his slouch in the chair when Sarah came running out of the Drexel Building with a bag, shot across the street to the shine stand, flung open the door and stepped inside. She slammed the door close.

"Where's Robert?" She asked.

"He didn't make it in this morning, and from the way it looks outside I probably shouldn't have come in either."

Sarah pulled two pair of black shoes out of the bag and tried to hand them to Dick. He pulled his hands back.

"I don't want them," he said.

"They from Mr. Sandler on the second floor," Sarah said. "He asked me to bring them over here for Robert to shine."

"That's why I ain't gonna take 'em."

Sarah placed the shoes in the vacant shine chair and folded up the bag. "You ain't going to shine them?"

"Hell no, he didn't send 'em over here for me to shine, did he?"

"But he wanted me to come and get them in an hour."

"You can come and get 'em, but they won't be shined. Robert got his customers, and I got mine. You can tell Sandler that Robert wasn't here, but he'll be here tomorrow and he can get 'em then."

"What you been doing, anyway?" Sarah asked.

"I been working, trying to make some money."

"What'd you do while I was in Kansas City?"

"Same thing you did while you was in Kansas City," Dick chuckled.

"I don't know what you mean by that."

"I mean if you did something with your ex-husband while you was up there, then I did the same thing."

"That's just silly. I was there to get my divorce, not go to bed with him." Sarah climbed up and sat in the other shine chair.

"Girl, what you doing?" Dick shrieked. "You know you ain't suppose to be over here messing around."

"Why not? What they going to do to me for just sitting over here talking to a Negro? And anyway, I got a reason. Sandler wants his shoes shined."

"How about the elevator? Who's operating it?"

"Nobody right now. Ain't nobody in and out of the building 'cause of the rain."

Dick's expression changed, as he turned to better face Sarah. He had a slight smile across his face. "Sarah, have you ever heard of the numbers game called policy wheel?"

"Yeah, some of the businessmen in the Drexel Building play it everyday."

"What, you know about it?"

"Moses collects numbers from the businessmen and places them with some man in Greenwood."

"Moses, the building custodian?"

"That's the only Moses over there."

"Why you ain't told me this before?" Dick frowned. "Damn girl, that's extra money we could've been making."

Sarah crossed her arms. "Why would I tell you? I didn't know you were interested."

"I'm interested in anything where I can make some money."

"What's that got to do with me?"

"We could be making that money. I know Roscoe Wright, and he'd let me work that building for him instead of old ass Moses. Shit, that man makes two to three dollars a day. And if he places numbers with his two dollars and hits, he wins big. Even if you only bet a nickel on your three numbers, you can pocket nine dollars."

With arms still crossed, Sarah looked straight ahead and her body stiffened. "Dick, I'm not interested in any kind of business like that. I'm only interested in you."

109

Encouraged by her admission of interest in him, Dick leaned closer to her. "Then you'll help me get that business from Moses," he seductively whispered. "We get enough money, and we can leave out of this old backward ass town. We can go on up to Chicago or maybe even New York. I hear there's a revolution in thinking taking place in a place called Harlem, and Black and white live together with no problems."

Sarah took both hands and pushed him away. "How you know what's going on up there?" She asked

"The porters bring back all kinds of news 'bout what Negroes are doing in New York and Chicago."

"I ain't no Negro so I don't care about all that, and I ain't interested in no business you talking about doing in the Drexel Building. Probably end up getting me fired."

Dick reached out and tried to grab her around the waist. "But you care about this Negro, and I know you want to see me dressed in the finest clothes, and wearing big diamond rings."

"Stop, boy." Sarah pushed him away from her. "You crazy or something. White man see you touching me, and you're going to be killed."

"I'll stop when you agree to help me get that business." He again tried to grab her around the waist.

She pushed his hand away and jumped down out of the chair. "I need to get back."

Suddenly the door swung open and Robert rushed in, but abruptly stopped when he was face to face with Sarah. "What's going on? He asked looking directly at Dick.

"Nothing at all," Dick answered. "Sarah brought over two pair of shoes from…" he hesitated and looked at Sarah.

"From Mr. Sandler in the Drexel Building. Said he wanted these back this afternoon, and Dick refused to shine them."

"No, that's not what I said." Dick looked over at Robert. "What I said was that Sandler was your customer and I wasn't going to take your business."

"I think I better leave now." Sarah swung the door open and rain splattered in the shine parlor.

"You sure you want to leave right now, hard as it's raining?" Dick asked.

"Don't be funny. I have to leave; you know, I do have a job." She paused and looked directly at Dick. "Well?"

"Yeah, tonight at Pretty Belle's, around nine o'clock."

110

She turned and walked out into the rain, pushing the door closed behind her.

"I didn't think you was going to make it in today," Dick said as he watched Sarah run across the street and disappear in the Drexel Building. "What made you change your mind?"

Robert also watched Sarah, then turned and glowered at Dick. "Man, what the hell's wrong with you?"

"What you mean?" Dick asked smiling.

"You know damn well what I mean. I saw you grab at that woman."

"She's my woman. Why can't I show her a little affection?"

"Dick, don't do that kind of thing in here. White man see you with your hands touching that woman and he gonna lynch both of us." Robert paused to release a deep breath. "They ain't gonna care none that I ain't had nothing to do with it. All they gonna see is two Black men inside this little space with that white woman, and with one of them touching her, then every peckerwood in Tulsa will line up to put the rope around our necks."

"Your problem Robert is that you worry too much."

"And your problem is that you don't worry enough." Robert took the two pair of shoes and placed shoehorns inside. He then began to apply shoe polish to the first pair.

***

Dr. Jackson figured this would be the last time he would have to visit Luther's son. And as he stared out his office window at the rain, he also figured this would be a good time to do it. He doubted that anyone would visit the office in the next hour. If a patient planned to walk or catch a jittney, they would be soaked before they reached his office. His two appointments had already cancelled because they had no transportation.

With his car parked right out back, his exposure to the downpour would be minimal. The muddy roads could cause some problems but not to the degree that he need worry. His car was a

111

strong and sturdy vehicle.

The doctor packed his medical bag, walked out to the reception area and said to his receptionist, "Be back in about an hour. If anyone comes in tell them to wait and that I won't be long." He ducked out of the office, into his car and started up Greenwood to Archer.

Soon as Dr. Jackson made the left turn onto Archer, the rain seemed to come down much harder. Even with his windshield wipers going full blast, he could barely see the road in front of him. He slowed his speed down to ten miles per hour. He felt the change in the ride as he drove off the last of the cobblestone road onto the dirt. The rain had created large mud holes and every time he dropped into one of them, he feared the car would get stuck. Maybe this was not such a good idea after all. He considered turning around and going back. There was no traffic on Archer Street, no pedestrians outside, and it continued to get darker. The large drops of rain pelted against the roof and the hood and the car hit a hole causing him to jolt forward against the steering wheel.

Dr. Jackson's eyes squinted as he tried to determine the location of the alley for his right turn. If he missed the road, he would end up in one of the large drainage ditches and be swept down into the Arkansas River. He slowed his speed to five miles an hour. He immediately noticed someone moving around right outside the car, and knew he couldn't see them if they darted out into the street. Why would anyone be out in the rain, he wondered.

The doctor lost vision of the figure outside the car and slowed down even more. When he did, the figure jumped on the running board of the car and knocked on the window. Whoever it was couldn't get in, because he had locked the doors when he got inside. Evidently, the person held onto the door handle with one hand and continued banging the window with the free one. Momentarily, Jackson felt sorry for the person. He was soaked and had to be miserable, but he didn't dare open the door. Robberies and murders ran rampant in that part of town.

"Get off the car," Dr. Jackson shouted.

Outside noises and the pounding of the rain made it impossible for Jackson to hear what the man was saying. He figured the person was asking for help.

"I can't," Dr. Jackson hollered. "Get off my car."

Maybe if he sped up, he could jolt the person off the car. But then in the pouring rain, he might lose control and kill both of them. Again he glanced over at the person who was now holding something in his hand. It looked like a gun. The doctor had no choice. He had to get that person off his car. He was a sitting target for a bullet. In a series of repetitive motions of the car, he increased the speed and hit the brakes. Fortunately, the car did not spin out of control, but the person held on. But he did drop what was in his free hand because he began banging on the window again.

Dr. Jackson sped up and hit the brakes another time and heard a thud, looked over and the man was gone. Had he killed him? As a doctor could he just drive away leaving the man to die on the side of the road? After all, the reason he was in this situation was because he felt compelled to treat a young boy in a part of town that under normal circumstances he wouldn't visit. Dr. Jackson hit the brakes, put the car in reverse and slowly backed up to the spot where he figured he heard the thump.

He got out, and the rain and wind practically knocked him over. Instantly the doctor was thoroughly soaked. His calculation was correct as he almost stumbled over a man lying motionless on the side of the dirt road.

"Can you hear me?" he shouted.

The man did not respond so he knelt down in the mud and felt for a pulse. He got one and was relieved the man was not dead. He had to help him. He had to get him into his car and to a hospital for treatment. Getting to Luther's house was no longer a priority. Jackson grabbed the man under his arms and slid him in the mud to the car. He opened the back door and conjured up enough strength to hoist the man's body onto the floor of the car.

113

The doctor climbed back into the drivers seat, closed the door and cautiously made a U-turn. He had to get to the hospital, and it had to be Frissel Memorial, the Black one. No way could a Negro take a white man to the white hospital and convince them that he had nothing to do with his condition. And he dare not tell them the injury happened when he forced him off the running board of his car.

Fortunately the rain had slackened, giving him minimal visibility. He could see at least a half block ahead. He still drove slowly, and let out a sigh of relief when the car finally reached the paved road. Hopefully, Dr. Bridgewater would be at the hospital, and the two of them could save this man's life.

Dr. Jackson reached Greenwood and turned right heading for Brady Street. For the next five minutes he prayed that he wouldn't get stopped by the police he spotted driving on the other side of the street. He didn't and finally turned left going west on Brady to the hospital. When he arrived, he went in the emergency entrance, parked the car right out front and ran inside and got two orderlies to help him get the man out of the car.

As they carried the man down the hallway, Dr. Bridgewater waited for him.

"What in the world happened to you? He asked. "My God man, you are filthy. Have you been rolling around in the mud?"

"Not quite—"

"And who is this man?" Dr. Bridgewater cut him off. "How in the world did you manage to bring an unconscious white man into this hospital?"

"He jumped on my running board and tried to force his way into my car. He fell off when I hit the brakes."

Dr. Bridgewater leaned over the man and began to examine him. "And once we save his life, what do we tell the people across the tracks?" He asked.

Dr. Jackson came in close to Dr. Bridgewater and also began to examine the man. "If we save his life, why will we have to tell them anything?"

114

"Because more than likely he's going to go hollering to the sheriff that a Negro driving a fancy car tried to run him over." Dr. Bridgewater stopped his examination and stared at his friend. "Why didn't you just leave him out there?"

"You know why," Dr. Jackson shot back. "We do our job believing in the oath we took as doctors."

Dr. Bridgewater returned to the examination. "Looks like

he might have a few broken bones, but it doesn't appear to be anything real serious."

"Can he stay here for the night?" Dr. Jackson asked

"Only if you're willing to admit him as a patient. You know the rules."

"I know the rules and the rule says no white can be admitted to this hospital just like no Black can be admitted to their hospitals."

Dr. Bridgewater again checked the man's pulse. "I'll put a sling on him, and that's as much as I can do."

"The rain has stopped, Dr. Bridgewater," one of the orderlies said as he passed by the examination room.

"I'm going to find some clean clothes for this poor man, and I think you need to take him back to where you found him."

"I know where I can take him," Dr. Jackson said. "As soon as he wakes up, and he gets dressed, I'll get him out of here."

"Looks like that's about to happen," Dr. Bridgewater said. "He's coming to."

The two doctors stood on different sides of the bed and glared down at the man.

"You had a pretty bad accident," Dr. Bridgewater said.

"You?" The man tried to raise his hand, but couldn't. "You're the one who tried to kill me," he glowered.

"No, I did not try to kill you, but I'd like to help you," Dr. Jackson said.

The man tried to rise up but couldn't. "What's wrong with me?" He asked.

115

"You had a real nasty accident," Dr. Bridgewater repeated. He pointed to Dr. Jackson. "This is Dr. Jackson, and I'm Dr. Bridgewater. We need to get you out of here and to the other side of town. Do you have a home?"

"Yeah, the railroad tracks," the man answered.

"You have to live somewhere," Dr. Jackson said.

"Yeah, in the box cars with the rest of the niggers."

"Watch your mouth," Dr. Bridgewater scowled. "We just saved your life and will not tolerate that kind of language in here."

"Where am I?"

"You're in the hospital," Dr. Bridgewater replied. "Dr. Jackson found you lying in the street up by the Frisco tracks and brought you in here." Dr. Bridgewater paused and looked over at Dr. Jackson. "But you can't stay in here, and Dr. Jackson has a place to take you."

Again, the man tried to rise up and with his good arm searched his body, obviously looking for something. "Where's my gun?" He shouted.

"You didn't have a gun when I found you lying on the ground," Dr. Jackson said.

"You're a damn liar, give me my gun back, you nigger," the man continued to shout.

"I told you to watch you language in here," Dr. Bridgewater's voice also rose.

Dr. Jackson grimaced as he listened to the abusive language coming from this man's foul mouth. How dare he use such language disrespecting the two men trying to treat his injuries? Where do these kind of men come from he wondered. And more important, would they ever change? If he didn't really believe they could, there would be no way for him to continue treating Luther's son, and certainly not help this foul mouth man any more than he already had.

"You need to relax and let us treat your wounds," Dr. Jackson advised the man.

116   "Don't put your monkey hands on me," the man shouted. "Let me out of this nigger hospital."

"That's it," Dr. Bridgewater scowled. He looked at Dr. Jackson. "Get him out of here."

"You think he can walk?" Dr. Jackson asked.

"I don't care; let's get him out of here. He's nothing but trouble for us."

"You know there's going to be repercussions," Dr. Jackson

admonished his friend.

The two doctors grabbed the man under his arms and lifted him up.

"Ahh, stop. That hurts," the man screamed.

Jackson momentarily froze.

"Don't you dare," Bridgewater exclaimed.

Despite the man's pain, they lifted him out of the bed, dragged him out of the room and down the corridor without the use of the gurney.

"Whatcha gonna do with me?" the man shouted.

Orderlies and nurses gathered around to observe what was happening. They had shocked expressions all over their faces, undoubtedly wondering if these two doctors would shove this man out the door.

Dr. Bridgewater and Jackson kept dragging the man to the front entrance where Jackson's car was still parked.

"Do you want to drive him or just throw him out front?" Dr. Bridgewater asked.

"Try to put him in the backseat, and I'll drive him over to the Frisco tracks. He said that's where he lives, so that's where I'll drop him off."

"Only if one of the orderlies goes with you," Dr. Bridgewater insisted. "George," he called to one of the orderlies.

"Yes sir, Dr. Bridgewater," a stout young Black man hurried up to where they stood at the entrance.

"Ride with Dr. Jackson to drop this person off at the Frisco tracks," Dr. Bridgewater instructed the young orderly.

"Yes sir," George complied.

The three of them dragged the man outside and pushed him into the backseat of the car.

"I'm in pain," the man shouted. "You got to treat me. You're a doctor, and you can't do this."

Dr. Jackson slammed the door shut. George climbed in the

passenger side seat and Jackson in the drivers seat. He grabbed the crankshaft and handed it to the orderly. "You know what to do," he said.

"Yes sir," George said as he gripped the crankshaft and got back out of the car. He hurried to the front and turned the shaft while Jackson started the car. Once the engine was running, George climbed back in the car and they drove off.

"You can't do this," the man shouted. "You gotta treat my injury. You're a doctor."

"Shaddup, or we'll drop you right in all this mud right now," Dr. Jackson said.

"You at least owe me a meal," the man said.

"I don't owe you anything," Dr. Jackson said. "You're going to be fine."

At the Frisco tracks just beyond Archer on Greenwood, Jackson pulled over to the side of the road. George opened his door and before Dr. Jackson could get out, he said, "I got this Doc, stay put." He opened the back door, reached in and grabbed the man by his arms and pulled him out of the car. He dragged him over to the train station.

"This ain't over yet, you fucking niggers," he shouted just as the orderly was climbing back into the car.

George abruptly stopped right where he was and glared over at Dr. Jackson. "What did that peckerwood say?" He didn't wait for Dr. Jackson's answer. He jumped back out of the car and started toward the man.

"No," Dr. Jackson shouted.

118

George didn't stop. Evidently he didn't hear the doctor or ignored his shout.

"Oh God, no," Dr. Jackson jumped out of the car and rushed to catch George before he did something that would get them all in trouble. If he hit that white man, then they would lose and the man would win. He had to stop his orderly from pulverizing that white man.

Just before George reached the man, Dr. Jackson stepped in

front of him, blocking his path.

"You're not going to do this," Dr. Jackson said. "If you do, we all lose."

"You nigger, you coon, come on," the man shouted.

"Shaddup," Dr. Jackson shouted. He had to end this situation before the strong young Black man took the man's head off.

Dr. Jackson reached in his pocket and pulled out a five-dollar bill. He held it out for the man. "Take this and get out of here."

The man snatched the five-dollar bill. "This ain't over you bunch of filthy niggers," He shrieked, then turned and limped off.

Dr. Jackson wrapped both arms around the young orderly. It took all his strength to hold him back. "George, get back in the car, and let's get out of here," he said. George kept pushing forward. He did not want to be contained.

"Let me get at him, Doc," he pleaded.

"He's not worth it."

"But he can't talk to you like that."

"He can because the law says he can."

"Just let me have him for a couple minutes. I'll teach that peckerwood to respect you."

"No, George, you can beat a man like that to within a inch of his life and he won't have learned a thing."

"Doc, that don't sit well with me. He can't talk to you that way when I'm right here to stop it."

"Save your fight for when the right one begins. Leave him alone," Jackson coaxed the young man to stop trying to move forward.

The man had disappeared between the boxcars, and just as he had abruptly walked into Jackson's life, he was now gone.

Dr. Jackson and the orderly stood there for a few minutes, then got back in the car. Jackson pulled back onto the road and drove back down Greenwood. The sun had begun to break through the clouds and created a beautiful rainbow right in front of them.

"Our day is coming, young man," Dr. Jackson said. He knew George was angry. "Someday all these white folks will pay for all their abuse and name calling." He paused and looked over at George then back at the road. "White folks going to pay real bad for all the terrible things they've done to our people. Just be patient; the time will come."

FOURTEEN

Veneice sat staring at Mrs. Jackson's back in her American Literature class, as her teacher wrote the topic for today's discussion on the chalk board: PHYLLIS WHEATLEY: THE FIRST GREAT NEGRO POET. She kept staring over at the door waiting for Verby to make his entrance into the room. She wondered if he would ever ask her to be his girlfriend. No doubt he liked her a whole lot and she liked him also. But it was the boy's responsibility to make the first step in the beginning of a relationship. He needed to hurry up because she was getting a little impatient. She'd never had a boyfriend before, and the anticipation of that happening was maddening. What was he waiting for? In less than two months, school would be out, and then the only time she might see him would be at Williams Confectionery, whenever Poppa allowed her to go on a Saturday afternoon.

Finally, she smiled and blushed as Verby strolled through the door and took his seat right behind her. How was she possibly going to concentrate on the discussion for the class knowing he was probably staring at her? Veneice, concentrate on the class material, she told herself.   She jerked forward as Verby tapped her on the shoulder.

"Hey, I got something to give you," he whispered.

Veneice turned around to look at him, and he handed her a folded piece of paper.

"Read this after class and then give me an answer," he said.

Veneice took the paper and turned back around.

"Good afternoon, class," Julia said as she walked and stood right in front of her desk.

"Good afternoon, today we will…" she stopped abruptly as a

hall monitor walked into the class . "Yes, what is it?" she asked.

"Principal Woods wants to see Veneice Dunn in his office," the young boy said.

All eyes turned and looked at Veneice. She felt a nervous tinge shoot through her entire body. Why would the principal want to see her? Was it because she had a tendency to daydream in class, and her teachers had admonished her on several occasions to pay attention?

"Veneice, did you hear?" Julia snapped her out of her musing.

"Yes ma'am," Veneice answered. She got up, still aware of all eyes on her, and could hear some of the students snicker as she walked out the door.

Veneice slowly made her way down the steps from the second floor to the first, and the closer she got to Principal Woods office the more nervous she became. Her seventeen-year-old brain thought back over all her activities since the first of the week. Usually Principal Woods did not let issues involving students linger, so if he had a problem with something she did, it had to have occurred that week. It was now Thursday afternoon and she couldn't think of what it could be.

She finally reached the first floor and walked into the principal's office. Principal Woods' secretary looked up. "He's waiting for you," she said. "Go on in."

Two other students, Billy Williams and Harold Mackey, both seniors were already standing to the side of Principal Woods' desk as she walked in.

Principal Woods looked over the top of his wire-rimmed glasses. "Miss Dunn, come on in."

122

He didn't look angry, and her two fellow students didn't have long faces so it couldn't be that bad. She hurried over and stood next to Billy.

"Uhum," Woods cleared his throat, put his pen down and looked over at the three students. "You all know that the junior and senior prom is coming up the first day in June."

"Yes, sir," they all said in unison.

"I assume all three of you will be attending," he said.

"Yes, sir," Billy and Harold answered. Veneice remained silent, hoping that the principal did not detect her failure to respond. The prom was a discussion she needed to have with her mother so that she could then bring it up with her father.

"I am pleased to inform the three of you that I have chosen you all to represent your classes on the committee planning the prom. I've cleared it with your teachers who all agree that you are an excellent selection. I know it's getting late and you don't have a lot of time for planning, so you and Mrs. Jackson, who is the faculty advisor, need to get busy and within the next week find a location." He paused to push his glasses back up on his nose. "I think the best place to have the prom is in the ballroom at the Stradford Hotel. I've already talked with John Stradford regarding the cost and he promised me a good deal. However, the choice is up to you all, but I think you should go with the Stradford."

Veneice and the two boys stood and listened as the principal rattled off the plans he had already put in motion for the prom, even though he did make them feel like they would have some say in the final decision.

"Do any of you have questions?" Principal Woods asked.

"No sir," they said, even though Veneice was tempted to ask him why he needed them if he had already made all the decisions. But then on second thought, that might not be a wise question.

"Are you listening to me Miss Dunn?" he asked, snapping her back to the situation at hand.

"Yes, sir, Principal Woods," she said.

"There you go letting your mind wander off," he said. "Your teachers have mentioned to me that you've been doing a lot of that lately. Is something bothering you?

"No, sir."

"Then pay attention. It should be an honor to represent your class."

"Yes, sir, it is."

"Billy, you will be the leader of your team. Harold, you will be second in charge, and, Veneice, you will represent the eleventh grade. I want you all in my office at eight o'clock sharp in the

123

morning, and we will continue to lay out the plans and I will also let Mrs. Jackson know. Do you all understand what you will be doing?"

"Yes, sir."

"Good, now you need to tell your parents when you get home about this honor."

"Yes, sir," only Billy and Harold replied.

"Is there something bothering you, Miss Dunn?" Principal Woods asked.

"Oh, no, sir," she quickly answered.

"Good, then back to your classes and no lingering in the halls."

The three students turned and hurried out of the principal's office. As they ambled down the hall, Billy came up next to Veneice.

"Hey, what's happening?" He asked as they kept walking. They dare not stop.

"You know how Poppa is," she commented as they started up the stairs.

"I know, your dad doesn't like dancing and doesn't like nothing but church music, but he got to let you go to your prom."

"Maybe your daddy can talk to him. Our daddies are close friends, being the two best mechanics in all of Tulsa, and he might be able to talk Poppa into letting me go."

"I don't know, but I'll try," Billy said as they reached the second floor, and he headed down the hallway back to his class.

"Please try Billy. I want to go real bad," Veneice said and continued down the other end of the hall back to her class.

"Girl, you so lucky," Esther said as the three girls crossed over Greenwood on their way home from school. "Mr. Woods picked you to represent our class and that is quite an honor."

"Yeah, everybody likes Veneice, even the teachers," Ruth said and she chuckled. "I guess even Verby likes you."

Veneice's enthusiasm increased. "He gave me a note to read just before classes started. With all that happened, I didn't get a chance to read it."

"Where is it?" Esther's enthusiasm also rose. "Bet he's going to ask you to be his girlfriend?"

"Why you think that?" Ruth asked.

"There's no other reason for him to give her a special note."

Veneice dug in her pocket and pulled the paper out. "Maybe it's just some kind of joke or something he couldn't tell in class."

"Boys tell jokes to each other," Esther said. "Not to girls."

"Hurry up, girl," Ruth urged her on.

"Okay, okay, you'd think he wrote to you all." Veneice said opened the paper and started to read the contents. As she did, a wide grin spread across her face.

"What's it say? Come on, share it with us," Ruth prodded her.

Veneice held the paper close to her heart and spun around in the middle of the dirt trail. "He wants to know if I'll be his girlfriend?"

"Ooooh, ooooh," both Esther and Ruth shouted, and the three girls hugged and began to jump up and down where they stood.

"Girl, you got a boyfriend," Ruth shouted.

"Veneice is the first one to get a boyfriend," Esther exclaimed..

"You going to kiss him?" Ruth asked.

"I don't know. I don't even know how to kiss."

125

"You just close your mouth and put your lips against his, I guess," Esther said.

"Then you got to hug him and hold him close to you," Ruth added.

"You all going to get me killed. If Poppa ever saw or knew that I put my mouth next to a boy and was that close, he'd kill me and then the boy."

"How you gonna be boyfriend and girlfriend if you don't do those kind of things?" Esther asked.

"I'll be his girlfriend, but the most we going to do is hold hands," Veneice said.

"At least that's a start," Ruth said.

They stopped in front of Veneice's house. "You so lucky," Ruth continued. "Not only do you get to represent our class at the prom, but you got a boyfriend to take you there."

"I don't know about the last two of those things. I have to first confront Poppa and according to what he says the only thing I might be able to do is represent our class, but not at the prom. I'll see you all in the morning." She stuffed the paper back into her pocket, turned and headed into the house.

"That you, Veneice," Momma shouted from the kitchen as soon as she walked into the living room and headed toward her bedroom.

"Yes ma'am," she replied. Veneice dropped her books off in her room and walked to the kitchen where Momma was breaking string beans and tossing them into a container of cold water.

Veneice hugged Momma, then grabbed some of the string beans, began breaking them into pieces and tossing them in the container.

"No, girl, break them into four pieces," Momma said. "They still too big if you only break them one time."

Veneice grabbed two at a time and broke them into four pieces. "Momma, I got a big complement from Principal Woods today," she said.

"Good, what did he say?"

"It's not what he said," she paused.

"What are you talking about?" Momma's tone was harsh. "Why you afraid to tell Momma what he said and what you're thinking.

"Momma, it's not about you at all, 'cause you don't see nothing wrong with other music and some dancing, do you?"

"Girl, if you don't stop playing with me?" She now chuckled.

"Okay, Momma, Principal Woods appointed me to be on the junior and senior prom committee to help plan the prom for this year," Veneice said and hesitated for a minute to determine her mother's initial response. But she couldn't wait too long. "Momma, Poppa's got to let me go." Excitement flowed through each word.

"Then I guess you'll just have to ask him."

"You know I can't do that. I mean, he'll tell me no, and I'll just die."

"Oh, girl, stop being so dramatic." Momma stopped snapping string beans and turned to Veneice. "You can't be afraid to talk to your Poppa. He loves you kids and would do anything in the world for you."

"He won't let us play music, and he sure won't let us dance and we can't have no boy company."

"I guess you're right. There are limits."

"So you'll do it for me, please Momma? If I can't go to the prom I can't be on the committee, and I'll just die."

"Quit saying that. You're not going to die. In fact, you're going to live a very long life. God got a lot of work for you to do."

"I know it, but will you do it for me?"

"Here's what we'll do. Let's finish cooking a real fine dinner for your Poppa, and once his belly is full of good food, the two of us will talk with him."

"Do I got to be there?"

"You mean do I have to be there. I know Mrs. Jackson is teaching you English better than that." Momma returned to snapping string beans. "And, yes, you have to be there. This is something you want real bad, and when you want something bad enough, you'll have to learn to stand up and go for it."

"Tonight, Momma. We going to ask him tonight?"

"Yes, we are. Finish those string beans and get over to peeling those potatoes so I can make some potato salad. Remember, it has to be a very special meal to get what you want."

FIFTEEN

———————

Nothing, absolutely nothing could stop O. B. Mann and his men from marching in the Memorial Day Parade next month. He had to make the organizers of the parade recognize his determination. As he rode his big stallion down Greenwood toward the *Tulsa Star*, he knew Smitherman must agree to run a series of articles in support of his position on this issue. These articles would help rally the Greenwood community to his cause. The men looked to him to get this done and he couldn't let them down. Just maybe the articles would convince white Tulsa that the Negro veterans deserved to march also.

He guided his stallion off the paved streets onto a muddy side alley where he came to a stop right in front of a shanty. He whistled loudly and dismounted. The same young boy who had tended to his horse before came running out the front door and took the reigns. Without a word spoken between the two, the boy led the horse to the side of the shanty and O. B. walked down the alley until he came out on Greenwood.

Smitherman looked up with a surprised expression on his face as O. B. barged right into his office. He'd never just shown up at the *Star* without calling ahead of time.

"Good afternoon, O. B.," Smitherman said as he placed his pen down on top of the paper he'd been writing on. "This is a surprise."

O. B gestured, pointing to one of the chairs in front of the desk.

"Yes, yes, certainly have a seat," Smitherman said. "To what do I owe this visit?"

"You know what happens every year at the Memorial Day

Parade?" O. B. asked.

"Well...yes, veterans march down Main Street for about four miles," Smitherman replied, not sure that was the answer O. B. expected.

"We all know that it's a parade," O. B. exclaimed. "I mean something more than just that."

"I have to admit I'm somewhat stumped. I'm not sure what you're driving at."

"This is shameful when your own people don't acknowledge the sacrifices we made for the country."

"What are you talking about, O. B.? We've honored you and the other veterans every year on Veteran's Day."

O. B. shifted his position in the chair and leaned forward. "That's not what I'm talking about."

"Then tell me what you're talking about?"

"We Negro veterans feel that we should be able to march in the city-wide parade. We should be able to strut down Main and be acknowledged by the entire city for our sacrifices."

"That's what brought you into my office this morning?"

O. B. reached into his pants pocket and pulled out a crumpled piece of notebook paper. "Exactly," he said. "I've written an account on how we're being mistreated and why we shouldn't be."

"O. B., I got news for you. All Negroes in Tulsa and for that matter the state of Oklahoma and in fact all over this country are mistreated." Smitherman leaned forward with elbows resting on the desk to make his point.

130

"That mistreatment is different from this. Don't get me wrong, it's all disgraceful, and someday we going to have to fight these peckerwoods. But the mistreatment I'm talking about right now concerns men who went and fought for this country and then weren't recognized for their valor when they come home."

"And the way you get that recognition is marching in the Memorial Day Parade in front of a bunch of white folks?"

"Hell, yeah, why not?"

Smitherman now leaned back in his chair. "What is it you want me to do?"

O. B. pushed the notebook piece of paper across the desk. "Publish this and publish something about the abuse we get every year on Memorial Day."

Smitherman gave him a hard look, then picked up the paper and opened it. He read the entire contents and again looked across the desk at O. B. "This is pretty powerful stuff, but is it all true?"

"Every bit of it. All of it."

Smitherman finally placed to paper back on his desk, folded his hands and continued. 'This is some pretty damnable information against the United States Army but I don't see how it's going to help get you all to march in that parade."

"That's how they treated us overseas and that's how we're being treated right here in Tulsa. They both tie together," O. B. scowled as he moved around in the chair as if trying to restrain a nervous anger.

"Let me get this straight, you're saying that a Brigadier General issued a general order prohibiting Black soldiers from speaking to French women, even over in France?"

"I'll swear by that. Two buddies in my unit were arrested and thrown in the brig for walking down the street with French women."

"That's disgraceful," Smitherman said. "Why did you all continue to fight?"

"We were soldiers, and we wanted to help defeat people who we thought were the worst in the world, actually the devil."

131

"You changed your mind?"

"Yeah, because the worst people in the world are these white people right here in Tulsa." O. B. dug in his pocket and took out an additional single piece of paper. He stuck his large arm out and handed it across the desk. "Here, take this."

"What is it?" Smitherman took the paper and unfolded it.

"It's an official order given by General Pershing," O. B. said.

"How'd you get it?"

"Not every white officer agreed with what they were doing over there." Again, nervous energy forced O. B. to scoot up to the very tip of the chair and lean forward. "Read it."

Smitherman stared at the paper, looked up at O. B., then back at the paper. He then read the contents aloud. "We must prevent the rise of any pronounced degree of intimacy between French officers and Black officers. We may be courteous and amiable with the last, but we cannot deal with them on the same plane as with the white American officers without deeply wounding the latter. We must not eat with them, must not shake hands or seek to talk or meet with them outside the requirements of military service."

"That's what the white soldier took overseas and poisoned the minds of all our allies against the Negro troops."

"How were you all able to fight under those conditions?"

"We knew we had two enemies, the Germans and our so-called fellow white soldiers. But we were trapped. Where could we go? So our better judgment dictated that we fight the Germans 'cause they were trying to kill us. The white soldiers were not going to shoot us, just embarrass us." O. B. paused to consider what he wanted to say next. He decided and continued. "Sometimes I wish we'd shot those white racist pigs, first. Then when I see these bastards march on Memorial Day just like they're the only ones that fought for this country, makes you want to kill all over again."

"I can think of a lot better reasons to want to kill white folks, but I see what you mean." Smitherman reared back in his seat. "I think I'll run a series of articles about this and maybe the *Pittsburgh Courier* and the *Chicago Defender* will pick it up and run it also. What unit were you in?"

132

O. B. sat straight up and stuck his chest out. "I fought with the greatest fighting unit in the entire United Sates Army, the 92nd Division. You couldn't find a better group of fighting men nowhere in the military." O. B. again paused remembering some of their battles. "We took poison gas, bullets, but the worse were the flyers they would drop all around us from airplanes.

"A lot of propaganda?" Smitherman asked.

"No, not really propaganda, and that's what makes it so bad. What they wrote in those flyers was the truth, and that's what hurt the most."

"You say it was the truth. What kind of truth?"

"About our pathetic condition in this country." O. B. fumbled around in a bag he carried with him. Finally, he pulled out a red colored paper with large black print and tossed it on the desk.

Smitherman again looked at O. B., then picked up the flyer and read the contents aloud. "People of African heritage stolen from your beautiful homeland and forced to work as slaves and now still treated as slaves by the worst of the Caucasian race, white people in the United States, why do you take up arms against the German people who feel nothing but compassion for your plight and contempt for the ugly Americans who have treated your ancestors and you in such a brutal and sadistically sick way. These monsters lynch your boys and rape your girls. Why would you as second-class citizens fight for them? Why would you fight for a people that hate you? Now is your opportunity. Lay down your weapons and the German people will welcome you to our country with open arms." Smitherman paused for a minute. "Did any of our boys take them up on their offer for a better life?"

"Not anyone from my unit. We heard that a couple boys from a different unit actually did try to cross over, but got caught."

"I can imagine what happened to them."

"You got that right. A legal lynching courtesy of the United States Army."

"Why did you stay loyal?

133

"I don't know. I guess most of us believed that we could really make a difference. You know, go fight for your country. Show you're willing to put your life on the line for the good old U.S.A. and you'll be rewarded. And I think we were all out to prove that we could fight just as well as they could. We got tired of hearing about how the Negro won't fight, how he's a coward, or he's too lazy, too dumb or too scared. Well, we proved them liars on all three counts."

"I'm starting to get the feel for a real story," Smitherman said. "How many more of these flyers you all got?"

"That's my only one but some of the other boys got some."

"I think I can write a good story about what the Germans was dropping from planes was called propaganda, but in reality was the truth." He grabbed both pieces of paper and held them up. "You'll get your story, O. B., but it's going to be much bigger than about a Memorial Day Parade."

"But don't forget the parade. We got to be able to march or there shouldn't be a parade."

"I won't. I most definitely will not forget."

O. B. pulled his large frame out of the chair. "All the promises they made us and they haven't kept not one of them. In fact, things done got worse out here since the war ended."

Smitherman also stood up. "O. B. let me ask you a question." He walked from behind the desk. "Are you sorry you did it now?"

"Only thing I'm sorry about is that I had my gun aimed at the wrong enemy." The two men shook hands.

"I'll be in touch with you about the story." Smitherman stood there while O. B. turned and walked out of the office just as abruptly as he had come in.

***

Veneice had made up her mind that she would tell Verby "yes"about being his girlfriend. She just wasn't sure how she should do it. Sitting in her bedroom with her youngest sister, Olivia studying at Venice's desk instead of her bedroom, she decided to practice on her. It was a little after seven o'clock, and they were waiting for Poppa to get home so they could eat. There was one hard and fast rule in the Dunn household; no one ate before Poppa. Usually they would have eaten right after six, but evidently he'd gotten tied up at work and was running late. They all had to wait, and that gave her the opportunity to practice what she would say to Verby.

"Olivia, I want you to do me a big favor," she said.

Olivia, busy doing her homework looked up. "What kind of favor, and what am I going to get for doing it?"

"Just do me a favor and don't worry about what you going to get." Will you or won't you do it?"

"What you want me to do?"

Veneice got up from her bed, walked over and sat next to her sister at the desk. "I'm going to tell you something and you got to agree not to tell anyone, not even Momma and especially not Poppa."

"I ain't gonna make no promise like that. You trying to get me in trouble?" Olivia closed her book and concentrated all her attention on her sister.

"No girl, I ain't going to get you in trouble, but you got to promise me. It's really important. The only other two people that know about this are Ruth and Esther."

"How they know, and I don't know?" Olivia asked.

"They're my closest friends in the whole wide world and we share our secrets with each other."

"That ain't fair. I'm your sister."

"I know, but you don't want to keep it a secret, and they will."

"Okay, I will too," Olivia finally agreed.

Veneice leaned in closer to her sister. "You remember I mentioned this boy name Verby who is in my sixth period class?"

"Yeah, what about him?"

"He asked me to be his girlfriend," Veneice whispered.

"Oh wow, you got a boyfriend?" Olivia shrieked.

"Ssh girl, I told you this is a secret."

"Oops, sorry. What did you tell him?"

"I haven't had a chance to tell him nothing. He wrote me a letter asking me to be his girlfriend, and I didn't read it until after school was out today. That's why I need you to do me a favor."

"You want me to tell him yes for you?"

135

"No, nothing like that." Veneice heard Momma walking outside the room and stopped talking for a moment. Once she was sure her mother wasn't listening outside the door, she continued. "I need to practice how I'll tell him yes, and I need you to pretend you're him and I'll practice with you."

"What? I don't want to be no boy."

"You don't have to be a boy, just act like you're one."

"Okay, what I got to do?"

"I don't know," Veneice's voice now rose out of frustration.

"How am I supposed to know what to do if you can't tell me? I ain't ever been a boy."

"I know you haven't, but just say, 'Veneice I want you to be my girlfriend.'"

"Okay, Veneice, I want you to be my girlfriend."

"No, at least try to talk like a boy."

"I can't talk like a boy. Why don't you get Ruth to do this?"

"'Cause I won't see her before tomorrow, and I got to give him an answer in the morning."

"Why don't you just write it and give him your answer that way. He wrote you to ask you to be his girlfriend, so just put on paper yes, hand it to him and walk away."

"Veneice, your Poppa's home so you girls come on out here for dinner," her mother called out from the hallway.

"See, now I didn't get a chance to practice," Veneice said. The two sisters got up and walked out of the bedroom.

136

"Too bad," Olivia whispered as they made their way to the dining room. "Just write him and say yes."

"What are you girls whispering about?" Momma inquired.

The two sisters took their seats at the table.

"Nothing, Momma," Veneice answered.

"How you girls doing?" Poppa said as he walked into the dining room and took a seat at the head of the table. "Bow your heads, and let's pray."

Veneice bowed her head while Poppa prayed over the food. But this time she really didn't concentrate on his prayer; instead her head was swimming with all the issues that needed to be resolved in her life. Olivia wasn't any help at all. She'd probably just scribble out one word on a scrap of paper and give it to him in the morning and that would be over. The other issue that had to be resolved that evening with Poppa was the prom. That made her nervous for fear he'd say no.

"Veneice, Principal Woods came to visit me this evening," Poppa said breaking her musing. He'd finished his prayer and shocked her when he called her name. "Told me something about you being picked to represent your class in organizing the prom this year."

"Yes Poppa," Veneice said, also shocked that her father knew about the prom and her appointment made by Principal Woods. She sat there, nervous that the next possible information from Poppa would be about Verby.

"Principal Woods is an excellent principal because when he detects something wrong in an outstanding student he has no problem sharing it with the parent. And that's why he stopped by to see me. He said he understood how I felt about other music besides religious songs, and knew your lack of enthusiasm was due to your fear that I wouldn't let you participate." He paused to take a drink of water and dug into the food waiting in the middle of the table.

Once he got his portions, Momma and Olivia started to get their food. Veneice remained still, unable to move for fear of what she might hear next.

137

"I thought about what he had to say on my way home this evening and agree with him that this would be a good thing for you. Since he is our most educated man and the leader of our high school, then I think it's important that parents accept his advice."

Enthusiasm about the direction of her father's comments built up in Veneice. Sounded like this might work out just fine. But she wouldn't believe it until he actually said she could go.

"For those reasons, I'm going to allow you to attend your

prom."

"Oh, Poppa, thank you," Veneice screamed, jumped up from the chair, ran over and hugged him. "Thank you, Poppa. You've made me the happiest girl in the world."

Her father hugged her and then pulled away. "Girl, get hold of yourself. But you cannot have a date pick you up at this house. I will not allow that, do you understand?"

"Yes, Poppa," Veneice agreed.

"Now get your food before it gets cold," Momma said. "I guess we don't have to have that talk after all." She smiled at her daughter

"We sure don't." Veneice also smiled. Half the battle was won, now she just had to deal with Verby but after this good news she knew that would be relatively easy.

SIXTEEN

Dick climbed the fifteen steps in the narrow dark stairwell to the third floor at the Savoy Boarding House, one block up from his home on Archer Street. Reaching the top floor, he strode down the hallway to the last apartment door on the right. After knocking twice and waiting a half-minute, the door swung open and a very large, brown skinned man waved Dick inside without speaking a word. The room was small and extremely hot. The only furniture was a card table with four metal chairs, a worn out couch that sunk low and a ripped leather chair. Three other men sat in the metal chairs so Dick sat on the couch. The large man who met him at the door sat in the leather chair.

"Smooth Diamond Dick, how you doing, young fellow?" the man asked.

"I ain't doing no good Roscoe 'cause I ain't making no money."

"And that's why you at Roscoe's door, this evening."

"You got it. I need to make some money so I can get up and out of here."

"Where you wanna go? Ain't nothing out there much better than Tulsa," Roscoe said.

"I need to find out myself. Got to be something better than shining peckerwoods shoes all day and having to take their shit just to get a dime tip."

"Damn, that's all you get is a dime?" Roscoe pulled a small bottle, with a white powder inside it, out of his pocket. "Damn man, I see why you up here visiting with Roscoe." He took off the cap to the bottle, and then removed a small object resembling a spoon on a big chain from around his neck. He took the small bottle and the spoon and held them out for Dick. "Want a hit?" He asked. "Some of the best cocaine out there in a long time."

Dick shook his head no and pulled his body back onto the couch. "I don't use that stuff."

Roscoe put the cap back on the container and put it back in his pocket, then put the chain back around his neck. "If I can't interest you in any drugs, how about a Choc beer?" Roscoe asked.

"Yeah, I'll take a beer."

Roscoe snapped his finger at one of the men sitting at the table playing cards. The man jumped from his chair, went into the kitchen area and returned with a beer. He handed it to Dick and returned to his game of cards.

"Thanks," Dick gestured to Roscoe.

Roscoe didn't acknowledge the thank you, but instead turned to the business at hand. "Let me get this straight," he started. "You want to work the Drexel Building; is that correct?"

"It's perfect for me," Dick said as he gulped down the beer. "I know the men over there and the ones I don't know, Sarah does."

"You still messing with that ofaye?"

"Every once in a while we might do something together."

"How you know she ain't already working that building for me?"

Dick could only hope that Roscoe was probing, checking out Dick's response to see if he showed any signs of anger. He wasn't going to play in his game. "You know some of these ofaye girls will do anything to make a dollar," he said.

140

"Ain't she your girl?" Roscoe sounded much more serious. "And if she is, why she ain't already cut you in?"

"Maybe I don't want to be dependent on no ofaye for making money."

Roscoe seemed to be satisfied with how Dick handled his question. "Problem is I already got somebody working there," he said.

"Oh yeah, who's that?"

"The old janitor over there."

"You mean Moses?"

"Yeah, Moses,"

"I'll be damn, Moses that good Negro. The one those white folks just love 'cause he always bowing and shuffling all day long."

"Seems to me he ain't doing nothing different than you," Roscoe guffawed.

"I ain't no Uncle Tom."

"You shine them peckerwood's shoes, don't you?"

"But I don't kiss their ass." Suddenly a smile spread across Dick's face. "And I get even with them every night I lay between them thighs of their most precious prize." Dick again took a gulp of the Choc beer. "One thing a white man can't stand is the thought of a Negro laying up with one of his women."

"That ofaye girl got any friends?" Roscoe asked.

"Naw, I ain't ever seen her with no one, but then I don't ever go in her neighborhood so I really don't know what she got."

"Why don't you find out and if she does and they think like her, y'all can come on by here and we can all have some fun. Then I might find it more beneficial to have you working Drexel instead of Moses."

"I can do that."

"Yeah, it might be a good set up if you can get that ofaye girl of yours to collect the numbers from the businessmen in Drexel."

"Seems like you got a good business head." Dick started to get up.

"What's your hurry?" Roscoe motioned for Dick to sit back down. "Got some real good gin coming soon. I know you can stand a little before you hit the clubs tonight."

Dick sat back down, reared back and relaxed. "Sounds good to me," he said.

The extended invitation was a good sign. Everybody knew

141

Roscoe was not a friendly man, and asking Dick to stay meant that his chances of picking up the Drexel Building were getting better. He now only had to make Sarah find a white girlfriend who liked to play across the tracks and he would be in business.

Dick lay next to Sarah in the bed in his upstairs bedroom staring up at the ceiling fan whizzing around, providing them with some cool air against their hot, naked bodies. Aunt Damie had decided to visit friends in Vinita for the weekend. She'd left earlier that Friday morning. After Dick left Roscoe's, full of gin and ready to sin, he met Sarah at Pretty Belle's and they went straight to his place. He didn't want to hang around the club just in case Ethel might come in and make a scene. On the occasions that Aunt Damie was out of town, he'd have Sarah over for the night. His room and home were much more comfortable than the cheap motels they'd usually end up at when they dated. Not only was it more comfortable, he also felt more secure. The possibility of some irate white men breaking in on them while in bed was always in the back of his mind. That thought had a tendency to affect how much pleasure he experienced while in the act with her. In his room, he was assured maximum pleasure.

Although this time there seemed to be something missing. The flair wasn't there. His thoughts kept slipping back to the last time he was with Ethel. With her the sex was much more intense but she wasn't white and that made the difference. Ofayes had the advantage because they were white and that's why Roscoe told him to get one of Sarah's friends over to his place and he'd make sure Dick got the Drexel for his numbers.

142

"Boy, you were in rare form all night long," Sarah said as she turned to her side facing him and breaking his concentration on other matters. "What got into you tonight?" she asked.

"You got into me," he said rubbing his hands through her sweaty, stringy hair. "And it's always more comfortable when we don't have to be down on First Street."

"Yeah, you're right about that. I wish your mother would let me move in here with you."

"Why should she do that when, first of all, we ain't married, and second I can't even visit you at your place."

"Okay, let's not even have that conversation. Let's leave it alone 'cause it always causes a fight. I ain't responsible for the racist idiots, but there ain't nothing I can do to change it."

"I know, and I don't blame you," Dick kissed her on the lips and pulled her naked body close to him. "You know, if we got enough money we could move right out of this part of the country to where they don't care about things like race."

"Where's that?"

"Chicago, New York and even Kansas City."

Sarah propped up, resting her head in the palm of her hand. "But we ain't got no money so we stuck having to sneak and see each other."

Dick also scooted up in the bed. "But there is a way we can make some fast money."

"No," she shrieked. "I will not get involved in your little illegal scheme."

Dick lay back down and again stared up at the ceiling. She was staring at him but he continued looking up. "I never told you I got two sisters." He finally broke the silence.

"No, you didn't," Sarah rejoined. "I thought Miss Damie was the only family you had."

"Naw, Aunt Damie ain't really my momma."

"That explains a lot. I always wondered why you called her Aunt Damie."

"Why didn't you ask me?"

"I don't know. I figured you'd tell me when you was ready." Sarah also lay back down.

"Aunt Damie took me in when I was six years old. She ran a one-room grocery store with some vegetables, some fruit and a few canned goods. Store was there to serve a bunch of farmers who lived in the country. But every Tuesday she'd bake corn bread, wrap it up and sell it in pieces. Man, you could smell that corn bread a block away." Dick paused and a smile spread across his face.

He turned on his side facing Sarah. "Me and my sisters were orphans but we was orphans with no where to live. We slept under bridges and in the woods. When it got cold, we'd sneak in somebody's barn and sleep with the animals. One time an old farmer come out to check on his cows and caught us in his barn. By the time he loaded his rifle we was out of there, and thank goodness he was a terrible shooter or one of us might've been dead that night."

"Where was your family?"

"Don't know. My sisters thought they was somewhere in Texas, but we really didn't know."

"Nobody tried to find you someplace to live? You know some family to take you in or something like that?"

"Be serious. We're Negroes, and don't nobody want that responsibility," Dick exclaimed with a frown. "Anyway, let me get back to my story. I used to go into Aunt Damie's store on Tuesdays and steal some of that corn bread. Then one day I must've got careless, 'cause she caught me."

"And she still took you in?"

"Yeah, she did. Called my sisters to her house and told them that she'd take me off their hands. Said I could earn my keep by sweeping and helping to keep the place clean. She didn't have no bed for me, not even a couch, so I slept on a small cot on the floor until we left there and moved up here."

144 "She took you in and seems like you all are doing okay." Sarah squeezed in her comments while Dick paused for a moment.

"Yeah, she did, and I'll always love Aunt Damie. But I want so much more 'cause I had so little. And most of all, I want to get out of here. Move somewhere else where the Negro is treated like a man and not an animal. That's why we need to make some real good money."

"Let me think about it," Sarah said.

Dick smiled and then kissed her. "Think right, baby. Think

right, and in less than a year we can be out of here. Just the two of us with a pocketful of money." He kissed her again, only this time a long passionate one. He was about to get busy again when suddenly he heard screaming.

"Get off me and get away from me you no good Black bastard," a woman's voice shrieked from the room next to Dick's.

"Oh, shit, not again," Dick scowled and instantly rose up in the bed.

"What the hell is that?" Sarah asked.

"That's the man who rents a room from Aunt Damie," Dick said as he jumped out of bed and started to get dress.

"Dick, what's going on?"

"Get up and get dressed," he ordered. "If I can't calm them down, police will be here in ten minutes, and they going to search the entire house."

"Why is that a problem? We ain't doing nothing wrong."

"I can't have the police coming back here on Monday and telling Aunt Damie that I had a white woman in her house while she was gone. Now get up and get dressed." Dick slipped on his shoes, scrambled over to the door and opened it. "I'll be right back."

He rushed down the hall as the screams continued, pounded on the door and shouted. "Damit Jake, open this door."

He raised his fist to bang again but the door swung open and Jake stood there only in his underwear. A woman who Dick recognized as a prostitute over on First Street sat up in bed with the covers pulled over her body.

145

"Jake, what the hell's going on in here?" Dick asked.

"Ain't nothing wrong, jest a little disagreement." Jake slurred his words as he answered. His eyes were blood shot red and his entire body wobbled.

"What the hell you thinking about with all that screaming?" Dick walked past Jake. "Georgia what you screaming like that for?"

"Golden Diamond Dick, the young man all the ladies like to dance with, how you doing, boy?" Georgia smiled. She was one of the older ladies of the night and her face showed the wear of time over the years working the streets of Tulsa. Jake seemed to be sweet on her and brought her to the house whenever Aunt Damie was out of town.

"You know you can't be carrying on like that. Police come up in here and then tell Aunt Damie, and we'll all be in trouble," Dick fussed. "You just better hope the neighbors didn't hear that screaming and didn't call the police."

"Hold up now young fellow," Jake scowled. "I pays my rent to Miss Damie every month right on time, and I got a right to have my company."

"Jake, don't be no fool. You know Aunt Damie don't care nothing 'bout no money. If she find out Georgia been laying up in this house all night, she gonna put you out and give you your money back. Man, you got a damn good thing here, don't mess it up."

"You right," Jake conceded. He walked over to his dresser, took some bills from his pocket and handed them to Georgia. "I'm sorry baby girl, didn't mean to make you mad, but you better go before the police show up."

Georgia pushed the covers back exposing her naked body. Dick turned and hurried out of the room. "Make it quick 'cause if my calculations are right, we have less than fifteen minutes before the police are knocking on the door," he said while walking out of the room.

He hurried back into his room where Sarah was fully dressed, sitting on the side of the bed waiting for him. "You ready?" he asked.

"Yeah." She got up and the strolled out of the room and started down the stairs. Georgia and Jake were already at the front door.

Dick came to an abrupt stop as he heard an extremely loud knock on the front door.

"Oh, shit," he exploded, grabbed Sarah by the arm and started back up the stairs pulling her behind him. "Come on, you got to get back in the room."

"Hold up there," a voice shouted from downstairs. He stopped, turned around and glared down at Jake and Georgia next to the wall and a white police officer at the foot of the stairs. The Black officer was talking to Georgia.

"You all come on down here," the officer at the stairs ordered.

Dick recognized both the policemen. They patrolled the red light district off First Street. He and Sarah made it down to the bottom of the stairs.

"Are you a prostitute too? The policeman asked Sarah.

"Wait just a minute." Dick jumped right in front of the officer. "You got no right to ask a guest in my house a question like that."

"Shaddup boy," the officer shot back. "I'll ask her any damn question I want." He turned to face Sarah. "Were you the woman screaming?"

"No," she answered in a very low voice.

"It was me," Georgia said. "Leave 'em alone. They ain't had nothing to do with it."

"Why were you screaming?" The officer closest to Georgia asked.

A grin spread across Georgia's face. "Hell, man, ain't you ever screamed when that lovin' got that good to you?" She asked. "This boy laid old Georgia out for the count. Shit was so good, I just had to holler."

"Neighbor who called us said it sounded more like a scream and not like a holler."

"Holler or scream, what difference do it make?" Jake asked. "I do my job well."

Georgia gave Jake a hard look and Dick caught it, and chuckled to himself. "Lookit, this has been a bad mistake, but I think it's all worked out now. Can we please get our privacy back?"

"Girl, you'd better get yourself over where you belong," the white officer said to Sarah. "And boy you'd better stop playing with fire. The Klan find out about this and they going to be burning

147

crosses on your momma's front yard."

Dick's first inclination was to come back at him with some choice words but the situation was contained and his better judgment told him to leave it alone. "You're right officer. We sure don't need no problems like that." He started to turn and go all the way back upstairs with Sarah right behind.

"Girl, didn't you hear what I said?" the white officer shouted. "You need to get out of here before you cause trouble for everyone."

Sarah stopped and turned around. She glared hard at Dick, and he looked away. She lowered her head and walked down the stairs and straight to the door. The two policemen followed close behind her.

Dick stood at the top of the stairs as Jake and Georgia walked back up.

"Dick, you going to get all these Black folks killed behind one little white girl," Jake said as he passed by him and went back into his room. "Come on woman, I still got something coming from that extra money I gave you," he finished and closed the door.

SEVENTEEN

"The problem with the Negro man is that he has an animalistic appetite for the white woman," the fiery, racist South Carolina Senator Ben "Pitchfork" Tillman preached, as he stood at the podium in a special banquet room at the Hotel Tulsa. Harry Sinclair of Sinclair Oil had flown him down from Oklahoma City where he'd spoken at a Monday morning prayer breakfast at the Southern Baptist Convention. It was a little after one in the afternoon.

Lloyd Jones, one of the invited guests to the private lecture sat right up front absorbing all that the senator chose to share with the distinguished leaders of Tulsa's business community. It had been a last-minute decision to fly the senator in, because a small cadre of leaders, including the editor of the *Tulsa Tribune*, believed the white people living in South Tulsa had become too complacent about the race issue. In fact, it had been Jones who made the initial pitch to the oilmen of the city. Everyday he stared down on First Street and saw the immorality of those people. Prostitution, bootlegging and narcotics ruled day and night over there. It was nothing more than illicit, reckless behavior, and something had to be done about it.

Jones constantly reminded his readers of the danger lurking so close to the civilized people in his town, but at times he felt that was not enough. Bringing a real expert on the evil effects of the Negro on the white race would serve to keep the decent citizens alert. He smiled as he relaxed in his chair and listened to the message Tillman brought to this group of leaders.

"If the Negro's animal instincts are not checked by the white man, then our women will never be safe in their own homes or anywhere else," Tillman continued to rail on. "Recently in

Columbia, South Carolina, I had to visit a precious thirteen-year-old angel of a girl who had been attacked by a nigger. He raped and beat her and took her innocence away. When I left that hospital, I wanted to kill that monster with my bare hands. The good white people of the town found that nigger and immediately took him to a tree with a good hanging branch. They strung that coon up feet first, cut off his genitals, all while he was still alive, then took a match and some kerosene and burnt his filthy body." Tillman paused, obviously to allow the magnitude of the story to sink in. "And that is the only way to deal with those animals cause you got to realize they are not fully developed human beings. They are part ape and still have that beastly nature. So when you lynch a nigger isn't no different than shooting a rabid dog or any wild animal. I have three daughters, but so help me God, I had rather find either one of them killed by a tiger or a bear and gather up her bones and bury them, conscious that she had died in the purity of her maidenhood, than to have her crawl to me and tell me the horrid story that she had been robbed of the jewel of her womanhood by a Black fiend." He stopped long enough to take a drink from the glass of water sitting on the podium. "There have been a number of studies done over the past twenty years by some very smart men up North at Harvard University, that prove through scientific studies that the Negro is an inferior creature to the white man. And if God created him inferior, who are we to go against God's design?"

"I say let's kill everyone of them got damn Black animals," a man sitting in the back of the room shouted.

"Why do we tolerate them in our city?" another businessman also shouted. "We need to do them the same way we did the savages, either kill 'em or put 'em on reservations."

150

"Then who's going to wash your laundry, cook your meals and clean your house?" Still another man said, and the entire room of businessmen broke out in laughter.

Jones smiled as he gave a quick look at Sheriff McCullough as if to say now you see the people are on my side.

After the laughter stopped, Tillman continued. "No my friends, let's be careful to distinguish between the old Negro and this new one. There is some semblance of respectability and decency among some of the Negroes. There are the older ones who are a carryover from the good old days and who still understand their place in a white man's country. They readily accept the superiority of the white race and are happy to serve us. My own servant is part of our family, and every one of my children would give that boy their last crust of bread." He chuckled and said, "Sometimes I don't know if I belong to Joe or he belongs to me." He stopped while the crowd released a controlled laughter.

Jones again peered over at the sheriff, and he was not laughing. The sheriff was becoming somewhat of a problem. Hopefully, he wasn't becoming a nigger lover. That would not bode well for him. He needed to get in line and join the chorus of important leaders insisting that something be done about niggertown.

The Senator continued, "If I die first, I know old Joe Gibson will shed a sincere tear for me as I would do for him. But," his voice shattered the hushed atmosphere and his huge fist came slamming down on the podium sending the glass of water to the carpet, "it's these new niggers that must be dealt with. While boys like old Joe, born a slave, had benefited from the discipline of slavery, it's their sons and daughters and grandsons and granddaughters who no longer know their place in a white man's world. They are inoculated with the virus of equality and that virus must be, sometimes to the point of death, beaten out of them." Again a pause as he reached for his glass not realizing he'd knocked it over.

A Negro waiter standing by the wall in the back of the room taking this all in, poured water in a clean glass and ran it up to the podium. Tillman snatched the glass out of his hand. The waiter turned and hurried back to his place in the back of the room.

"What's your name, boy?" Tillman asked then took a drink from the glass.

"Sir, I'm sorry—'

"Don't be sorry, nigger. Tell these people your name." Tillman cut the man off.

"My name is Otis," he said in a very low voice.

"Now that's a good nigger there," Tillman said. "He ran up here with my water and ran to the back of the room. Now you all know why he ran? He knows his place is to be out of sight and not seen. A good nigger is invisible when they're cleaning your house or your clothes, and when they're ironing and cooking. And especially when they're serving white folks food at dinnertime. And a good nigger doesn't even hear what you're talking about over dinner. They're just supposed to stand there and the first words they should hear is 'Come here boy' or 'Come here girl.' A nigger who knows too much can be dangerous. So that's a good boy, and I bet he's from the old school." Tillman dug in his pocket and pulled out a nickel.

"Come here, boy," he shouted and at the same time waved Otis back to the podium.

Otis didn't move. Instead he looked all around him and stayed frozen in place.

"Ain't nobody in here going to bother you, boy," Tillman again shouted.

"Get your ass up there, boy," a white man with a very deep and commanding voice shouted.

Otis seemed to recognize the man's voice. He ran back up to the podium

"Good boy," Tillman said and handed him the nickel. "Look like y'all might have your darkies trained well."

"Not all of them, Senator," Jones stood up. "If you don't mind, sir?"

"You're the young brilliant editor and publisher of one of your local newspapers, aren't you?"

"Yes Senator, the *Tribune*."

"Go right ahead. Let me hear what you got to say."

"I believe we got way over our share of the new Negroes. You know the uppity niggers that don't know their place. A large number of them own their businesses and aren't dependent on us."

"All niggers got to be dependent on white people or we'll lose control. Understand something very important: A segregated society depends on the total and complete subjugation of the niggers. That subjugation has to be voluntary as it seems to be with Otis back there and Joe my boy, or it must be forced. One way or the other, it must be."

Jones really liked this man. Leaders in his city didn't have this kind of firm handle on the racial situation in Tulsa. What an excellent idea it had been to bring this giant of a leader to Tulsa. He had one more question to ask. "The Negro leaders in North Tulsa or what they prefer to call Greenwood plan to bring that rabble rousing, trouble maker Mr. Du Bois to speak to them this month. How should we handle it?" Jones deliberately stared hard at Sheriff McCullough and then sat down to listen to the answer.

"Undoubtedly the most dangerous nigger in the entire country," an aroused Tillman scowled. His face turned beet red just at the mention of Du Bois' name. "He's a threat to our democracy and all our God given freedoms. The Justice Department recently placed him on a list of dangerous individuals to be watched. And our newly appointed head of the Federal Bureau of Investigation is also closely watching his every movement. Your authorities here in Tulsa should be on alert and watch him closely while he is here."

Suddenly Jones sprang to his feet, turned and glared back at the sheriff. "You should be telling that to the sheriff, Senator." Just as quickly as he had gotten up, he sat back down. Silence engulfed the room momentarily. The men stared down McCullough. Finally, Tillman broke the silence.

"I'm sure you have a capable sheriff who will know how to handle riff-raff like Du Bois. If there are no other questions, I want to thank you fine citizens of Tulsa for this wonderful hospitality. I will carry the word back to South Carolina that y'all are fine people and have the graciousness of the South. But before I step down from the podium let me ask you a question. What do you have when you have one thousand niggers at the bottom of the Arkansas River?"

The audience remained silent.

"A good start." The entire audience erupted in laughter with Tillman as he returned to his seat.

As Jones started to the exit, he noticed Sheriff McCullough standing near the door. Jones approached him, and McCullough

153

stepped right in front of him.

"You're really starting to get out of line," McCullough said, staring him right in the face.

"Somebody in this damn town got to speak up for the white folks of this city who are deathly afraid that those animals from North Tulsa going to invade their privacy."

"I keep order in this city, and I don't need you creating any doubts about how well I do my job. And especially to a United States Senator."

"Then do your damn job, starting right now," Jones scowled. He would not back down to this confrontation. "Go on over to the *Star* and tell them niggers to back down and don't bring that troublemaker to our city."

"Did you ever think that those folks over there are citizens also and do have the right to have speakers come into their community just like you had the Senator in here today?"

"Are you comparing that communist nigger to a very fine and distinguished senator?"

"I wasn't making any comparisons," McCullough shot back. A small crowd had surrounded the two men. "But those people have a right to have speakers just like you do. Stop trying to do my job. Don't try being sheriff, and I won't try writing a newspaper. You'd better back off." McCullough finished and turned to walk away.

"You'd better do your job and keep this city safe or we'll do it ourselves." Jones shouted as McCullough disappeared out of the room.

154

***

Gurley felt nervous and unsettled after receiving a telephone call from Cleaver asking that he agree to a meeting with Sheriff McCullough and himself. No doubt they wanted to talk about the Du Bois trip to Tulsa. Sitting in his office in the hotel, Gurley felt uncomfortable with such a meeting. The Du Bois visit was set in stone, and the man was scheduled to lodge in his hotel. Even if he wanted to cancel it, he didn't have the kind of clout in the community to make that happen. The sheriff should be talking with Stradford and Smitherman. They got this Du Bois nonsense started and stirring up all the people, expecting this man to come in here with some kind of answers to their problems

Extremely uncomfortable in anticipation of the sheriff coming to his place, Gurley busied himself rearranging all the objects and pictures on top of his large oak desk. He positioned his wedding picture first to the left side and then over to the right side. He smiled while reminiscing on those earlier years the two of them had spent building their financial empire in Tulsa. Emma had been with him every step of the way, from Pine Bluff, Arkansas, to Perry, Oklahoma, and finally to Tulsa.

His pleasing memories were interrupted when Edna knocked on the office door, opened it and escorted Sheriff McCullough and Cleaver inside.

"Afternoon, Sheriff McCullough," Gurley greeted them from behind his desk and signaled for the two men to have seats.

"Thanks for seeing us on such short notice," Cleaver said as the two took their seats. "But earlier this afternoon a guest speaker aroused a crowd of businessmen. They're concerned about what you all are doing over here."

"Whenever our distinguished sheriff and his deputy ask to meet with me, of course I'm going to be accommodating. Can I offer you some coffee or a soft drink?"

McCullough moved right to the tip of his chair and leaned forward. "O. W., what are you all trying to prove?" he asked.

155

"You're talking to the wrong person," Gurley countered, not bothering to act like he didn't know what the sheriff was talking about. "I opposed the decision to have the man come here."

"But you're letting him stay at your hotel."

Gurley's entire body jerked back in his chair. How did the sheriff know the man would be staying there? "How could I not allow a distinguished Negro scholar and leader to lodge in my hotel, sheriff?"

McCullough raised both his arms high in the air and brought them crashing down on his thighs. "Hell, man, I don't know," he scowled in frustration. "But you people keep playing these games with the white folks in this town, and it's not going to fare too well for you all."

"I'm sure you and your deputy will keep everything under control," Stradford said standing at the back of the office. "May I come in?" he asked.

"Certainly," a relieved Gurley said. "Let me get you a chair."

"No, I don't plan to stay long. Actually I was on my way to a meeting with Andrew Smitherman about the Du Bois visit when I saw our distinguished Sheriff walking into your building."

"I was planning on dropping by to see you and Smitherman," McCullough said as Stradford made his way to the front of the room and stood next to Gurley's desk.

"Is that so, sheriff? Glad I could save you the trip."

"You boys need to think about what you're doing when you bring Mr. Du Bois down here," McCullough said.

"It's Doctor Du Bois, not mister," Stradford said. "And I'm afraid it's too late to cancel his visit. We have already purchased his ticket and expect him to arrive on Saturday afternoon."

"You crazy people actually paid for his train ticket?"

"I believe that is the proper thing to do when you invite a distinguished leader to your city as a guest speaker. I understand that you all went further than that when you brought Senator Tillman here. You provided him with a free plane ride," Stradford said.

156   "What is it you all want?" McCullough's eyebrows furrowed. "You two are the richest Negroes in Tulsa. Between the two of you, you got more wealth than most of the poor whites, and you're still not satisfied."

Gurley recoiled. He detected anger in the Sheriff's words and in the past when uttered by a white man to a Negro, that meant trouble. He didn't quite understand how Stradford could stand there and show no fear of the awesome power this white man possessed.

Stradford did not back down. He moved a little closer to the sheriff.

"Years ago, sheriff, I paid three dollars and sixteen cent for a first class train ticket from Arkansas City to Tulsa, and for that I was kicked off the train and arrested. They took my money and still denied me my rights by forcing me to sit in a segregated car right up front where all the exhaust and heat from the train filled the room."

"We all have sad stories to tell," McCullough said. "But that doesn't change the fact that if you insist on bringing this man to our city, there could possibly be trouble."

"Like I said before, we will look to you and your deputy to make sure that trouble does not interfere with our plans."

"And like I said before, you're pushing your luck and taking us down a road I'm not sure any of us can handle." The sheriff rose up out of his chair, as did Cleaver. "It's my duty to keep our streets safe for all our citizens and that's exactly what I plan to do, even for you two."

"Thank you, sheriff," Gurley said and also got up. He hurried from behind his desk and all four men stood for a moment in the middle of the floor.

"I would suggest that you convince your boy next door at the *Star* to keep some of those fiery editorials to a minimum. He's really starting to anger a lot of good folks," the sheriff continued.

"First Amendment protections apply to Negro newspapers just like the white ones," Stradford retorted as they all walked out into the lobby of the hotel.

"First Amendment rights won't mean a damn thing if you got an angry mob of white folks breaking down your door. Good day, boys." Sheriff McCullough and Cleaver strode across the lobby and out of the hotel.

157

"We need to talk about this situation," Gurley said to Stradford as they both watched the lawmen leave the hotel.

"It's too late for talk," Stradford said. "In the meantime, don't let that man scare you because that's always their way to keep us subdued." He patted Gurley on the back and headed for the exit.

EIGHTEEN

Gurley hurried out the front door of his hotel and started across the street to confront Stradford. On Monday as his friend left the meeting with the sheriff, he had told Gurley it was too late for talk, but with the latest developments he couldn't accept that answer. He had a copy of the Thursday afternoon *Tulsa Tribune* under his arm in case his friend hadn't yet seen the story about Dr. Du Bois.

Crowds of young men and women as well as some older people packed the streets on Maid's day off. They were either heading to either the Dreamland Theater for a matinee or to Williams Confectionery next door. Gurley planned to take Emma to the afternoon show Sunday after church since Loula had filled her head with how good and proud it made her to see a movie produced and directed by a Black man.

Gurley zigged-zagged across the street, having to duck in and out to steer clear of the buggies and cars. His mind was so occupied with the story in the *Tribune* that he just missed getting hit by a car. The driver had to let out a loud blare of his horn to alert him to move out of the way. All the hateful talk just led to articles like the one that appeared in the *Tribune* that afternoon.

Having walked the additional half block, he swung the door open and proceeded into the Stradford Hotel. He didn't see Stradford in the lobby, so he stopped a bellhop.

"Is Mr. Stradford in today?" He asked.

"Yes sir, he's back there in the main ball room with the high school students," the bellhop said. "They're in there talking about decorating the ballroom for their senior and junior prom."

"Thank you." Gurley turned and hurried his steps to the double ballroom doors, pushed them open and walked in.

Stradford stood in the center of the ballroom looking up at the beautiful chandeliers that hung down like icicles made of crystal. He was busy explaining something to the three students from Booker T. Washington High School and Julia Jackson, who had taken their lunch period to come over and check out the ballroom recommended by Principal Woods for the prom.

Gurley didn't want to interrupt, but his concern had to be dealt with immediately. He waved, hoping he would catch Stradford's attention. He kept moving his arm sideways until Stradford finally looked his way. He said something to Julia, and they started walking toward Gurley.

"O. W., this is the student delegation from the high school," Stradford said. "They're trying to make a decision where to hold their senior and junior prom this year"

"Mrs. Jackson, it's good to see you, and your students," Gurley said. "You couldn't find a better and more suitable place for your prom than right here in this beautiful ballroom."

"I'm sure you know young Billy Williams, John and Loula's son, and Harold Mackey." Julia said. "Billy is chairman of the committee for the senior class and Harold's second in charge." Julia put her arm around Veneice's shoulder. "Veneice Dunn represents the junior class."

"I know all these young people and their parents also," Gurley smiled. "How you young people doing?"

"Fine, thank you," Billy answered for all of them.

"I think the committee has pretty much made up their mind that they want to hold the prom right here, Mr. Stradford," Julia said.

160

"That's fine with me, and I'll draw up our contract next week," Stradford said. "What was the date again? I want to make sure I put the right date in the agreement."

"June 1, from seven to twelve p.m.," Julia replied.

"I assume you'll be the responsible adult?" Stradford asked.

"That's right, and we will have plenty of chaperones for the evening."

Stradford swung the ballroom door open, and they all walked out. "That's good to know. The ballroom will be available for decorating as early as May 30."

The two men and Julia marched out of the ballroom, followed by the students right behind them. Julia suddenly stopped as they came upon a portrait hanging on the wall in the lobby. On the bottom of the portrait the words, "Julius Caesar Stradford: A Proud Black Man Who Refused to Remain a Slave," were inscribed. They all stared at the picture.

"Your father?" Julia asked.

"Yes," Stradford answered.

"You look a lot like him," she said. "When did you hang this picture? It wasn't here the last time I was here."

"About a month ago. It had been in my home but I decided to share him with all the guests that will pass through this hotel in the future."

"Mrs. Jackson, is it all right if I ask Mr. Stradford a question about the caption under the portrait?" Veneice asked.

"Certainly, you can ask him."

"Sir, how did your father not remain a slave?"

"Young lady, have you studied the underground railroad in your history class?"

"Yes, sir, it had something to do with our ancestors escaping from slavery," Veneice answered.

"You're right; it does," Stradford said. "My father was born a slave in Kentucky but escaped across the Ohio River, and there he received help from both Black and white people who escorted him, giving him protection all the way to Canada. Once in Canada, he was safe from the slave hunters and their hounds. He made it to a place called Stradford, Canada and changed his name to Stradford. After the big war, he came back and got me, my brothers and sisters and our mother.

"That's just like Eliza in *Uncle Tom's Cabin*," Veneice said, as she turned and looked directly at Julia.

"You're absolutely right, Veneice, but with Mr. Stradford's

161

father, it was not a novel, but real life."

"So his daddy is proof that our ancestors didn't like being slaves like they try to say in our history books," Billy chimed in.

"You're right," Stradford said. "They hated slavery and every chance they got, they escaped."

"Your daddy is a real hero to our race, and I'm going to tell all the students in our English class tomorrow," Veneice said. "Is that okay, Mrs. Jackson?"

"Yes, Veneice, that's okay," Julia said. "Children, we'd better get back to school so that these men can take care of their business. It looks like we're all set," Julia said. "Call me when the contract is ready. I'll pick it up for Mr. Woods's signature. Let's go children." They started for the front door. "Good day, Mr. Gurley."

"Good seeing you again Mrs. Jackson and please say hello to your husband. We are so proud of him," Gurley said.

I'll be sure to do that," Julia said and she, along with the kids, disappeared out the door.

Stradford and Gurley watched as they walked out the double doors to the hotel.

"Let's go to my office," Stradford said.

The two men walked to the other end of the lobby and into his office. Stradford sat in one of the large leather chairs in front of his desk, and Gurley in the other one.

"My God, man, you stormed in here like something drastic happened," Stradford said.

"It might not be drastic yet, but if we don't put an end to these back-and-forth verbal attacks between the *Tribune* and the *Star*, something drastic just might happen," Gurley said as he handed Stradford the *Tribune*. "Read Jones' editorial today. We got to stop feeding that man fuel for his fires."

Stradford unfolded the paper and slowly read the editorial aloud. "Little Africa has gone too far this time. They have invited the most dangerous and volatile Negro in this country to speak in our city Saturday evening. The citizens of Tulsa do not need a rabble-rouser like this man coming down here and stirring up

162

trouble between the Negroes and the law-abiding white citizens. This dangerous radical socialist wrote in his magazine the *Crisis* only a few years back the following, 'We raise our clenched hands against the thousands of white murderers, rapists, and scoundrels who have oppressed, killed, ruined, robbed and debased their Black fellow men and fellow women, and yet today, walk scot-free, un-whipped of justice, un-condemned by millions of their fellow citizens, and un-rebuked by the President of the United States.' We understand that the FBI has placed Du Bois on the radical subversive list and are watching him very closely. We must approach our better Negroes and convince them to dis-invite this troublemaker."

Stradford handed the newspaper back to Gurley. "You're not surprised that this riff-raff newspaper and its publisher would print that hatred, are you?"

"You know I'm not, and you know I don't agree with anything he writes," Gurley answered. He folded the paper and laid it on his lap. "But he's a very dangerous man because he has the ability to provoke the rednecks out there who are jealous of our success and are looking for any excuse to come after us."

"Any redneck that comes on this side of the tracks is going to get exactly what he deserves," Stradford said.

"See, that's what I'm talking about," Gurley retorted as he squirmed around in his chair. "You have built a financial empire here in Greenwood. In fact, together, you and I made a decision way back to build a Negro community that is financially solvent on its own." Gurley stopped to catch his breath. He was breathing deeply and began to shake. "Together we started this back in 1909, and now you talk about fighting peckerwoods, and for what reason? Pride."

163

"You're damn right, pride." Stradford sat straight up in his chair as if to emphasize his point. "You saw that picture of Poppa out there hanging in the lobby. I put it out there because everyday I am here in this hotel, it reminds me that I come from a stock of men that were proud and refused to remain caged up like animals, taking orders from some tyrants who wanted to be called their masters. I will never back down to another man simply because of the color of his skin. And you need to stop backing down and acting like you fear those bastards."

As Stradford's anger rose, so did Gurley's state of nervousness. "I'm just saying that maybe we should ask Smitherman to stop the negative attacks on white people. I'm not saying Dr. Du Bois shouldn't speak here, and I'm proud that he'll be lodging in my hotel during his stay. But we need to keep the waters calm until he gets here and then leaves."

"I'm sorry, O. W., I can't tell Smitherman what to print in his paper," Stradford said in a much calmer manner.

"You know what these white folks did in Atlanta back in 1906, in East St. Louis and even Chicago up North. They burnt Black folks out of house and home. Destroyed their businesses and everything. Smitherman's got to know they don't care. They got some kind of sickness when it comes to us."

Stradford leaned toward Gurley, "Have you ever asked yourself what we ever did to those people to make them hate us the way they do?" he asked, but did not allow Gurley to answer. "If anyone should hate someone, we should hate them. They've done nothing but make the lives of Black people all over the world miserable. They lynch our men, they rape our women, and they drain our manhood right out of us. And then have the nerve to get upset when we dare to protest." Stradford moved in even closer to Gurley for greater effect. "The nerve of any race to think they have a right to mistreat other people the way white folks do is sickening. If Du Bois preaches about it and Smitherman writes about it, and O. B. Mann wants to fight about it, then good." He finished and relaxed back in his chair.

"I just don't know what to do," Gurley also relaxed back in his chair.

164

"Don't give in to their threats and intimidation. Our problem is that we are too passive and forgiving. Quite frankly, we need to kick some ass. That old Booker T. Washington approach is over. For the first time I believe Negroes are ready to die instead of continuing to be kicked around."

Gurley recognized the futility in his request and rose up out of his chair. "I was just hoping that we could get Smitherman to slow down on his articles."

Stradford got up and placed his hand on Gurley's shoulder. "We got each other's back and we're not going to let anything happen to our people down here in Greenwood. Those white folks know that, so they're not about to come down here making trouble." He walked Gurley to the door, opened it and the two men stepped out into the lobby. "I think both races have a pretty good understanding. They don't come down here messing with us, and we won't go on the other side of the Frisco tracks messing with them. That understanding will keep the peace between us."

As they approached the double doors, a bellhop rushed and opened the door.

"I pray that you're right," Gurley said and walked out into the warm spring air.

***

"You've got to stop this race baiting," Sheriff McCullough advised Jones as he sat across from the publisher who relaxed in his chair at his desk. Jones received the sheriff's call and agreed to meet with him at his office, despite their confrontation after the Tillman visit. Sitting across from McCullough and listening to his opening comments, he now knew the reason for the meeting. He also had a pretty good idea how it would end.

"Pretty strong terms, don't you think, sheriff?" Jones asked without waiting for an answer. "The race baiter is that so-called smart ass nigger that'll be bringing his hate-the-white-man-because-he's-done-you-so-wrong bullshit here to our otherwise peaceful city on Saturday."

165

A slight smirk broke through McCullough's solemn expression. "You been here a little over two years, Mr. Jones, and you think you can intimidate those Negroes over in Greenwood? Well, you really don't know those people. Race baiting and intimidation just won't work with them."

"You're right, sheriff, I've only been here two years, but I've been all over this country, and one thing I know about the darkies is if you be nice to them, they'll forget their place. If you keep a foot in their ass, they'll always know their place."

"You have a different brand of Negro here in Tulsa. They're more independent, tougher and quite hard headed."

"That's exactly why you can't afford to let up on them."

Sheriff McCullough leaned forward and glared directly into Jones' eyes. "Let's stop the bullshit," he scowled. "What's your real motivation, Mr. Jones?"

Jones was not about to be intimidated by this man whom he really did not like or respect, a man he believed was much too soft on crime and too friendly with the Negroes. He also leaned forward.

"My real motivation, sheriff, is to keep the good citizens of Tulsa aware of what is happening right before the eyes and ears of our law enforcement agencies." He abruptly got up, hurried over to the window and stared down on Archer Street. "Right down there on Archer and on First streets there is prostitution, illegal drugs and booze available to anyone who has a little money." He turned to look back at the sheriff. "You care to look down there?"

McCullough did not budge.

Jones continued. "Down there you got white whores and Black whores, you got white pimps and Black pimps, you got white and Black drug users and dealers. But the worst of all, is a nigger with some booze, a gun and an attitude that he isn't afraid of the white man. With that kind of coon, you got real trouble."

McCullough still did not budge. Jones wandered back to his desk and fell back into his chair. "I simply print the truth sheriff, only the truth."

166

"Excuse me, Mr. Jones," McCullough exclaimed. "But that is a bunch of horse shit. You've found a way to compete with the *Tulsa World,* and you're exploiting it for all it's worth. You know there are enough nigger haters out there that'll buy your paper just for the constant barrage of editorials attacking the Negro.

"I have more than editorials in my paper," Jones retorted.

"Yeah, but the normal news stories are also in the *World.*

Face it, your only exclusives are the editorials you write attacking Negroes."

Jones folded his hands together and began moving his thumbs up and down. He did that whenever he felt anger building up inside him. "What is it you like about the nigger race?"

Again the sheriff smiled and leaned back in the chair. "My job is to keep the peace on the streets of Tulsa," he said with calmness in his voice. "The most effective way I know to keep the peace is to prevent trouble from happening. And, Mr. Jones, you are trouble."

"Sheriff, I do believe I am within my First Amendment rights. I am a law-abiding citizen who performs a service for the people of Tulsa. I plan to continue writing about what I feel needs to be expressed."

"You're right, you are within your First Amendment rights. I just thought maybe you'd have the best interest of our city as your primary concern."

"I do, sheriff, I do."

Sheriff McCullough rose up from his chair and fixed his eyes on Jones. "We both know what is your primary concern. Just remember, law and order is my primary concern, and I'm going to make sure no one upsets the peace in my city."

"I appreciate that sheriff, and I will keep that in mind every time I look down on the filth below me," Jones said.

"We'll be having this same conversation again," McCullough finished, turned and left Jones' office.

NINETEEN

Determined not to look up from the textbook on her desk in Mrs. Jackson's class, Veneice concentrated on the poem, "We Wear The Mask," by Paul Laurence Dunbar that was to be the topic of discussion that afternoon in class. She must have read the poem a dozen times and practically knew it by memory. Her attention to the words had nothing to do with her intense concentration. If there was any problem at all, it had to do with Verby. Yesterday after class, she'd handed him a short note that read, "Yes I will be your girlfriend," but then ran off with Esther and Ruth before he had a chance to respond. But now in their sixth period class on Friday afternoon, she had to confront him, and that was her dilemma. She didn't know how to act as a girlfriend. It was something she had never experienced before in her seventeen years and knew she would melt right there on the spot the first time he looked at her in this new role as girlfriend.

She looked up long enough to glance over at Esther who snickered then tapped Ruth, sitting right in front of her, on the shoulder. Ruth also snickered as she looked over at Veneice. Not happy with her two friends, Veneice frowned and stared back down at the poem. She didn't appreciate her best friends poking fun at her during this moment of crisis. At least she did have a boyfriend; the two of them didn't. They had no one to dance with the night of the prom. Even though Verby wouldn't be allowed to pick her up at the house, he'd be there waiting for her at the ballroom. That made her feel special, just like a princess.

Finally, she felt Verby's presence right behind her. She could hear him as he scrambled around and finally settled into his seat. Her eyes stayed riveted on the lines, "We wear the mask that grins and lies. It hides our checks and shades our eyes." No way would she turn around and look at him. He had to make the first move.

Verby did, as he tapped her on the shoulder. "Hi, Veneice," he said.

She froze and stiffened up. Veneice just didn't know what to do next.

"I'm happy you're my girlfriend," Verby continued.

Don't be so silly and childish, she thought. After all, she wasn't twelve or thirteen anymore; she was seventeen and needed to act like a mature, young lady. If they were going to be boyfriend and girlfriend, she had to talk to him. Without turning to look around she said.

"Hi Verby."

"You going to be able to come by Williams Confectionery tomorrow afternoon?" he asked. "Bunch of the kids from the school going to meet over there for sodas."

"You know I can't—"

"Good afternoon class," Julia interrupted Veneice. "Today we'll discuss the meaning behind Paul Laurence Dunbar's poem, 'We Wear the Mask.'"

"I'll tell you after class," Veneice whispered while looking at Mrs. Jackson.

"Veneice, do you have something you'd like to share with the rest of the class?" Julia asked.

"No ma'am," Veneice replied.

"Then I suggest you stop that whispering and pay attention."

"Yes ma'am."

170   "Since you were whispering, Veneice, why don't you explain to the rest of the class what our great Negro poet, Paul Laurence Dunbar, meant when he wrote that poem," Julia instructed.

Veneice stood up at her desk. "I believe the 'we' in the poem refers to the Negro race living in the South," she said. "And the mask means that we can never reveal our true selves in front of white people. We always have to wear a mask of deception."

"Very good," Julia said. "Now Verby, since Veneice seemed to be whispering something to you, why don't you tell us why Mr.

Dunbar felt Negroes had to wear a mask."

Verby stood and said. "Because we can never tell white people what we really think and feel about them." He paused, looked around the room and smiled. "We always got to be acting like someone we're not."

A young boy sitting in the back of the room raised his hand just as Verby stopped talking and sat back down. He didn't wait to be called on.

"Mrs. Jackson, my daddy said he ain't ever going to be putting on and acting like he's someone else other than who he is. He said it's about pride and dignity."

"There are a lot of Negroes in this city and all over the country who feel the same way as your father does, James," Julia said. "But let's stay focused on the poem, and watch your use of 'ain't' in this class." She didn't want to get distracted as they did when discussing *Uncle Tom's Cabin*. How does this poem differ from others written by Mr. Dunbar?"

This time Esther raised her hand just before Ruth did.

"Yes Esther." Julia looked directly at her.

"Most of his poetry is in old Negro dialect; this one isn't," Esther said while standing.

"Why do you think he decided not to write this one in dialect?" Julia asked.

Ruth not only raised her hand but jumped to her feet before anyone else.

"Go ahead Ruth."

"I asked my brother who graduated from Tuskegee Institute, and he told me it was because Mr. Dunbar was trying to make a statement. And he couldn't make that statement in dialect."

171

"And what was the statement he was making?" Julia continued with the drill.

A young girl, sitting in the front row to the left of Veneice, raised her hand and also stood up at the same time.

"Paul Laurence Dunbar was the greatest Negro poet in the history of our people, and—"

"No he wasn't; Phyllis Wheatley was," Esther interrupted the young girl.

"Esther, how rude," Julia scowled. " Please, do not interrupt her. Continue, Alice."

Alice glared over at Esther and continued. "Mr. Dunbar was very upset because he was forced to always write one way only and that was in dialect if he wanted to get his poems published by the white publishers. And part of the whole idea of the mask was that we, as a people, had to act out roles to suit the idea of what white people think of us."

"Very good, Alice, and very good class. Now for the remainder of the time, I want you all to write a short essay on how Mr. Dunbar's message in his poem affects you." Julia finished, walked over and sat at her desk while the students began to write their short essays.

Ten minutes after the students began their writing, Principal Woods stepped into the class and strode over to Julia. He whispered something in her ear. She clapped her hands and said, "Students, please listen up. Principal Woods has something he must share with you." Principal Woods stood right in front of Veneice's desk and said, "I have chosen this class to attend the special lecture of the great scholar and Negro leader Dr. W. E. B. Du Bois, tomorrow night at the Dreamland Theater. Your parents have all been contacted and notified that you will be in attendance. And I am happy to report that all of them planned on attending also. You will have an assignment to write a paper about Dr. Du Bois and what his speech meant to you. I will be there to take attendance. A special section will be set-aside for students from our school. Feel honored that you have been chosen to hear this great man speak." He finished and walked out of the classroom.

Mrs, Jackson watched as Principal Woods disappeared out the door. She smiled as she addressed her students. "Feel honored that you will have an opportunity to hear a great leader speak. You are fortunate to live at a time when he is our spokesman and this will be an experience that will be with you all your life. Now finish your essays and I will see all of you

172

tomorrow evening at the event."

Veneice and Verby walked together up Independence Street after school with Esther and Ruth right behind them.

"I don't know why I can't come to your house to see you," Verby said.

"'Cause Poppa isn't going to let me entertain any company."

"How you know unless you ask him?" Verby stopped and looked at Veneice.

"Boy, don't stop walking." Veneice grabbed his hand and jerked him forward. "You know Principal Woods is in that window looking at everybody, and he don't allow no students to stop and talk when leaving school."

"Okay," Verby said and started walking again. "But how do you know unless you ask him?" He continued.

"I know my Poppa," Veneice answered.

"Are you going to tell him that we are girlfriend and boyfriend now?"

"Not right away," Veneice said. "After a little while I'll tell him."

"Girl, what's the sense in me having you as a girlfriend? It's already frustrating having you as a girlfriend"

"I'll be at the prom," Veneice said smiling. "And I promise that I won't dance with no one but you."

"You better not. You're my girlfriend." The two stopped walking. 173 Verby had to go up Greenwood while Veneice would continue on Independence. Esther and Ruth also stopped right behind them. "You never did tell me if you'll be at the confectionery tomorrow?"

"Yes, I'll be there, but I'll be meeting with Billy, Harold and Mrs. Jackson. We'll be discussing the prom."

"At least I'll see you there, even if I can't sit with you."

"Okay, I'll see you then," Veneice said, still a little nervous because she wasn't sure what he would try next. She wasn't ready to kiss. Holding hands was sufficient for the time being.

Verby took her right hand, kissed the top of it. "See you tomorrow." He then started walking up Greenwood.

"See you, Verby," both Esther and Ruth shouted.

Verby held his arm up and waved it from side to side without turning around and looking back. The three girls strolled up Independence toward Kenosha.

"Looks like you going to have problems with a boyfriend," Ruth said.

"Yeah, 'cause you can't ever go nowhere and he can't even come to your house," Esther added.

Defiantly Veneice responded, "At least I got a boyfriend."

"I could get one if I wanted to," Esther countered.

"Yeah, me too," Ruth said.

"Who could you get?" Veneice looked at Esther.

"I could get Ronnie. He likes me a whole lot," Esther answered.

"And Arthur already told me he's just going to dance with me at the prom," Ruth said.

"But he won't be your boyfriend," Veneice rejoined.

"After prom night, he will," Ruth said.

"Hey, you guys coming by Williams Confectionery tomorrow?" Veneice asked as they stopped right in front of her house.

174

"I'll be there about twelve," Ruth answered.

"And I should be there about twelve-thirty," Esther said.

"Good, see you there," Veneice finished.

"See you, girl," Ruth said and along with Esther they started walking up the street.

Veneice watched as her two best friends finally disappeared around the corner, then went inside feeling good because she had broken the ice with Verby and was now officially his girlfriend.

TWENTY

Veneice hurried into Little Rose Beauty Salon on Saturday morning at eleven o'clock. She was on her way to meet with Billy, Harold and Mrs. Jackson. She hoped to also see Verby there. But first she had to talk with Mrs. Mabel about doing her hair for the prom. Everyone knew Mrs. Mabel was the best hairdresser in all of Tulsa, and Veneice wanted the very best to make her look pretty for her special night. Veneice knew she'd be a few minutes late for her meeting, but that was okay. They would all understand. She scurried over to the hostess who stood behind a podium greeting customers as they entered.

"Young lady, may I help you, and do you have an appointment?" the hostess greeted Veneice. Because without an appointment there is no way we can squeeze you in. We're booked all day long. Everybody wants to get their hair done for the big event tonight at the Dreamland Theater with Dr. Du Bois."

"No, ma'am," Veneice answered. "I only need to talk to Mrs. Mabel for a minute."

Mabel looked up from working on a customer's hair when she heard Veneice call her name.

The hostess smiled at Veneice and said, "I'm sorry, she's busy with a customer right now. Would you like to leave a message?"

"I...I guess so," Veneice stammered, feeling a little intimidated by the denial.

The hostess handed Veneice a notepad and a pencil. "Write it out, and I'll make sure she gets it."

Veneice took the notepad and pencil, but just as she began to write her message, Mabel called out to her. "Come on over here, child. Lou Ann, take that pencil and pad from that child and let her come on over here."

Veneice handed the pencil and pad back to Lou Ann, smiled, then hurried over next to Mabel.

"What is it, child? Why you want to talk with me?" Mabel asked without looking up.

"Mrs. Mabel, our senior and junior prom is next month, and my Poppa said I could go this year since I'm a junior and doing real good in my studies," Veneice said.

"That's wonderful, baby," Mabel said still not looking up. "Go on."

"Everybody in Greenwood know you the best hairdresser in town, so I was—"

"Who told you she's the best," a young hair stylist in the chair next to Mabel interrupted Veneice. "She can't carry my hot iron, let alone style hair as good as me," she continued with a big smile all over her face.

Veneice turned toward the hairstylist. "I'm sorry ma'am...I mean, I didn't mean no harm."

"Leave that child alone," Mabel spoke up. This time she looked up from running the hot comb through her customer's hair. "Quit teasing her. Can't you see you making her uncomfortable?" She finished, then looked at Veneice. "Go ahead baby, finish telling Mrs. Mabel what you want."

"I was hoping that you'd be willing to do my hair on the morning of the prom."

176 "What day is the prom?" Mabel asked,

"June 1st, ma'am."

"Let's do it on May 31st, just in case something happens to me on June 1 and I'm not here. Don't ever wait until the last minute to do things."

"Yes, ma'am, May 31st." A smile spread across Veneice's face.

"You're one of Fritz Dunn's daughters, aren't you?" Mabel

asked as she looked at Veneice.

"Yes, ma'am."

"I thought so. You're the spitting image of your daddy. He's a good, hard working man and helped us out when our car needed some work. I won't charge you nothing 'cause you got such good folks," Mabel smiled at Veneice and then continued. "This child's daddy works on buses for the city. Got a real fine job and a real fine home over on Kenosha. Lou Ann, make sure you put her down in the appointment book for 9:00 a.m. on May 31st."

"Thank you, Mrs. Mabel." Veneice could hardly contain her excitement. "I'll be here and I'll be right on time."

"You'd better, because if you aren't, you won't get your hair done," Mabel said.

"May 31st." Veneice finished, turned and practically ran out of the parlor. "Bye everybody," she said and was out the door.

Billy and Harold sat at a table at the far end of the confectionery sipping on a sarsaparilla as Veneice bound through the front door, spotted them. As she made her way to their table, she noticed Verby sitting at the soda fountain with two other boys. He smiled at her, and she smiled back. She took one of the empty seats at the table.

"Where you been?" Billy asked.

"Sorry, but I had to stop to ask Mrs. Mabel if she'd do my hair for the prom," Veneice said. "Where's Mrs. Jackson?'

"In the back. She's talking with Momma about providing the refreshments for the prom," Billy said. "She'll be back out in a few minutes."

"Why'd you have to make a reservation so far in advance?" Harold asked.

"'Poppa always tell us that the early bird gets the worm and don't put off till tomorrow what you can do today," Veneice said.

"Man, you girls sure are different," Harold said.

"I'll get you a drink." Billy got up, walked over to the counter where drinks were kept, got one and hurried back to the table. He put the drink down on the table in front of Veneice.

"Thank you," she said and took a sip.

"We got a little over five weeks to graduation for some of us," Billy sat back down at the table. "And five weeks to the prom. We're going to have one heck of a good time."

"Yeah, and I'm actually going to get a chance to dance without worrying about Poppa walking in on me and scolding me for doing the devil's work," Veneice said.

"Your daddy really believes you're doing the devil's work if you dance?" Billy asked.

"Sometimes I get a chance to dance at home when he and Momma gone somewhere. But I can't do it long 'cause if he comes in that house and sees me dancing, he'll be awfully mad, and I'd be grounded for a very long time."

"Boy, I'm glad my parents aren't like that," Billy said.

"Who's gonna be your date?" Harold asked. " It must gonna be Verby Ellison."

"Why you think it's going to be Verby?" Veneice asked.

"Isn't he supposed to be your boyfriend now?" Harold queried.

"Boy, word sure gets around fast," Veneice said. "Yeah, and I'm going to dance all night just with him."

"Is he going to pick you up at your home or just meet you at the dance?" Billy asked.

178   A frown invaded Veneice's face. "You know he can't come to the house. This isn't really an official date, more like...oh, I don't know what." Veneice snatched her glass and gulped down her drink. "But we'll be together at the dance and he'll be the only boy I'll dance with." Her smile returned. "And I'm going to dance right up till the end."

"You know who's gonna be there, watching all of us to make sure we don't get out of line?" Harold asked.

"Principal Woods," Veneice answered.

"He's going have those old wire rimmed glasses way down his nose," Billy added as he lowered his head mocking the principal. "And he's going to be looking over the top at everybody."

Veneice and Harold laughed at Billy's imitation of Principal Woods.

Billy continued, "And as soon as he sees somebody getting too wild with their dancing, he's going to have them stop the music, walk right up to the students and tell them they can't dance any more."

"He might not be hard on us since it's prom night," Veneice surmised. "And after all, this is 1921 and not 1900. Things have changed a whole lot."

"Not that much," Billy responded. "He's harder than some of the preachers in this town."

"I'm not going to worry about it," Veneice said. "I'm just going to enjoy the night and remember it forever," she added as she watched Mrs. Jackson come out of the side room. She walked over to the table and sat down in the empty chair.

"How are you kids doing?" she asked.

"Just fine, Mrs. Jackson," they all answered in unison.

"We're set on the refreshments," she said. "We need to finish our work this afternoon because Dr. Du Bois is coming into town today."

"He's speaking at our theater next door. Our history class was picked as one of the classes that have to attend," Billy said. "Daddy been getting it all ready since this morning. They won't be showing any movies today, and a lot of people got mad. Saturday is when they come to the theater."

179

"Veneice's literature class was also chosen to attend. This is a very important man, and he's going to be talking about some very important issues," Julia said.

"Like some of the things we talk about in class?" Veneice asked.

"Yes, like some of things we discuss."

"My daddy said he is about the smartest man in the entire country and that the white people don't like him," Billy said.

"Yes, he is a brilliant man. He got his doctorate degree from Harvard University, the first Negro to do so," Julia added.

"Boy, we're pretty important if a man that smart comes to our town to talk to us," Harold said.

"Was he smarter than Mr. Booker T. Washington?" Billy asked.

"No, he couldn't be; they named our high school after Mr. Washington so he had to be real smart," Harold said. "He isn't smarter than Mr. Washington is he, Mrs. Jackson?"

"They were all smart men in their own way. Mr. Washington had his way of looking at how to advance the race and Dr. Du Bois has his way, and they differed but still respected each other."

"Do you think the white folks will try to make trouble when he gets here?" Billy asked. He didn't wait for an answer. "I heard my Daddy talking with some other men, and they said if the whites try anything, the Negro veterans gonna take care of them real good."

"Let's hope it doesn't come to that," Julia said. "We don't need any trouble, just a good eventful night for everyone." She folded up her papers and prepared to leave. "I will see you all this evening at the Dreamland Theater." She got up and started toward the door leaving the other three still sitting at the table.

"Do you think there's gonna be some fighting tonight?" Harold asked.

"I don't know but my Daddy said isn't no way the Negroes, especially the war veterans, going to let white people come over here and mess with their event," Billy said.

"Don't talk like that," Veneice cautioned. "Everybody always talking about fighting and killing. What's wrong with this world? Must be getting ready to come to an end." She watched Verby get up from his seat at the fountain and scurry over to the table.

180

"Hey, Billy, Harold, how's it going?" Verby asked. But he didn't wait for them to answer. He looked directly at Veneice. "Hi, Veneice, how you doing?"

"I'm okay. We just finished our meeting with Mrs. Jackson."

"Yeah, I saw that. You all are the big wheels at our school, meeting with the principal and Mrs. Jackson all the time." Verby put his hand on Veneice's shoulder.

She didn't push Verby's hand away, but felt just a little uncomfortable knowing that Billy and Harold saw him do it. "We were just getting ready to leave," she said.

"Yeah, 'cause I have to get home to clean my bedroom," Harold said.

"I wonder what happened to Esther and Ruth?" Veneice commented.

"Probably couldn't get away. You know they have to get ready for tonight," Verby offered.

"Man, we sure are lucky," Billy exclaimed. "Getting a chance to hear the greatest living Negro speak right here in our city. That's exciting."

"No, what would be exciting is if the veterans have to take out some white people 'cause they try to break up the event," Verby said.

"Shame on you," Veneice scolded. "Why do you want to have violence?"

"Not against us, but against them. They deserve it," Verby retorted. "They always beating up on Negroes.

"I have to get home," Veneice said as she stood up. She felt relieved. Verby had to remove his hand from her shoulder.

"I'll walk you half way," Verby said.

"Okay, but only half way, and you know why," Veneice said.

"Yeah, I know why. Because of your daddy."

Billy and Harold chuckled as they also got up and prepared to leave.

181

"You two make a good couple," Harold said. "I hope you stay together for a very long time.

"Yeah, like get married and someday have a whole lot of children that look just like both of you," Billy added.

Veneice blushed and said. "I definitely have to go. See you all tonight." She and Verby turned and walked toward the door and finally out of the confectionery.

TWENTY•ONE

The Baltimore and Ohio Train Number 65 from Chicago pulled into the Frisco Train Depot right at one o'clock Saturday afternoon. Smitherman and Stradford waited on the platform as the train came to a stop and the Pullman porters got off first to help the white passengers from the train. The two men walked to the front car and waited for the door to open from inside. Once it swung open, the third person to step onto the platform was Dr. Du Bois, dressed in a blue suit, white shirt, blue tie and vest and carrying a briefcase. He also had a copy of the *Chicago Defender* under his arms.

Just as Stradford and Smitherman walked toward him, a Pullman porter stepped between them and said, "Dr. Du Bois, it is a pleasure to have been on the same train with you." He grabbed Dr. Du Bois' hand and shook it. "I will definitely be there to hear you speak tonight. We been anticipating your visit for weeks."

Before Du Bois could respond the man turned and went back to his station at the door helping white passengers off the train.

"Dr. Du Bois, Andrew Smitherman of the *Tulsa Star* and my associate, John Stradford. We welcome you to Tulsa, Oklahoma." Smitherman shook Du Bois' hand, as did Stradford.

"Thank you, it's a pleasure to be in your city," Du Bois replied as he shook hands with both men. He looked directly at Smitherman. "So you are the man that is causing the entire southwest to get up in arms against your editorials?"

A smile filled with gratitude for the compliment covered Smitherman's face as the three men walked to the end of the platform and to Stradford's Ford.

"I get my encouragement from you," Smitherman said. "I read

the *Crisis* every month and of course I always read the *Chicago Defender*." He pointed at the newspaper folded under Du Bois' arm.

"Oh yes," Du Bois replied. "I read this last edition the porter got for me when I stopped in Chicago. He gave it to me last night. I saved it because it had a story about the new Wall Street in Tulsa. Mentioned you and your magnificent hotel, Mr. Stradford, and, of course, they wrote about the original pioneer O. W. Gurley. Hopefully, I'll have the opportunity to meet him."

"Not only will you meet him," Stradford interjected. "You're going to stay at his hotel. In his VIP room."

"That's fine with me, and I am looking forward to meeting many of the leading Negroes in the city. You all have accomplished so much, especially you, Mr. Stradford, with a hotel that is considered the largest and the best Negro hotel in the country. And I might add the rest of the country knows that your hotel can actually rival the best that Tulsa has to offer in the other part of the city."

Now it was Stradford's turn to beam. A compliment like that from the most important Negro in the nation brought a smile to his face.

Smitherman opened the car door, and Du Bois climbed into the back seat. He then walked to the front of the car and cranked it while Stradford turned the engine over. Smitherman walked back to the passenger side and climbed in the front seat. He positioned his body so he could talk directly with Du Bois in the back. Stradford pulled out of the parking area and down Greenwood toward the Gurley Hotel.

184   Du Bois stared out the window at the Williams Confectionery and the Dreamland Theater. He saw the Little Café and Little Rose Beauty Parlor, Elliot and Hooker's Clothing Emporium and the Gurley Hotel. The street was packed with Saturday afternoon revelers, out and about.

"What an impressive line up of businesses, just on this one side of the street," Du Bois said as the car pulled up and stopped in front of the hotel. A group of men and women stood outside the hotel in anticipation of their arrival.

"This is called Deep Greenwood, and it runs five blocks on both sides of the street," Smitherman said. "All of these businesses are a success because the community supports them." Smitherman got out of the car to open the door for their guest. "Looks like you have an official welcoming party," he said.

Du Bois stepped out of the car. "Welcoming parties always bother me because sometimes they are not all that friendly." He and Smitherman strode around the back of the car and met Stradford on the other side.

"Welcome to the greatest Black community in the entire country," a man standing in the front of the welcoming party said.

"You are now in the Black Wall Street," another man shouted. "Keep up the good work. Keep telling those white racists that we can't stand them."

"No, no," another man shouted. "Don't come in here and stir up these crazy white folks. You ain't never seen no white folks like these. They're crazy."

"Ain't nobody afraid of these peckerwoods," still another man shouted. "We got guns, too."

"You got guns, they got guns and everybody got guns," the other man shouted.

"Gentlemen, gentlemen, please stop this bickering." Du Bois stopped right beyond the two men. "There is still hope that we can get this all together. Let's not talk on the street about guns." He then followed Smitherman and Stradford inside the hotel.

Gurley, his entire staff and Emma stood in the lobby waiting for their guest. After they were inside, Gurley hurried over to them, followed closely by Emma and the others.

185

"Welcome to the Gurley Hotel," Gurley said and extended his hand to Du Bois.

"Thank you, it's my pleasure and honor to be able to stay here," Du Bois responded and accepted Gurley's handshake.

"We have a special VIP room all arranged and waiting for you," Gurley said.

Smitherman was pleasingly surprised at Gurley's demeanor.

He didn't appear nervous at all. In act, he seemed quite jubilant. But still, Smitherman felt compelled to follow Du Bois upstairs to his room.

"Let me show you where you'll be staying," Gurley continued. He walked across the lobby and started up the stairs to the second floor. Before they reached the top, they heard loud voices outside the hotel. Gurley stopped, turned around and looked past Du Bois at Smitherman and Stradford. The expression on his face was informative. He had told them this would happen.

Without hesitation, Smitherman took control. "Not to worry," he said smiling. "Just a little disturbance out front."

"And would that disturbance have anything to do with me?" Du Bois spoke up.

"We'll take care of it," Stradford joined in. "O. W. why don't you get our guest settled in his room. I'm sure he could do with a nap and then freshen up before dinner this evening."

"Oh yes, yes," Gurley rejoined. "I'll do that." He turned and continued up the stairs.

Du Bois smiled at Stradford then turned and followed Gurley. The other two men hurried back down the stairs, across the lobby and out to the front.

Cal, the man who had met with Jones, and four white men sat in a green Norwalk with shotguns resting across their arms. A contingent of Negroes still mingling out front, stood on the sidewalk facing the men.

"Is that nigger trouble maker staying here?" Cal shouted from the front passenger seat in the car.

"None of your business who's staying here," Stradford shouted back, having joined the men on the sidewalk.

"We know he is. The conductor on the 65 from Chicago told us he was," the man in the back seat shouted.

"Who stays in this hotel, as I told you before, is none of your business. You men better head on back across those tracks and out of our community," Stradford continued to shout.

"That man is a communist, and we don't want no dirty

commies fouling up our city," a skinny man wearing coveralls, and only a whit tee shirt yelled from the backseat.

"Where is McCullough now?" Smitherman asked.

"Dr. Du Bois is one of the most outstanding scholars in this country, and you'd best be on your way before this turns bad for you men," Stradford kept shouting.

"You threatening white men?" Cal scowled. "You see what happens when them uppity niggers from up north come down here?"

"Who the hell you think you're talking to?" Stradford started off the sidewalk toward the car.

Smitherman instantly caught up with his friend and pulled him back, just as Cal raised his rifle and aimed at him." Come on, John," he urged. "You're too valuable to lose because of these fools." He slowly pulled Stradford back onto the sidewalk, and Cal lowered his rifle.

"Good way to get killed," Cal yelled. "You boys better get that communist out of town or things just might not go so well for you this evening," he finished and the car sped off.

The two men watched as the car headed across the Frisco Railroad tracks back into South Tulsa. They then walked back into the hotel and met Gurley who stood by the stairway. Smitherman could detect the fear in Gurley's eyes.

"What in God's creation have you all done?" he asked as the two men approached him. "You brought this man to town, and now all hell is about to break out."

"Quit acting like such a coward," Stradford frowned. "Aren't you tired of letting them ignorant peckerwoods intimidate you?"

187

"Oh yeah, you're mister tough man all the time," Gurley groveled mockingly. "Let me bow to your courage while you get all of us killed."

"All right, let's not fight among ourselves," Smitherman intervened. "We got a situation that we must deal with. One fact we can all agree on and that is these white folks go crazy when it comes to Black folks exerting their independence. That's exactly what we've done and now we have to back it up. This evening those fools going to be perched out front of the Dreamland Theater trying to intimidate folks not to go in and hear Dr. Du Bois speak." He paused and stared at the other two men. "It's time to make a visit over on Lansing Street and get our own muscle."

"I'll go with you," Stradford said. "We'll be back right at six-thirty to escort Dr. Du Bois to the theater. Feed him when he gets up. And please do not tell him about all this."

"He already heard," Gurley said now calmed down.

"He heard but doesn't know the extent of the danger, and he doesn't need to," Smitherman said.

"What if he asks about it?" Gurley continued.

"Just tell him we'll have it all under control, and he'll be in no danger," Stradford advised. "And for God's sake, don't act like you're scared. Act normal, and we'll be here to get him over to the theater."

"Let's go," Smitherman said. "We don't have a lot of time to get this done," he finished and the two men walked across the lobby and out of the hotel.

***

At five o'clock Gurley, along with Edna, escorted Dr. Du Bois into the dining area of the hotel. Captain Townsend Jackson, Dr. Andrew Jackson, Julia, Mabel and Reverend Whittaker were already seated at a specially decorated table with a beautiful blue tablecloth, a bouquet of fresh flowers in a designer vase in the middle and eight elegant white plates with silverware wrapped in cloth napkins. The party seated around the table stood for introductions as Gurley, Edna and Du Bois approached them. Once they were all seated at the table, Du Bois initiated the conversation.

188

Turning to Captain Townsend he said, "Back East we have heard of the many accomplishments you have made over a very active lifetime. And I know you are very proud of your son who is recognized as one of the pre-eminent surgeons in the country." He looked over at Dr. Jackson.

"You're right, I'm very proud of Andrew as I am of all my children," Captain Townsend said.

"The American Negro is coming into his own, and that is a good sign that we as a people are leaving the old images and perceptions of us behind and are defining who we are ourselves. When we do that, we produce men like your son." Du Bois paused while the waiter poured iced water into the glasses next to each plate. "Thank you," he said, picked up the glass and took a sip. He continued, "There are wonderful things happening all over this country for the Negro, and the center of all the activity emanates from Harlem in New York City. You all must visit the cultural capital of our race and of course meet and talk with some of the many artists who now live there." Again he paused to drink his water, and Captain Townsend used that as an opportunity to ask a question:

"Dr. Du Bois, a few years ago we heard a great deal about the disagreement you had with Dr. Booker T. Washington before that great man died. Do you still believe that his expressed approach to our problems in the country was wrong?"

Du Bois remained silent for at least a minute. He adjusted his position in the chair and said. "Dr. Washington was a great leader for our people in the South. He, more than anyone else, offered them hope. But unfortunately that hope was built on a false premise. You see, he sincerely believed that if we stayed out of the white man's way, that is, didn't bother with politics or economic and social justice for our people, and if we worked hard and accumulated land and wealth, we would eventually be treated as equals."

189

"That's exactly what I believe, and that's what I've practiced all my life," Captain Townsend interjected, and Gurley smiled in support.

"That is a noble and honorable approach if dealing with honest and fair people," Du Bois said. "But I'm afraid history has shown us and is now showing us that approach will not work with these people. They do not want to see our race progress. When you're successful, they will make you pay. They have what are referred to as whitecaps, poor white framers throughout the South. What these farmers hate most is to live near a successful Negro family, especially if they are struggling." Du Bois again paused to catch his breath.

"I believe I heard that term used in Hominy. That's a small rural country town near Oklahoma City," Gurley said, allowing Du Bois a short reprieve.

"These southern whites have carried out a systematic attack on Black farmers who worked their land successfully," Du Bois continued. "One Black man who left Meridian, Mississippi, and moved to New York actually brought one of the signs they would place on Negroes' land. It read, 'If you have not moved away from here by sundown tomorrow, we will shoot you like rabbits.' That next day, the man packed what he could carry and got his wife and children out of there. They didn't stop until they got all the way to New York."

"That might be the case with other parts of the country," Gurley spoke up. "But here in Tulsa we have prospered as a Black community, and we just don't have to worry about those kind of things happening. We have a pretty good understanding with our white neighbors. We don't bother them, and they don't bother us."

"I certainly hope it can stay that way," Du Bois said.

The tantalizing aromas of ham, sweet potatoes, hopping john, corn bread and sweet corn filled the room as the three waiters assigned to the dinner brought the food in on trays.

"It sure smells good," Du Bois remarked.

"It's going to taste good also. Greenwood has some of the best cooks in the country," Gurley said. Once the plates of food were placed in front of the party, he then turned to Reverend Whittaker. "Please lead us in prayer."

190

***

Right at six thirty, Smitherman and Stradford strolled into the lobby of the Gurley Hotel, and the clerk signaled for them to go into the dining room. Smitherman walked in first. He proceeded over to the table where Dr. Du Bois and the guests were seated.

"Evening, Dr. Du Bois," Smitherman said as he and Stradford positioned themselves next to the guest. "I hope you had a good rest."

"Yes, I did," Du Bois answered. " I slept just like a baby for at least three hours. Guess that long train trip tired me more than I originally thought. But I'm feeling well rested and raring to go."

"We're expected at the Dreamland Theater at seven, so if you need to return to your room for a few minutes to freshen up, it'll take us less than five minutes to get there," Smitherman said.

"I'm just fine and ready to go meet the fine citizens of the Greenwood community." Du Bois pushed his chair back, got up and the others followed. "Compliments to the cooks," he said looking at Gurley. "It was a delicious meal, and I now see why you all are proud of the meals a person can get here in Greenwood." He followed the group out of the dining room.

As the entire party strolled across the lobby toward the front door, they heard a commotion outside the hotel. Smitherman and Stradford got out front of the entourage with Du Bois secured in the middle. They stopped right at the front entrance.

"Would you prefer to wait here inside until we find out what this commotion is all about?" Smitherman looked at Du Bois.

"Absolutely not," Du Bois answered with no hesitation.

"Are you sure?"

"Please, Mr. Smitherman, do not baby me. I am accustomed to conflict. Our days of being intimidated are over."

191

Smitherman glared at Stradford, smiled and swung the door open. The streets directly in front of the hotel swarmed with men wearing white robes, white masks and holding flaming torches high in the air. In their other hand they brandished shotguns and pistols. Cal, their leader stepped forward.

"That nigger will not speak here in Tulsa," he shouted. "Get him out of here tonight."

Unmoved by their attempt at intimidation, Stradford

continued out of the building followed by the others, with Du Bois comfortably snuggled in the middle. They turned right and slowly walked in the direction of the Dreamland Theater.

"We just have to make it to the opening leading back into the alley," Smitherman whispered.

"Stop or somebody's going to die right now," Cal once again shouted.

Led by Smitherman and Stradford, the party kept walking without looking out to the street where the white-robed men walked parallel to them.

Cal thrust his rifle into the air and fired off a couple rounds. "You niggers going to have to learn the hard way. Next step and you two coons up front die."

"We can't stop," Stradford whispered. "We're almost there."

No one stopped walking. They just looked straight ahead. At the alley Smitherman finally stopped, and suddenly O. B. Mann on his white stallion galloped out of the alley, followed by what appeared to be at least twenty men, armed with rifles and pistols. Men on the roof of the store where they stopped also appeared with rifles at the ready position. O. B. took the lead. He positioned himself in the middle of the road, blocking the movement of Cal and his men.

"It ends right here," O. B. shouted with rifle aimed at Cal. "We don't cotton to y'all bringing your weapons on our side of the tracks just like you wouldn't cotton us coming on your side."

Cal glowered up at O. B. atop his stallion. "You boys making a big mistake," he shouted.

192

"No, you the one that made the mistake thinking you can come over here and break up our peaceful assembly. We don't want no trouble, but we'll deal with it if you insist."

"Nigger, I could kill you right now," Cal screamed, but was careful not to point his weapon at O. B.

"And I could kill you too, peckerwood," O.B. challenged the man. "You might get me but my men gonna kill everyone of your boys."

"Come on Cal, let's get out of here," one of Cal's men shouted from the middle of the pack. "There's too many of them."

Smitherman stared over at his partner who helped plan this scheme of counterattack, and smiled. Looked like it was going to work.

"Yeah Cal, let's get our of here. To hell with that nigger; let him talk," another man shouted.

"Looks like your men not willing to die for your cause," O. B. snarled. "We're ready to die, and if you the only one ready to go, just try pulling that trigger."

The silence lasted for thirty seconds, and then Cal relaxed his entire body and shouted to his men. "Let's get out of here."

The hooded men lowered their torches and guns and marched up Greenwood toward the railroad track. Before turning to follow his men, Cal shouted, "You niggers outgunned us this time, but there will be another time and then we'll outgun you."

"Until that time comes, get the hell off our side of town," O. B. also shouted.

Smitherman thrust his hand toward Stradford and said, "It worked."

Stradford grabbed his hand and shook it. "It sure did. Now let's get our guest over to the theater. I understand they've got a lot of people waiting for him."

"You got it," Smitherman said.

The two men walked their group to the Dreamland Theater and entered to a full house. When the crowd inside saw them stroll into the theater, they all stood and applauded. Ten chairs were set up on the stage for the guest and distinguished members of the community. With the crowd still applauding, they made their way up on the stage and took their seats.

Stradford strode up to the podium set up in the middle of the stage and waved his arms for the crowd to sit and stop applauding. "It's only once in a lifetime that you might have the opportunity to come in contact with a giant of a man," he began after everyone had sat down and stopped the applause. "And you usually never have the opportunity to introduce that person at a gathering such as this. You all must know that I am overwhelmed by this opportunity." He paused and let out a deep breath. "We are so honored this evening to have in our presence the great scholar, sociologist, historian, writer and editor of the most widely read news magazine, the *Crisis*, The great Dr. W. E. B. Du Bois. Friends of Greenwood, I present to you the one and only, Dr. Du Bois." Stradford finished and returned to his seat, while Du Bois stepped up to the podium. He smiled as the crowd stood and clapped again. Finally after a few minutes, he signaled for them to stop and sit down.

Smitherman had waited a long time for this moment. As he looked at the man standing before him, he could hardly believe it was real. But as soon as Du Bois began to speak, he knew it was really happening.

"My fellow friends of the African Diaspora, thank you for allowing me the chance to share a few words with you. I want to first bring you greetings from the NAACP and the staff of the *Crisis*. Second, I want to inform you that the day of passive resistance is over. The Negro has been backed into a corner and must now begin to fight back."

Smitherman figured Du Bois would come out fighting, and it looked to be an evening of no holds barred.

"We have endured quite enough," Du Bois continued. "We endured the slaughter of our people in Atlanta, Georgia, in 1906, Springfield, Illinois, in 1907 and Chicago only a few years ago. And a full-fledged pogrom took place in East St. Louis, Illinois, where over thirty-nine Negroes were slaughtered. In fact, it was so God-awful Negro corpses were seen bobbling in the Mississippi River. But at least we fought back and took out eight of them before it was over. Now the final act took place in Houston, Texas, in 1918. Thirteen Negro soldiers were summarily executed for coming to the defense of a Negro woman being accosted by a white police officer."

194

Du Bois reached inside his suit coat pocket and unfolded an article. "I wrote the following editorial for the *Crisis* after the legalized lynching happened to those soldiers in Texas. It reads, 'We raise our clenched hands against the thousands of white murderers, rapists and scoundrels who have oppressed, killed, ruined, robbed and debased their Black fellow men and fellow women, and yet, today, walk scot-free, un-whipped of justice, un-condemned by millions of their fellow citizens and un-rebuked by the President of the United States.'" He finished, folded the article and placed it back in his pocket. "Yes, I included President Warren Harding because he is to blame too. He does nothing to try and stop these slaughters. He refuses to support anti-lynching legislation and is not a friend of the Negro. In fact the Negro has no friends or allies in any branch of government, not the Congress, not the Supreme Court and not the executive branch. We find that local and state governments are hostile to our requests to be treated as equals. But we must stay proud, head held high, un-bowed and un-bending to anyone." His voice rose. "We must begin to arm ourselves against the rogues of the white race, the racist, the rapist and the murderers who would dare claim they commit these acts in the name of the Lord. We must condemn the white church with their white Jesus, where in New Orleans they cordoned off a part of the back of the Catholic Church with a sign that read Negroes must sit here. That is their religion, that is their God who is not our God.

As Smitherman listened, he was more certain now than before that this was the man they needed in a national leadership position representing the Negro. Bringing him to Tulsa had been a good decision no matter what the outcome.

He smiled as Du Bois continued. "There is a new day dawning for the Negro in this country, and just a little bit earlier this evening we witnessed the mighty power and strength of the new Negro. White folks have to know that we own guns too, and we know how to use them." Du Bois again paused and took another sip of water. "I would like to conclude my talk with you very fine people by quoting from an editorial I wrote back in 1919 after the East St. Louis riot. I quote from it because it is still applicable today here in Greenwood and all over this country where our people are living under some unbearable conditions. It reads as follows, 'For three centuries we have suffered or cowered. But we have cast off on the voyage that will lead to freedom or death. For no race ever gave passive submission to evil a longer, more piteous trial. But today and everyday from this day forward, we raise the terrible weapon off self-defense. When the murderer comes he shall no

195

longer strike us in the back. When the armed lynchers gather, we too must gather armed. When the mob moves we propose to meet it with sticks, clubs and guns.'"

Du Bois finished and walked briskly back to his seat. The entire audience sprang to their feet and clapped. The great scholar and leader sat down, and the audience continued to applaud.

Smitherman sat there mesmerized by the speaker and his words. Du Bois was a man who had no problem talking to his people. The men and women in the audience really admired and appreciated what he had said and would be willing to do battle with any group that violated their humanity. Dr. Du Bois would be leaving in the morning, but he would leave a part of him right in Greenwood. And the part staying behind would be the fire in their bones to stand up and fight back.

TWENTY•TWO

"Them niggers pulled guns on white folks," Cal screamed at Jones in his office at the *Tribune*. "What the hell kind of city you all got here in Tulsa where niggers can pull guns on good white citizens," he continued as he turned and stared at Deputy Cleaver who had been instructed to attend this meeting by Sheriff McCullough. Hiram Rheingold from Mayor Thaddeus Evan's office was also sitting next to Cleaver.

Jones, who had been reclining back in his chair leaned forward and stretched his arms across the top of his desk. His face turned beet red. "You telling us, Cal, that niggers actually had their guns out in front of white folks," he asked then looked over at Rheingold.

"You damn right they did. And it was that big red nigger riding on top of a white horse told us to get out from on that side of town. Said they don't come on our side and we can't come on their side."

"That's pretty much been the arrangement around these parts for a very long time," Cleaver said.

"What the hell, you all got arrangements with niggers," Cal scowled. "The Klan always considered Tulsa ripe for growing the organization here in the southwest. But if you're telling me you all got arrangements with darkies, then I don't know if this is a place where we should be."

"Now don't get carried away," Jones said. "We have no arrangement with no got damn darkies. Why didn't you boys just open up and start firing at them?"

"We was definitely outnumbered. Must have been over a hundred of them. They just seem to come crawling out the gutter and everywhere else."

"So, they scared you?" Cleaver asked with a smirk on his face.

"They ain't scared nobody, boy, and you'd better take that damn smirk off your black face or I'll do it for you," Cal shot back.

Cleaver instantly put his hand on top of his holstered revolver. "I think you'd better watch who you're talking to," he said in a stern tone. "I ain't one of them you can push around. I'm a deputy sheriff, and you got to respect that position."

"All right, knock it off," Jones shouted. "Cleaver's on our side so lay off him. Take your aggressions out on those other bad niggers. He's a good one."

"If he's one of us, what's he gonna do about that nigger on that white horse?"

"Wait a minute," Cleaver's voice rose. "I'm not one of you all. In fact, I'm not one of this group or any other group. I am the law. You gentlemen should not misunderstand my position in what seems to be a growing and dangerous divide between Tulsa and Greenwood. Our job is to make damn sure all this don't explode into some kind of uncontrollable confrontation like what happened in Houston and East St. Louis."

"The mayor feels the same way," Rheingold spoke up. "He thinks that we need cooler heads on both sides of the tracks."

Cal jumped out of his chair, and ignoring Rheingold, pointed his finger at Cleaver shaking it in an almost uncontrollable motion. "That's the problem out here," he shouted. "You and that damn sheriff and even the mayor want to pacify them niggers who done forgot their place in this town."

198

'You better watch your language," Cleaver said as he remained seated.

"All right, Cal, that's enough," Jones said also in a calm voice. He didn't want to lose Cleaver, his only link to Greenwood and information about what was happening over there. "No need to be insulting to our deputy sheriff," he continued. "We appreciate what you're doing and agree that no one wants violence. But I got to side with Cal when it comes to them bringing that radical to town and then pulling guns on white men in order to protect him."

"This man has to understand," Cal scowled, "that decent white people, law abiding citizens will not sit patiently by while niggers pull guns on them."

"Come on Cal, you know they were just bluffing," Rheingold interjected. "They wouldn't have shot white folks."

"You better believe they would," Cleaver said. "Those men have been trained to kill, thanks to the United States Army." He pointed at Cal. "If this man here had aimed his weapon at those men, he wouldn't be standing here talking to us today."

"And all of them coons would be dead or locked up waiting a hanging," Cal's voice shrieked. "You hear me nigger? All them coons would be dead."

Cleaver sprang to his feet and moved in the direction of Cal. "You'd better watch your mouth," he shouted.

"It's time we ended this meeting before the two of you end up killing each other." Jones came around his desk and planted his body between the two men. "Deputy, Mr. Rheingold, thanks for coming by, and we'll continue working with the mayor and sheriff to keep peace in our city." He placed his arm around Cleaver's shoulder and moved him toward the door with Rheingold next to them. Cal remained standing and made no effort to leave.

They reached the door, and Jones swung it open. "But you all got to know we can't have them chocolate colored coons pulling guns on white people, not in this town or nowhere else in this county in 1921."

"I believe the mayor will support that position, and as the elected representative of the people of Tulsa he would be expressing their opinion also." Rheingold walked out in front of Cleaver.

199

Cleaver started out the door, but then stopped and turned back around. "You go across those railroad tracks and tell that to men like O. B. Mann and John Stradford," he said.

"That's your job, not mine," Jones rejoined. "Tell McCullough we're watching him, and I'll be writing about niggers carrying guns and threatening white folks and we'll see where it goes from there. Good day deputy." Jones finished, closed the door and hurried back behind his desk. He stood there staring off into space. He finally broke the silence. "Can you reach Elton Walker in Oklahoma City?"

A smile spread across Cal's face. "You bet I can," he said.

"Good, set up a meeting for me with him either up there or here. It's time we brought heavy hitters into Tulsa."

"Just what we been waiting to hear."

"And Cal, don't ever let a nigger know that he made you mad or got the best of you," Jones said.

Cal gave Jones a perplexed look. "Niggers always make us mad; that's why we kill 'em."

"I know but just kill 'em and don't let 'em go to their grave thinking they got the best of you."

"Yeah, you're right. A nigger should never be able to think he bested a white man."

"Now you're getting the picture."

Again Cal smiled. "You're a real wise man, Mr. Jones."

"I know, now go make that contact for us."

"You got it, Mr. Jones."

Jones watched as Cal backed up and disappeared out the door, closing it behind him. Things were moving along nicely and getting close to the breaking point when white folks would finally silence that arrogant group of uppity niggers across the tracks.

200

***

Dr. Jackson stood over the young boy and smiled. His recovery was complete. The fever had broken and disappeared, as had the rash. Color had returned to his face, and he was no longer an ashy white.

"How you feel, young fellow?" he asked.

"Okay," the young boy replied.

"Then give me a smile."

The boy managed a slight smile, then closed his eyes and turned on his side.

Standing back at the entrance to the room, Luther asked, "Is he all right now Doctor? Is my boy gonna live?"

"God willing, for a very long time," Dr. Jackson said. "The rash and fever are both gone, and he's just a fine, healthy young boy once again."

Luther walked into the room and stood on the other side of the bed from Dr. Jackson. His wife stayed back at the entrance to the bedroom. "Dr. Jackson, we'll never be able to repay you for what you done," Luther said with tears. "We just knew we was going to lose our son and we couldn't get any of them other doctors to come down here in this part of town and help us. But you did."

"I did it for two very good reasons," Dr. Jackson said looking up from the boy and over at Luther. "First reason is there was a young boy who needed medical attention, and any doctor who takes his commitment seriously could not and should not ever overlook his responsibility to aid and treat a sick person, regardless of their race or status in life, and the second reason is that you knew you were violating a taboo, almost a law against racial mixing, but that didn't matter to you. All that mattered was getting medical help for your son. No way I could turn my back on a father pleading for his son's life."

"You sure are different from all the other nig…Negro people in Tulsa," Luther said.

Dr. Jackson knew what word Luther meant to use and also knew what he was insinuating with his comment. He could ignore it or use it as an opportunity to try to change this poor man's wrong perception of the Black race in Tulsa.

201

"Exactly what are the Negro people like in Tulsa that makes them so much different than me?" He decided to pursue it.

"You know, Doctor, they're really not good people, especially them that hang out at the joints all up and down First Street and some on Archer, just up the road from here."

"You think that's how all Negroes are in Tulsa when you already know I'm different?"

"It just seems that they always want to fight and steal. I guess it ain't all of them, but sometimes it sure seems that way."

It was obvious that Luther felt nervous and uncomfortable answering these questions, which was a good thing. He'd shot off at the mouth about the Negro race. Dr. Jackson felt no need to continue the discussion and most importantly no need to come back. The boy was well, and that was all that counted. But he had to get one more dig in. He'd earned that right.

"You're wrong. Most Negroes living in Tulsa are just like me." He exaggerated, but in this case, that was all right. "They have good jobs, beautiful homes and fine automobiles. So this man who just saved your son's life is no different than the rest of his race."

"Sorry, Dr. Jackson," Luther said almost in a whisper.

Dr. Jackson also knew why Luther whispered his apology. He didn't want his son to hear him apologizing to a Black man. No doubt, it was time to go. "I think I'm finished here and your son is going to be just fine," he said as he closed his medical bag and started for the door. "Even though the dangerous time is over, I'd still keep him inside for a few more days."

"Yes, Dr. Jackson," Luther's wife spoke up. "And we'll always let him know who saved his life, and hopefully, some day he'll be able to thank you himself."

"That's fine," Dr. Jackson said as he walked to the door, opened it and stopped right in his tracks. He counted ten men surrounding his car, and when they saw him standing in the doorway, they started toward the house.

202

"Nigger, why you always up here at Luther's house lately?" A short stocky man took the lead.

Dr. Jackson struggled with the right words to say to these men. He didn't have to think about it too long as Luther shot right past him and out into the street.

"Jenks, this ain't none of your business why this man been at my house," he shouted at the leader.

"It's our business when a nigger spends as much time as this one does in our neighborhood and in your house."

"This man ain't no nigger." Luther kept shouting, as he got right in Jenk's face. "He's a doctor and he healed my boy from the fever."

"You got a nigger doctor treating a white boy?"

"I done tole you, he ain't no nigger so stop calling him one."

"He is to us, 'cause he ain't done nothing for our kids."

"Your kids ain't sick Jenks. What the hell's the matter with you?"

"Don't like seeing his kind up around our neighborhood."

"I was just about to leave and I will not be back." Dr. Jackson started walking toward his car, but the men blocked his pathway.

"We don't like your kind around here driving your big old fancy cars and acting all important," Jenks said, ignoring Luther. "We ought to put a good whipping on you for trying to show off in front of your betters."

"Come on now Jenks," Luther stepped between Dr. Jackson and Jenks. "You boys just turn around and go about your business."

"Luther done become a nigger lover," another one of the men shouted.

"Ain't nobody no nigger lover," Luther countered. "But you men gonna back up and let this man leave peacefully."

The other men moved in closer to Luther and Dr. Jackson. "You can't whip us all, Luther," another man shouted.

Dr. Jackson began to feel tense and nervous until he heard 203 the cracking sound of a shotgun right behind him. He turned and looked at Helen pointing the shotgun in the air after having fired it, and he looked back at Luther who also had a stunned expression all over his face.

"You men got this all wrong," Helen said in a calm tone. "This man saved my baby from certain death, and the first one who tries to harm him going to find himself full of buckshot. Now clear a path and let the doctor get to his car."

Dr. Jackson watched as the men blocking his way stood to the side providing him with a clear path to his car. He nodded his head to Helen, smiled at Luther and hastily made his way to his car. Luther followed close behind and cranked the car to get it started. He then moved away, and Dr. Jackson drove straight out to Archer, made a left and headed toward Greenwood.

TWENTY·THREE

May 1921

———————

Twenty-five men sat in chairs lined up in rows of two facing the podium placed in front of them in the back room of Mann Brothers Grocery Store. O. B. standing poised at the podium noticed a new face sitting in the back. He was a skinny frail looking man who carried the expression of someone that had lost all faith in himself. Mann knew the soldier but couldn't figure from where. As Chair of the Black Veterans of World War I, he usually held the meetings at his place of business. All the men, with the exception of the new person were armed with either a rifle or pistol. They had their "take care of business" faces on as Mann struck the gavel down hard on the podium.

"With your permission, men of the 92nd Fighting Division, the monthly meeting of Veterans of World War I will now come to order. Let's stand and pledge our allegiance to our country."

The men, with the exception of five in the back of the room, stood. O. B went through the same exercise every month with the same five men sitting together in the back.

"Claude, you men ought to stand to honor our country while we say the pledge," O. B. said.

Claude Washington stood up when his name was called. He was a short stocky man, who had one sleeve loosely hanging on the right side of his body, evidence that he had lost an arm. "We ain't standing up to honor no got damn country that don't honor us for our service," he said.

"Ain't the country you ought to be angry with, but the men who make the country look bad," O.B. shot back at him.

"But they always claim this country for their own, just like we don't belong here, till its time to go fight and die," Claude replied.

"Come on, O. B., You know they got no problem with us spilling our blood. Claude lost his arm fighting for this country, and they stole his land over at Glenpool when they found oil on it," a light skinned, heavy-set man sitting next to Claude spoke up. "Why should he want to stand up and salute these bastards?"

"Don't you know we all recognize the white man is the evil force that poisons the country with all his rotten prejudices," Peg Leg Taylor exclaimed. "We all done paid our dues one way or another, but that ain't no reason to give up on a country that's been our home all our life."

"Peg Leg's right," a heavy-set veteran spoke out. "Why we going to give up on staking a claim. I don't give a damn what no redneck peckerwood thinks. I'm gonna stand and pledge my loyalty and allegiance just like I kneeled, took aim, and blew them Germans away."

"Look at it this way," O.B. said. "We are pledging to our people and to our community right here in Greenwood and to nothing else, just like them bastards stand and pledge to their community and could care less about Greenwood."

"That's right, we can act like it's two different countries," Peg Leg Taylor said. "And just like we ran those peckerwoods out last week, we can do it again if they try coming over here."

"If you all feel that way, why are we trying to march in their Memorial Day parade in a couple weeks?" Claude asked.

"Because Memorial Day belongs to every soldier that died for the cause," O.B. answered. "I'm damn sure gonna honor the five boys from our community that we lost in the war. Memorial Day doesn't belong to the whites just like the pledge of allegiance don't belong to them, either."

206

"Come on, boys, show some unity," a much older man spoke up. "Hell, I fought at San Juan Hill, and President Roosevelt refused to give us any credit for winning that battle in Cuba, but it was the Buffalo Soldiers that kicked ass. But I don't care about what Roosevelt didn't do. I stand because this is the country I fought for, and I'm gonna march in two weeks right down Main out of respect for the boys we lost in the war."

"I'm waiting, boys," O. B. continued. "Listen to Mr. Howard.

He's one of our seniors and do it for him."

O.B's appeal worked, and the other five men reluctantly stood up. They refused to place their hands over their heart, but O. B. wasn't going to push his luck. The men recited the pledge of allegiance, sat back down and O. B turned his attention to the new member sitting in the back.

"I want to welcome a new member to our group," O. B. said, pointing to the back of the room. The other men turned around and looked. "What's your name friend, and where did you serve?"

"Name's Otis, Otis Martin, and I served with the 369th Infantry Regiment of the New York National Guard. Saw plenty of action in France and participated in the march down Fifth Avenue in 1919 when we got back from France."

"You served with Colonel William Hayward?" One of the other men sitting two rows back shouted.

"Sure did." Otis smiled. "Fought at Belean Wood."

"Welcome," O. B. said. "Where you been all this time and how long you been in Tulsa?"

"Come here from New York, looking for a better opportunity to feed my family. Harlem done got overcrowded with people coming there from the South, and there just ain't no jobs. The word back there is that this is the best spot in the country for a Negro to get ahead."

"Did you find work?" O. B. asked

"Not right away. It took me about a month, and I'd about used up all my savings when I finally got hired as a waiter over at the Hotel Tulsa."

207

"Hell, man, you over there dealing with the oil men. You got to be making good money in tips," one of the men in the back said.

"You make good money, but you pay a price for it," Otis said.

"What you mean?" The same man asked.

"Abuse," Otis answered with no hesitation but did not elaborate.

O. B. instinctively knew the reason for Otis's reticence. He came to his rescue. "It's hard to tolerate for any of us. Don't matter what you do or where you live, at some point you got to deal with their abuse. But here with us, you can drop the veil and just be yourself."

"I appreciate that," Otis said.

"All right, men,, it looks like we're getting the support from the *Tulsa Star*," O. B. said as he changed the subject and got down to the reason they were all there. "Mr. Smitherman has already run a story about us. And I heard its been picked up by the *Chicago Defender* and the *Pittsburgh Courier*."

"But will it make any difference in us marching in the Memorial Day Parade?" Claude asked.

"Don't know right now, but at least we know other parts of the country are learning about what these crazy white folks are doing down here," O. B. said.

"Hell, O. B., that don't matter," Peg Leg Taylor said. "These peckerwoods don't care so I say let's just have our own parade in Greenwood."

"That's a damn good idea," another veteran who hadn't spoken said. "We can start right on Greenwood, march down Archer and then at Main, cross the railroad tracks and march down to Third Street. What you think, O. B., that something we can do?"

"I like it," O. B. agreed. "We'll cover both sides of the tracks with our march, much better than what they plan to do."

"It's going to make a lot of them real angry," Otis joined in.

208

"Don't matter, they going to be angry no matter what we do," Claude said.

"Give me a show of hands if you favor that approach," O. B. instructed.

Every hand shot straight up in the air.

"Looks like it's settled. Question is do you all plan to participate?" O. B. asked.

Again, every hand shot up in the air, including that of Otis.

"If it means losing your job?" O. B. smiled as every hand still remained up.

"Good then we'll meet next Monday to decide the time we want to start." O. B. paused while the men rose to their feet. "Until next meeting let us repeat the adopted motto for all the Negro veterans across the is nation.

Together, the men shouted.

"We return

We return from fighting

We return fighting

Make way for democracy. We saved it in France and by the Great Jehovah, we will save it in the United States of America or know the reason why."

***

A blindfolded Jones sat in the backseat of a green Norwalk driven by Cal with another very large man sitting in the passenger seat. They had picked him up in front of his office building at a little after nine at night and were taking him to meet with Wash Hudson, a prominent Tulsa lawyer and one of the new leaders of the growing local branch of the Ku Klux Klan. Cal had set up the meeting on the instructions of Walker out of Oklahoma headquarters in Oklahoma City.

Klan leaders were cautious when inviting newcomers to meet with them for the first time, and Jones understood their apprehension because he was a newspaperman. But Cal told him 209 the Klan leaders did trust him somewhat because of the editorials he wrote attacking the crime, the sinful behavior and decadence of the Negroes, and acknowledging the need to eliminate them from North Tulsa. Even though Jones resented the blindfold, he was willing to accept it as a way to meet with these men he felt he needed at that time.

After a brief ride, the car came to a stop, the large man removed Jones' blindfold and Cal led him into a house in an area of the city he did not recognize.

"Where are we?" Jones asked.

"We're right outside the city," Cal said. "Don't worry, you're with friends." The three men walked to the back of the house, and Cal rapped on the door to another room.

"Yeah," a deep voice from inside shouted.

"It's Cal, with the guest."

The door swung open, and the three men walked inside a large room with a conference table positioned in the center. Four men looked up at Jones. The man at the head of the table smiled and said, "Come on in, Mr. Jones, take a seat at the table."

"Thank you," Jones replied and sat down near Wash Hudson. "How you doing, my good friend."

"Doing fine, but got some serious concerns about what's happening in North Tulsa," Wash replied.

"I share your concerns, and that's exactly why I'm here."

"What are we going to do with those coons?" Wash asked getting right to the point.

"I'd say tar and feather all of them, but that's too drastic for some of our soft hearted friends up North. It we tried doing that, we'd probably find ourselves in another civil war."

"But them people ain't nothing but a bunch of hypocrites. They don't like the darkies no more than we do."

"I'm sure they would love for us to do their dirty work for them if they didn't have to know what was going on. Just wake up one day and all the niggers be gone, compliments of the Klan."

Wash reared back in his chair and locked his hands behind his head. "What you got in mind?" he asked. "And can the Klan help you?"

Jones leaned forward and clasped his hands on the conference table. "I believe Tulsa is about at the breaking point. The niggers are getting bold in their confrontation with white men. I'm sure you heard about the way some of them attacked our men who were trying to stop that damn nigger communist from coming in there and poisoning our good niggers with all that talk of equality."

"Can you imagine that," Wash interjected. "A nigger thinking he can be equal to a white man?"

"We got to put a stop to all this nonsense," Jones scowled. "I'm damn sick and tired of it, and its got to stop."

"Just tell us how we can help."

"Don't quite know yet, but I believe those fools are going to give me the right ammunition to fire the gun that'll wipe them all out. They'll do something I can write about to incite our boys to action."

"What you got in mind?"

"Their leaders made it known they aren't going to stand for no lynching in their city. Can you just imagine what'll happen if those coons try to stop some of our boys from lynching a nigger if they figured he had it coming," Jones said and smiled.

"It'd be worse than Atlanta back in '06 or East St. Louis a few years ago."

"They'd be no match for our boys." Jones balled his fist and held it up for emphasis.

"It'd be just like a lynching holiday, and our boys would be right there with the rope," Wash concurred.

"Yeah, your boys did a good job on Roy Belton last year, and he was white."

"We did, but in a way that wasn't good."

"Why is that?"

"Because the last person to be lynched in Tulsa was a white boy. That's a fact that should be reserved for someone Black." Wash placed both hands on the conference table. "But I believe we got plenty of prospects for that honor all up and down First Street and over on Archer."

"Especially since there's a lot of interracial mingling in those clubs." Jones leaned closer to Wash. "If the opportunity comes will your boys be ready?"

"Absolutely ready," Wash answered with no hesitation.

"Now you and your boys got to understand taking on Greenwood isn't going to be like other cities. Most places you can lynch a nigger with no resistance. This time will be different. These boys will fight back."

"I haven't ever seen a nigger that can whip a white man at anything, especially fighting." Wash hesitated, obviously to let his words sink in with Jones. "We'll wipe them niggers out in less than an hour if they dare try to fight us."

"So all we need is the right incident to make this happen." Jones relaxed back in his chair, confident that all he had been working toward for the past two years would soon come to fruition.

"That's all we need 'cause white people all over this country are having to put them people back in their place. Since the war, they done come back here all cocky. Even had the nerve to march in New York like they're the reason we won that war."

"I guess you haven't been reading that nigger newspaper lately?" Jones remarked.

"I never read a nigger newspaper. Far as I'm concerned they shouldn't be allowed to publish no newspaper."

"The editor over there has written a couple editorials urging the city to let the Negro veterans march with the white ones on Memorial Day."

"That'll never happen," Wash bellowed and pounded his fist on the table. "That's exactly what I'm talking about. Since them boys came back they've been acting like they're equal to us. We have to put an end to that nonsense, and we got to do it real soon, right in Tulsa."

212

Jones slid his chair back and got up. Cal and the other man followed his lead.

"I believe we both feel the same way," Jones said as Wash also stood up. "Even if white men have to die, we got to put an end to this."

"You can count on us," Wash said. "Let's get it on and get it over."

"Won't be long now." Jones reached out and shook Wash's hand. He then started for the door and out of the house, followed closely by the other two men.

TWENTY•FOUR

"Girl, can you believe Jake had that old prostitute in my house, and Dick had that white girl there while I was in Vinita," Damie complained to Mabel while sitting in her chair in the beauty parlor. Mabel had just started to straighten Damie's hair when she opened up. "You know Henry Pack showed up at my house that night with another white police officer. They didn't arrest nobody 'cause old Georgia, you know her. I think one of your girls does her hair, told the policemen the hollering somebody thought was her getting beat was really screams of pleasure."

"What? You mean Officer Pack actually told you that?" Mabel stopped what she was doing and stared at Damie.

"Sure did, and was I ever embarrassed?"

"My Lord in Heaven, Damie, they going to think you running a house of prostitution instead of a legitimate boarding house," Mabel said as she put the hot comb into a portion of Damie's hair.

"I know, so I don't really know what to do. Jake knew my rules about carrying on like that. When I asked him about it, he was all apologetic. Explained by bringing her around when I was gone, showed the kind of respect he had for me. Said least he didn't bring her around when I was there and that he was a man who still had needs."

"But why he got to go get a prostitute and an old one like Georgia?" Mabel asked and again applied the hot comb to a portion of Damie's hair.

It got worse with Dick and that white girl," Damie continued. "Pack told me that the white policeman got all upset seeing that white girl with Dick. Said he was gonna tell her boss over at the

Drexel that she sleeping with a Negro boy, and that sure gonna get her fired."

"Who cares what happens to her?" Mabel snapped. "She over here getting that Black boy in trouble and possibly lynched if some hot head roughneck racist find out about them. First thing she going to holler is rape and they'll believe it 'cause they can't stand the thought that one of their girls would voluntarily have sex with a Negro."

"I got to tell you, it scared me half to death hearing about that. All I need is for some of them white folks to come over here and burn down my house. I just don't know what I'd do if that happened."

"I know you got on that boy real good."

"No, I ain't talked to him yet," Damie said. "I kinda feel bad trying to tell him who he can and can't see."

"I know, but it's for his own good." Mabel put the hot comb down, slid her fingers into a container of hairdressing, rubbed it into the palm of her hands and stroked it into Damie's hair. "I'm going to let that settle for a couple minutes," she said and then placed her hands on her hips. "You got to tell him for his own good. These white folks just like wild dogs. They run in packs, and a pack of them liable to surprise him one night. That'll be the end of him."

"That boy knows the danger of messing with one of them girls," Damie said. "I've told him over and over can't nothing good come out of that relationship. Only thing gonna happen is that them white folks gonna bring real trouble across those tracks."

214

"What you going to do with Jake?" Mabel chose to change the subject. She'd get nowhere trying to advise Damie of the dangers with her boy messing with that white girl. "You going to put him out?"

"I gave him a warning that if it happens again he's got to go."

"So you didn't put him out?"

"I just couldn't put him out on the street, Mabel," Damie said.

"So nobody got in trouble for abusing your home?" Mabel asked.

"I gave them a good fussing at," Damie rejoined.

"A good fussing at when Jake brought that prostitute into your home," Mabel said adamantly.

"She comes in here to get her hair done; what's the difference?"

"The difference is that she doesn't apply her services for money when she's in here," Mabel answered.

"But you make her all pretty so that she can go out and get money for applying her service. You make it possible for her to do what she does."

Damie's words hit Mabel like a sledgehammer. "I never thought of it quite that way," she said and again ran the hot comb through strands of Damie's hair. She decided to change the subject. "I didn't see you at the Dr. Du Bois lecture last month."

"No, girl, I ain't about all that politics stuff," Damie said.

"You got to be concerned about politics. What them white folks do affects our lives over here."

"I know, but it don't matter. They gonna do whatever they want to anyway."

"Well, I think something bad going to happen here in Tulsa. I've been reading all them articles by Smitherman in the *Tulsa Star* and them in the *Tribune* and they both sound like they about ready to start fighting." Mabel finished with Damie and removed the full-length apron. She reached back, picked up a small round mirror and handed it to her. "I done made you look awfully pretty," she said smiling.

"I'm ushering at church on Sunday, so I need to look my very best when I'm doing the work of the Lord." Damie handed the mirror back to Mabel.

"Ain't that the truth," Mabel said as she placed the mirror back on the counter.

Damie took both hands and patted her hair. "Can I pay you later today when Dick gets home?" She asked. "He told me he'd treat me because he's trying to make up."

215

"You know you can," Mabel said.

"Can you mark it down in your book?"

"I don't need to mark it down in no book. I know everybody that owes me. I may not be the smartest woman in town, but I sure can remember when it comes to money." Mabel took a small swish broom and ran it across Damie's shoulders.

Damie started for the door. "You got any plans for Memorial Day?" she asked.

"We're going to have a special service at the church. If you're not doing anything come on by." Mabel followed Damie to the front door.

"I just might do that," Damie said. "I been meaning to get by and attend service in that new church you all got over there. It sure is beautiful."

"Come on by and pray with us." Mabel swung the door open, and Damie walked out into the warm rays of sunshine beating down on Greenwood. "What a blessed day," she said as she stood to the side while two young girls loosely dressed like women of the night strolled into the parlor.

Damie smiled. "Remember our earlier conversation," she said, then turned and walked up Greenwood toward Archer.

***

Cleaver stared across the counter at O.B. right inside the front entrance of the Mann Brothers Grocery Store. The inside was packed with veterans standing in the aisles and surrounding the deputy. Cleaver had unexpectedly showed up at the final meeting before the march on Memorial Day. Peg Leg Taylor stood behind the counter with O. B. as did McKinley.

216

"You boys just can't do what you're planning for Memorial Day," Cleaver said. "If you cross that boundary line at the Frisco Tracks into South Tulsa, I guarantee you, there'll be trouble."

"Why you always doing the white man's dirty work for him?" O. B. asked.

"Whether or not I'm doing the dirty work for anyone at all is not the issue," Cleaver rejoined. "The issue is that you all are about to cause a great deal of turmoil in this town, and I'll be caught in the middle because I'm obligated to uphold the law."

"Even if those laws are harmful to your people?" Peg Leg Taylor asked.

"The law is the law," Cleaver exclaimed.

"Ain't no law that says we can't march downtown," O. B. countered.

"You need a permit to march in that part of town," Cleaver snapped back. "Them's the rules, boys," Cleaver said in a much calmer voice. "I don't make 'em, I just enforce 'em."

"And what' going to happen if all these veterans of the war decide not to obey that law and still march across that railroad track?" McKinley jumped into the fray.

"There'll be a whole lot of veterans in jail," Cleaver answered.

"And if we resist arrest?" O. B. scowled. "If we come over those tracks with bullets in our rifles, what are you going to do? You gonna shoot your own for breaking a white man's law who is not one of your own?"

"I will if I have to." Cleaver paused and looked around the room. "Come on, boys, we been knowing each other for a long time. Some of us went to school together." He looked over at one of the men standing in the aisle. "Bobby, we played baseball together, man," he said. "How's it gonna look us fighting each other?"

"You done gone to the other side, Barney. You done become one of them. You ain't with us no more." Bobby said. "When you can stand there and tell us you'd be willing to shoot and kill one of your own, you done left us. You ain't the same person I grew up with." Bobby finished and looked away.

"There you have it," O. B. said. "Looks like these boys ain't about to change their minds."

Cleaver again gazed at all the men standing in the aisle of the store. He then looked back at O. B. "You boys be careful out there." He finished and hurried out of the store.

217

TWENTY•FIVE

The morning of Memorial Day, Veneice could hardly contain her excitement as the prom committee, along with Mrs. Jackson, strolled into the ballroom at the Stradford Hotel with boxes of decorations. Besides Billy and Harold, Esther, Ruth and Verby had volunteered to help decorate. Actually, Veneice, who insisted that her boyfriend should be willing to help with the decorations, drafted Verby into service.

Once inside the ballroom, Veneice ran down to the far end and hollered back to the others. "I'll start down at this end hanging streamers."

"Get back down here, girl," Julia said smiling. "We're going to be much more organized as to how we go about doing this."

"Yeah, get back down here," Billy said. He and the others broke out laughing

"You all don't laugh at her," Julia scolded. "At least she's showing some enthusiasm."

"We're enthused, Mrs. Jackson," Harold declared.

"Good, because you all represent both classes that will be here for the prom, and if you all show a lot of enthusiasm, the rest of them will do the same," Julia advised.

"We got to get this place so pretty," Veneice said as she trotted back to the front. "I can just see it now. The music playing and the dance floor filled with us all dancing away." She began to dance with herself, moving to the left, then the right, and spinning around.

"You don't even have no music," Ruth said.

"Watch your double negatives," Julia admonished.

"You don't even have any music," Ruth corrected herself. "Is that better, Mrs. Jackson?"

"Remember back when we were discussing *Uncle Tom's Cabin*?" Julia asked. "You told the class the reason you didn't like Topsy was because she was an embarrassment to the Negro race."

"Yes ma'am," Ruth answered.

"You're doing the same thing as Topsy when you use improper English."

"Where you want us to start?" Billy asked while still watching Veneice dance solo.

Julia handed him an orange colored banner that read in big black letters. "CONGRATULATIONS CLASS OF 1921."

"Find a good place to hang this banner," Julia said.

Billy read it, and a frown surfaced on his face. "Mrs. Jackson, I don't know where to hang it."

"I'll help you find a place," Esther said.

"And I will too," Ruth joined in.

"I have an idea," Julia said. "The three of you go back to the entrance and when you first walk through the door, imagine you're looking at the banner and where you would be looking. Now go back there and let your imaginations do the rest."

Billy, Esther and Ruth walked back to the entrance, turned and stood like they had just walked in.

"I picture it all the way at the other end of the room," Billy suggested.

220   "No, that's too far away." Esther disagreed.

"Okay, then where do you picture it hanging?" Julia looked directly at Esther.

Veneice had ended her solo dance and stood next to Verby. They both were looking around the ballroom. She was imagining where she would hang it.

"I got it," Ruth blurted out before Veneice could make her suggestion. She pointed toward the middle of the room where the Booker T. Washington High School band would play. "Right above the bandstand," she said. "Everybody going to be facing the band so that way it will always be in sight."

"Excellent idea," Julia said. "What do you all think?"

"That's perfect," Verby said.

"Okay," the others agreed.

"There you go, Billy," Julia said. "You got your spot so go to work."

"I'll help you," Harold offered.

"Me too," Verby joined in.

The three boys took off toward the spot they'd chosen to hang the banner.

"All right, young ladies," Julia turned to the girls. "Here are some streamers you can hang from the chandeliers." She handed four boxes of streamers to Veneice. "The custodian told me there is a ladder in the closet back there in the corner." She pointed to the far end of the ballroom. "Get the ladder out of the closet and you can take turns hanging the streamers from the chandeliers."

"Yes ma'am," Veneice said. "Come on, let's get to work." The three girls practically ran down to the closet to get the ladder and go to work.

***

Dick felt his nerves coming unglued as he sat high up in the shine chair and watched the crowd gather along the curb right outside the parlor on Main Street. The parade was set to begin at ten o'clock, and it was only nine. Mr. Simon had insisted that he and Robert show up on Memorial Day just in case there might be a flood of business after the parade ended. But it had rained earlier that morning, the clouds still lingered like it might rain again and chances were negligible that men would want shines that morning.

Lack of business, however, was not his biggest problem that morning. He hadn't seen or talked to Sarah since the incident at his house last month. For the past three Friday nights, usually their night together, she failed to show up at Pretty Belle's. He ended up spending this past Friday night with Ethel who teased him that the white girl had dumped him for one of the oil millionaires. Now on Monday morning he wondered if Ethel had been right. He needed to know exactly what was going through Sarah's mind. Was it the fact that he'd asked her to help him get the numbers business in the Drexel Building from Moses or was it because the white police officer confronted her that night at his home?

Dick glanced over at Robert whose head kept nodding He instantly looked out the window and spotted a girl running across the street toward the shine parlor and briefly thought it was Sarah, but no such luck. The girl reached his side of the street and took off running toward the tracks. He knew Sarah was at work because many of the businessmen with offices in the Drexel would probably use the elevator after the parade ended. He also knew that she wasn't really busy because of the parade. She was deliberately avoiding him, and he had to get to the reason why. As a rule, women didn't avoid Diamond Dick, but to the contrary, they usually flocked to him. What he did know for sure was that his relationship with Sarah seemed to be in jeopardy. He needed to squash any potential problems right away.

The best time to confront Sarah was early while things were still rather slow. Dick glanced up at the clock on the wall. A little after nine. He had close to an hour to get across the street and talk to her. Again, he looked at Robert whose head remained drooped forward.

Dick nudged Robert. "I got to take a leak," he said.

Robert jumped straight up. "What?"

222

" I got to take a leak," Dick repeated with more emphasis.

"Man, you going over there to mess with that white girl since she ain't been over here to see you," Robert said.

"No, I really do have to use the bathroom."

"You got to be careful today." Robert sat straight up in the chair and stared out the window. "Ain't gonna be your usual business people around here. It's gonna be a lot of those rednecks that work out at the wells. They see you talking to that white girl, ain't no telling what'll happen."

Dick jumped down from the shine chair and slid the door open. "Told you before, you worry too much," he said.

"And I told you before that you don't worry enough. Don't go over there and get us both killed," Robert rejoined.

"Relax, I'll be back in less than fifteen minutes." Dick finished, strolled out into the warm air and closed the door behind him.

Dick stepped off the curb, waited for a couple of cars to pass by and then ran across the street. On the other side, he had to step back off the sidewalk to make room for a man, his wife and three children. As they passed him, he looked down at the pavement. Every time he had to do that, he could feel a knot right in the pit of his stomach. The law that forced him to give up the entire sidewalk to white people was bad enough, but then having to look down at the ground for fear he could be accused of looking directly into the eyes of a white woman was aggravating. Once they past, he got back on the sidewalk, and trotted to the Drexel Building.

Dick entered the building and peered down at the far end. The elevator door was closed, which meant Sarah was either on the second or third floor. As he strolled down the long corridor, he glanced to his left. Renfeld's was open. Evidently the owner was not going to miss that holiday traffic. Posters advertising Memorial Day Specials hung throughout the store as did the sign that read, "WE SERVE WHITE CLIENTÈLE ONLY." He had stared at the sign so often it didn't bother him anymore. But having to get off the sidewalk and look down at the ground did, and that, he would never get used to doing.

The insult gave Dick even more reason he needed to see Sarah. She had to help him get Roscoe's business in the Drexel. 223 Working the numbers, he could save enough money to get the hell out of Tulsa, and go up north where he wouldn't have to put up with that kind of nonsense. He'd finally reached the back end of the building and stood right in front of the elevator. He waited a few minutes after ringing the buzzer, and it still didn't come. He decided to walk the two flights of stairs and check at each floor to see where Sarah was hiding.

Dick ran up the stairs to the second floor, swung open the

door leading into the hallway. The elevator was not there. Sarah had to be on the third floor. He shot up the stairs to the third floor and swung open the door. He glared down at Sarah sitting right outside the elevator reading a magazine. Dick closed the exit door and briskly walked toward the elevator.

Sarah looked up, jumped from the chair and into the elevator.

"Wait," Dick shouted. "What are you doing? Hold up." He ran down the hall and before Sarah could close the door, he squeezed inside.

"What's got into you?" he asked.

"Nothing, now get out of here."

"Why you acting like this all of a sudden?" His voice raised a couple decibels.

"I can't keep doing this with you, at least not here in Tulsa." Sarah's tone was shrill. "They almost fired me, Dick," she continued. "Officer Carmichael told my boss that I was at your house, and he threatened to fire me." Tears filled her eyes, and she struggled with her words. "Now you got to leave me alone." She turned the handle, and the elevator started its downward movement.

"But we can get away from here if you'll only help me work the numbers." Dick allowed a little pleading in his words. "I figured it out, in six months I can make enough money with Roscoe for us to get out of here."

"You make enough right now, but you too busy buying new clothes and diamond rings," Sarah exclaimed now with anger lacing her words. "And who is the woman named Ethel?"

224   A stunned expression appeared on Dick's flushed face, his brows furrowed. "How you know about her?"

"So it's true," Sarah countered as the elevator came to a stop on the first floor.

"How you know that?" Dick shouted as he moved in close to her.

"I know it 'cause I came by Pretty Belle's on Friday, and one of them nigger whores got a great deal of pleasure in telling me you already left with some woman named Ethel. So it was true."

"That ain't none of your damn business and don't you use that word around me," he scowled.

"Nigger, nigger, nigger," she shrieked as the elevator door swung open. "Now get off the elevator, boy."

Dick grabbed her by both arms, but she broke his grip and ran outside the elevator and down the hall. "Help me," she shouted. "Someone help me, please."

Suddenly a white man ran out of Renberg's Clothing Store and toward Sarah.

Dick was also running toward her from the elevator. He stopped and froze in place when he saw the man.

"What's wrong, ma'am?" the man asked.

"That boy down there grabbed me while just the two of us was in the elevator. I was able to break loose and run out after the door opened. Don't let him hurt me."

"You stay right here," the man said and ran toward Dick.

Just as the man reached out to grab him, Dick stepped to the side and got around him. He shot down the hall; pass Sarah and right out the door. He forced himself through the crowd lining up for the parade and headed toward the Frisco Railroad tracks, and into Greenwood where he figured he'd be safe, at least for a while.

TWENTY • SIX

A proud smile spread across O. B.'s face as he gazed at all fifty men in their military uniforms lined up right outside the grocery store. Some men wore the uniform of the Buffalo Soldiers, and all the others wore their World War I uniform with one exception. Eighty-five-year old Nate Hampton stood proudly right in front of all the men in his Union uniform from the Civil War. Nate had contacted O. B. a week ago and informed him that he planned to participate in the march. O. B. knew Nate's arthritic legs and weak heart would prevent this old warrior from completing the entire march, but it was symbolically important that he start it with them.

Nate had been a twenty-seven-year-old South Carolina slave when he crossed over to the Union Army in February 1863. The entire plantation of over three hundred slaves had been told of the Emancipation Proclamation, signed by President Abraham Lincoln, that freed them on January 1, 1863, and they all had decided to take their freedom by joining the Union Army. Now, fifty-eight years later, Nate told O. B. it was time to march for equality, just like he had fought for freedom in the past.

O.B. was pleased to see most of the men had brought their Winchester rifles and he was pretty sure they had the ammunition to go with them. No soldier carried an unloaded weapon into battle. And from what he could gather, these old soldiers were ready to do battle with their real enemies across the tracks. Hopefully, it wouldn't come to violence, but they wouldn't run from a fight. On many occasions, these men had expressed a feeling that they had been fighting the wrong enemy all along. Germans way across the ocean were never a threat to them,, white folks right across the tracks were. O. B. felt the same way and had no doubt he'd be right there on the front line when the gunfire broke out. Those were his thoughts as he saw Captain Townsend Jackson turn the corner onto Lansing and walk briskly toward them. It was unusual to see the old man on O. B.'s side of town. Had to be something important to bring him way over here.

The Captain strolled right up to the front of all the men who were still lining up in formation. He glared over at O. B. "I need to talk to your men about what you all are about to do," he said in a stern tone.

"Something wrong, Captain?" O. B. asked, still perplexed and not sure what this man, whom he respected, was doing here.

"Yes, there is," Captain said and pointed to O. B's rifle. "All these rifles and guns."

The men who had been chatting among themselves heard the Captain and stopped to listen. All eyes were riveted on the young warrior and the elder statesman who appeared to be on their way to a possible confrontation.

"Captain, these men feel it necessary to arm themselves because they are determined to march across the Frisco tracks and up Main Street, just as the white veterans do on every Memorial Day," O. B. said.

"My concern is not with the march, but with all these weapons. What you plan to do, shoot your way up Main Street if necessary?"

"Yes, if necessary," O. B. did not hesitate to answer.

"O. B., I've known you since you were a little boy running up and down these muddy roads over here on East Lansing. We all know you aren't afraid, and it was a magnificent stand you made when those Klan folks tried to stop Dr. Du Bois from speaking. That was a time to make a stand. This isn't." Captain paused to catch his breath. He then stared disapprovingly at all the men. "This just is not the cause to die for. Believe me when I tell you, if white people keep acting crazy, the time will come. But don't be no setting targets in the middle of Main Street. Pick your time to fight better than that."

"We're going to march, and we ain't going to be stopped," Peg Leg Taylor stepped forward and declared..

"I didn't say nothing about you not marching," Captain snapped back. "Hell, if my legs weren't so weak, I'd be marching

228

right along with you. But I'm saying don't die."

"Captain, you know damn well if we march across those tracks, them peckerwoods from the oil fields going to be armed and they liable to start shooting."

"They got guns, you got guns." Captain waved his arms around in the air for emphasis. "Everybody got guns, and everybody going to have a grand old time shooting each other."

"What would you have us do when we dealing with a race of people who don't like us and sure as hell don't respect us?"

"Just leave your guns here," Captain encouraged them. "March for the Greenwood community and the hell with them."

"You telling us to confront those peckerwoods without our guns," Peg Leg Taylor spoke up again. "You know what happened a few weeks ago when Dr. Du Bois was here."

"Lookit, men, I'm only trying to prevent a major catastrophe from happening," Captain said with some remorse, evidently resigning himself to the fact that he would not change their minds. "I give up." He turned and started to walk away.

"No, Captain Townsend's right," Nate said as he made his way to the front. "We can march, but without the weapons," the old man continued. "Now you got your two senior warriors, veterans of battles long before most of you were born, least you owe us is to listen to what we're telling you." He stood next to Captain Townsend, "I'm going to march with you, but without a man-made weapon. I got God as my weapon against evil."

Nate's comments made O. B. cringe. He knew from experience overseas that God probably wouldn't protect them. They had to protect themselves. But the old man was right. The younger men owed a certain amount of respect to their elders. With great reluctance, he said.

229

"All right, men, let's cache our weapons inside the store and this one time we'll make a concession." He paused and frowned at both Captain Townsend and Nate. "But please don't ask us to make this sacrifice in the future."

The men fell out of formation and took their weapons back inside the grocery store. Once the weapons were all inside,

McKinley locked the front door, and the men got back in formation.

"We still going to march across the tracks?" One of the men asked.

"You damn right were are," O. B. answered.

"What's going to happen if them peckerwoods start shooting?" Another man called out.

"Let's just pray that Nate is right and God will protect us," O.B. said.

The Captain stood there watching as the men began their march up Lansing to Archer. Now that he'd convinced the warriors to go toward a potential battle without their weapons he also would pray that Nate was right and God would protect them.

***

Dick startled Aunt Damie when he bolted through the front door, slammed and locked it closed, then ran into the kitchen. She'd just finished washing the dishes and planned to head out to Archer and Detroit to watch Greenwood's heroes march by. Most of Greenwood would line both sides of the street all up and down Archer, but no one would cross the tracks and stand along Main.

"Boy, what you doing home already?" she asked.

"I believe I got big problems," he exclaimed.

She knew it had to do with that white girl. She could tell by the expression all over his face. "They after you?"

230

"How'd you know?"

"'Cause everybody in Greenwood who know you messing with that girl figured someday this would eventually happen. How bad is it?"

"Could be pretty bad," Dick answered. "All according to what Sarah told that white man."

Aunt Damie's hand came up across her chest, she breathed deeply and fell back into a kitchen chair. "Dick, what did you do?"

She asked in a shrill voice.

"She ran out of the elevator hollering and acting like I attacked her," he said and also sat down in a chair across from Aunt Damie.

"Boy, you tell me the truth. Did you attack that white girl over on that side of town?"

"No, Aunt Damie I didn't attack her. I ain't crazy." He paused long enough to get up, walk over to the fountain, grab a glass and pour some water into it. He leaned against the counter and drank from the glass, then ambled back to the chair and sat down. An abundance of nervous energy was taking control of his equilibrium. "I grabbed her on the arms 'cause she all of a sudden started shouting nigger for no reason at all. And I almost lost it when she called me a boy."

Aunt Damie shook her head from side to side. "What is wrong with you Negro men you can't leave them white women alone? You know they ain't nothing but a whole lot of trouble, but you just won't leave 'em alone."

"Aunt Damie, I swear to God I ain't gonna let no white person call me out of my name. Sometimes them white men will call me boy when I'm shining their filthy shoes, but I got to take it or I won't have a job. I ain't gonna let no woman do it."

"What you gonna do now?"

"I don't know."

She got up, walked to the other side of the table and put her hands on Dick's shoulders. "Tulsa ain't gonna be safe for you if word gets around about what happened." She moved right in front of Dick and placed her hands on each side of his face just as she did in the past when he got in trouble. This time, however, it wasn't a child's mischievous behavior. Dick was a grown man, and there might not be an easy way out.

231

"You have to get out of Tulsa for a while. You might have to go up to Vinita."

"I don't want to go up there, Aunt Damie. And even if I do go, that's the one place they'll look, since they know that's where we came from."

"Then maybe you need to catch any train tonight no matter where it's going, and get out of here."

"I can't run." Dick lowered his head and covered his face with his hands.

"Why can't you run?"

He looked up at Aunt Damie. "Colored people been running from white folks for too long." He took another sip from his glass. "I should've stayed right there and fought that white man."

"And you'd be in jail right now and a lynch mob would be gathering right outside hollering for your hide."

Dick finished his glass of water and jumped to his feet. "Probably ain't nothing gonna happen. Sarah ain't gonna tell the police nothing, so they won't have no reason to bother me."

Aunt Damie looked up at her son. "I'm going to pray awfully long and awfully hard tonight that you're right."

Dick walked over to Aunt Damie, leaned down and kissed her on the forehead. "I'm going upstairs, close my shades and stay there till this whole thing blows over."

Aunt Damie got up from the chair. "If I hear any talk while I'm at the parade, I'll tell you when I get back."

The mother and son stood there and stared at each other, and Dick could feel the desperation between the two of them. Without saying another word, he turned, walked out of the room and up the stairs.

TWENTY•SEVEN

O. B. led his men west on Archer across Greenwood toward Main. As they marched in perfect cadence, a quartet consisting of a trumpet, drums, saxophone and clarinet added marching music for entertainment of the crowd. A young boy, no more than ten, carried the American flag. Greenwood residence lined both sides of Archer Street all the way up to Main.

Old Nate marched right next to O. B. His adrenaline was obviously pumping overtime, and he showed no signs of dropping out. After crossing over Detroit Avenue, O.B. began to get nervous. He had no idea what lay ahead as they got closer to Main. Hopefully, he hadn't made the wrong decision when he conceded and the men left their weapons behind. Without them, they'd be sitting targets for whatever might be waiting on the other side of the tracks.

"You are our heroes," a lady shouted from the crowd. "We love you men."

"God bless you all," still another lady called out.

O. B. looked over at the crowd and tipped his head in recognition of the women who'd called out to the marchers. It made him feel good to know that what they did during the war was much appreciated by his people on this side of the tracks. He realized their celebration couldn't compare to the great march back in 1919 when the Fifteenth Regiment of New York's National Guard proudly returned to Harlem, led into the Black metropolis to the music of Lieutenant James Reese Europe's famous band with Bill "Bo Jangles" Robinson as the regimental drum major. O. B. was very much aware that Greenwood was not Harlem nor was Tulsa New York City. But just as the fighting men of Harlem made sure they were honored for their valor, the men of Greenwood were doing the same.

O. B. stayed out in the lead as the men approached Main, went to the left and marched across the railroad tracks onto a deserted street. The crowd, there earlier for the white parade, was gone, and all that remained was a lot of debris. As the veterans marched parallel to the Drexel Building, more than a dozen white-robed men dashed into the street with weapons at the ready position and stood right in front of O. B. and the men.

"Niggers, turn around and go back to niggertown." Cal ripped his white mask off and hollered.

O. B.'s eyes shot daggers at Cal. Evidently Cal wanted the veterans to know who it was behind the mask. "No weapons," O. B. whispered to himself. "Why did I listen to Captain Townsend?"

"Now, we 'preciate what you niggers did during the war. But that is now over and things in this country is back to the way they always been. You stay on your side of town," Cal shouted.

Old Nate broke from the formation and limped out in front of O. B. "Just look at you pathetic men," he also shouted right in front of Cal.

Cal took the butt of his rifle and pounded it into the old man's stomach. Nate gasped and fell to the ground.

"You son of a bitch," O. B. shouted and lurched toward Cal. He pulled up when Cal thrust the barrel of his rifle into his stomach.

"Come on nigger, give me the pleasure," Cal blustered. "Please come on and give me the pleasure of blowing your guts open. I told you that one day we'd be back, and we'd have all the guns."

234

O. B. wanted to grab this little man and choke the racist life right out of him. Instead he backed up to where Nate still lay on the ground. He picked the old man up in his arms, turned and walked back toward the railroad tracks. The rest of the men also turned and headed back to Greenwood.

"That's right nigger, turn and run just like the coward you are," Cal shouted. "Now you know what it feels like to turn and run. Don't ever come on this side of the tracks again."

O. B. listened to Cal's words and his blood rushed to the top of his head in anger. He could literally tear that man apart with his bare hands. But this was not the time. He needed to get his men safely back on their side of the tracks. He knew, however, the opportunity to even the score would come and he would be ready.

***

Police Chief John Gustafson looked up from reading the morning edition of the *Tulsa World* when Klan leader Wash Hudson, along with Cal and Jones burst into his office unannounced.

"You got to arrest Dick Rowland," Jones exclaimed loudly as the men took seats around the Chief's desk.

"What are you talking about?" Gustafson folded up the paper and pushed it to the side. He knew exactly who Rowland was and what had happened earlier that morning in the Drexel Building. His two officers, Pack and Carmichael, had responded to the call from Renberg's reporting a possible assault by a Black man against a white woman. But he had no eyewitnesses and the girl refused to cooperate so there was no reason to arrest the boy. Now these men come busting into his office insisting they do just that.

"We're talking about attempted rape," Jones continued. "And it's your job to arrest this man and make him pay."

"I don't need no civilian telling me how to do my job," Gustafson scowled.

"All right, cool down, chief," Wash spoke up. "We're not trying to tell you how to do your job. It's just that we can't let no nigger get away with putting his foul hands on the purity of a white woman."

235

"My boys went down there after we got the call, but there were no witnesses, and the girl wouldn't say nothing," Gustafson said in a shrill voice.

"Didn't a white man come to her aid and didn't she tell him that the boy grabbed her?" Jones asked.

"Oh now you wanna play cop? You wanna do my job?"

"Not at all, chief," Jones said also in a calmer tone.

Satisfied that Jones had cooled down and backed off, Gustafson relaxed. "We got a much bigger problem with the girl and her story," he said.

"What's that?" Wash asked.

"Last month, Carmichael and Pack got a call about a disturbance at the boarding house where Rowland lives. Seems as though some whore was screaming, but when they got there, she told them it was a scream of pleasure and not distress. Well, they both knew better 'cause don't no damn whore get pleasure from having sex, but there wasn't anything they could do."

"What's that got to do with what happened in the Drexel Building this morning?" Jones asked, now sounding somewhat impatient.

"The girl was there with Dick Rowland, and it wasn't just a casual kind of visit. She would have spent the night if Officer Carmichael hadn't made her leave."

"You saying they're lovers?" Wash asked.

"They sure are unless he kidnapped her, and she didn't act like she was there against her will."

"That's what I'm talking about," Cal exploded. "We can't allow that kind of thing happening in Tulsa." He pounded his right fist in his left open palm. "That's why we got to get that nigger. We got to make an example of him, just like we got to do that with the big yellow nigger who tried to march downtown this morning."

"Calm down, Cal," Wash said. "We're going to get both of them. But the first one's going to be that coon who thinks he can sleep with white women." He momentarily paused and then looked over across at Gustafson. "I don't care how you do it or for what reason; you got to arrest that nigger."

"I can arrest him, but I don't think we can make a case against him if the girl won't testify."

"You just arrest him, and I'll take care of the rest," Jones said.

"Why the hell didn't you ask McCullough to arrest him? He's the sheriff and has the authority," Gustafson complained.

"Because there's no way he'd cooperate with us," Wash said. "He doesn't like us and he doesn't like the Klan."

"Next election we're gonna get rid of him. The Klan is growing, and within a year we'll be controlling a lot of elected offices like we do down in Texas," Cal said.

"I guess I can bring him in for questioning, but that's about the best I can do," Gustafson said.

"That's all we want," Jones said. "When can you do it?"

"I'll put Carmichael and Pack on it in the morning."

"That's all we can ask," Wash said.

"I'm writing the lead story for tomorrow's edition around his arrest, so try to get it done no later than noon tomorrow," Jones said as the three men walked out the door just as abruptly as they had come in.

TWENTY•EIGHT

Mabel smiled as she turned onto Greenwood and walked toward the beauty parlor. As she made that turn, she saw Veneice standing out front. She had two other young girls with her. Mabel had told her to be on time, and she had complied; it was five minutes to nine. But why were the other two girls with her? Maybe just to be there while she did Veneice's hair. All three of the young ladies smiled as Mabel strolled up to the parlor and said, "I am certainly pleased to see you here right on time."

"Yes ma'am, no way I wouldn't be," Veneice said.

Mabel pulled out a key and unlocked the front door. She turned and looked at Veneice. "And who are these two other young ladies?"

"This is Esther," Veneice put her hand on Esther's shoulder, then placed the other hand on Ruth's arm. "And this is Ruth. They are my very best friends, and Mrs. Mabel they need to get their hair done too."

Mabel still stood right outside the parlor holding the door open. "Why didn't they do like you did and make an appointment ahead of time?" she asked but didn't wait for an answer. "I'm not sure I have any openings." Mabel paused and looked directly at Esther. "Why didn't you come down here earlier and make an appointment?"

"I wasn't sure Momma was going to have the money for me," Esther said. "She does domestic work over on Girard across the tracks and was able to talk the folks she works for to give her an advance so I could get my hair done."

"And you?" Mabel looked at Ruth. "What's your excuse?"

"I'm sorry, ma'am I ain't got no money. But since both my

friends were going to get their hair done, I just wanted to come down here with them. Momma told me if she had to pay money for me to get my hair done, then I just wouldn't be able to go to the prom. So, Veneice, Esther and I figured we could do my hair ourselves. It won't be as nice as theirs, but at least it'll look pretty good, I hope."

"My God, child, what kind of language is that, I ain't got no money?" Mabel admonished.

"I'm sorry, Mrs. Jackson always gets on me about my grammar. Told me the other day that I'm acting like Topsy."

"Who is Topsy?" Mabel asked.

"Have you read *Uncle Tom's Cabin*?" Veneice asked.

Mabel waved the girls inside just as two of her beauticians came around the corner and walked up to the door. "No, I don't know anything about it," she said.

They all walked inside, and Mabel closed the door. The other beauticians hurried over to their chairs and began to prepare for their first customers.

"Get in this chair, girl," Mabel said to Veneice. She then turned to Ruth. "So you don't have any money?"

"No ma'am," Ruth replied.

"We'll all cover for her," Esther said. "We talked about it on our way over here. We are willing to come in and clean up the shop for as many straight weeks as you think we should for doing her hair today."

"I see, you're the little negotiator, aren't you?" Mabel smiled. She then turned her attention to the two beauticians whose chairs were at the far end of the shop. "You girls have any customers before eleven?" She asked.

240

"I sure don't," one of the girls replied. "I was hoping we might get a few walk-ins."

"You got one," Mabel said. "Esther go on down there to Helen's chair. How about you Ella, you got any customers this morning?"

"Got someone coming in about ten, that's all."

"Well, they can wait just a little while. We have a real emergency. This young lady needs to get her hair done so she can look real pretty at her prom tomorrow night. I'll cover her." Mabel then looked at Ruth. "Get on down there before someone else comes in here with some money."

"Yes ma'am." Ruth ran down to the chair and flopped down.

"Okay, now we're set; let me make you beautiful, young lady," Mabel said to Veneice.

"Thank you, ma'am, and we'll work for nothing until we pay you back for Ruth."

"I know you will, baby, that's why I'm so proud of you all."

***

By eleven in the morning, Dick felt confident that nothing would happen as a result of his encounter with Sarah yesterday in the Drexel Building. The police hadn't broken down his door, and it was now over twenty-four hours since the incident happened. He sat relaxing in the overstuffed chair in the corner of his room. He'd only gone out for a half hour to grab some breakfast earlier in the morning. He ate a couple eggs and toast and washed it down with a glass of milk. By eight thirty he was back in his room, still nervous that he might hear the knock on the front door.

At a little past eleven, the sun shone brightly into his room, and that added to his restlessness. He needed to get out and get some fresh air. Sitting there in the room worrying about his problem, all he wanted to do was sleep. Dick climbed out of the chair, grabbed his toiletries and headed down the hall to the bathroom to get cleaned up. He was going to get out of the house, regardless of the consequences.

241

As he bounced down the stairs, he heard Aunt Damie in the kitchen talking with Jake. He decided to by-pass them; he wasn't in the mood to talk. He swung the front door open and stepped out into the bright early afternoon sunshine. The hot rays seemed to give him a new lift of energy. He was more than confident that nothing would happen as a result of his brief encounter with

Sarah in the Drexel Building. But he also realized that he had to reconcile with Sarah, and the both of them had to get out of Tulsa. He needed to talk to her, convince her that nothing had happened with Ethel, and she was the only woman that he loved. As he walked up Archer and crossed over Greenwood on his way to Main and the Drexel Building, he could only hope she would be there and willing to listen to reason.

Dick had been concentrating so much on Sarah that he didn't notice the police jitney that pulled up next to him on the street.

"Dick Rowland," Carmichael shouted from inside the vehicle. "Hold it right there where you are. Don't move."

Dick couldn't have moved if he wanted to. The actual reality that the police had finally caught up with him meant yesterday's problem did still exist. He froze right there in place. Pack and Carmichael got out of the police jitney and walked up to the sidewalk.

"Looks like your messing around where your black ass had no business has caught up with you. Chief Gustafson wants you arrested," Carmichael said.

"You're not actually under arrest," Pack said. "Don't do that to him." He glared at his partner. "We've been asked to bring you in for questioning about the incident that happened in the Drexel Building. At this point it's just a formality, nothing serious."

Carmichael stared hard right back at Pack. "Anytime you're taken into police headquarters, it's serious. Put your hands behind your back."

Pack's correction of Carmichael made Dick feel some relief, but the handcuffs caused his stomach to get wheezy. What next, he thought, as Carmichael clicked the handcuffs tight around his wrist, pushed him into the backseat of the police jitney and drove off.

242

Dick's entire body went numb as they pulled up in front of the city jail on Second Street. Carmichael and Pack led Dick inside where Gustafson and his Chief Detective James Patton waited for him. Carmichael took the handcuffs off and escorted the young man to a room, followed by the chief and Patton. Pack forced Dick down into a chair while Gustafson and Patton sat down right across from him.

Carmichael and Pack stood against the wall just in case the prisoner tried to get out of the room. Dick's apprehension increased when Patton sat down right across from him. The detective had a reputation of beating confessions out of prisoners. And his beatings were known to get real severe if the suspect was Black. A few months ago, rumors spread throughout Greenwood that Patton had beaten a Negro woman with a rubber tube, practically killing her. Dick expected the rubber tubing would come out before this was over. He also knew that no one in that room would try to stop Patton from beating him to death. He had plenty reason to be scared.

"You scared?" Gustafson asked.

"Should I be?" Dick replied.

"Not if you haven't done anything wrong," the chief said. "But if you tried to rape that young girl, then yes, you got a lot to be scared of."

"I didn't rape nobody."

"Young lady said you grabbed her by her arms in the elevator in an attempt to rape her. Is that true?" Detective Patton asked.

"No way, I didn't touch her." Dick jerked back as Patton jumped out of his chair and stood right over him.

"Boy, you calling a white girl a liar?" Patton screamed right in Dick's face and hit him a hard blow with his fist to the head.

Dick fell sideways to the floor. He looked up at Patton standing over him and expected the rubber tube to come crashing down on his head. Instead of hitting him again, Patton held out his hand to help him up.

243

Dick ignored the detective, got to his feet and sat back in the chair. His only thought at that moment was he'd love to get this white asshole over in Greenwood in one of the back alleys. Patton hid behind the protection of the police and his badge. Take them away from him, and Dick knew he'd wail his ass all day long. But back to the matter at hand, he had to try and survive until Aunt Damie could get him out of this terrible predicament.

***

Jones finally had what he needed, a reason. He could hardly contain his excitement. A Negro boy was in jail for assaulting a young white girl. The perfect scenario for what he wanted to do, and now the rest was up to him. He couldn't understand why Gustafson and his men weren't able to get the girl to cooperate. They needed her testimony. Actually they needed her to act the role of the victim. Poor innocent white girl attacked by the brute, the monster, the nigger. Maybe the problem is they didn't know how to talk to her. Convince her how important her testimony was to make sure that the monster never attacks another innocent white girl. Jones figured he was just the right person to get the job done.

He grabbed his suit coat and hurried out of his office, slowing down on his way out to say to his secretary. "Tell them to hold the press for this afternoon's edition. I'm going to bring back the story of the year." He finished and shot out the door.

Jones walked the six blocks over to Main Avenue and toward the Drexel Building. As he passed by the shoeshine stand, he shook his head. He knew something was wrong with that boy. He had gotten a bad feeling every time he sat in his shine chair, and then only a few months ago, the boy had the nerve to wear a ring that looked like it was mounted with a real diamond.

Jones finally crossed the street and walked into the Drexel Building. He spotted Sarah sitting outside the elevator reading a magazine. All the times he'd been in that building, he'd never paid any attention to her. Now, as he approached her, he was struck by her good looks. If she was sleeping with Dick Rowland, he couldn't understand why such a nice looking white girl would want to mess with a coon? It made no sense at all.

244

"Miss. Page," he said as he stopped right in front of where she sat. "My name is Lloyd Jones, and I own the *Tulsa Tribune* newspaper. I'd like to talk to you about the assault yesterday."

Sarah folded her magazine and placed it in her lap. "I got nothing to say about yesterday."

"Miss. Page, I just want to get the facts straight so that we can report the story exactly how it happened."

"Look, mister, didn't nothing happen."

This was going to be more difficult than what Jones first thought. "We have it on record that you screamed for help and a salesman from Renberg's ran to your rescue. You pointed to a Negro boy as the one who attempted to rape you, now is that true?" Jones was more aggressive with the question.

"How many ways and how many times I got to tell you, didn't nothing happen."

"Why are you protecting this monster? If you don't help us put him away, he'll only do it to some other poor unsuspecting white girl. Do you want that on your conscience?" Jones paused to let her think through all that he'd said.

"It was just a misunderstanding. I didn't call the police, the salesman from Renberg's did. It was just a misunderstanding, and that's all I have to say."

"What do you mean, a misunderstanding? That means you knew this man personally and what Officer Carmichael told us earlier today is true."

What'd he tell you?" Sarah seemed to tense up.

"Told us that he caught you at that boy's house at three o'clock in the morning, and if he hadn't made you go home, you'd probably spent the rest of the night there. Now is that the story you want me to print in the paper?"

"No, you can't do that," she shrieked. "If it's in the paper, I know I'll get fired. Only reason I didn't get fired before is because it wasn't public. You can't do that."

"I can do it and will do it if I don't get better cooperation from you. Tell me what I need to help save your reputation," Jones ordered. He opened a note pad and took a pen from his pocket. "I want to hear about the brutal assault perpetrated on you by that monster."

TWENTY·NINE

Veneice knew she would never in life feel this good again. At seventeen, she had reached the pinnacle, and nothing could be better than this moment as she got out of Mabel's chair and stared at herself in the mirror. Her hair had never looked as good as it did right now, and the first thought that crossed her mind was she had to roll it before going to bed so it wouldn't lose any of its curls for the prom.

"Thank you, Mrs. Mabel," she finally said.

"I was wondering if you were ever going to stop admiring yourself in the mirror and say something to me."

"I'm sorry, but it just looks so beautiful. This is the first time I ever been to a hairdresser to get my hair done. Momma usually just puts the hot comb to it. But you sure did something special," Veneice said and scurried down to Esther who had just gotten out of the chair. "We're going to be the prettiest girls in all of Greenwood tomorrow night." She looked directly at Esther and then over at Ruth. "Just look at you and Ruth."

"And look at you," Esther said. The three girls wrapped arms around each other and danced in a circle.

"All right, you all need to get on home," Mabel said. "Save all that dancing for tomorrow night with your little boyfriends."

"Let's go," Veneice said, and the three friends headed toward the door. "Thank you, Mrs. Mabel. We love you." Veneice finished and they ran out of the shop.

"I love you all, too," Mabel shouted as the girls closed the door and briskly walked up Greenwood Avenue.

"You going to pick up your dress this afternoon?" Esther

asked Veneice.

"No, Momma already picked it up. How about you?"

"Momma finished sewing mine last night," Esther said.

"And I got an old one from my sister that she wore two years ago," Ruth added.

"Hey, how we going to get to the hotel?" Esther asked as they cut across the street on Greenwood and walked up Elgin.

"Poppa going to take me and I can have him pick you all up," Veneice offered.

"Oh yeah, your daddy's got that big Ford. We'll be the envy of every girl there if we drive up in that big car," Ruth said.

They reached Kenosha and stopped outside Veneice's house.

"Then it's settled; we'll all go together," Esther said. "I know your daddy's going to be right there at midnight to get you, so I'll tell Momma that I should be home by twelve thirty."

"Me too," Ruth added.

"Why don't you all spend the night here, and then we'll be together all day tomorrow as we get ready for the prom?"

"When we going to get ready if we're here in the morning?" Esther asked.

"Well, we can at least spend the morning together," Veneice suggested.

"You sure your momma won't mind?" Ruth asked.

"Positive," Veneice said.

248   "Okay," Esther agreed.

"Sounds like a good idea, but I got the outside corner of the bed," Ruth said. "I ain't going to get caught in the middle."

"Boy, this has all worked out fine. Nothing can stop us now," Veneice shouted. "We're going to the prom. But I got just one final question for you all."

"Yeah, what's that?" Esther asked

"Since I have a boyfriend to dance with all night long," she paused for emphasis. "Who are you going to dance with?" She finished laughing and ran up the steps to the front porch.

"We'll get you for that," Esther said also smiling. "We'll see you in a couple hours."

"Yeah, that wasn't fair, but we'll forgive you," Ruth and Esther waved good-bye to their closest friend and walked up Kenosha.

***

Stradford ran across the street and down Greenwood Avenue to Smitherman's office at the *Tulsa Star*. He charged into his friend's office and slammed the afternoon edition of the *Tribune* on his desk.

Smitherman looked up at Stradford and then down at the paper. He pulled back in his chair as he stared at the words in big, bold, black type across the front of the paper:

NAB NEGRO FOR ATTACKING GIRL IN ELEVATOR.

He again looked up at Stradford and then read the story. "A nineteen-year-old Negro bootblack has been arrested and charged with assault of a seventeen year old white elevator operator in the downtown Drexel Building. The young girl, Sarah Page, noticed the Negro looking up and down the hallway on the third floor. Apparently that is where he planned his assault but actually carried it out after he got in the elevator and she was taking him to the first floor. The Negro boy attacked her, scratching her hands and face and tearing her clothes. When the elevator stopped on the first floor, the young girl was able to break from his grip and run out into the hall, where she was saved by a salesman from Renberg's Men's Store. The brute ran out of the building but was apprehended this morning by the Tulsa Police."

249

Smitherman gazed up at his friend. "Looks as though Jones has finally gotten what he's wanted all along," he said.

"It gets better," Stradford bellowed. "You have to look at his editorial page."

Smitherman opened the inside of the paper to the editorial

page, and a shocked expression shot all across his face. For a minute he could only stare down at the paper.

TO LYNCH A NEGRO TONIGHT!

"This is beyond shameful," Smitherman said.

"It means war," Stradford pointed at the ominous words. "That racist pig has been waiting for the opportunity to cause a race war in Tulsa, and if they try to lynch that boy, that's exactly what they're going to get. When word spreads that they are about to lynch a Negro out of Greenwood, all hell's going to break loose."

"I'm afraid the tiger's out of the bag," Smitherman said. "By now this paper has been bought out, and Negroes all over Greenwood have read it."

"Yeah, and so have all the roughnecks from the oil fields still in town from the holiday yesterday," Gurley said as he rushed into Smitherman's office. He stood next to Stradford in front of the editor's desk.

"Calm down," Smitherman said. "We might be jumping the gun. The boy's locked up in jail, and I'm sure Chief Gustafson's going to give him some protection."

"I think O. W.'s right this time, Andrew," Stradford rejoined. "Them roughnecks from the oil fields are angry 'cause many of them been out of work for months. They've been drinking for the past twenty-four hours, and they're itching for a fight, especially against us. First thing they're going to want to do is tighten the noose around that boy's neck."

"There's no way we can let that happen," Smitherman said. "And there's no way O. B. and his boys going to sit around and let a bunch of peckerwoods lynch someone from our community."

250

Gurley started pacing over to the window looking out and then walking back and standing behind one of the chairs in front of the desk. "That man's a ticking time bomb over there on Lansing with all that military marching and bragging about fighting over in Europe." Gurley's brows furrowed; his forehead wrinkled.

"What do you suggest we do if the *Tribune's* right and they plan to lynch that boy tonight?" Smitherman looked directly at Gurley.

"Sheriff McCullough is not going to let that happen," Gurley answered. "Not on his watch."

"Have you forgotten what happened ten years ago when they hanged that boy, and there wasn't a whole lot of proof that he was guilty," Smitherman said. "McCullough was the sheriff back then, and he couldn't do anything to stop it."

"That was different; the boy had been found guilty," Gurley rejoined, his voice becoming shrill. "That wasn't a lynching; it was a legal hanging."

Stradford was tempted to choke some sense into his old friend. Instead, he pointed his fingers at him. "Every time they hang a Negro in the South, it is a lynching. I don't care if it's after one of their so-called trials or if they just drag the poor victim from his jail cell without going through the process of having a jury find him guilty. Look what happened to Roy Belton last year."

"He was white," Gurley retorted, determined to stand his ground.

This time Smitherman exploded. "What are you talking about he was a white man? If these people will lynch one of their own, you know what they'll do with one of ours." He stopped and took in a deep breath and released it. "Right now they're holding him in the city jail. That's the police chief's jurisdiction, and you know none of them over there will lift a finger to protect that boy."

"Lift a finger, they'd probably participate," Stradford added. "Everyone knows Gustafson and that detective are sympathetic to the Klan."

"All I'm asking is that we wait and see what happens, you know, take it slow," Gurley said allowing slight pleading in his voice.

251

"Taking it slow will get that boy lynched," Smitherman shot back. "The time to act is before the lynching starts and not after it gets started. Then it's too late."

"I agree," Stradford said. "Our indecisiveness will get that boy killed." He got up and pulled out his pocket watch and checked the time. "It's four thirty right now. Let's wait until after the folks across the tracks get off work and see what they do. We'll let their actions determine ours, and if they show any signs of trying to lynch Rowland, then we'll organize all the manpower we can get to make sure that doesn't happen."

"Why don't we all meet back here in an hour and do another assessment," Smitherman suggested.

"I'll contact Cleaver to find out what protections they're going to put in place," Gurley said.

Smitherman walked from behind his desk and accompanied the two men to the door. "But keep in mind, the boy's in the city jail right now, not county. The man you need to talk to is the police chief, and I'm not sure that'll do any good."

"I'll do my best," Gurley said as they all walked out of Smitherman's office.

THIRTY

"What in hell was Jones over at the *Tribune* thinking about when he wrote this editorial?" Police Commissioner James Atkinson asked as he sat in Mayor Thaddeus Evans office. The Commissioner, Gustafson and McCullough sat across from the mayor's desk. Usually the two lawmen never appeared together because of the extreme animosity between the two. Sheriff McCullough was very vocal about the corruption that existed in the police department. But Jones's editorial made it necessary for all law enforcement to put aside differences and figure out what to do with this potentially explosive crisis.

"The man has been nothing but problems since he took over that newspaper," Atkinson continued. "This time he's gone too far. Before the sun sets you're going to have a crowd out front of the jail. And they're either going to participate in the lynching or they're going to watch."

"How safe is that Rowland boy in the city jail?" Evans asked.

"Major problem is that the jail cells are all on the ground floor and easily accessible," Gustafson said. "We'd have to set up a fortress of officers on the outside to prevent a mob from getting to him."

"And that would mean a lot of white men would die trying to protect one stupid nigger," Atkinson said. "That would also mean we would be defeated in the next election." He looked directly at the mayor.

"You all forgetting one other thing?" McCullough asked.

"What's that?" The mayor asked.

"The Negroes are not going to sit around and allow one of

their own to be lynched. They've made that very clear in that newspaper."

"If them niggers come anywhere near my jail, their blood will cover the street," Gustafson snarled.

"Quit talking tough, and let's talk sensible," McCullough's voice rose. "Let me assure you those boys can fight, and they will fight. This is not Mississippi or Alabama where they sit around and do nothing when one of their kind is lynched."

"What are you becoming, a nigger lover?" Gustafson's voice also rose.

"Okay, let's knock it off," Mayor Evans intervened. "Name calling and fighting among ourselves is not going to solve this problem. What we need to do before the mob has a chance to gather is move the boy from the city jail to the more secure facility at county."

"You're right," McCullough said. "Our jail is on the fourth floor, and the only way to get up there is up a narrow flight of stairs or by elevator. We can disable the elevator and lock the door to the hallway from the stairs. And then we can also double lock the doors leading into the jail area. All that will discourage a mob and lessen the chance of white men having to die to protect a Negro."

"How soon can you move him?" Atkinson asked.

"As soon as we can get out of here," McCullough said.

"We need to get that done right away," Mayor Evans added. "And the two of you better find a way to get along until this all blows over." He looked a both Gustafson and McCullough. "Now get out of here and go and move that prisoner."

254

***

McCullough and Cleaver walked into the city jail on Second Street a little before four o'clock. Gustafson, sitting at his desk, gave them a very hard stare, then got up and met them in the middle of the room.

"You're fortunate there is no crowd building up outside yet," he said. Without waiting for a response, he then turned and walked in the direction of the cells. The two men followed closely behind. "You'd be smart to take him out the back way and up the alley instead of on the street,"

"That was our plan," McCullough said as they stopped right in front of the cell. He glared at Dick who sat on the side of the bunk, staring off into space. "So you're the boy that's caused all this ruckus," he said.

Gustafson unlocked the cell door and stepped inside. "On your feet. Time to move you to another location."

Dick stood up next to the side of the bunk. "Where you taking me?" he asked.

"You'll find out soon enough," Gustafson said.

"Put your hands behind your back." Cleaver walked behind the young prisoner and tightened his hands in the cuffs.

"When do I get a chance to contact my Aunt Damie?" Dick asked as Cleaver led him out of the cell and McCullough followed.

They walked over to the back door. Gustafson swung it open and looked in both directions. "No problem back here," he said and moved out of the way. "Wait here, I'll get the car and bring it around the back." He finished and walked to the front of the jail and out the door.

"You got no reason to be doing this to me," Dick screamed at McCullough. "I didn't do nothing to that girl. You got no right to do this."

"You'll have your day in court," McCullough said.

"I'll never make it to court; you know that." Dick looked directly at Cleaver who looked away. "Come on Uncle Barney, you know me and you know I didn't attack that girl, and if she said I did, she's lying."

"Sheriff told you that you'll get your chance to prove her wrong," Cleaver finally spoke up.

The police jitney with Gustafson behind the wheel pulled up to the back door. "Let's get him in the backseat. I'll drive," he said.

"What way you gonna go?" McCullough asked, as they

255

forced Dick into the backseat and Cleaver got back there with him. McCullough hurried over to the passenger side and climbed in.

"Gonna take the alley all the way up to Sixth and the street to Boulder. That way no one will know we're bringing him over there. We shouldn't have a welcoming crowd," Gustafson said.

"Why you going up alleys?" Dick shouted. "I thought I didn't have anything to worry about. What's going on?"

"Shaddup, you're safe," Gustafson also shouted. "The sheriff is a better person than me. If I had my way, I'd throw you to the wolves and let them devour you."

Gustafson drove the jitney out of the alley and onto Boulder Street for the final two blocks to the county courthouse.

"For precaution, let's take him in the back way," McCullough advised.

"You got it," Gustafson said.

Right at the corner of Fifth and Boulder, he turned into the alley, drove a couple blocks and stopped in front of a steel door. Cleaver got out of the car, grabbed a key and opened the door. He held it open while McCullough led Dick inside the county courthouse. Gustafson climbed back inside the jitney and drove off.

Once inside and with the door securely shut, McCullough and Cleaver escorted Dick up four flights of stairs and through an enormous set of doors and finally locked him in a cell on the fourth floor. With their prisoner securely locked behind bars, the two men took the elevator back down to the first floor and into the sheriff's office.

256

"How long do you think it'll take before the trouble begins?" Cleaver asked as he sat in a chair in front of McCullough's desk.

"Don't know," McCullough mumbled. "I'll give it an hour, and then they'll be banging on that door."

"Gustafson's going to tell them where he is?"

"No doubt, he's probably told them already."

"What about the boys across the tracks. You were right when

you told the mayor that they're not going to sit around and allow a lynching to take place."

McCullough got up and walked over to the window looking out to the front of the courthouse. He stood there for a minute. "Them boys might be able to put up a fight but they're going to lose, 'cause they'll be fighting the entire power of the Oklahoma law enforcement." He said with his back to Cleaver.

"It's almost five o'clock," Cleaver said. "We'll know what the Klan's going to do soon after they all start to get off work."

"I'm not worried about the Klan, but about all them workers from the oil field that been coming into town and talking about how well the Negroes have it across the tracks. If them boys come over here, that's going to be reason for them to start shooting." McCullough turned, sauntered back and sat at his desk. "You got to go talk to that boy's Aunt Damie and let her know we got him locked up over here. Let her know that I am not about to let that boy be lynched and that she needs to get him a lawyer for his arraignment in the morning."

"You want me to come back here after I talk to her?" Cleaver asked.

"No, you'd better go by the newspaper office and see what's happening there. That's where them boys will plan whatever they're going to do. Whatever it takes, you got to convince them they can't come across those tracks with weapons. Let them know that if they do, I may not be able to control what happens after that."

Cleaver got up, but hesitated. "This city may be on the verge of making headlines all over the country, but not for the right reason." He turned and walked out of the office.

257

THIRTY•ONE

Damie could feel in her bones that something was terribly wrong. While sitting in the kitchen talking with Jake earlier in the day, she heard Dick when he left the house. She didn't think he should leave, but knew telling him so wouldn't keep him inside. Now, it was nearly five o'clock, and she sat in that same chair at the kitchen table peeling potatoes for a salad she planned to make to go along with baked chicken, collard greens and corn bread for dinner that evening.

Her son hadn't called or come home, and she began to worry. Damie knew he didn't go to work and he surely wasn't with that white girl. She'd caused enough trouble for him, and there was no way he'd gone back up to the Drexel Building to patch things up. For once she prayed that he was over on First Street at one of the choc joints or at Pretty Belles. She felt confident he wasn't in trouble despite the feeling she felt in her bones.

Damie finished peeling her potatoes and just as she got up to cut them into small chunks in a bowl, she heard the loud banging on the front door. The feeling she had deep in her bones had been right was her first thought. She put the potatoes in the bowl and walked hurriedly to the door. She opened it, and her heart sank.

"Good afternoon, Miss Damie," Cleaver greeted her. "May I come in?"

Momentarily, Damie did not respond. She simply stared at Cleaver as if she was looking at a ghost.

"Miss Damie, may I come in?" Cleaver repeated.

"Oh, certainly," Damie said and swung the door open so he could get in. "Forgive my manners, Deputy Cleaver."

Cleaver walked into the foyer and waited for Damie to close the door.

"Please come on into the parlor," Damie said as she walked in front of him. "Have a seat?"

"Oh, no, ma'am I can't stay," Cleaver said.

"Fine, then can you tell me why you're here?" She asked.

"Yes ma'am. Dick Rowland has been retained in custody for questioning of a possible assault on a young girl who operates the elevator in the Drexel Building over on Main Street."

Damie fell back into a chair and felt that she might faint. She knew that was the worst charge a Black man could receive and usually a death sentence.

"Are you all right, Miss Damie?" Cleaver asked.

She took in a deep breath and released it. "I'm fine," she said. "How is he?"

"He's doing just fine. Sheriff McCullough promised that he would be treated just like a white prisoner."

A smirk spread across Damie's face. "He sent you all the way over here to tell me that as if I'd believe it 'cause you're Black. Well, I don't care who the messenger is, I won't relax until I see him walk out of that jail unharmed."

"If he's innocent, he don't have nothing to worry about," Cleaver said.

"Nothing to worry about," Damie said in a shrill voice. "You got my son in jail, accused of raping a white girl, and you can stand there and tell me I don't have anything to worry about. How can you possibly do that white man's evil work?"

260

"Miss Damie, your boy did this to himself," Cleaver said. "People all over Greenwood been telling him to stop messing around with that white girl, but he just wouldn't listen."

Damie buried her head between her hands and sobbed. She knew Cleaver spoke the truth. On many occasions, she'd told her son the very same thing. To even look at a white woman was taboo. He'd gone much further than just looking. He'd actually slept with her. She finally stopped crying.

"I know you're a deputy and have to be on the side of the law, but you're a Negro also. You got to feel something for my boy. He's only nineteen and if we can't help him, he might die. It just ain't right."

"There's a lawyer who is one of the best in town; he can help you," Cleaver said. "Sheriff McCullough told me to give you his name and for you to get over there and talk to him."

"Can he really help my boy?"

"If anyone can, he's the one. He knows all the judges."

"You have his name and address?" Damie asked feeling better that there was someone out there who would help Dick.

"Wash Hudson," Cleaver said. "His office is over on Second and Boulder near the city jail."

Damie got up from the chair. "I need to go see him right now," she said.

"Come on, I'll drive you over there," Cleaver volunteered.

"No, I don't want to put you out," Damie said.

"It's on my way, and it's no bother. It's the least I can do to help you out."

"Give me a minute to get my purse." Damie hurried out of the room. "Thank you and I'm sorry for what I said about you earlier," she said and disappeared into her bedroom.

***

Fear shot throughout Gurley's entire body like a cannon shot when he turned onto Boulder off Third and scowled at a crowd of at least one hundred white men dressed in coveralls, standing in front of the county courthouse. His initial thought was how could he get into the courthouse to talk with the sheriff with a mob building up right outside the door. They would possibly make him the first victim if he tried to negotiate his way through them. But it was imperative that he speak with the Sheriff. He promised the men back across the tracks that he would get assurances from McCullough that Dick was safe.

He pulled over and parked his car on the corner of Fourth and Boulder. Just as he cut off his engine a police jitney pulled up right behind him. He turned and looked at Cleaver as he got out and walked toward him. He quickly exited his car and turned to greet Cleaver.

"Why is the crowd outside the county courthouse?" Gurley asked. "I thought Dick Rowland was in the city jail."

"We moved him over here for safety reasons," Cleaver said as he approached his friend. "But how in hell did all these folks find out he'd been moved over here?"

"I don't know," Gurley said, "but I got to talk to the Sheriff. We're getting our own mob building up at Smitherman's place, and they want some assurances that the Rowland boy ain't going to be harmed."

Cleaver turned around and said, "Come on, get in. We'll go in the back alley way." The two men climbed into the police jitney, and Cleaver drove up the alley and stopped in front of the steel door.

"Come on in this way." Cleaver got out and unlocked the back door. He left the jitney blocking the alley as the two men walked to the front of the building and ducked into McCullough's office.

The Sheriff stood staring out the window when the two men came in. He turned and faced them.

"Mr. Gurley, I thought I might be seeing you sometime this evening," he said.

"What the hell happened?" Cleaver asked. "How did they know we'd made the switch?" He pointed his finger at the window.

"Either Patton or Gustafson and maybe both of them. They probably couldn't wait to spread the word that Rowland was over here," McCullough said.

"That's going to be a real problem," Gurley said. "If they get wind across the tracks that a mob has gathered over here, then I don't believe I'll be able to stop them."

"What's wrong with them boys over there?" McCullough

asked. He didn't wait for an answer. "Don't they know they can't whip a mob of white boys? The odds are against them."

"You got a bunch of hot heads like that Army boy and the few that follow him. They believe that they aren't men if they allow another Negro to be lynched without putting up a fight," Gurley said.

"Are they ready to die?"

"They're ready to do whatever it takes to make sure that boy gets a fair trial and won't be hanging from a tree in the morning," Gurley said.

McCullough placed both hands on his desk and leaned forward. "You go on back over there and tell them boys there won't be no lynching on my watch. But them boys better be careful. White men don't have much patience when Negroes forget their place. You'd better be sure to let them know that." He paused and glared at Gurley, "I might be their only friend on this side of the tracks."

Gurley stared back at McCullough. If he was the only white friend Negroes had in Tulsa, then they essentially had no friends at all. Men like Stradford and Townsend Jackson and himself were practically twice his age and he referred to them as boys and not men. He felt like shouting at this man that they all had paid their dues to be respected as men just as he expected respect as sheriff. But he wouldn't do that because it was not his nature to be confrontational. Instead he said, "I'll let them know that, and I'm sure they'll appreciate your friendship. I'll let them know they have your assurance there will be no lynching tonight or any other time."

"Let's go out the back way, and I'll drive you to your car," Cleaver said.

263

"I'd appreciate that," Gurley said, and the two men walked to the door.

"Cleaver, why don't you just stay over there and call me to let me know what's going on and I'll keep an eye on those fools outside."

"Got it," Cleaver said, unlocked the door and the two men stepped outside.

***

Damie had been waiting almost two hours before Wash Hudson opened his office door.

"I'm sorry, Auntie," he said. "Been taking care of some important business. Come on in." He waved her into his office.

Damie took a chair in front of his desk while Wash walked back behind it and sat down.

"How can I help you?" he asked.

"I've been told that you are about the best lawyer in town in getting people out of trouble," Damie said. "I'm sure you heard about the colored boy who was arrested earlier this morning and accused of assaulting a white woman."

"Yes, I did hear something about that."

"That boy is my son, Dick Rowland. I'd like to hire you to be his lawyer."

"Seems as though they caught him putting his hands on the girl who runs the elevator in the Drexel Building." Wash leaned forward across his desk.

"There's no truth to that," Damie fired back. "My boy ain't touched that girl. Now will you take his case or not?"

"Easy Auntie, slow down," Wash said. "It's going to cost you because representing a nig…" Wash caught himself, "Nigra against the charges he's going to face is going to take a lot of my time."

264   Damie went into her purse and pulled out a wad of bills all rolled up. This was the money Dick had given her over the years to buy something nice for herself. Instead, she'd always saved it for him. Someday she figured he might need it, and that day had come. She counted out five dollars and stuck it back into her purse. That was the money she owed Mabel for doing her hair last Saturday.

"How much money you got there, girl?" Wash asked.

"Over three hundred dollars." Damie handed the money

across the desk to Wash.

"This should take care of it," he said. "I'll do my best to make sure your boy gets a fair trial. I tell you, though, I won't make any friends defending him. A white man defending a Nigra boy is dangerous for his career."

"You can do it, can't you?" Damie asked.

"Yes, I can do it," Wash said. "First thing in the morning, I'll get over to the jail and talk with him before arraignment. I know all the judges in the courthouse, and when they see me defending him, they'll make sure he gets a fair trial." Wash stood up. "Is there anything else?"

"No, only that I want my boy to walk out of that jail alive." Damie stood up.

"I'll talk to you tomorrow after I meet with your boy. Come back by here about eleven, and I should know something by then."

"Thank you, Mr. Hudson." Damie finished, turned and walked out of the office. She had no choice but to believe that this white man was sincere when he took her money and promised to help her boy. But that old uncomfortable feeling in her bones indicated otherwise.

THIRTY•TWO

O. B's veins pulsated and his blood rushed to his head. He threw the *Tribune* down on the counter in the grocery store and glowered across the top at Peg Leg Taylor and Otis, who stood waiting for his response.

"They think they're going to lynch Miss Damie's boy, we gonna have a real surprise for them," O. B. said.

"It's just like they didn't even listen to us when we told them we ain't having no lynching in Tulsa, less they want to do it to one of their own," Peg Leg Taylor said.

Two more veterans from the march strolled into the store with their rifles.

"Figured we might need these after word got to us they planning on stringing the Rowland boy up tonight," one of the veterans said.

"We with you, O. B. This going to be just like France, only this time we get to fight our real enemy," the other man added.

"Welcome to the new war, boys," O. B. exclaimed.

"Y'all ready to die if necessary?" Peg Leg Taylor shook hands with both men.

"Ready if we have to," the first veteran said. "I couldn't live with myself if I just sat around and let them disrespect that boy."

"Not only disrespect that boy," Otis spoke up, "but disrespect us. I done been disrespected so many times by them folks, I don't respect myself." He held his rifle high in the air. "I'm ready to win it back and be a man for the first time since I moved to this city."

"What are we going to do, O. B.?" Peg Leg Taylor asked.

"Right now we going to wait and see what happens and wait for more of the boys to show up."

"They'll be here," the first veteran into the building said.

O. B. walked from behind the counter with a shotgun under his left arm and a pistol holstered around the right side of his waist. "I'm gonna ride up to Greenwood and Archer so I can get a good look at what's happening."

"Need us to go along?" Otis asked.

"Naw, I need you all to stay here while I scout it out." O. B. finished and walked out of the store and to the back.

He rode his big white stallion up to Archer Street, then went west to Greenwood, up the back alley, dismounted and whistled. The same young boy who'd taken care of his horse when he visited Smitherman came running out of the shanty. O. B. handed him the reins and walked up the alley to Greenwood and into Smitherman's office.

Stradford and John Williams sat on one side of the desk and the editor on the other side when O. B. walked in and interrupted their conversation.

"We got to go across those tracks and rescue Miss Damie's boy. Ain't no way we can let them harm one hair on that young man." He pulled his revolver from its holster and slammed it on the desk. "This is just one of the five weapons I'm ready to use if necessary."

Gurley burst into the room right after O. B. He stopped in his tracks as he stared at O. B's weapon on the desk. He frowned at the men and finally made his way to the front of the room.

268

"We don't have any problems," he said in a shrill voice. "I talked with Sheriff McCullough, and he assured me that the boy will be safe in the county courthouse jail."

"They're lying to you," O.B. scowled. "The paper said the boy was being held in the city jail, and you know damn well that Gustafson will do nothing to protect him. Hell, he'll probably cross over and join the mob."

"No, see, you don't know what you're talking about," Gurley

fired back. "The sheriff was concerned for the boy's safety, so they moved him over to county, which is a much more secure facility."

"That's a good sign," Stradford said.

O.B. and Gurley finally sat in the two empty chairs, also in front of the desk.

"Remember what happened over in Oskogee last year," Smitherman said.

"I damn well remember," O.B. snarled. "Negroes got there too late to help."

"That's exactly right," Smitherman continued. "When they got there, the poor boy had already been taken from the jail. Them peckerwoods lynched that boy and didn't care if he was guilty. They just said he raped a white girl, and that was enough."

"You all know Miss Damie and how much she loves that boy," O.B. practically shouted. "He's all she's got, and if something happens to him ain't no telling how she'll handle it."

Exasperated, Gurley asked, "What do you want us to do?" He didn't wait for an answer. "Go rushing over there into a mob of drunk white men who sure enough gonna open up firing on us?"

"Why you such a coward, old man?" O.B. snapped.

"It ain't about being a coward," Gurley also raised the volume in his voice. "You want to cause a race war over a boy who ain't been nothing but a troublemaker since he dropped out of school."

"Okay, hold up," Stradford intervened. "We aren't going to let those people lynch that boy, I don't care what kind of person he is."

"That's right," John Williams finally spoke up. "He is one of ours and that's all that matters. And for me, it's much more than about Dick Rowland. It's all about dignity."

"John, you got a whole lot to lose if this gets violent," Gurley said.

"We all have a whole lot to lose," Smitherman said. "But we've known that for a very long time, and all we did was prolong the inevitable believing in what Booker T. Washington constantly preached before he died. Well, we took his advice and sacrificed

269

dignity for financial security, and I'd say today we don't have either."

"Ain't that the God's honest truth," O.B. said. "Me and my men are just aching to take back the dignity we gave up for money. Some of us went all the way to France just to prove we were as good as them at killing other men. Why are we always trying to prove our worth as men to them when really they should be trying to prove they deserve our respect? My days are over trying to prove a damn thing to them. I'm gonna take my respect." He snatched his pistol from the desk and jammed it back into the holster.

"Don't leave," Stradford said.

"I've seen and heard enough," O.B. said as he started to get up.

"No, no, wait," Stradford put his hand on the big warrior's shoulder. "It's a little after seven, and if those boys are going to do something, it should happen real soon. I'm going over to the courthouse and check to see if things have cooled down. Promise, I'll be back in a half hour."

O.B. sat down and relaxed. "I can wait," he said. "Don't matter if I kill them peckerwoods now or hours later."

***

Each time Sheriff McCullough walked over to the window and looked out at the front of the building, the crowd had grown larger. He stood staring out at what had to be over five hundred people many still dressed in business suits. Evidently, they had come over to the courthouse as soon as they got off work. But most of the men were from the fields. There was also a contingent of women and children scattered throughout the crowd.

Suddenly, three men dressed in business suits walked up the steps. Evidently they had plans to enter the building. That was something the sheriff could not allow to happen. Walking briskly, he swung the door to his office open, walked down the court corridor and out the front door. He met the men at the top step.

270

"We want no trouble with you, Sheriff," one of the men said. "But the good white people of Tulsa need answers to what happened over at the Drexel Building yesterday morning."

"You all will get your answer when the prisoner appears before a municipal court judge in the morning," McCullough exclaimed. "Now I need for you to march back off these steps before others are encouraged to join you up here."

"Sheriff, why are you protecting that brute who attacked an innocent white girl?"

McCullough wrapped his right hand around the revolver resting in the holster on his hip. "I am protecting a prisoner who will be either officially charged tomorrow or will be turned loose. Now please don't force me to have to shoot you. Turn around and get out of here."

"I'm not sure the people out there are going to be satisfied with your answer," the man said, and the three of them turned and walked back down the steps.

McCullough glared at the men as they made it back down to the bottom and huddled with five other men in business suits. The sheriff did not recognize any of them in the group. They had to be either strangers passing through who decided to join in the excitement or members of the Klan who were in Tulsa to recruit. Either way, they seemed to have an effect on the crowd. McCullough listened as the same man he'd warned to get off the steps to the courthouse again walked up five steps, turned and shouted.

"Friends, this is a very sad day in Tulsa, Oklahoma. A day for which we all should be ashamed. A day when a brute nigger was able to attack and rape a young white girl who is an orphan and was working to earn enough money to go to business school. I understand she is in a state of shock right now and her future may have been ruined. Now the rest of the country will know that Tulsa is a city where the white men cannot protect the innocence of the women from the brutality of the niggers."

271

Listening to this nonsense caused McCullough's blood pressure to rise. This man was attacking him and every other law enforcement officer in the city. The man continued his diatribe.

"The rest of the country is going to know that the niggers run Tulsa. If the sheriff does not move out of the way and let us have that animal hiding behind sheriff's threats to hurt good white people, then the word will spread as far away as Texas that the niggers run Tulsa."

That was enough. McCullough had to put an end to this kind of talk. He scrambled down the steps and stood next to the man.

"That's it," he shouted. "I want you off these steps or I'm going to arrest you."

The man turned and confronted the sheriff. "For what Sheriff? You got no reason to arrest me."

"I'll deal with the reason later. But right now you're building this crowd up to an unhealthy fever pitch, and someone is bound to get hurt." He finished, turned and looked out at the crowd. "I want you all to disperse," he shouted. "There will be no mob rule this evening, and I will shoot the first person who tries to take my prisoner out of this jail. I promise you he will receive punishment for his crime, but it will be through the courts. Now I want you all to go home." He placed his hand on the revolver just to let the mob know he was serious.

He watched as some of the crowd dispersed and returned to their cars or just walked off. The three men who first confronted him, hurried back out into the crowd. Suddenly, the mob turned back around and began to shout.

"We want the nigger, we want the nigger." They started to move toward the steps, and McCullough pulled his revolver from the holster and fired into the air.

272

"The next shot will be aimed at the first person that attempts to climb these steps," he shouted.

"You can't kill us all," a man at the front of the crowd shouted.

"Yeah, but I sure as hell can shoot you." He pointed his revolver right at the man's chest.

The man froze. "You ain't nothing but a nigger lover," he screamed, but turned around and walked back into the middle of the crowd.

"All right now, your fun is over, and you all need to go on home and call it a night." McCullough finished, walked back up the steps and into his office. He hurried over to the window. Evidently, most of the crowd had not taken his advice. It looked to McCullough that the crowd had grown even larger. It was time to take further actions to protect his prisoner.

The Sheriff ran out of his office, into the corridor and over to the elevator, got in, turned the handle and rode to the fourth floor. When the door opened, he turned the elevator off and walked in the jail. He had five deputies up there all waiting for orders.

"It looks like we're in for a very long night. A crowd has built up outside and might attempt to force their way in and take the prisoner." He paused to let his words register with his deputies. "That will not happen under my watch. When I walk back out of here, I want you all to bolt the door from the inside. Do not open it for no one but me. I want two of you out on the roof with rifles pointed down on that mob." The men looked ready for action and he was sure would not abandon their responsibility as officers, despite how they felt about Rowland. "Get to it," he ordered and walked back out the door.

McCullough could hear the locks snap shut from the inside as he hurried down the hall to a door, opened it and walked down the four levels of stairs to the first floor. If the intruders forced their way inside the building, he would climb the four flights back up to the fourth floor and plant himself right at the top. The stairwell was so narrow, only one intruder at a time could enter, and he would shoot each and every one of them, one at a time. The Sheriff felt flushed and angry. His anger targeted the Negroes for not staying in their place, the mob for defying his orders to disperse, at the Rowland boy for his arrogance, but most of all at Jones for printing that inflammatory editorial that led to all of this mess.

273

THIRTY•THREE

Stradford turned the corner at Third and Boulder and quickly pulled his car over to the curb. He looked down Boulder at the large crowd standing in front of the county courthouse. There was no way he'd make it down there and get inside to possibly talk with the sheriff. He knew why they were down there, either to participate in the lynching or to stand by and watch it happen. He figured there were over five hundred men, women and even some children out there just waiting for the action. He also figured that no matter what McCullough said to them, they were not going to be dissuaded from what they came there to do. No need for him to try to get through that mob and talk with the sheriff.

The possibility of communicating their differences and prevent what was about to happen was gone. He needed to go back to the men and tell them that there was an awfully strong possibility that the mob was going to get to Rowland and unless they struck first, there would be a lynching in Tulsa that night. A despondent Stradford turned the car around and drove back to his side of town.

He parked right in front of Smitherman's building, exited the car and hurried up the steps into the *Tulsa Star* office. As he walked into the room, Captain Townsend, Gurley, O. B. and Smitherman all turned and looked at him. They remained quiet until Stradford flopped down in a chair right next to Gurley.

Smitherman stood up and placed his hands, palms down, on the desktop. They all had an anxious look on their faces. The leaders of Greenwood were there, and now some hard decisions had to be made.

"What's it look like over there?" Smitherman asked.

"You want the truth? It doesn't look good," Stradford said. "It's a mad house and it don't look like McCullough's going to be able to maintain order. Must be at least five hundred men out front of the courthouse."

"No, that can't be," Gurley said. "Sheriff guaranteed me that the Rowland boy would be safe."

"I believe the Sheriff really meant well, "Stradford said. "But he's going to need a lot of help keeping the crowd under control."

"Just what I knew would happen," O.B. exclaimed. He jumped up from his chair. "I did just what you asked," he continued. "I waited, and now the waiting is over. We got to strike before it's too late."

"What are you talking about?" Captain Townsend spoke up. "The man just told you there are over five hundred men over there. How many men you got?"

"I got enough that's ready to go across those tracks and rescue that boy," O.B. replied.

"O.B., you going to get that boy killed for sure as well as yourself and all your veteran friends. Them white folks going to kill you dead if you cross those tracks carrying guns," Captain Townsend admonished.

O.B. stood erect. "Old man, you talked us out of carrying our weapons yesterday, and we got ambushed and embarrassed. That ain't going to happen a second time." He started toward the door.

"What you plan to do?" Stradford asked.

"I plan to get as many men as possible and go over and assist the sheriff in protecting that boy," O.B. said.

The door swung open, and Cleaver hurried inside the room. "I just finished talking with the sheriff and he told me that it's under control over there. In fact, the crowd has started to break up," he said. "So don't nobody panic and go do something stupid."

"When did you talk to him?" Smitherman asked. "John just come from over there, and he said it looked like it was out of control."

"Sheriff said there were a few hotheads who tried to stir things up, but they had failed and now they've left." Cleaver paused for a moment. "Said he took the elevator to the fourth floor and turned it off, and they locked all doors leading into the jail cells up there, and he got men on the roof of the building who have orders to shoot anyone trying to come into the building. Nobody needs to go over there. Sheriff's got it all under control."

"Now, there you have it," Gurley said. "No need for us to do anything."

"What you think?" Smitherman asked Stradford.

"I don't know; it looked pretty bad when I was over there. But if the sheriff says he's got it under control, I agree we should just leave it alone tonight. When that mob finds out there's no way to get inside, they'll get frustrated and leave for the night."

"Then what happens in the morning?" O.B. chimed in.

"I think we should worry about that in the morning," Stradford answered O.B.

"You put too much faith in white people," O.B. grimaced, turned and walked to the door. He glared back at the others. "You put too much faith in white men and the only thing I put my faith in is my Winchester and my pistol." The giant of a man walked out the door, slamming it shut behind him.

O.B's words resonated throughout the room. The others sat there silent for a moment. No one could stop the big giant and his men from going across those tracks and trying to get Dick out of jail.

"We have to beat O. B. to the punch," Smitherman said. "We have to go over there and help the sheriff before the others get there."

277

"I'm going this time," John Williams said. "I'll meet you all out front. Got to get my gun." He hurried out of the room.

"Who's all going?" Stradford asked.

We're all going," Gurley said. "I don't have no gun, but I'm going anyway. You with us Deputy?" Gurley asked Cleaver.

"I'd better go," Cleaver said. "I'm not sure the sheriff will be in the mood to see you all unless I'm with you."

"You with us, Captain?" Stradford asked.

"Might as well," Captain said. "Maybe there's still some hope we can stop all this violence from happening."

The four men practically ran out of the building and piled into Stradford's Cadillac. They pulled up in front of the confectionery, and John Williams shot out of the building, climbed into the backseat with his rifle, and Stradford started up Greenwood across the Frisco tracks.

Stradford's adrenaline was pumping so fast he could hardly steer the car when he made a right turn off Fourth Street onto Boulder and drove directly at the crowd still mingling in front of the courthouse.

"Turn right here at Fifth and take the alley," Cleaver said from the backseat. "We can go in the back way. I got a key."

Stradford followed the deputy's instructions and drove up the alley to the back of the building. He stopped right in front of the back door. Cleaver jumped out, ran around the car and unlocked the back door.

"Come on, hurry," he instructed.

The men piled out of the car and briskly walked into the building, down the hall and swung the door to the sheriff's office open.

McCullough, standing at the window staring out, swung around and pulled his revolver from its holster. He pointed the gun right at Cleaver who was the first one through the door.

Cleaver threw his arms in the air. "Hold up, Sheriff."

278   "What the hell do you think you're doing?" McCullough shouted as he put his gun back in the holster.

"Didn't mean to scare you, boss, but I thought it best we come in the back door so as not to excite the crowd and have the boys up top take shots at us," Cleaver said.

"You didn't scare me, but you sure as hell come close to getting yourself shot," McCullough scowled. "What are you all doing here?" he asked as he looked past Cleaver at the other four men who'd come in right behind the deputy.

"There's a gang of men across the tracks determined to make sure nothing happens to that boy you got in custody," Stradford spoke up. "From the way it looks outside, they may have reason to be concerned."

"You men get it through your heads that I'm the sheriff in this town, and ain't nobody going to enforce the law here but me. I'm not going to be pushed around by that mob out there or by the mob that might be organizing across the tracks."

"Help us out, Sheriff," Smitherman said. "Give us some kind of assurance that this boy will make it to court; then we'll go back and try to stop them boys from coming over here."

"I'm sure Cleaver told you that I got sharp shooters on the roof of this building with strict orders to shoot the first son of a bitch who charges up to that front door. That includes them folks out there, and that includes your boys organizing to come over here and try to do my job."

"Where's the boy?" Stradford asked.

"Got him locked up on the fourth floor in a cell behind locked doors with two more deputies ready to shoot any bastard that tries to come through those doors. I disabled the elevator so the only way up there is up a narrow stairway, and if it gets to that point, I'll be sitting at the top of them stairs ready to shoot."

"I'm satisfied," Gurley spoke up. "There's no doubt the Sheriff's got the situation under control. We can all go home and rest easy."

McCullough ignored Gurley's comment and instead stared intently at Smitherman. "You need to stop encouraging your people to fight white folks," he said.

279

"Encouraging people to aspire to be treated as equals is not encouraging them to fight anyone," Smitherman replied without hesitating.

"Looks like we're through here. "Cleaver jumped in the conversation. "I believe we can feel relatively safe nothing is going to happen tonight. Let's get back across the tracks."

"You people are fighting for something you will never get in this country," McCullough ignored his deputy's attempt to bring the discussion to an end. "The government, the people, everybody who is important in this country is against you all being equal to white people and quite honestly, I'm against it. Now I'm gonna protect the boy up there because it's my job, but I'll use the power of my badge to stop you all from upsetting the peaceful relationships we have in this city. You all stay in your place, and there'll be no problems. You keep trying to change things, then somebody will get hurt."

Silence engulfed the room. Suddenly the chatter from outside began to increase.

"Give us the nigger. Sheriff McCullough's a nigger lover," the crowd repeated.

"I need to get back to protecting my prisoner," McCullough said as he turned and walked back over to the window and looked out.

"I think this meeting is over," Stradford said. "Let's get out of here."

The five Black men walked out to the car still parked in the alley and drove back across the tracks and up Greenwood Avenue to Smitherman's office building.

***

The entire crew that marched on Memorial Day crowded into the Mann Brothers Grocery Store. This time they did not wear uniforms but had weapons. O.B. stood behind the counter and checked to make sure his pistol was loaded. He looked up just as a young boy came running through the front door.

280

"They getting ready to lynch Dick Rowland," the boy shouted. "I watched them as they were forcing their way up the steps at the courthouse," he continued, gasping for air. "I ran all the way over here from downtown, Mr. Mann. If you all don't act real soon that boy gonna be swinging from a tree branch."

"That's the word, men," O.B. said. "What more do we need to hear?"

"Let's go," Peg Leg Taylor shouted.

"We'll drive just to the other side of the tracks and march the rest of the distance," O.B. said. "Remember what we want to do, and that is help the sheriff protect the prisoner."

"What if he doesn't want our help?" Otis, standing next to Peg Leg Taylor, asked.

"This time he don't have no choice," Peg Leg Taylor fired back with an answer. "We will defend our manhood no matter what."

"We going to let those other folks up at the *Star* know what we're doing?" Claude stepped forward and stared at O. B.

"Yeah, we owe them that much," O.B. said. "I'll go in and let them know we're on our way to defend Miss Damie's boy."

"What if they try to stop us?" Claude asked.

"We're stopping by there only to inform them what we're doing, not to get their permission," Peg Leg Taylor this time answered.

Old Nate made his way up to the counter. "I want to be out front," he said.

"No, Nate, it might get a little nasty out there," O.B. said. "You need to stay back."

"I might need to, but I ain't going to," Nate fired back. "Negroes done lived with the lynching and the rape from them people for too long. After the big war we thought, give it a little time and all the hatred toward us would end. Those peckerwoods only needed some room to heal was the thinking. That's been over fifty years ago, and they ain't healed or changed yet. I'm going with you, and I'm gonna be right up front. I'm feeling like I wannna be a man tonight. No longer a boy or uncle, or nigger no more. Let me go with you, O.B. You got to let me go with you."

"How can I argue with any man who after seventy-five years, insists on being treated like a man."

The other men surrounded Nate, and some patted him on the back. A couple of the older veterans hugged him. O.B. felt the strength of a comradeship building up among these men. Their

281

cause was one and the same. They insisted on manhood.

"We got three trucks and a bunch of cars out front," O.B. said. "Our first stop is on Greenwood." He counted fifty men as they rushed out the door. He was determined to be able to count fifty when they returned from saving that boy's life.

THIRTY • FOUR

Jones smiled across his desk at Wash and Cal sitting in chairs right in front. "You mean she actually gave you three hundred dollars to defend her boy?" he asked.

"Yeah, I actually felt a little guilty taking it," Wash said. "Can you imagine how long it took for her to save that kind of money?"

"I'm sure she had to scrub a whole lot of floors," Cal added.

"You know that boy's going to be out of jail by tomorrow afternoon because they have to drop the charges," Wash said. "I checked with the city attorney's office, and they can't get that girl to confirm anything you wrote about the incident."

"He might be better off hiding in county jail since the crowd outside the courthouse is getting pretty rowdy," Jones said. "They want that boy for their own justice."

"I was down there about an hour ago," Cal said. "And there had to be at least five hundred ready for some action."

"You know them boys across the tracks claimed they won't stand by while one of their kind is hung," Jones said.

"Let 'em try something, and that'll be the end of niggertown," Cal said. "Them boys downtown are armed and ready to use their guns if them coons try anything."

"They'll probably do the same thing they did yesterday when our boys stopped them from marching down Main Street," Wash added. "Thanks to Cal they didn't get very far."

"No, they just turned and retreated like a bunch puppies with their tails between their legs." Cal chuckled.

"What you going to do when the mayor and commissioner

learn that you lied in your story about what that girl said happened to her?" Wash asked.

Jones leaned across his desk. "It's my word against her's. I'm an upstanding newsman, and she's nothing more than a little whore' who you think they going to believe?"

"I better get back down there and take charge," Cal said. He got up out the chair.

"Yeah, I'm going back to the office and kind of monitor what's happening in front of the courthouse from my window," Wash said and also got up. "What you going to do this evening?" Wash asked Jones.

"Tonight is my night to relax," Jones answered and also got up. "Tomorrow I'll be writing about how the Negroes were upset because one of their own was arrested, but they were unable to do anything to help him because of the superior physical capabilities of the white man." He strolled from behind his desk and escorted the two men to the door. "I want them men out front of the courthouse to hang that nigger. It'll be good for our reputation across the country. People will know we maintain strict discipline with our niggers."

Jones placed his hand on Wash's arm. "Tomorrow the Rowland boy will either be released from jail or lynched. Either way he won't go to trial. Are you going to give that old woman her money back?"

"Hell, no," Wash scoffed at the thought.

The two men opened the office door and left.

***

"O.B. you can't be serious?" Gurley shrieked.

Smitherman's office was overflowing with men who had heard what was happening and rushed down to the *Star* office.

"We are serious, and we invite any of you to join us," O.B. said as he stood at the back of the room right in front of the door to the office. "They will not touch a hair on the head of that boy. If they do, blood will be flowing down Boulder Avenue."

"We got the sheriff's word nothing will happen to him," Smitherman spoke up. "He's determined to protect him."

"Yeah, just like they protected the Belton boy last year," O.B. said.

"Looks like you men are ready to fight the war all over again, only right here in Tulsa," Stradford interjected. "It would be better if you could wait until the sheriff called us for back up."

A smirk crossed O.B.'s face. "You know that's not going to happen. He'd let them take that boy and lynch him before he called us to help. I just don't see where we have a choice anymore. We got to go."

"Sounds like you boys going over there looking for a fight and not just to offer help to the sheriff," Smitherman said.

"No, you got this all wrong," O.B. rejoined. "We're going to offer our assistance in case them men attack the courthouse."

Captain Townsend had remained silent all this time, but finally spoke up. "I convinced you boys to march without your weapons yesterday, and that turned badly for you," he said from his chair on the other side of the room. He stood erect just as an old warrior would do. "This time I won't tell you to do that. Just remember when you pull that trigger if you have to, you can't take it back. No matter how much you might regret it, after it's all over, you just can't take it back." Captain slowly walked over to the door and opened it. As he started out he said, "You can't take it back." He finished and closed the door behind him.

"I'm going with you, boys," John Williams said and stood up.

"What?" Gurley said. "You're going back over there after hearing the sheriff promise nothing will happen to that boy."

"I heard him, and I believe he'll do his best. But I also heard him tell us we'll never get equality in this country. He even told us he was opposed to it, so what do all these material possessions mean if he's going to tell us we'll never be equal? 'Bout time we made a statement, and I'm ready to do that." John Williams paused for a moment, then looked directly at O.B. "I'll meet you out front. Got to get my rifle." He hurried out the door.

285

Smitherman finally stood up. "Don't get yourself killed over there," he said. "Don't start nothing with them drunk peckerwoods."

"I gotta go now," O.B. said. "We'll be back when we're satisfied that young fellow is safe." O.B. had tired of all the talk. No need for any more. He closed the door, hurried out of the building and climbed back in the truck. They drove the half block up the street, stopped and picked up John Williams and drove straight up Greenwood Avenue and across the tracks where they planned to settle the score.

Men and women strolling up and down Greenwood Avenue stopped and stared at the caravan of cars and trucks filled with men carrying rifles driving up the street toward the railroad tracks. O.B. could imagine what they must be thinking. He doubted it would be that these Black men had the nerve to invade white Tulsa with weapons.

One man standing at the corner shouted, "Good luck."

O.B. saluted him. The caravan crossed the tracks and traveled toward Sixth Street. They were getting close. O.B. turned around and looked at Nate. The old man's expression was somber and at peace. Momentarily the young warrior's thoughts slipped back to Europe when they marched toward the French front to confront the enemy. This was a new front, however, not in a foreign country but in his hometown. At that moment, it seemed just as foreign as Europe had several years ago. Maybe it was and they had never realized that they were living in a foreign land, even though it was the only home they'd ever known.

The caravan approached the corner of Sixth and Cincinnati, and O.B. signaled for them to all pull up to the curb. The vehicles behind his lead truck pulled over and parked. A cloud cover blocked the moon and stars from providing some light. They couldn't see the four blocks up to Sixth and Boulder. They had no way of knowing the size of the mob out front.

286

"Line up in twos and keep your weapons at the ready position, and let's march forward." O.B. glanced over at Nate who stood on his right. "You all right, old man?" He asked.

"Good as an old man can be, young man," Nate replied.

"Let's move out," O.B. shouted, and the men began a slow trot forward.

O.B. counted the blocks to Boulder as they passed by each one. Finally he could hear the mob calling out to McCullough.

"Why you protecting the nigger?"

"Sheriff McCullough ain't nothing but a nigger lover."

"Maybe we need to hang him along next to that boy."

O.B. could now see the crowd. It was massive, larger than what he'd expected. He took note that they were gathered at least fifty feet back from the building. That gave his men enough room to take positions between the building and the crowd.

A hush came over the crowd as O.B. and his men with guns at the ready position slowly moved in front of the building and faced the mass of men staring up at them. O.B. turned his back to the crowd and called out, "Sheriff McCullough, the veterans are here to offer you support in defense of Dick Rowland, Miss Damie Rowland's son. We promised her that we would return her son to her unharmed."

The silence of the crowd made O.B. wonder why someone in the didn't open fire. He knew they had weapons. Maybe fifty Black men facing them with no fear at all was a daunting sight to them. Just as he turned back to face the door, it swung open and Sheriff McCullough ran out and stood at the top of the stairs.

"What the hell do you think your doing?" the Sheriff shouted.

"We're here to give you backup," O.B. yelled back. "Make sure nothing happens to Miss Damie's boy. Look like you could use some help judging by the size of that crowd out there."

287

"Are you crazy, man?" McCullough walked down a couple of steps. "Do you know what you're doing?" he asked but didn't wait for an answer. "Evidently you don't. Let me inform you those people out there are going to kill all of you if you don't hurry up and get out of here."

"Appears to me they're pretty subdued, not saying anything."

"Man, don't be fooled. Ain't no way white men gonna allow all you to come over here with guns and try to intimidate them."

"We ain't trying to intimidate nobody. Just want to offer our help and make sure that boy is safe."

"I really don't need your help, and that boy is safe. Can't nobody get to him." McCullough pointed to the roof. "First son of a bitch who reaches the top of these stairs going to be shot dead. And that goes for you and your boys, too."

"Can I see the boy? Make sure he's okay."

"Hell, no, you can't see my prisoner. But I guarantee he is safe. The girl has told authorities that Rowland did nothing to her and that she over reacted. They got no case against him, and he'll probably be released in the morning."

"What the hell's going on up there?" A man hollered from the crowd.

Instantly, the veterans aimed their rifles out at the crowd.

"Nothing, and just shaddup out there," McCullough shouted. "Damit man, tell your men not to point their weapons at the crowd," he said to O.B. "Somebody out there gonna get nervous and start shooting."

"Stand down," O.B. shouted, and the veterans returned their weapons to the ready position.

"Now I'm telling you that boy is safe and he'll be released probably sometime tomorrow."

"Why can't I see him?"

"Because we have secured the building so nobody can get up to the fourth floor. Go home so I can get the crowd to also go home. It'll be all right and you all will see that boy tomorrow."

288

O.B. glared hard at McCullough for a good minute, then turned and started back down the steps. "Fall out men, we can go back home," he said.

"We ain't gonna fight?" Otis asked.

"Remember, we only fight when it's necessary, and it ain't necessary right now. Let's get out of here." O.B. led the men back down the steps. When he reached the bottom, Cal jumped in front of him.

"You remember me, don't you nigger?" He asked

"Yeah peckerwood, I remember you," O.B. replied.

"I told you yesterday don't come on this side of town. And what you doing with a gun?"

O.B. pulled his revolver out the holster and pointed it at Cal. "I'll use it if I have to." His words rolled like thunder.

"Nigger, give me that gun," Cal shouted and reached toward the gun in an attempt to wrench it out of O.B.'s hand.

O.B. tried to swing the gun away from Cal so that he couldn't grab it, but the white man took hold of O.B.'s wrist before he could move out of his way. Instinctively, the veteran pulled the trigger.

The shot rang out making a piercing sound, and Cal fell backwards, blood gushing from the wound to his chest.

"That Black son of a bitch shot Cal. He killed him," a man in the crowd shouted.

"It's on, let's get them niggers," another man shouted, and bullets shot out of the guns at the veterans who, outnumbered, began to run for cover.

"The alley," O.B. shouted. "Get over to the alley, take cover and fire back." He noticed Nate had fallen behind; he went back, grabbed him and pulled the old man forward. "Come on, I got to get you to safety," he said.

John Williams kneeled on one knee, aimed his Savage rifle at the crowd and opened fire. The white men stopped to take cover, and that gave O.B. time to get Nate to the alley. He then knelt also and fired back into the crowd. Three of his men were down and gasping for air. Blood covered them, and O.B. knew they would die. His anger was boiling over. He stood and fired away. Peg Leg Taylor grabbed him by the arm and pulled him toward the alley.

289

"That's not the way to do it," Peg Leg Taylor shouted over the sounds of gunfire. "We got to get back across the tracks and secure our position."

O.B. turned to run back into the alley and stumbled over a body lying face up on the ground. "Oh, hell, no," he shouted. "Nate, can you get up?"

Nate did not move. Blood flowed freely from a gunshot wound to his stomach. He showed no signs of life. "No, no, not Nate," O.B. continued to shout.

"He's gone, O.B.," John Williams shouted also. "Nothing you can do for him. Let's get out of here."

"Hell, no, I'm not gonna leave him here so these bastards can kick, stomp and spit on his body." O.B. handed John Williams his rifle, reached down and picked up the old man. He threw him over his shoulder and ran with him toward the alley.

John Williams again got down on one knee and covered the two men until they disappeared into the alley. He then got up and moved backward while still firing at the mob until he also made it to safety in the alley. Using the alleys, they made it back to the cars, and O.B. put Nate down in the back seat, climbed in the front and the driver took off back across the railroad tracks. Most of the men had already loaded back into the cars and were also crossing over toward Archer Street, making their way back to Greenwood Avenue where they would position themselves for the shoot out.

"We need to make a stand right at Greenwood and Archer," O.B. said to John Williams and Peg Leg Taylor.

"We'll have a perfect shot at them from the second story windows of the confectionery," John Williams said. "They'll be setting ducks if they cross the tracks there, if they're coming."

"You know damn well they're coming 'cause we left at least ten of them dead in the street," O.B. bellowed. He watched as the other cars drove in different directions, some turning on Detroit Avenue, some on Elgin. Their driver turned onto Greenwood Avenue, pulled up and parked in front of the Williams Confectionery. O.B. jumped out and carried Nate's body up the stairs to the second floor with John Williams and Peg Leg Taylor following closely behind.

A shocked Loula stood in the middle of the living room as the three men rushed past her and young Bill to the bedroom. O.B. gently placed Nate's body on the bed; then he and Peg Leg Taylor knocked out the two windows facing Greenwood. John Williams took a position in the adjoining bedroom, and the three men prepared for the invasion from across the tracks.

THIRTY•FIVE

"It's like a got damn madhouse out here," McCullough shouted into the phone at Mayor Evans. "All hell has broken loose. Them damn Negroes came here with loaded weapons, and when I'd convinced them that I had everything under control, that damn Klan member attacked the leader of the Negroes and all hell broke loose."

"What's happening now and how many white men are dead or wounded?" Mayor Evans asked.

"The boys chased them back across the tracks, so everything is calmed down over here. We got six dead bodies still in the street."

"They're all Negroes?"

"No, two of our boys got killed, including Cal."

"Damit, Blacks killing white people. We're in for a long night. When white folks find out about this, they're going to cross those tracks and kill every black person over there."

"I don't know if we have enough men to put this down," McCullough said.

"Talk to Gustafson and get the local police on the job. We got to stop this from becoming an outright slaughter. Got to try to keep the mob on this side of the tracks and get them that already crossed over, back here. I'll call Atkinson and make sure he pressures that sorry son of a bitch Gustafson to do his job."

"Mayor, I think you'd better alert the governor and Major Bell of the National Guard. I can hear a second wave of people building up right outside the building. Now with the two dead white men they're going to want Dick Rowland more than ever."

"I'll do that, but you need to get those dead white bodies off the street."

"I can't move my men, especially not now."

"Then call Gustafson and tell him to get some of his boys over there to move those bodies. The longer they lay out there, the angrier those boys going to get. I'll call Governor Robertson as soon as we get off the phone."

McCullough hung up the pone and quickly moved back over to the window. He peered down, and what he saw shocked him. A massive gang of men, women and children had gathered out front. He couldn't actually believe that they seemed so joyous and excited, just as if some great festivity was about to begin.

"What's wrong with these people?" he whispered as he walked back over to his desk and picked up the phone to call Gustafson. "Police Chief Gustafson," he said to the operator. The police chief picked up on the first ring.

"What the hell did you let happen over there?" Gustafson yelled into the phone.

McCullough held back. Instead of attacking this man, he calmly said, "We got a real problem building up over here. We got dead bodies out in the street, and we have an angry crowd outside the courthouse.

"What the hell do you want me to do? That's your problem," Gustafson continued yelling. "They figured you could handle the prisoner better than me, so now you handle it."

The Sheriff wanted to explode, but again reason prevailed over emotions. "Lookit, chief, this is not time for us to fight. We got a much bigger battle on our hands than the one that exists between us. We're law enforcement for the city and county of Tulsa, and now its time for us to exercise that collective power together and put an end to this uprising. The mayor instructed me to contact you, and tell you that your men need to get over here and help out."

"I'm short of men tonight," Gustafson said in a much calmer tone. "I got three men and myself. The rest of my men are out on patrol. We'll come over there and see what we can do."

292

"Hurry before this thing explodes. We got to get these dead white men around to the back alley. We don't need nothing to rile these people anymore that what they already are. Some of them got a gun in one hand and a bottle of whiskey in the other."

"We're on our way," Gustafson finished, and the two men hung up the phone.

***

From his perch in a second story bedroom of the confectionery, O.B. could see down Archer back toward Cincinnati. He watched as the first wave of white men ran up Archer, obviously prepared to shoot any Negro found out on the street. He knew they were in for a surprise because his men had positioned themselves tactically after crossing the tracks and heading back toward Greenwood. He was right. Just as the white men reached the crossing at Archer and Cincinnati, his men opened fire from inside homes and businesses along Archer. The white men instantly stopped as five of their men were shot on the spot. They turned around and ran back toward the tracks into South Tulsa. In this exchange, O.B. did not lose any of his men. A victory for the good guys, he thought. But white men lay dead on the ground, and for that reason he knew the peace would not last.

He looked over at Peg Leg Taylor who was perched at the other window in the room. Now with a break in the shooting, he had a minute to reflect on what was happening and on the death of Nate. The old man had told him that he wanted to be a man before he died. He had accomplished that when he stood up before being shot down. O.B. felt the same and knew he would die that night before he would concede his weapon and his dignity to any man.

Peg Leg Taylor finally looked his way. "You think it's over?" he asked.

"Not by a long shot," O.B. answered. "They're coming, and it's going to be in large numbers."

"I ain't afraid to die," Peg Leg Taylor said. "Old Nate died a man and I wanna die the same way."

"Ain't nobody gonna die. We'll weather this storm, and maybe after this, they'll leave us alone."

Suddenly, flames from a fire down Archer at Cincinnati lit up the sky.

"Hell, they're lighting fires," O.B. shouted.

John Williams ran over to the room. "Look at what those rotten bastards are doing," he yelled. "That's their plan. They're going to burn us out.

O.B. felt helpless as he watched at least twenty white men cross over the tracks and run up Archer. Seconds later, at least thirty Black veterans stepped out from the alley and fired at the white men. They hit four who fell to the ground and the others scattered, running for shelter behind a building on the railroad grounds. The shooting stopped, and O.B. ran into the dining room area, grabbed the telephone and dialed the fire department.

"You have to hurry to Cincinnati and Archer," he yelled into the phone. There's a fire burning out of control."

"Sorry, we've been given orders not to cross the tracks for any fires between Cincinnati and Greenwood on that side of town," a voice said on the other end.

"What the hell? You just going to let the building burn down?" He asked.

"Ain't nothing we can do; you'll just have to let the fire burn out."

O.B. slammed the phone back into the cradle and hurried into the bedroom. "I think you're right," he said to Peg Leg Taylor and John Williams. "Fire departments got orders not to come on this side of town to put out the fires."

"What else could you expect from these peckerwoods?" Peg Leg Taylor said. "How long you expect we ought to stay here?"

"Till morning, O.B. said. "Ain't nothing we can do with that fire, and those boys will probably stop the mob from coming back over starting any more fires. Just in case they try the same thing here, we'll be ready for them. Then we'll see what happens in the morning."

"Daddy, you think it's over?" Billy suddenly appeared at the

294

entrance to the room. "We got our prom tomorrow night."

"Yeah, son it's over," John Williams said and looked over at O.B. and Peg Leg Taylor. "Go on back to bed, and everything will be just fine."

Billy stood there and stared at the three grown men who stared back at him. He then turned and ran back to the other end of the apartment.

***

All three girls had squeezed into Veneice's bed. They lay there staring at the ceiling, each lost deep in thoughts. Images of dancing tomorrow night at the prom made it practically impossible for Veneice to fall off to sleep.

"I can't believe it's almost here," Ruth finally broke the silence.

"I know, and I won't be able to sleep tonight," Veneice said. "First thing in the morning I'm going to lay my dress out and have everything ready when it's time to get dressed."

"Why I got to sleep in the middle?" Esther complained. "I'm a guest, and, Veneice, you should be in the middle."

Veneice jumped out of bed. "I'm getting me some water, I'm thirsty. I'll get in the middle when I come back." She left the room and crept down the hall toward the kitchen. But she suddenly stopped when she heard Momma and Poppa talking.

"They killed some white men over at the courthouse," Poppa said.

"What were they doing over there, anyway?" Momma asked.

"Claimed they was trying to help the sheriff guard Dick Rowland from being lynched."

Veneice felt a chill shoot through her body. In history class at school they had read about a number of lynchings in Texas, Mississippi and Louisiana, and now they were talking about lynching Dick Rowland. All the girls had a crush on him because he was so cute.

"With them Negroes having killed them white folks, no telling

295

what's going to happen in the morning," Poppa said.

"What you mean?'

"If them white folks invade this side of town, them veteran Negroes and some of the other men gonna fight back."

Veneice couldn't hold back. She might get in trouble, but had to know. She ran into the room. "Poppa, they're not going to call off our prom, are they?" she asked.

"Girl, what you doing out of bed?" Momma asked.

"I was thirsty and wanted something to drink," Veneice answered. "Poppa, they ain't going to mess up our prom tomorrow with no lynching are they?"

"No, baby, everything'll be all right; now get your water and get back in your bedroom with your friends."

Veneice walked back out of the parlor and into the kitchen. She filled her glass with cold water, gulped it down and ran back to the bedroom.

"What's wrong?" Esther asked.

"Nothing." Veneice climbed over her friend and settled in the middle of the bed.

"Something's wrong," Esther persisted. "You got this funny kind of look you get when you ain't sure of something, don't she, Ruth?"

"Yeah, like all the times you didn't know how to tell Verby yes. You had this old pokey look on your face." Ruth twisted her face in order to imitate Veneice. She and Esther laughed.

"I'm ready to go to sleep," Veneice scowled.

"Okay, if you say so," Esther said. "But you're in the middle for the rest of the night."

"I know it."

"Yeah, something's bothering you." Esther turned her back and settled in. "Hope you're in a better mood in the morning. Tomorrow is a very special day, and we don't need no unhappy face."

THIRTY•SIX

Gustafson along with Pack and Carmichael stopped dead in their tracks as they stepped outside police headquarters. A large contingent of men was marching down Second Street toward them. The chief figured the crowd had come from the county courthouse to the city jail, and that meant they planned to confront him about the killing of white men by a mob of niggers. He stood there prepared as the irate men approached him.

"Niggers killing white men and that damn sheriff ain't doing a damn thing about it," a man who was out in front shouted. "We were invaded by a mob of niggers, and now we got to go take over that part of town, all of them coons and I mean all of them and put them in cages where they'll never be a threat to white people again."

"I don't have enough men to do nothing like that," Gustafson shouted. "Tonight there's just me and my two deputies and five men out on patrol."

"Then, got dammit we'll do it ourselves," the lead man shouted.

"You all can't take the law into your hands," Gustafson continued shouting. "I can't let you do that." He had forgotten about his conversation with McCullough. He had his own crisis to deal with.

"You're gonna turn against white people too?" The man approached the chief. "You gonna have white people fighting white people to protect niggers."

Carmichael moved in close to the chief and said. "Deputize them, then we won't have to fight them."

Pack who had also moved in close exclaimed. "No, you can't do that. You can't give these people that kind of power. They'll go over there and destroy everyone and everything."

"Step back," Carmichael growled.

"Okay, stop it," Gustafson intervened. "Pack, go home and get your family out of the Greenwood area."

"Chief, you can't do this. It'll be a slaughter," Pack pleaded. "Most of the people over there don't even know what's going on. You'll have a lot of innocent victims."

"Your people should have thought about that before they killed them white folks. This isn't about that boy in jail no more. This is about power," Gustafson said. "Niggers got to be taught a lesson. Got to be beat into submission."

"Chief, you can't—"

"Go home, Pack," Gustafson cut him off. "Get out of here. Go on back across the tracks before these folks forget you're a good nigger."

Pack glared at the chief, then stared out into the crowd. "God help us," he said, turned and went back into the building.

"All right, I want you men to line up right out front," he shouted. "We're going to deputize all of you and then we're going across those tracks and arrest them niggers who caused all this trouble."

***

Pack scrambled across the tracks and up Greenwood past a marauding group of veterans who had strategically positioned themselves along the streets. He had no trouble making it to the Gurley Hotel. He ran through the lobby and up the stairway to the third floor, down the hall and banged on the door to the apartment.

"Mr. Gurley, you gotta open the door," he shouted. "You gotta open the door."

After a couple minutes the door swung open. "What's going

on?" Gurley asked. "Homer, you look like you saw a ghost."

"Mr. Gurley, it's worst than a ghost," Pack exclaimed as he stepped inside the apartment. "You gotta warn the people that they coming after them. They're angry 'cause white men got shot and killed by them veterans."

"Calm down, man," Gurley said. "Come and sit in the kitchen." The two men walked into the kitchen and sat at the table. Emma came out of the bedroom and stood in the doorway.

"What happened this evening?" Gurley asked.

"Evidently, O.B. Mann got into a fight in front of the courthouse with a man named Cal who was a known member of the KKK." Pack paused to catch his breath.

Emma rushed over to the kitchen counter, grabbed an empty glass and filled it with water. She gave it to Pack.

"Thank you, ma'am," he said as he gulped it down. "Once O.B. shot that white man, all hell broke loose. You haven't heard any of the shooting?"

Gurley looked over at Emma. Neither of them had heard the shooting. "No we didn't," Gurley said. "What's happening right now?"

"Them veterans done set up outlook posts right at the corner of Greenwood and Archer and all down Archer Street to Cincinnati, and they just waiting for them white folks to come across the tracks with their guns blazing.

"Did you tell Gustafson what's happening?"

"Hell, he's deputizing the mob so that he won't have to fight white folks to protect Negroes. By deputizing them, the mob becomes the law."

"You mean the chief is joining in with the mob?" Emma asked from back at the entrance.

"Yes ma'am, I guess that's one way to look at it." Pack turned and looked back at Emma.

"You tell anybody else about this?" Gurley asked.

Pack looked back at Gurley. "No, I came right over here."

"So the veterans are positioned to fight right at the corner of Archer and Greenwood?"

"That's where they are right now, at least some of them. I heard that they're located all along Archer and ran some white boys back over the tracks up around Cincinnati." Pack swallowed the rest of his water. "Mr. Gurley, you and Mrs. Gurley got to get out of here before that mob starts across them railroad tracks. If you don't, I'm afraid it's going to be too late." Pack jumped up from the chair. "Please, Mr. Gurley you're a good man and I don't want to see anything happen to you, that's why I risked my job coming over here. You got to get out now."

Gurley also got up and walked Pack to the front door. "Thank you," he said, opened the door and watched as one of the only Negro policemen on the Tulsa Police Force disappeared down the steps.

***

Stradford briskly walked the block and a half, crossed over Greenwood and hurried up the stairs to the Williams' residence on the third floor of the confectionery. He knocked once, and the door swung open.

"There in the back in the bedroom," Loula said and waved him inside.

"Evening, Loula," Stradford said as he walked past her, down the hall and into the bedroom. He glanced at Nate still on the bed.

O.B. looked at Stradford from his position in front of the window. Peg Leg Taylor had drifted off to sleep.

"What happened over there?" Stradford asked.

"We did what we had to do," O.B. said.

"And what was that, to get into a shoot out with a bunch of people who far outnumber us?"

O.B. banged his huge fist down on the windowsill. The sudden sound caused Peg Leg Taylor to jerk straight up. "What the hell was that, a gunshot? They started shooting again?"

O.B. ignored the question. "We didn't go in there looking for a fight. That little peckerwood who confronted us when we marched yesterday tried to take my weapon, and I shot him."

"You just shot him? You didn't try to talk to him?" Stradford asked.

"The time for talking to these peckerwoods is over. Now it's time for fighting.

"Just how do you plan to win this fight?"

"By shooting more of them than what shoots us," O.B. fired back.

Stradford shook his head from side to side. "You just started a race war."

Again, O.B. banged his fist on the windowsill, harder this time than the first. "We didn't start nothing," he shouted. "They started it when they hung that young boy in Muskogee a few years ago and when they rape our women and every time they call men like you and me, boy or nigger."

"And when they laid my leg across the railroad track and laughed when the train cut it off," Peg Leg Taylor chimed in. He'd never before told anyone how he had lost half his leg. This was the right time and the right folks to hear it.

"What the hell are we supposed to do? How much abuse is one race of people suppose to take?" O.B. asked rhetorically. "Not any more."

"All right, I'm with you all, and the first one of them bastards that tries to harm my family or destroy my property, I'm going to lay them out on the street. But you boys know damn well we can fight, but we can't win."

301

"Yes, we can, Mr. Stradford. Yes we can," Peg Leg Taylor said. "We lose only if we throw these guns down and fall back in line like the safe Negroes they want us to be. Sometimes death can mean freedom."

John Williams walked into the room with his Savage rifle on his shoulders. "Old Nate was willing to die to be a man." He glanced over at the body still on the bed.

Stradford also stared down at Nate.

"His body's dead, and his spirit is free," Peg Leg Taylor added.

"Looks like you boys made up your mind," Stradford said.

"You going to join us?" O.B. asked

"I'm going to join you, but not here. If they come across those tracks ready to fight, then I'll join and fight back. I will protect my property and my family."

"That's all a man can be asked to do," John Williams said.

"That's all a man should be expected do. I'm going on back to my business, load my guns and wait to see what happens." Stradford stared hard at each of them.

"Tomorrow is Thursday, and let's hope our streets and your hotel and my theater are filled with the maids and all the men folk that come to party on maid's day off. Let's hope everything is back to normal," John Williams said.

"Let's do more than hope. Let's pray," Stradford said. "Good luck to you boys, and maybe we'll see each other in the morning for breakfast at Pressley's." Stradford finished, turned and walked away.

THIRTY•SEVEN

After his confrontation with O.B., Captain Townsend decided to go home and pray that those men wouldn't get killed going across those tracks with all those guns. He had already missed the weekly family dinner at his son's house and thought about going over there after leaving Smitherman's office, but felt too exhausted.

Captain Townsend sat on his couch in the living room and opened up his Bible, but his thoughts kept racing back to his younger days in Memphis, Tennessee, when he had the same fire in his belly as the Mann boy did. But white folks had an answer to that fire, and it was the rope and the mob. He barely escaped that fate back in 1888 when he had to get out of Memphis because white folks thought he had become too uppity. Enough lynching, whippings and rapes have a tendency to take the fire right out of a man. It forces him to make adjustments in his life and rationalizations for his submission to abuse. Negroes couldn't be men and expect to survive in the South, and that to him was the tragedy of being born a man and black. Those were his thoughts when he heard the first shots ring out.

The Captain put his Bible down, hurried over to the front door and opened it. The sound was deafening as he heard repetitive gunshots that seemed to be moving closer to Archer Street from across the tracks. He stepped all the way out on the porch. At the same time, a number of neighbors also stepped out onto to their porches. Staring up Cincinnati toward the railroad track he finally saw what he had feared from the moment O.B. told all of them that he and his men were going into Tulsa to rescue the boy. There had to be at least thirty Black men running back toward Archer Street. They ran about a hundred yards, stopped, kneeled down and fired their rifles at a mob of white men chasing and firing at them.

One of the retreating men was hit in the back and fell to the ground. Instead of stopping to help the man, the veterans kept firing and retreating. Instantly, the mob was upon the wounded man. A short stocky man who Captain had seen on numerous times aimed his rifle down at the wounded man and pulled the trigger. The veteran's body gyrated for at least thirty seconds and then went still.

At that moment, the veterans knelt down and blasted two white men. They lay there as the mob either walked around them jumped over them, ignoring their wounded and bleeding bodies. The veterans crossed over Detroit Avenue and kept running toward Greenwood. Again, one of retreating men fell to the ground while the veterans turned, knelt down and released another volley of shots piercing to the ears. The air smelled of sulphur. Suddenly, the whites stopped their hot pursuit and started running back toward the Frisco Railroad Depot.

The Captain had positioned himself on the side of his house facing away from Archer for safety reasons. A volley of shots rang out as the mob continued its retreat back across the tracks. Not far behind them were at least forty Blacks firing away. These men were not a part of O.B's original crew. The Captain could only surmise that word was spreading throughout Greenwood that whites had invaded, and were set on destroying the Negro community.

The commotion had quieted down, and Captain Townsend walked back inside his house. He hastily returned to the couch, exhausted from the confusion that seemed to be gripping Greenwood and turning it into a killing field. He waited a few minutes, then snatched his Bible and leafed through it until he came to the right chapter and verse. "And when they shall have finished their testimony, the beast that ascendeth out of the bottomless pit shall overcome them, and kill them." The Captain closed his Bible shut, grabbed his favorite picture of Sophorina and hastened out of the house. He needed to get to his son's house and warn them that the beast of "Revelations" was loose, and even though he had momentarily retreated back across the tracks, he would be back.

Captain Townsend felt exhausted as he flopped down on the

couch in Dr. Jackson's parlor. No one had answered when he knocked on the front door, and knowing that often they would be upstairs and not hear a knock, he let himself in and called out, "Anybody here. You need to get down here right away. All hell has broken out, and we need to get out of Tulsa tonight."

He laid his head back, closed his eyes and a vivid picture of the slaughter passed through his mind. How did those boys ever believe they could win this battle? Put up a good fight maybe, but in the long run they would lose. But it was too late for reflection and contemplation. It was important that he save his family, his two sons and his daughter and her family.

"Poppa, you all right? How long you been here?" Julia asked as she strolled into the parlor.

"None of us are all right," he exclaimed "Where is your husband?"

"He went over to Frissell Hospital. Evidently there was some kind of gunfight around Greenwood and Archer. White folks shot some Negro veterans in a skirmish."

"That's why I'm here," Captain's voice continued to rise. "According to 'Revelations,' the beast is loose and is about to attack our community and destroy us all. We have to get out of here before it's too late. You need to call Andrew and tell him to get back over here."

"Slow down, Poppa. What are you talking about?"

"Evidently them war veterans went over to the county courthouse to save the Rowland boy and ended up shooting some of them white folks. That's unleashed the beast and I watched some of the shooting from my yard."

"You're not making sense talking about shootings and quoting from 'Revelations.' Are you sure you're feeling well?"

305

"I'm feeling fine, Julia, now please call Andrew and tell him to get on home so we can get out of here."

Julia walked over to the table and removed the phone from the cradle. "Yes give me Frissell Hospital, please," she said while still staring at her father-in-law with a worried expression across her face.

***

Mabel and Pressley reserved Wednesday nights for the detailed and tedious work involved in owning two businesses. They sat at one of the tables in the restaurant with receipts and money spread out in front of them. Tomorrow morning, Mabel would take the week's earnings and deposit it in the bank. She sat quietly doing the chores in front of her when she heard a loud bang, breaking her concentration. Momentarily, she glanced over at the door and then at Pressley.

Pressley jumped up and walked briskly to the front, peeked out the window, turned and looked at Mabel. "It's Officer Pack," he said, then unlocked and opened the door.

"Evening Officer," he said. "What brings you around here this time of evening?" He waved Pack inside.

"There's been some shooting going on at the courthouse, and its spread to this side of town," Pack said.

Mabel stopped counting the money and scrutinized Pack. "Shooting? What kind of shooting?' she asked.

"The veterans shot up some white men over at the courthouse, and now the whites are organizing to get even. I believe sometime tonight or tomorrow they going to come over here looking for the veterans who participated in that attack. It might not be safe for you all to be out tonight," he said.

"Heaven help us," Mabel cried out..

"I knew that hothead O.B. Mann would eventually cause something like this to happen," Pressley said. "What should we do?"

"Probably go home but lock up real good," Pack advised. "Try to weather this storm, and hopefully everything will be calmed down by tomorrow morning."

"You think they going to come this far across the railroad tracks?" Mabel asked.

"I really don't know," Pack answered. "But when I left from over there, the chief was deputizing everybody who had a gun and a desire to kill Negroes."

"How many been killed?" Mabel asked.

"Don't really know. But there was a lot of shooting over at Cincinnati and Archer. Left bodies all along the road, both white and Negroes."

"We'd better get out of here," Pressley said.

"Yeah, and I need to hit some of these other businesses if they're still open," Pack said walking back over to the door. "And I sure got to get over to Miss Damie's and warn her. They sure going to come looking for her."

"Thank you," Mabel said as she watched Pressley unlock and open the door. "Let's pray this passes."

"I'll be back for breakfast in the morning," Pack said to Pressley.

"We plan to be open," Pressley said as the two men shook hands and Pack disappeared out the door.

Pressley closed and locked the door then stood staring back at his wife with his hand still on the knob. "You worried?" he asked.

Mabel sat back down at the table and stuffed money into a satchel. "Not for us but for all those men involved in the shooting," she said without looking up. "They're going to catch them men, and they'll kill them."

"We need to get home," Pressley said.

"No, we need to get over to the church and pray," Mabel corrected him. "It's Wednesday, and usually prayer service goes on until eleven. Let's hurry and we can catch the last of prayer service. Mount Zion's going to be a praying church tonight." 307

THIRTY•EIGHT

"The niggers killed Cal. The niggers killed Cal," Gustafson heard the continuous repeated chants outside police headquarters. Just an hour ago, he had deputized over five hundred men, but the crowd had increased since then and these men were waiting for some action. He looked out the window and frowned as the crowd had doubled. Their attitude was changing, becoming more belligerent and loud. The chief knew that was the result of the alcoholics joining the crowd. The later in the night, the more drunks would show up. He also knew nothing would satisfy the appetites of the men but nigger blood.

"What's a nigger doing with a gun anyway?" Someone in the crowd shouted.

"Yeah, we need more weapons and ammunition," still another man shouted.

"Across the street," someone called out.

Willard's Sporting Good Shop, Gustafson thought. Damn, they're going to break in across the street. Just as the thought hit him, he heard the crashing sound of glass. He rushed to the door and looked out at pandemonium. Men came running out of the sporting good shop with rifles and pistols and were stuffing ammunition in their pockets. He had no way to stop them with only himself and two other officers in the building. Gustafson needed some backup. He went back into his office to the desk and picked up the phone.

"Connect me with Major James A. Bell," he said. After a short pause, Gustafson continued. "Major, I believe we're going to need some help this evening. The niggers been driving around town in a threatening mood, talking about killing white folks."

"That must be why some white men tried to break into the National Guard Armory and steal weapons," Major Bell said on the other end.

"They already broke into a gun shop over here and loaded up on weapons and ammunition," Gustafson said.

"Who, the niggers?"

"No, the white men. If we don't get some help, there might be a race war tonight."

"I'll contact Lieutenant Rooney and have him alert the Guard and get them down to the police station in the next couple hours."

"That'll do the job," Gustafson said, and the two men hung up.

"We got one," the crowd roared. "We got one. Somebody get a rope."

Carmichael flung open the door and ran inside. "Got damn if they don't have a nigger," he shouted. "It's blind Tom from the corner."

"Blind Tom, the crippled?" Gustafson asked as he walked to the door still halfway open.

"Where you going?" Carmichael asked as he followed the chief out the door.

"They can't lynch blind Tom," the chief scowled. "That poor boy ain't never hurt nobody."

"Try telling that to them men out there."

"I plan to." Gustafson rushed out the front door of headquarters and ran into the street. "My God, what's happening?" he whispered as he fought his way through the throng of men, all staring down Sixth toward Main at something that had captured their attention. Gustafson couldn't see over the top of the crowd, and his movement to the front where the action was going on slowed to a snail's pace. But the periodic cheers from the mob told him something was happening.

Instantly, the men broke out in loud and raucous laughter. What the hell could they possibly be doing to the blind nigger that it caused such laughter, he thought, as he pushed harder and elbowed his way forward.

Just as Gustafson neared the front of the crowd, the mob cleared the street as a car slowly worked its way toward where the chief stood. The men were pointing to the back of the Ford and laughing. When the car finally passed by, Gustafson looked down at blind Tom dragging behind with his head bouncing up and down on the cobblestones. The man was screaming. Gustafson was too late to help him. Once the Ford cleared the crowd, the driver floored the accelerator and headed for Greenwood where they probably would deposit the body. The Chief slowly walked back to his office listening to the cheers of the mob and feeling sick to his stomach.

***

O.B's eyes were heavy and his head started to fall forward just as he saw the black Ford speeding across the tracks and come to a stop right at Greenwood and Archer. He stared at the two white men who jumped out of the car and ran to the back. He couldn't figure out what they were doing.

"You see them peckerwoods get out that car?" He asked Peg Leg Taylor who had just looked up.

"Yeah, what the hell they doing?"

"Don't know but it can't be good." O.B. took aim, fired one round and hit the driver just as he had run back to the front and was about to open the door. The man instantly fell to the ground.

"I got the other one." Peg Leg Taylor took aim and squeezed the trigger. The bullet hit the man and practically lifted him off his feet as he fell backward to the ground.

"Good shot," O.B. said.

"Back at ya," Peg Leg Taylor agreed.

"Gotta see what they were so anxious to drop off in the middle of the street," O.B. said. He got up from his prone position on the floor. "Cover me," he said and scrambled out of the room.

John Williams met O.B. in the hallway. I'll go down with you."

The warriors made it down the steps and out into the street.

311

"We got you covered, O.B.," a voice called out from the other side of the street. He looked over at Hal's Pool Hall directly across the street and saw at least a half dozen men with guns pointed toward the railroad track.

"The men are ready and waiting," O.B. said to John Williams.

O.B. cautiously approached the Ford on the driver's side, and John Williams from the passenger side. As he neared the rear of the vehicle O.B. felt sick to the stomach. Blind Tom's entire body was drenched in blood, and his right arm had been practically severed from his body.

"Those animals," John Williams shouted coming up on the other side. "Those sick bastards."

"How the hell did we get stuck in this world with these people?" O.B. asked.

In a sudden burst of energy, John Williams aimed his Savage across the tracks and began firing. "Come on you sick bastards. Come on," he shouted.

"No John," O.B. said. "Save that ammunition. We gonna need all we got. They just let us know they're coming."

O.B. handed his rifle to John Williams, took his knife and cut the rope from Blind Tom's body. He picked the dead man off the ground. "I'm going to carry him down the street to Jackson's. They can take care of his body the right way. Then I'm gonna carry Nate over there. Mr. Jackson gonna be real busy tonight."

O.B. walked past the confectionery, down the block to Jackson's Mortuary. John Williams followed closely behind in order to protect his friend.

312

***

Another roar of the crowd in front of the police headquarters brought Gustafson back to his feet, and he rushed over to the window. He figured the crowd had probably found a second victim to torture. Peering out the window he thought that maybe it hadn't been a good idea to deputize all those men. He might not be able to control them when they finally decide to invade Greenwood.

But then it wasn't his fault, and he had no reason to feel guilty. The damn niggers should never have come across the tracks with weapons, and they sure as hell shouldn't have shot a white man. After all these years, they knew the rules of the game. When the servant disobeys the master, he must be punished, and blind Tom was simply a warning to the niggers.

The crowd's cheers grew much louder as Gustafson watched the National Guard unit march down Second Street toward the police station. "Thank God, maybe we can get some order around here," he whispered, then scurried over to the door and made it outside just as the Guard stopped right in front of the headquarters.

Lieutenant Rooney met Gustafson at the front of the building. His men stood right behind him.

"Thank God you all are here," Gustafson said as he shook Lieutenant Rooney's hand.

"Major said you got some problems across the tracks," Rooney said.

"Niggers are out of control. They attacked some of our men over at the courthouse earlier this evening," Gustafson answered. "Heard they'd planned to break that boy who attacked a white girl yesterday out of jail."

"We'll see about that," Rooney said. "We're going to set up some road blocks on all the streets leading from North Tulsa over here. And we're going to send patrols up and down the main thoroughfares over here, and start arresting any Negroes on this side of the tracks."

"Do you need any of my boys to help?" Gustafson asked.

"Yeah, you need to deploy them at all points along the railroad tracks and tell them to hold off attacking until we got everything lined up just right. You got men down here and you got some over at the courthouse. We need to get them all deployed strategically."

"Anything I can do to help?" Gustafson again volunteered

"Not now," Rooney answered. "We'll take it from here. Our men and your deputies will go in together." Rooney turned and faced his guardsmen along with the men who had been deputized earlier. "Listen up, men, if you follow orders and do what I ask you to do, we should be finished here and home early in the morning. Sergeant, get the men positioned at the locations we discussed earlier and make sure everybody's got plenty of ammunition. When the whistle sounds, we'll be ready to teach them animals over there what happens when you challenge white people."

Gustafson smiled as he listened to the lieutenant lay out the battle plan to obliterate the niggers. It was just too bad that white men had to die to make this finally happen, but a few lives were worth what obviously was going to be the end result.

***

"What the hell's happening down there?" Governor James Robertson asked the mayor.

Evans held the telephone receiver in one hand while staring out a third floor window in the Tulsa Hotel. For the past four hours he'd watched the crowd build up at the police station. By his estimation now there had to be over a thousand men carrying guns and liquor bottles crowding the street. He'd also watched as the two men snatched Blind Tom off his cart, tied him behind their car and drove down Second Street with his head bouncing against the cobblestone. He glared down at the local National Guard when they showed up and just mingled with the crowd, evidently with no intention of policing the situation. He knew all hell was about to break out, and it was time for the state to get involved.

"It's about time you sent the National Guard unit from Oklahoma City down here," Evans said. "About an hour ago, the men tied an old blind and crippled Negro behind their car and drug him to the other side of the tracks. We need help, Governor, and we need it before this becomes a national tragedy."

314

"State law requires me to get something in writing, signed by you, the sheriff and a state judge before I can intervene. Can you get that to me in the next couple hours? In the meantime, I'll notify General Barrett to prepare the National Guard Unit from up here to prepare to move out and be down there by the morning."

"I'll get on it right away, Governor, and make sure they get down here as fast they possibly can. We are in serious trouble."

"You get done what you have to, and we'll put an end to this right away."

Evans hung up the receiver and then dialed another number. "Give me Judge Ralph Hanson."

"Mayor, do you know what time it is?"

"Hell, yes, I know what time it is. Now get the judge on the damn phone."

***

This silence was menacing, almost threatening in some bizarre way. O.B. had experienced this same kind of quiet over in Argonne Forest in France. To the men in the trenches, the silence was deafening because they anxiously waited for it to be shattered with a barrage of gunfire. He had no idea what was happening across those tracks. Even though he couldn't hear the sounds over there, he knew there was a lot of activity. That activity would soon come hurtling across the tracks at them.

After dropping Blind Tom's body at the mortuary, O.B. had climbed the steps at the confectionery and picked up Nate and carried him over there also. Two Black men dead, and no telling how many more scattered on the grounds between Greenwood and Boulder and Sixth Avenue where it all got started. There was no way this could end well, and had he decided when they left earlier in the evening to go over to the courthouse that he might have to give up his life. He was all right with that possibility.

O.B. took his eyes off the street long enough to look at Peg Leg Taylor whose head kept nodding as he dozed off. He pulled out his pocket watch and checked the time. Four thirty, and they had just about made it through the night with very little fighting. 315

"Whatcha gonna do if we make it through till tomorrow and nothing happens?" He asked Peg Leg Taylor.

"Go home, take a bath and sleep all day. How 'bout you?"

"Go pray somewhere at some church."

"You starting to feel the worst part is over?" Peg Leg leaned way up on his shoulders.

"If that's true we got through this with very little damage."

"Yeah, you're right, that is if you consider at least ten men dead to include Blind Tom and Nate that lightly."

"I guess you're right," O.B. conceded.

"By no stretch of the imagination is this over," Peg Leg Taylor sighed.

"You know they're coming and they're gonna want to kill us all," O.B. said.

"Let's make sure we kill them first," Peg Leg Taylor rejoined. "That way we don't have to worry about dying, at least not now."

Both men looked back at the doorway as John Williams walked in. "I just sent Loula and Billy out of the county till this is over. They're on their way to Vinita."

"That makes sense," Peg Leg Taylor said.

"What the hell are they waiting for?" John Williams asked.

"This is the first phase of the punishment," Peg Leg Taylor said. "Work on our minds."

"Germans were great at that," O.B. added.

"What's the second phase?" John Williams asked.

"To attack and kill as many as they can and all of us if possible." Peg Leg Taylor got up to stretch.

"Well I got the third phase," O.B. said.

"What's that?" Peg Leg lay back on his side.

316 "Kill as many of those folks as I possibly can."

"Think we ought to try and rest 'cause when it happens, we're gonna be awfully busy," Peg Leg Taylor suggested.

"You all go on and rest," O.B. said. "Not me. I want to be wide awake when the first one of them peckerwoods sets his feet on this side of the railroad tracks.

THIRTY•NINE
June 1, 1921

O.B's head snapped straight up as the loud shrill sound of a factory whistle broke the silence of the early morning all over north Tulsa. His sight zeroed in on the railroad tracks as he detected movement. Instantly, what sounded like a machine gun began firing down on Greenwood and Archer. The gunfire seemed to be coming from Middle States Mill near First and Archer. In the next ten seconds, a green four-door Franklin with no top sped across the tracks with five men brandishing rifles inside.

"Wake up," O.B. shouted to Peg Leg Taylor. "They're coming."

Peg Leg Taylor rose up from his position and took aim. "Let's get them bastards in the car," he said.

"I got the driver," John Williams shouted from the other room.

The three men opened fire, and within a minute all five invaders were dead. The car careened off the street and crashed into the pool hall. The car didn't harm the men inside as they began to fire at the out-of control vehicle.

O.B. scanned both sides of the railroad track. There had to be at least five hundred men running and shouting toward Archer. He knew there was no way they could hold off that many invaders. They didn't have enough men or weapons and ammunition. They would soon be surrounded and pinned in.

The invaders began to fire at the building, forcing the men to duck down for cover. The firing stopped and O.B. looked out the window and the building across from them was on fire. He spotted three men also tossing what looked to be rags soaked in kerosene. As soon as the men placed them at the base of the buildings they tossed a match onto them, and they lit up like fireworks, ignited the building and quickly spread from the front to the back.

"Those bastards," O.B. scowled, took aim and fired, hitting one of the men. The others leaped for cover. Immediately after O.B. fired, the men coming across the railroad tracks opened fire on the building, forcing him to go down to the floor.

"They're going to burn us out," Peg Leg Taylor shouted.

"We'd better get out of here," John Williams said as he kneeled in the door entrance. "It's just a matter of time before they torch the whole neighborhood."

A barrage of bullets from the machine ricocheted throughout the room, forcing the men to lay flat on the floor. Once the firing stopped, O.B. sprang back to the window and stuck his rifle out. He was about to squeeze off a round but the men who had been firing from the building across the street, came out of the burning building with their arms high above their heads.

Within seconds, the whites opened fire, killing all ten of them right on the spot. O.B. closed his eyes and turned his head away.

"What happened?" Peg Leg Taylor asked as he rose and looked out the window. "Oh shit," he shouted. "These peckerwoods don't plan to take no prisoners."

Again a barrage of bullets forced them to dive again to the floor. O.B. knew they were being torched. "We got to get out of here," he shouted. "This place is going to go up in flames any minute now."

"We can't go out the front way," Peg Leg Taylor also shouted.

"Come on, we got a back way out of here," John Williams said. "Leads to the alley. If they're not back there yet, we can escape over to Cincinnati using the back alley."

318 Just as John Williams finished, another volley of shots hit the walls in the bedroom and forced the men to again dive for the floor.

"Everybody okay?" O.B. asked.

"Yeah, but not for long if we don't get out of here," John Williams called out.

"Whatcha waiting for?" Pet Leg Taylor shouted.

John Williams led them down the hallway but instead of going out the front, they took the stairs in the back of the building.

O.B. could smell the smoke and knew the fire was making its way up to the top floor. They were lucky. It was still in the front of the building. Now their good fortune needed to stick around long enough for them to clear the alley on Cincinnati before the mob caught up with them.

***

Luther felt the hype of the mob. It was catching, and all fifteen of the men in his patrol were ready for some blood. He initially had refused to join the patrol when Jenks had knocked at his door about three o'clock in the morning. Jenks and four of his neighbors, the same men who had accosted Dr. Jackson in front of Luther's home when his wife fired the warning shot in the air, insisted that he join them in the fight to whip the niggers. Luther knew he had no choice. After defending Dr. Jackson, he now had to prove to these men that he was still one of them. Despite his wife's pleas not to go, he grabbed his weapon, ran out of the house and followed the men up Archer toward Greenwood. His patrol was finally ordered over to Archer and Detroit with instructions to remove all the niggers from those beautiful homes. He distinctly remembered this was the same street the one Negro he admired lived on.

His patrol met little resistance as they crossed over Archer and started up Detroit Avenue. Sergeant Murphy was assigned by Lieutenant Rollins to lead his team into the hinterland. They approached the first house on the street with weapons at the ready. Luther stood back and watched while four of the men hurried up to the front door. The lead man kicked the door open and with rifles still at the ready position, they charged inside. Minutes later, a brown-skinned man and a light-skinned woman were pushed out the door and shoved down the sidewalk.

"Stay there," the Sergeant shouted at them. "Okay, burn it."

"Wait a minute, Sarge," one of the deputized men called out. "Can't we see what they got inside?"

"No, you can't burn my home." The man rushed back up the steps toward the porch.

319

One of the deputized men took aim and fired two shots into the man's chest. He fell to the ground. "Yes, we can burn it," the deputy said. The other men broke out laughing.

Luther glanced over at the man's wife who had fallen to her knees and buried her face between her hands. Momentarily he thought of his wife. He wanted to rush over to her but knew better. He already had the reputation as being soft on the niggers because of Dr. Jackson.

"Go ahead and hurry up and get what you want," Sarge shouted, paying no attention to the killing that had just occurred in front of him. "Make it quick. We got to make it all the way down to Standpipe Hill."

The men ran inside and began to ransack the house. Luther stood at the entrance way and watched as they drug out clothes, jewelry and an old Victrola.

"You don't want none of this?" Sarge asked, staring at Luther.

"Don't think so," Luther answered. He looked hard at his two neighbors, Jenks and Ronnie as they examined the items brought from inside the house. What they were now doing was worse than what the Negroes had been accused of doing.

Once the men finished ransacking the inside, they walked back out to the street.

"Hold up," Sarge called out. "Some of you get that nigger's body and toss it back in the house."

Two of the men grabbed the dead man and hauled him back inside the house while two others dipped rags in kerosene and placed them all around the base of the house, then dropped matches on the rags and the house went up in flames.

320

"No, Lordly, no," the woman screamed and tried to run back up to the house.

Jenks took aim and fired, hitting the woman in the back. She fell to the ground and didn't move. "Got her," he said. "One more dead nigger."

"Should we throw her body in the house?" One of the men asked.

"No, leave her there," Sarge answered. "They'll be coming around picking up bodies when we're finished. They'll toss them in the Arkansas River so they won't stink up the city. Let's move on. We got a whole lot more niggers to get rid of."

It finally hit Luther that the other patrols were probably doing to same thing on all the streets across Greenwood. He took note that they only burned the east side of the street. The other side was the white side.

Before they reached the next house, three men, three women and two children ran out and kept running north on Detroit Avenue, away from the invaders.

"Look at them nigger coons run," Jenks said as he broke out laughing.

"Just like monkeys in the jungle," Ronnie added also laughing.

"Y'all watch this," still another man said. He aimed his rifle, squeezed the trigger, and one of the men running fell to the ground and grabbed his right leg. The two other men stopped and helped him up. Limping, the man held his leg as he tried to keep up with the others.

"What the hell you doing?" Luther charged up to the man. "We were specifically told not to fire unless fired on." He couldn't handle any more of this brutality.

The man didn't back down. He stood right in Luther's face. "I thought he was going to stop any minute and start firing at us," he said. "And what's your problem? Wasn't nothing but a nigger."

Jenks grabbed Luther by the arm and pulled him away from the man. "Hey what's wrong with you?" he shouted. "You ain't going soft on niggers 'cause that nigger doctor treated your son?"

Luther pushed Jenks back off him. "No I ain't going soft on no niggers," he shouted.

Sarge walked up and stood between the two men, turned and faced Luther. "You all stop fighting between yourselves. This is war, and we can't have no traitors." He finished and walked ahead of them toward the next house. "You take the lead going into the next house," he said to Luther. "If there's anyone inside, get 'em out to the street." He pointed to two of the younger deputized men.

321

"You all go in with him."

Luther glared at the two young boys assigned to invade the house with him. They couldn't be any older than fifteen. What the hell were they doing participating in a police action? He gave them a final glance and then tried the doorknob to the house. It was locked.

"I'll get it opened," one of the young boys aimed his rifle at the doorknob and when he fired, half the door flew off the hinges. The other boy kicked it open and Luther followed them inside.

The front of the house was empty. One of the boys kicked the bedroom door open and shouted, "I'll be damn, look what we got here. An old uncle and auntie." He laughed.

Luther walked into the room and looked at the old man and woman sitting on the side of the bed. Their heads were bowed and hands clasped together as if in prayer. A Bible was on the bed between them.

The boy, who had blown the door open, walked up next to the old couple and hit the man in the head with the butt of his rifle.

The old man fell back on the bed, and the woman stayed frozen in her position, hands clasped together and head bowed.

"You got orders to take them out to the street," Luther shouted. "Not hit them with your weapon, so cut it out."

"Go to hell," the young boy also shouted. He pointed the rifle at the old woman's head and pulled the trigger. The old woman fell back on the bed as blood shot all over the room.

"What the hell did you do?" Luther screamed and started toward the boy.

The boy quickly pointed his rifle at Luther. "Back off, old man," he shouted. "We was told to teach niggers lesson. This here is a lesson."

"Why you feeling sorry for these got damn niggers?" the other boy also shouted. "They kilt white folks." He pointed his rifle down at the old man and pulled the trigger. Again, blood shot all over the room. The old man's body lifted up from the impact of the bullet then settled back down on the bed.

Luther turned, ran out of the house and out to the street.

"What the hell's wrong with you?" Sarge yelled.

"They just killed two old people, just up and shot them for no reason."

"Yeah, we did have a reason," the first boy shouted as they walked up next to Sarge. "They was niggers, they was old and they wasn't worth a shit to no one."

"All right, what's done is done," Sarge said. He then turned to three men with the rags. "Okay boys, it's ready."

The men ran up to the house, lit the kerosene soaked rags and tossed them inside. Instantly the house caught fire.

"On to the next house," Sarge shouted. He pointed to three other men and said. "Next one's yours. He looked at Luther. "Don't kill the niggers unless you have to."

FORTY

———————

Damie rushed up the stairs to Jake's room and pounded on the door. "Jake, you got to get up, they're coming for us. They're killing all the Negroes. Come on man get up."

Just fifteen minutes earlier, Pack had banged on her door, awakened Damie and warned her that she needed to get out of Tulsa, go somewhere else because they sure would be coming after her. Before she went to bed she'd heard the gunshots outside but thought nothing of it, because that was a common occurrence since she lived so close to First and Archer. Even though she was still angry with Jake for bringing that prostitute to her home while she was in Vinita, she still had to warn him.

Damie anxiously waited for Jake to open the door, but he didn't. Damie knew he was in there; she had heard him come in last night. Suddenly, it hit her. He'd told her about ten o'clock that he was going out for a little while and would probably get back in pretty late. That was just before she went to bed. She thought nothing of it at the time; he often went out late at night. After all, he was a single man. She'd never known, before officer Pack told her about the incident at the house while she was in Vinita, that he was bringing Georgia into her house. He'd probably snuck her in late last night and planned to get her out before Damie got up. Just as she figured out what was happening, she heard another round of gunfire and again banged on the door.

"Come on man, I know you got Georgia in there with you. That don't matter right now. We all got to get out of here." She turned the doorknob, and the door swung open.

Jake, holding his pants, pulled them up over his waist. Georgia covered her naked body with a sheet. "I'm sorry Miss Damie, we was going to leave before you got up," Jake said.

"Don't matter none," Damie shot back. "You all got to get dressed 'cause they done started killing Negroes on account of Dick. We all got to get out of here." She turned and stared at Georgia. "Hurry up woman and get dressed."

Damie waited in the hall until Jake and Georgia came out of the room, and they all hurried down the stairs. Damie unlocked the front door, opened it and they were met by three young boys, wearing deputy badges, standing on the porch. They couldn't have been any more than fifteen years old.

"Where you niggers think you going?" One boy shouted. "Get your ass back in that house. We know this is a nigger whore house."

Jake stepped up next to the boys. "Let the women be," he scowled. "Take me and let 'em go. They ain't never done nothing to you."

One of the young deputies took the butt of his rifle and knocked Jake back inside the house. They then pushed Damie and Georgia back inside also.

"We know this one's a prostitute," the same boy said and looked at Georgia. "I bet she got some nice titties and good pussy."

"I ain't never seen no nigger titties and ain't never had no nigger pussy," one of the other boys exclaimed

Jake wiped the blood from the gash in his head. "Leave her alone," he shouted.

"This nigger here wants to play hero," the third boy snarled.

Georgia stepped between Jake and the deputies. "I know what you boys want," she said. "Let them go and we can go on upstairs for a little while."

"No, that ain't about to happen." Jake rushed them and snatched the rifle out of the hands of the third boy who was standing closest to him.

326

Before he could aim and fire, the first boy hit him across the head. He fell to the ground and dropped the rifle. "You damn nigger fool." The boy aimed his weapon right at Jake's face and shot three times.

Damie covered her mouth to stop from screaming. She glanced over at Georgia who stared down at Jake's motionless and blood-drenched body. She showed no expression on her face, but then looked back up at the deputies.

"I thought you boys was here to have fun, not kill people?"

They looked at each other and then smiled at Georgia. "What you gonna do, nigger?" The first boy asked.

"What you all want to do?" Georgia asked.

"All three of us?"

"If you let this lady who ain't done nothing to none of y'all leave out," Georgia said.

The lead boy turned and glared at Damie. "She ain't worth fucking no way. Get on out of here," he shouted.

Damie stared at Georgia but did not move.

"You heard him," Georgia yelled. "Get on out of here. They don't want nothing to do with you. They want old Georgia who knows how to make them scream." She motioned with her head for Damie to leave.

Damie moved in close to Georgia and tried to hug her, but got no emotional response. Just a cold and stiff feeling from the woman. Georgia didn't look at her and instead seemed to be staring into space. Damie quickly moved toward the door and ran down the steps. She kept running north up the alley.

After running a block, she stopped for one minute and gazed back at the house. Jake was dead and Georgia would be raped, and all of this because her son couldn't leave that white girl alone

***

Gurley cringed as he stared out his apartment window at the fires and smoke ravaging down Greenwood Avenue from Archer. Men, women and children scrambled and pushed their way north of Archer trying to escape the fires and the bullets. National Guard soldiers and men wearing police badges forced the ones not lucky enough to escape to put their arms above their head and line up in the middle of the street. Gurley had never seen anything quite so horrific, not even during the years he lived in Alabama and Arkansas before the turn of the century.

327

"My God, they're treating people like they're prisoners," he exclaimed to Emma who walked up and stood next to him.

"They're being rounded up just like a bunch of cattle."

"Yeah, cattle to be slaughtered," Emma said with disdain.

Gurley turned and stared at her somewhat surprised at her response. Emma was always so even tempered. "I guess they'll burn down the entire Greenwood community and put all the Negroes in jail," he said.

"At least that's something you don't have to worry about," Emma placed her hand on Gurley's shoulder. "They always looked at you different. The white folks trust and respect you."

Just as Emma finished, Gurley watched the mob toss torched rags into the building right next to the hotel. "I think they're going to burn us all out," he said.

"No," Emma shrieked. "They wouldn't dare burn down the hotel."

"I think we'd better get downstairs and get all our guests out."

"We just going to leave everything here?" Emma screamed.

"We got no choice." He grabbed his wife's hand and hurried out of the apartment and down the stairs.

Gurley was surprised that most of the guests had already exited the hotel. The few still in their rooms rushed out and followed Emma and him down the stairs. The employees on the first floor and in the lobby had already left. Gurley led the few guests who came with him out the front door first, then he and Emma followed them outside. He again grabbed Emma's hand, and they both ran out into the middle of the street. They started running right behind a crowd when a shot rang out and Emma fell to the ground pulling Gurley down with her.

" No, oh my God, no," Gurley shouted. "You got to get up: we can't stay here," he pleaded with Emma as he tried to lift her off the ground.

"No, no, I can't move," she agonized. "You need to get away. You got to follow the others."

"I'm not going to leave you here," he said. "When they come out that building next to ours, they going to torch the hotel and probably shoot you."

"I'll be all right," Emma pleaded. "You have to save yourself.

328

Please just go."

Gurley stared at his wife, struggling with the fact that he had to leave her behind. He leaned down and kissed her then started walking alone up the street. He made it to the corner just as five guardsmen came around and stood directly in front of him, with rifles pointing at his head.

"Put your hands above your head and march back into the middle of the street," the lead man said.

"Don't shoot me," Gurley said. "I'm O.W. Gurley. I know Sheriff McCullough and Chief Gustafson. They both can vouch for me."

"I'm afraid they're not here so get your hands up and get your Black ass out into the middle of the street."

Gurley put his hands above his head and marched to the middle of the street where another dozen Negroes who had been guests at the hotel joined him. They marched back to where Emma was still on the ground.

"Can I help my wife?" Gurley asked.

"No, she'll be all right. There'll be a truck coming along picking up the dead and wounded."

Gurley marched past Emma who looked up at him and managed to smile while holding her hand against the right side of her body. He tried to manage a smile also, but failed. He couldn't possibly smile knowing this might be the last time he'd ever see his beloved Emma.

The guardsman walked up next to him and poked him in the side. "Hurry up, nigger, we ain't got all morning."

329

FORTY•ONE

A young boy no older than thirteen ran through the front doors of the Stradford Hotel, through the lobby and into the ballroom where a large contingent of men, women and children had congregated, trying to find safety from the violence engulfing the streets. The boy spotted Stradford standing at the far end of the room talking with two other men. He ran up to him.

"Sir, Mr. Gurley been captured by the white men, and his wife been shot," the boy shouted, practically out of breath.

"Calm down, young fellow," Stradford said. "Do you know if Emma is still alive?"

"Yes, sir, they took her off in a truck with a lot of dead bodies. They been dropping dead bodies off in the river and taking the live people to the jail."

"Stay inside where it's safe,"Stradford instructed the young man. He then ran out of the ballroom and up the stairs and out on the balcony. He stared out over the top of the rail as two more buildings, one on each side of Greenwood Avenue went up in flames. Five other men who had brought their families to the hotel for safety followed him out on the balcony. They had rifles and were ready to fight. But how much damage could they do against such lopsided odds.

Stradford's forehead wrinkled, and beads of perspiration trickled down into his eyes. He wiped the sweat away and gripped his pistol tightly as he watched the invaders running out of the Gurley Hotel with jewelry. One man had a fur coat wrapped around his shoulders. They dragged chairs, couches and tables from the lobby into the street. One man came running out with a Victrola in his arms. Stradford frowned as three other men poured kerosene onto a stack of rags, lit them and tossed them inside the building. Instantly, fire and smoke shot out of the windows and rose toward the sky. He shook his head in disgust as he watched the confectionery, Dreamland Theater, Little Restaurant and the Little Rose Beauty Parlor all begin to crumble from the flames. No doubt these animals intended to burn down all Greenwood.

Suddenly the roaring sounds coming from the skies above caught Stradford's attention and forced him to look away from the carnage destroying the first two blocks of Greenwood. He stayed focused on the sight where he heard the sounds and then fell back in disbelief as two airplanes came into view. The pilots brought the flying machines down low and tossed explosives from the cockpit. As the incendiary devices hit the ground they spread uncontrollable fires, causing more destruction. The planes stayed low as they flew north on Greenwood Avenue out of the business district to the residential housing that consisted primarily of weakly constructed bungalows. No, these bastards wouldn't dare, he thought. But he was wrong, they would and they did. He watched in horror as the entire blocks beyond the business district lit up ablaze with smoke billowing skyward. Men, women and children running up Greenwood dived for cover to avoid the fire. One man wasn't so lucky as the fire caught him, and he dropped in the middle of the street. The others screamed as they watched him burn.

Finally the mob that had been occupied looting and burning their way north were only three blocks from the Stradford Hotel. It was time for the people inside the hotel to make their exit and run for safety. He figured they had a good twenty minutes before the killers reached him as they continued to burn and pillage each building on their way down the avenue.

"We probably need to get out of here," he shouted to the other men, even though he never planned to leave. "Let's get back downstairs and get these families out of here."

Stradford, followed by the men, rushed down the stairs through the lobby and back into the ballroom. His eyes lit on the banner that read, "CONGRATULATIONS GRADUATING CLASS OF 1921." It still hung high above the ballroom floor, and for a moment he felt sad for the young kids who would not celebrate their achievements that evening. But there was no time to ponder what should have been, only on what was. Standing in the doorway, he shouted, "You all got to get out of here. The killers are only a few blocks away."

"Where we going to go?" An elderly woman standing at the front of the group asked.

"Try to make it to the alleys and side streets," Stradford said. "Let's hurry."

The congregation of men, women and children flooded out of the ballroom through the lobby and out into the street. Stradford stood at the entrance to the ballroom watching his people run for their lives. He then closed the door, stopped in front of the picture of his father and removed it from the wall. He strolled over to the registration desk and leaned against the counter. He had told O. B. that he would defend what he struggled so long to build. With the picture in one hand and his pistol in the other, he would wait for the first invader to violate his property and then take action.

***

Smitherman stared out his living room window in his home on Detroit Avenue and saw the fire and smoke leaping high in the air on Cincinnati Avenue. He knew that after it was over, he would be blamed for the carnage. They would write that he encouraged bringing the troublemaker, Dr. Du Bois to town, and he often had made it clear in his newspaper that no Negro or anyone else would ever be lynched again in Tulsa. But he also knew that he would not stay there and be the scapegoat for this crime occurring on the streets of Greenwood. Earlier last evening, he'd sent his wife and three children to Vinita. They were safe and now he had to make his escape before it was too late.

333

He unlocked the front door and stepped out on the porch. He could hear the gunshots and the roar of the two airplanes. Everywhere he looked, black smoke rose toward the sky. The fires of Greenwood were now burning out of control. He had to escape so he could write about this massacre and what a city filled with mad white men did because of their hatred toward a race of people.

Smitherman briskly stepped back into the house and hurried into the parlor. He snatched pictures of his parents, of his wife and him on their wedding day and one of his children recently taken at the Kirby Studio near the office of the *Tulsa Star,* two buildings he assumed were burnt to oblivion. With these cherished treasures of memories past, he climbed into the drivers' seat of his car, started the engine and drove north on Detroit Avenue for three blocks in front of the mob. Smitherman was determined to drive until he made his way out of the state of Oklahoma. Once safely out of the South, he would send for his family. He had no desire to ever live in Tulsa again, but he did still possess that fire in the belly that Dr. Du Bois talked about to right the wrong happening all around him, and to set the record straight about the true animalistic nature of the white race in Tulsa.

FORTY•TWO

O.B. with Peg Leg Taylor and John Williams had made it safely to Standpipe Hill located right at the foot of Detroit Avenue. He knew this was about as far as they could go and still put up a fight. To continue north would be the safest escape since the mob seemed to have invaded from every possible direction into Greenwood with exception of the northern boundary. Everywhere he looked was fire and smoke. And everywhere he looked, his people were running with children, babies and whatever precious commodity or memorabilia they were determined to save. He and his men needed to provide his people with cover from the killers until they were safely out of Tulsa.

Thinking as a military man, O.B. calculated that there were two strategic positions they could take to hold off the onslaught. "You know we're going to lose this battle," he said as he watched, pleasingly surprised as fifteen of his veteran fighters came down Standpipe Hill toward the three men.

"O.B., if you ain't a sight for sore eyes," Otis shouted.

"Where the hell did you all come from?" Peg Leg Taylor also shouted as he hugged Otis who had been in charge of the men, and then hugged all the others.

"Been up on the hill waiting for those ass holes to get within shooting range," Otis said. "We're ready to fight. Killed a bunch of them peckerwoods on our way over here last night."

"No way we're gonna win," O.B. repeated. "But at least we can offer our people some cover until they get out of Tulsa."

"Then what?" One of the other veterans asked. "Don't matter where we go, they going to have men waiting for us."

O.B. chose to ignore the man's comment. "Peg Leg, you take

Otis and five of the men back up the hill where you'll have a clear shot at them when they come up Detroit. Me and John going to take the rest of the men and climb up to the top of Mount Zion. We gonna have a clear shot from there. By the time it's over, they gonna know they was in a fight.

"You gonna use the church?" Another veteran called out.

"You got a better plan?" O.B. asked. "It's the steadiest structure and we'll have a clear shot from the belfry.

"I don't think God going to appreciate using His place of worship as some kind of fortress," the same man said.

"Just pray that He'll forgive us, but right now we need to get over there." O.B. pointed to five of the ten men. "You all come with us; the rest of y'all head back up the hill. Let's do as much damage as possible."

"We gonna kick some ass," Peg Leg Taylor shouted as he and Otis along with the other men headed back up the hill.

O.B. watched them for a moment and then said. "Let's move out. Time to fight our own Alamo like they did down there in Texas." The men followed him down Easton to Elgin toward Mt. Zion.

***

Veneice woke up to what she thought were firecrackers. She climbed over the top of Esther, ran over to the window and opened the blinds. Her entire body weakened and she felt a tightness in her stomach. She saw smoke and fires leaping toward the sky. She ran back over to the bed and shook Esther and then Ruth. The two girls both rubbed their eyes and sat up in the bed.

"What's the matter, you couldn't sleep?" Esther asked.

"No," Veneice quipped. "You got to see this, come on." She ran back over to the window, motioning her two friends to follow her.

Ruth and Esther ran over to the window and looked out.

"Oh my God," Esther exclaimed. "What's going on?"

"Is the world coming to an end?" Ruth shrieked.

"I don't know but it can't come to an end," Veneice said. "The prom is tonight."

A knock on the bedroom door caused all three of them to jump.

"Veneice, hurry, you girls have to get up and come on out," Veneice's mother said. "Don't worry bout washing up making up the bed. Come on out in your pajamas. We have to get out of here. Your sister's already downstairs with Poppa."

Veneice scrambled over to the door and opened it. "Momma what's happening? We looked out the window, and it looks like everything's burning up."

"It is, and the white folks are killing the Negroes," her mother said. "Now you all come on. Your daddy's out front with his gun. He's not going to let them people hurt you children. That's why we have to get out there before the white folks show up. They'll kill your daddy, because he's sure going to kill them before he lets them hurt you kids."

Veneice backed up in the room and ran to the closet. She grabbed her blue dress. "Momma, I can't leave my dress. 'Cause wherever we go I got to get ready for the prom tonight."

"Honey, I'm sorry but there won't be a prom tonight. Your daddy said Mr. Stradford been took prisoner by the white folks, and his hotel been set on fire like every other business on Greenwood. Put that dress down and come on."

Esther and Ruth had already stepped out of the bedroom and stood in the hall waiting for Veneice.

337

"No, Momma, please don't make me leave my dress, please Momma." Veneice couldn't hold back the tears.

"Honey, I'm sorry. Now put that dress down and come on before you get your father shot and killed. Certainly he is more important to you than a dress."

Veneice laid the blue dress neatly across the unmade bed and backed up to the door while still staring at the dress. "Momma, will my dress still be here when we get back?" she asked as she walked out of the room and joined the others hurrying down the hall toward the door.

"I got to go home," Esther said as they walked outside and joined Fritz.

"You can't do that," Fritz said. "It's much too dangerous up Lansing. You'll be killed."

"I wanna see my Momma," Esther screamed and started to run out of the yard.

Fritz caught here and lifted her in his arms. "I'm sorry I can't let you go," he said. "You'll be killed."

Just as he picked her up, a truck came screaming down Kenosha. Fritz put Esther back down next to Veneice and lifted his pistol ready to fire, but quickly put it down. The truck came to a stop right in front of Fritz. Veneice recognized the driver. It was Mr. Nicols, Poppa's boss at the auto shop.

"Come on, Fritz, get your family inside before it's too late."

"Mr. Nicols, thank God," Fritz exclaimed. "You are an angel of mercy."

Veneice's mother climbed in the truck with Olivia holding her hand, and the three girls followed her. Fritz jumped in the passenger seat and Mr. Nicols drove off.

"Where's he taking us, Momma?" Veneice asked.

"Probably to his home where it'll be safe," she said.

The three girls got in a circle and hugged. Esther and Ruth were crying because they had to leave their families behind. Veneice was crying because she had to leave her blue dress and because she wouldn't have the opportunity to dance the night away at the high school prom that night.

FORTY•THREE

Luther felt nauseous as he watched while the men with him killed and burned their way up Detroit Avenue. Now that the Negroes had been wiped out and no longer were a threat, they began to enjoy themselves as if it was all a big party. They methodically approached each house, kicked in the door and proceeded to loot the place. The drunker they became, the more damage they did. They no longer worked in teams, but instead every man was on his own, free to take whatever appealed to them. He glared at a man so drunk he staggered out of the house in front of them with an expensive Hamilton watch he flashed in front of the others. Another man had what appeared to be very expensive china and two other men actually pushed a piano off the porch, into the front of the yard. The men then tossed kerosene soaked rags inside the home and cheered as it went up in flames. Everywhere Luther looked, he could see fires burning out of control.

"Okay men," Sarge shouted. "Next block is the five hundred block and where all the elite niggers live."

Luther immediately recognized the house he had sought out that night his son's condition worsened. It was the third one on the block. He had to inform the National Guardsman in charge that they should leave the doctor's home alone. Just like they weren't burning white houses across the street, they shouldn't burn the doctor's. But a much more frightening thought crossed his mind. What if Dr. Jackson was home? What if he hadn't run like the rest of his neighbors? Luther knew these men would kill him if he put up any resistance or was found in possession of a weapon. He needed to hurry ahead of the others and warn the doctor of what was in store for him if he stayed inside. But if he did that, the men would consider him a traitor and nigger lover. They'd probably shoot him right on the spot. As the men attacked Smitherman's house right next to Dr. Jackson's, he could only hope that the man who saved his son's life had already abandoned his property.

"Look at these got damned houses these niggers got," one of the men who was extremely drunk shouted. "It's a got damn shame when coons can live better than white folks." The men had just finished taking all the valuables they could handle out of the fiery editor's house. "Everybody out of there," Sarge asked one of the looters who ran out of the house with a bunch of shirts and ties.

"Yeah, ain't nobody in there."

"Good, 'cause I got something for them niggers," the extremely drunk man shouted before Sarge could give his order to burn it down. Not hesitating to wait the order, the man ran up on the porch, tossed some kerosene soaked rags right inside the house and torched them. He ran back to the front of the yard, threw his arms in the air and shouted, "Yowee," as the fire spread inside the house.

Sarge shouted to the men," Okay, let's move out and get the next house; we got a lot—"

"Sarge, can we spare the next house?" Luther interrupted the sergeant while pointing to Dr. Jackson's house.

"What the hell," Sarge scowled. "Spare it for what reason? White folks don't live on this side of the street."

"I know, Sarge," Luther continued. "But the man who lives here is a doctor, and last month he saved my boy's life. He's a good man that—"

"This is the nigger doctor's house," the drunk, boisterous man interrupted Luther. "This is the nigger that hit me with his car last month and left me to die on the railroad tracks.

"You're lying," Luther shouted. "He's a doctor. He'd never leave someone to die." Luther moved in closer to Sarge. "This is a fine and decent man: Sarge, can't we spare his house?"

The drunken man moved in closer and pushed Luther, causing him to stumble backward. Instantly Luther regained his balance and lurched forward toward the man. Sarge stepped between the two men.

"Knock it off," he ordered. "We're burning everything owned by niggers. I don't give a good got damn if his name is Jesus and he's a nigger, it's coming to the ground. Prepare to go in," he shouted.

Just as the men moved forward toward the house, the front door swung open and Dr. Jackson, Captain Townsend and Julia walked out on the porch.

"We want no fight," Dr. Jackson called out. The three of them put their hands clasped together above their heads. "We have no weapons, and we do not plan to fight you."

One of the men raised his gun and pointed it at Captain Townsend, another did the same, aiming at Dr. Jackson and still another aimed at Julia.

"Hold up, don't fire," Sarge ordered. "Come on down, keep your hands high above your heads and line up in the middle of the street."

Doctor Jackson walked down the steps first. Captain Townsend and Julia followed close behind. They reached the walkway and cautiously moved toward the street.

Abruptly the drunken man who had pushed Luther stood directly in front of the Doctor. "Remember me, nigger?" he shouted. "Remember how you tried to run me over and how you tried to kill me at the railroad tracks." He lifted his gun chest high to the Doctor.

Doctor Jackson glared at the man and said, "I didn't try to kill—"

"No," Luther screamed and propelled his body toward the man.

341

The shot rang out, and Dr. Jackson dropped to the ground, blood gushing from his chest area.

"You bastard," Captain Townsend shouted and rushed toward the man who then pointed his gun at the Captain. Before he could pull the trigger, Luther's full body knocked him to the ground.

"Oh my God, what have you done?" Julia's voice shrieked. She dropped to the ground taking Dr. Jackson's limp body into her arms. "Somebody help my husband," she screamed. She placed her hand on his chest as if that would stop the blood gushing out of the wound. "Oh my God, you've killed my husband."

Luther knocked the gun from the drunken man's hand and began wailing at him, throwing lefts and rights to his head and body. "You son of a bitch. You bastard. You've killed the man who saved my son's life," he shouted as the blows continued. "I'll kill you, I'll kill you."

Captain Townsend fell backwards from the impact of Luther's attack on the drunken man. He stumbled and caught himself before he hit the ground. He turned and fell next to Julia, tore off part of his shirt and applied it to his son's wound. But it failed to stop the bleeding. He and Julia were soaked in blood.

"Don't die, Andrew, please don't die," Captain Townsend pleaded with his son who did not move. He listened for a heartbeat and looked up at the Sergeant. "He's still breathing. You got to get him some help."

Sarge paid no attention to him as he swiftly accosted Luther and pulled him off the drunken man. "What the hell you think you're doing?" He shouted as he and two other men finally pulled Luther off the man. Sergeant took the butt of his rifle and hit Luther in the head. He fell to the ground and did not move. Blood gushed from the blow to his head.

"Get them two off the dead man," Sergeant shouted to the other men, pointing at Captain Townsend and Julia. "Get them damn niggers into the street, and a truck will be along any minute. Throw this dead nigger into the back of the truck."

"Please sir, let me stay here with my son," Captain Townsend begged the Sergeant. "I'll ride with him in the truck. Please sir,"

Sarge stared at Captain Townsend for a moment and said. "Okay, you can stay with him but the woman's got to go with us."

"Thank you, sir," Captain Townsend said, then turned to Julia. "It'll be all right. He's still breathing, and when we get to wherever they're taking us we can get him some help. You go with the others. I'll find you later."

Julia hugged the Captain, looked down at Dr. Jackson and

then marched with hands above her head out into the street where she joined a number of Blacks who had been pulled out of some of the other homes.

"Burn it," Sarge shouted. "And pick up this nigger lover and get him some help," he said, looking down at Luther. We'll deal with him later."

Four of the men laughed as they took rags and soaked them in kerosene. They then ran up the steps and into the house. Minutes later when they came back out, the house went up in flames. The men then joined the others as they continued their march with the prisoners up Detroit Avenue.

"Let's hurry, we got a couple blocks before we get to Standpipe Hill," Sergeant said.

The Captain fell back to the ground next to his son. He again placed his torn shirt on the wound and applied pressure in an attempt to stop the bleeding. He noticed his son's color slowly dissipating from his face. He placed the back of his hand on Dr. Jackson's forehead, and it felt cold. Tears streamed down the Captain's face. He knew his son was fading.

He looked up at the burning house and visibly cried as all his dreams, his trust in his country and his years of dedication to a belief went up in flames with the home that his son so loved.

FORTY•FOUR

General Charles Barrett, Commander of the State of Oklahoma National Guard gazed out the train window in awe as the special train carrying one hundred and thirty men pulled into the Frisco Station. Everywhere he looked north of the tracks, he saw red flames rising through roof tops, dead bodies lying along the street and swarms of men with rifles running and shooting at anything that moved in front of them. What the hell is going on in this city, he thought. Governor Robertson had simply instructed him to get down to Tulsa because the niggers were causing an insurrection. But as far as he could see and surmise, it was the whites that were causing the problem. All the windows in the Frisco station had been smashed and bullet holes riddled the building. Did the governor expect his men to kill white folks? Because that's all he saw? As the train pulled up and stopped, the general knew he'd need a lot more information and the blessings of the city officials before his men jumped into the fray. They had to know who needed killing.

"General Barrett, the men are ready to exit the train. They're just waiting your orders," a young national guardsman wearing a starchy clean uniform with lieutenant bars said after walking into the car where the general was seated.

General Barrett pulled his large frame up from his seat and turned to face his underling. "Have the men fall out and line up next to the train station," he said. "Don't shoot unless shot at first," he ordered. "But keep their rifles at the ready position." He then walked to the back of the car and out the door onto the platform.

"General Barrett," Gustafson called out as he and Detective Carmichael walked up to meet the general. "Thank God you're finally here." He stuck his hand out to the general. "This whole mess has gotten out of hand. Them niggers have gone wild just attacking white people."

"Where the hell are they? All I see is white folks," General Barrett snarled.

"They pretty much done got beaten down and have retreated across the tracks," Gustafson said.

"Then why the hell you need us?"

"To help bring order back to this town," Gustafson shot back. "It's all about control."

"I can do that, but first I have to talk to the mayor and the sheriff as a courtesy. I just can't come in here and take control without their knowing what I'm doing. As the police chief I guess I know you support us. Best way to restore order is to get the governor to declare martial law and put all control in my hands." He paused and looked hard at Gustafson. Satisfied that the chief agreed he said. "In the meantime I need to get my men fed."

"I can take you to the mayor who's stationed himself over at the hotel but I haven't the slightest notion as to where you're going to find Sheriff McCullough."

"Where can my men eat breakfast?" General Barrett asked, ignoring the chief's comment.

"My detective can take them over to the Second Street Cafeteria, two buildings down form the police station and I can take you to the mayor," Gustafson suggested.

"Let's get moving." General Barrett waved the lieutenant to come over. "This detective's going to take you and the men to get some breakfast. The men need to eat before we go to battle. The chief here is picking up the bill. Detective Carmichael will show you how to get to the cafeteria."

346

"Yes, sir," the lieutenant replied and looked at Carmichael. "The men are good and hungry. Can we move out?" He waved for the men to march over to him.

"Men, it'll probably be an hour or so before you see any action," General Barrett said as the men fell in formation in front of him. "In the meantime, go fill up your bellies. We'll meet back here at eleven hundred hours. It's now nine-thirty. Now move out."

"Yes, sir," the lieutenant said. He looked at Carmichael. "Lead the way."

As the men marched across the tracks into South Tulsa, General Barrett said, "Let's go and get these approvals so that we can bring order back to this city. It looks like a fucking war zone."

***

"Are you happy now, Mr. Newspaperman?" Mayor Evans shouted as he barged into Jones' office.

Jones, standing by the window looking at the damage along Greenwood, didn't immediately turn around. He just kept looking out the window watching as new fires broke out across the tracks. He gazed at the two airplanes as they descended on Greenwood, and moments later flames from a new fire jumped toward the sky.

"You hear me, Jones?" The mayor kept shouting. "Your bullshit editorial is responsible for all this got damn carnage in our city."

Jones calmly turned to face the mayor. "Don't seem to me that the carnage is in Tulsa, but in niggertown where it should be," he said. "You worried about what's happening to a bunch of niggers who killed some good white boys? Them niggers shot and killed my friend Cal. I hope they all burn up."

"And once you kill all the niggers, who's going to do the nigger chores that got to be done everyday?" Mayor Evans taunted. "You going to clean up white folks' kitchens? You going to clean the shit houses or pick up the garbage?'

"It'll get done. The men ain't going to kill all the niggers, just the bad ones. By tomorrow the good niggers will be able to go back to work, and they'll be just as happy like nothing ever happened at all."

"You're so dumb; I doubt if you know to lift the toilet seat before you take a piss. Have you even looked at that mob out there on the loose? They've been reading your editorials, and they don't

347

believe there is such a thing as a good nigger. They're all bad to them right now."

Jones' face flushed red with anger. "They can't kill all nine thousand niggers living over there. They'll run out of bullets first. Let's just hope they kill the bad ones."

Mayor Evans moved forward and stood right in Jones' face. "When this is over I'll see you run out of this town," he snapped.

Jones didn't budge. "When it's over, the good white folks going to say good riddance to you at election time. We'll see who's going to be run out of town."

Abruptly the door swung open and Gustafson with General Barrett, briskly walked into the room. "We been looking for you," he said to the mayor. "This is General Barrett and he—"

"I know who General Barrett is." Mayor Evans interrupted the chief. "Welcome General, and thank God you're finally here." The two shook hands.

"Looks to me like your men got everything under control," General Barrett said. "Don't look much like a fight when we rode in this morning."

"But we got to stop the burning." The mayor bristled. "We got to call the boys off before this becomes a total massacre."

"We're going to do that," General Barrett replied. "But first I have to inform you and Sheriff McCullough that I plan to declare martial law and clear all the streets with a curfew."

"Okay, you informed me, so now go out and stop this fiasco."

348   Jones finally strode over and stood behind his desk. "It's good to have you in our city, General," he said. "But it's not quite as bad as the mayor seems to think it is. Our boys just got tired of the niggers forgetting their place and went over to spank them a little bit."

"And who are you?" General glared at Jones.

"I'm publisher of our local newspaper and have been writing all along that the niggers need to be tamed and put back in their cage."

General Barrett again looked directly at Mayor Evans, ignoring Jones comment. "Since my men had to head over here to Tulsa before they had a chance to eat breakfast, I sent them over to a cafeteria by the jail to eat. Your cities going to pick up the cost."

"If that was the only cost we'd endure, I'd be a very happy man," Mayor Evans lamented.

"Where is Sheriff McCullough?" General Barrett abruptly asked, changing the subject. "I need to inform him of our intent to declare martial law, and then my men can get busy."

"I'm afraid you're not going to be able to reach him," Mayor Evans said. "He snuck out about four hours ago to take the prisoner over to Muskogee for safe keeping."

"What?" Jones shouted. "You took him out of this jurisdiction, and this is where he should be tried."

"There's not going to be a trial after that boy raped a white girl?" General Barrett sounded incredulous.

"There won't be a trial because the girl refuses to sign a sworn statement about what happened in the elevator and also refuses to press charges."

"You're not serious," General Barrett scowled. "All this damage and nothing really happened. How dumb are you people down here in Tulsa?"

Mayor Evans glowered at Jones. "I'm afraid it appears that we are quite dumb," he answered.

"I need to use your phone and call the governor." General Barrett couldn't hide his disgust. It showed all over his face. "He has to declare martial law, and then my men can go to work and clean up this real mess you all made down here."

349

"Certainly." Jones pointed to the phone on his desk.

"If there wasn't no rape, then you all done killed and burned all these Negroes for nothing. That's going to haunt this city for a very long time." The general paused for a moment and then spoke into the phone. "Give me the governor's mansion in Oklahoma City." He paused again and fixed his eyes on Jones and the mayor. "Tomorrow you all had better be thinking of ways to cover this up, and at the least place the blame on the Negroes." He turned his back and said. "Evening, Governor Robertson, I believe it's time to take this city out of the hands of the mayor, the police chief and the sheriff, and declare martial law."

FORTY·FIVE

Luther knew he had a very short time to break from his squad and return to Dr. Jackson in order to help Captain Townsend get his son to the Frissell Hospital where he could get medical attention. The wound to the doctor was pretty bad, and if he weren't attended to he would die within the next few hours. Luther watched from the street as the men ran out of another house with as many belongings as they could steal. His best chance to disappear would be when Sergeant asked for volunteers to torch the house. He waited patiently, intent on being one of the men.

"Let me have four men to torch it," Sergeant called out.

Instantly Luther moved to the front of the men and picked up a small container of kerosene and rags from the ground next to the sergeant. Along with three other men, he ran up the steps and into the house. But instead of stopping in the front hall, he kept going to the back. He lit the rags and tossed them into the kitchen. He then shot out the back door and ran down the alley back toward the doctor's burning house. He knew the sergeant would take note that he didn't come back out with the other men and might send a squad looking for him. He had to move fast and get to the doctor before they caught up with him.

Luther reached the back yard to the doctor's house and ran toward the front. Captain Townsend, still on the ground next to his son, held a rag to Doctor Jackson's wound. He wasn't too late. Chances were good that he could help save the life of the man who had saved his son from certain death. The Captain's body stiffened when he saw Luther come from between the two houses.

"Not to worry, sir," Luther said out of breath. "I'm going to help you get Doctor Jackson out of here and to the hospital."

"He's still alive," Captain Townsend exclaimed. "He's not

gone yet."

"Good, where are the keys to his car?" Luther asked.

"Upstairs in his study on the desk. Hurry, man, we don't have much time. He's hardly breathing, and the bleeding won't stop."

"I'm on my way." Luther tore up the steps and into the house. He shot up the stairs and into the study. "The keys, the keys, where are they?" he whispered as he looked all over the desk. "Damn, they're not in here. Where would they be?" He thought for a second and then ran over to what appeared to be the master bedroom. He spotted some keys on the night stand on the side of the bed. He grabbed them and ran back down the stairs and out of the house. "I got 'em," he shouted and again ran over to the Ford parked in the driveway. He climbed in the front seat and turned the ignition, hoping the engine would turn over without being cranked. It did, and leaving the engine running, he jumped out and hurried over to the doctor.

Captain Townsend got up from the ground and put both hands under Doctor Jackson's arms. "Help me pick him up," he said.

"I got him," Luther replied as he gently lifted the Doctor's legs and the two men carried him over to the car and placed his limp body in the back seat.

The two anxious men climbed in the front seat, and Luther backed the car out of the driveway. "You'd better put your head down in case we run into a unit."

Captain Townsend slid down in the seat. "They're going to know this isn't your car," he said.

"I know." Luther forced a smile. "They'll just think I'm stealing it. So many cars being stolen they won't pay no attention to me." Luther turned off Detroit Avenue and headed toward a street where they wouldn't recognize him. He would then find a way to get to the hospital and if possible save the Doctor's life.

352

***

"Mabel, we got to get out of here," Pressley pleaded with his wife as they sat in the front pew of Mount Zion Baptist Church.

The sanctuary was crowded with men, women, children and small babies all seeking protection from the mob making its way up Elgin toward the church.

Mabel ignored her husband and instead looked over at Lucinda. Her stomach tightened as the older woman gripped the child in her arms and closer to her breast. Every time the sound of gunfire exploded throughout the sanctuary Lucinda seemed to jump and look all around her as if she anticipated an attack. Mabel had to calm her friend down. But first she had to respond to Pressley's plea to leave.

"I can't leave my church," Mabel exclaimed. "We just got to pray that God won't let nothing happen here. They already burnt down our businesses, and by now they probably have burnt our home. I can't let them burn my church, too."

"How you gonna stop 'em," Pressley tautly replied. "They've gone crazy and they're intent on killing all of us and burning us out. We can't save anything now but our lives."

"We're going to pray," Mabel said. "Be patient and be prayerful, Pressley." She got up and walked over and sat next to Lucinda.

Lucinda didn't acknowledge Mabel because her eyes remained tightly shut. Mabel touched her on the arm. "It's going to be all right; we're in the house of the Lord, and He surely will not allow the devil to invade his sanctuary.

Lucinda jerked at the touch and opened her eyes. She looked intently at her friend and managed a smile. "This child here is my great granddaughter. Only nine months old."

Mabel couldn't help but notice the sadness that spread across Lucinda's face.

353

"They already killed my granddaughter's husband," Lucinda lamented. Thank God my daughter was up in Oklahoma City with my granddaughter when this mess got started. Me and this baby just got away when all those men come running and yelling and shooting them guns. Only place I knew to come was here to the church." Lucinda's eyes filled with tears, and her voice cracked "I can't run from them. My legs are too tired and old. But I can't let them kill this baby. If they come through that door you got to take this child. You can't let them kill her."

"We'll be just fine. God ain't going to let anything happen to us."

"Promise me …promise me you'll take this child to safety."

Mabel ran her hand along the side of Lucinda's face trying to wipe away the tears. "I promise I'll take both of you to safety."

Instantly, the front door swung open, and for a moment fear shot through Mabel's body. But then she relaxed as O.B., John Williams and five veterans hurried inside the sanctuary. They stood in the back.

"Sorry, didn't mean to scare you all," O.B. shouted. "But I'm afraid that this is not a safe place for you all. You got to get out of here and into the countryside. If you stay here, you might be killed."

"This is the house of the Lord," an older, gray haired lady standing closest to O.B. rejoined. "If it ain't safe in here, then it's not safe anywhere."

"It's not gonna be safe in here 'cause this is where we plan to fight them. Some of the men going up to the belfry and others gonna position themselves wherever they can get a clear shot."

"You can't fight from in here," Mabel shrieked. "This is the house of the Lord."

"I'm sorry, Mrs. Mabel but we got no other choice," O.B. exhorted. "We got men over on Standpipe Hill, and we're here. We can fight them off long enough for all of you to get to safety out in the countryside."

"They done burnt down everything, haven't they?" Pressley asked from the other side of the pew.

"Afraid they have," O.B. answered. "They'll probably burn down this church. They already put the torch to Mount Vernon."

"Heaven help us," Lucinda shouted.

"There is no way I'm going to allow them to damage this church," Mabel's voice rose. "They've destroyed my businesses, my home and I'll die before I let them damage this place. We spent too much money and waited too many years to build it and overnight they think they're going to destroy it?"

Pressley hurried across the aisle to his wife and placed both arms around her. Mabel was physically shaking. "You all need to get out of here," he shouted. "Now get on out of here before them devils find out you're inside and start shooting up the place." Pressley exhaled while glaring at Mann. "You done brought all that violence and killing back from overseas. You killed them white folks knowing darn well they would retaliate and kill us. Innocent people, who don't care nothing about hating and fighting, are suffering because of you. Ain't you did enough damage?"

A loud explosion shook the church and shattered the windows in the front. The ground shook, and the women screamed. Mabel looked at Lucinda. Her entire body tensed up and fear dominated her face.

O.B. ignored Pressley's attack; instead he and John Williams ran to the front of the church and swung the door open. He heard the roar of the airplanes and looked up just in time to see them descend toward the ground and bomb right at the foot of Standpipe Hill.

"Got damn them," O.B. shouted as he thought of Peg Leg Taylor and the other men over on the Hill. Both O.B. and John Williams ran outside and started firing in the air, in a futile attempt to hit the plane in the right spot and force it to the ground.

The plane turned and headed right toward O. B. and John Williams. They kept firing until O. B. had a clear view of the pilot who was smiling and obviously enjoying this attack. He watched as the pilot picked up an object in his right hand and reared back to toss it directly at him. Just as the object started its descent, the two men ran back inside the church and O. B. shouted to the other men who had followed him outside, "Look out, get back inside." The men scrambled back inside the church.

355

Within seconds, they heard and felt the explosion. O.B. knew the airplanes were clearing a path for the invaders to attack. The men began to knock out windows, crouch down and position their weapons on the windowsill in anticipation of the invasion.

"What are you doing?" An older lady sitting on a pew in the back of the church stood up and shouted. "How dare you destroy

God's sacred property."

O.B. had put up with just about as much as he was going to tolerate from the very people he and the men were willing to sacrifice their lives to protect. "Listen up all you self righteous, sanctified people," he shouted. "Those animals out there don't give a damn about God's precious property, and they're gonna come in here in the next half hour just burning and killing." He paused, looking into the faces of the people he loved and would die for if necessary. But they needed to face reality. God was not about to send a bolt of lightning down from Heaven and wipe out all those drunken fools with guns. "I'm telling you to get out of here and run to the country. These men will protect you all until you're out of the church and cross over Pine Street to safety. Now you can either take our protection or sit here and wait for God's protection." O.B. finished, turned and hurried up the stairs to the belfry, with John Williams right behind him.

Pandemonium erupted throughout the church as everyone started talking at the same time.

"People, please quiet down," Reverend Whittaker shouted as he came in from the side door to the church.

"Reverend Whittaker, where you been?" Mabel shouted also.

They all looked to the side of the church, and silence engulfed the sanctuary.

"I been over at the hospital," Reverend Whittaker answered as he walked down the middle aisle to the front of the church. "My God in Heaven, they are slaughtering our people. They're actually dropping firebombs from airplanes. Some poor souls over there are burnt so bad you can't recognize them. You all have to get out of here and run for safety. Our men in the belfry going to slow them down, but only for a little while. There has to be at least ten thousand devils on the loose out there."

356

"Why ain't God going to protect us?" A lady hollered from the middle pew. "We spent all this money to build His house of worship, and He don't care enough about it to save it and save us?"

"Stop that kind of talk," Reverend Whittaker admonished. "I'll have none of that talk in this church. You are in no position to question what God does or does not do. Do you all understand there will be no questioning of God?"

Again silence prevailed.

"Now I want you all to line up in the middle aisle. Please men, let our ladies and children, and of course our elderly go first," Reverend Whittaker instructed.

Tears blurred Mabel's vision. She felt emotionally drained as her church family followed their pastor's instructions and lined up in the middle aisle. She would wait and leave with Pressley. It was important to her that she be with him.

Mabel smiled at Lucinda as she got in line, still clinging to her great grandchild. Unlike Pressley, Mabel was not angry with O.B. and the other veterans who had initiated the confrontation. They were protecting Damie's boy and in doing so, making a statement about lynching. But she knew after this was over, the question would linger for a very long time. Was the life of one boy worth the tragedy thousands were suffering?

"I'm going to stay with the men and fight." Pressley snapped her out her musing.

"What are you talking about?" Mabel snarled. "You'll do no such thing. You know nothing about killing people and shooting guns."

"These men doing something Negroes should have did a long time ago. I want to be a part of that," he rejoined. "You go on with the others. I'll be all right."

"No, Pressley." Mabel's voice was strained. "Please, Reverend Whittaker, tell him he got to go with me." Tears flowed out of her eyes. "Pressley, you can't do this. Tell him Reverend." She grabbed Reverend Whittaker by the arm, as he stood right in front of them. "He ain't cut out for this kind of fighting. I don't believe Pressley ever fired a gun." 357

"You need to go with your wife," Reverend Whittaker said. "I know you want to help, but these men are well trained at warfare. You don't want to get Mabel killed, do you?" Reverend asked but did not wait for an answer. "'Cause that's what might happen. She's not going anywhere without you."

"That's right," Mabel agreed. "I'll stay right here with you if you don't leave."

"Why you want to deny me a chance to be a man?" Pressley asked.

"You are a man." Mabel took her husband's hands into hers. "Killing people don't make you no man. You don't call them fools out there burning and killing, men. You call them animals."

"She's right," Reverend Whittaker said. "Now you'd better get going before it's too late. Your wife will not leave without you, and that's something you'd never be able to live with, if something happened to her."

The sanctuary had emptied, and only the three of them remained inside.

"What are you going to do, Reverend?" Pressley asked.

"As soon as I know everybody's safely out of the church, I'm going to pray and then leave."

Pressley smiled at Reverend Whittaker; then he grabbed and hugged him. "When this is over and if they burn our church down, we're going to come back and rebuild it all over again."

Reverend Whittaker broke from Pressley's hug. "That's why we need you all to get out of here so we can rebuild and start all over again, if necessary." He patted Pressley on his back. "Now get out of here and let these warriors do their job. I'll be along directly."

Pressley squeezed Mabel's hand, and they hurried down the center aisle and out of the church.

358

***

From the belfry at the top of the church, O.B. watched as Mabel and Pressley hurried north on Elgin Avenue to safety. Less than five minutes later, at least two dozen white men came running up Elgin from the other direction. Unless stopped, they would eventually catch up with Mabel and the others before they could make it deep enough into the woods. O.B., John Williams and the veterans had to stop them before they passed the church. They would catch the invaders by surprise because they probably didn't think that fire fight would come from the church.

"Get ready," O.B. shouted to his men. "They're coming." He stretched his rifle out the window right next to John Williams.

"Was it like this over in France?" John Williams asked without looking over at O.B.

"Yeah, something like this," O.B. said as he kept his sight on what was happening outside the church.

"I missed all that action." John Williams also kept his sights outside.

"Don't matter," O.B. exhaled. "'Now you're participating in the real war. Them's our enemies." He began firing, as the invaders got close. The other veterans also opened fire. Four of the white men fell to the ground. The others either dived for cover or turned and ran back the other way.

"Great shots men," O.B. shouted. "But stay prepared because they'll be back." He looked back over at Standpipe Hill. Peg Leg Taylor and the other men were busily engaged in a fire fight. They seemed to be holding their own. But then he heard the roar of the airplanes. They appeared from the south and flew low over the Hill. Right after they passed over, fires shot straight up. The invaders were going to flush Peg Leg Taylor and the other veterans out of their cover by setting Standpipe Hill on fire. He knew they would stay put as long as they could and then take off north into the woods. Hell, the damn crackers wouldn't dare burn up the entire wooded areas just to destroy a few men. The Hill was burning, and the fire spreading at a rapid rate. No doubt Peg Leg Taylor had taken off to find cover. O.B. and John Williams along with the other men were the last of the fighters, and he knew their time was also numbered.

359

Minutes later, a flatbed truck rumbled down Elgin, turned around with the back positioned toward the church. One of the men removed a canvass, and another loaded ammunition into a machine gun mounted on a tripod. Another man began firing rounds of bullets into the church frame. Bricks and mortars began to crumble under the onslaught, and within five minutes bullet riddled openings began to loosen the entire structure. Windows were shattered, and the foundation began to weaken. As the men continued the attack, O.B. knew it was only a matter of time before the entire structure crumbled. They had stayed as long as they could and long enough for everyone who had been inside the church to safely escape into the woods. O.B. got to his feet and shouted.

"Let's get out of here while the building's still standing."

The men followed O.B. and John Williams down the stairs. With the bullets whizzing around them they ran out the front door, made it to the side of the church and kept running until they reached Frankfort Avenue. They ran north on Frankfort toward the woods.

Breathing heavily, O.B. yelled. "You men got to keep moving north till you are as far away from Tulsa as possible. Don't get caught 'cause they sure enough will kill you on sight."

"Which way you heading?" John Williams asked.

"Gonna keep going east till I know it's safe to rest," O.B. said between breaths. "I'm gonna get as far north and east as I can go. When this is all over, gonna send for my family. But one thing I know for sure, I'll never set foot in Tulsa again."

"We did what we had to do." John Williams declared.

"Yeah, for sure we did what we had to. We stood up for our manhood and our God given rights." O.B. hugged his friend. "Which way you heading?"

"To Vinita to get my family. Maybe someday when this all dies down, I'll come back and start all over again."

360

Suddenly a burst of flames leaped toward the sky back in the vicinity of Mount Zion.

"I'll be damn, they torched the church," another veteran shouted.

"We need to keep moving," O.B. ordered. "You got six or seven white men laying in the street dead from our guns. Them white folks ain't gonna let that die down. We need to get as far away as possible so they can't associate any of us with the shooting."

"You think Peg Leg made it?" a veteran bringing up the rear asked.

"No doubt," O.B. said. "Ain't no way he was gonna let them folks capture or shoot him. He's probably half way to Oklahoma City by now." O.B. hugged the other men and then turned back to John Williams. " Let's get out of here."

The men scattered in different directions. O.B. began running east of Greenwood. He looked back over his shoulder at the center of what had been dubbed the Black Wall Street one final time. He cringed at the fires blazing from the buildings that once represented the pride of the community.

O.B. then looked straight ahead and kept running, and knew he would not stop until he was all the way out of the country that he loved and would always claim as his own.

FORTY·SIX

"It's time to bring this madness to an end," General Barrett shouted to his troops. "Our orders are to spread out all across the Negro section of town. When you see white men with guns, inform them that the entire city of Tulsa is under martial law by orders of the governor, and they are to return to their homes. When you see Negroes on the loose, arrest them and take them to the convention center or to the ballpark. We are setting up camps to keep them under arrest and try to determine the ones that participated in this riot. The only way they are to be released from incarceration is if someone white vouches for them." Barrett paused to catch his breath. "No doubt by the morning white folks will be looking for their maids and servants. In the meantime, spread out, starting on Archer and patrol every street between Archer and Pine going south to north and Boston to Lansing going west to east. Now get busy."

General Barrett backed up a bit and stood next to Mayor Evans and Gustafson. He watched as his men formed into small details for patrol duty. Barrett knew their work at this point would be primarily cleanup, picking up the strays that the local National Guard hadn't already captured and taken to jail. Gustafson had informed him just before he went outside to address his troops that the jail was overflowing, and his men and the national guardsmen already had begun to deposit the Negroes either at the convention center or McNulty Baseball Field. The cleanup would take the rest of the afternoon. Now he only needed to set up his command post.

The General turned to Mayor Evans, "I hear the Hotel Tulsa is a pretty nice place."

One of the very best hotels in the southwest." Mayor Evans smiled. "I guess you want to set up your operation there."

"Exactly."

"No problem. Let's go."

***

Captain Townsend gaped in disbelief at the flames and smoke that engulfed the Frissell Hospital. Brady Street was crowded with injured and sick people as well as nurses and doctors who had evidently gotten out before the hospital was torched.

With a forlorn expression over his face, Luther turned to Captain Townsend. "What do we do now?" he asked.

"I don't know," Captain Townsend stammered, at a lost for words because of the site before him. He turned and glared at Luther. For a moment, he wanted to attack this white man, take all his pent up aggressions that laws and customs forced him to hide inside. He wanted to rip off that veil that Black men were forced to wear in order not show their anger, just be himself and tear this white man apart. Instead, he looked away from Luther and out the window at the calamity. He replaced the emotion of anger with one of sorrow. His son would die, and dealing with that emotion was much more important than what was happening outside the car.

"We must get my son's body to an undertaker who will give him the proper treatment," he said contritely. "I can't let them throw his body in the Arkansas River or just dump it out in the woods. I have to take him to Guthrie and bury him next to his mother. Sophorina would like that." Captain Townsend Jackson was a tough man, but not tough enough to hold back the tears.

364

"But there's only one nig…" Luther caught himself.

"You were going to say one nigger undertaker, weren't you?" Captain Townsend asked but did not wait for an answer. "What's wrong with you people? You use insulting words on us, you kill and burn. Just look at all this around you. How can you possibly hate a race of people to the extent that you would do all this?"

"I'm sorry, Captain Townsend," Luther said with his voice trailing off almost to a whisper. "We ain't all like that."

"No, you're not all like that. But enough of you are to cause all this damage and to kill my son."

"I loved your son for what he did for me."

"My son dies and yours lives. And that is something I'll never understand."

Luther thrust his revolver into Captain Townsend's hand. "If it'll make you feel better, you can shoot me. If that's what it takes to even the score, then I'm willing to die. But you got to know I'm hurting too, 'cause the only man I looked up to and admired is dead, and that was your son."

Captain Townsend peered into Luther's eyes. They were filled with tears.

"Go ahead and even the score. Think of me as all them people out there and kill me, so my death can pay back the debt white folks owe you."

The Captain tossed the gun on the floor inside the car. "We need to get out of here before they spot us," he said.

"We can take the doctor's body over to my house," Luther volunteered.

"And do what with it there?" Captain asked. "We got to get him to an undertaker."

"Mr. Rosewood," Luther blurted out. "We'll take him to Mr. Rosewood. He's a good man. Often times he'll prepare bodies for burial for families like mine that can't pay. He lets us pay a little over time."

"Burying poor whites is much different than preparing a Black man," Captain Townsend rejoined.

365

"I know you think all white people hate your people, but that's not true. There are some of us that don't live by the rules of racism. Can't we at least try?"

Captain Townsend forced a smile. "Yeah, I guess we can try."

"The mobs have moved way north of Brady Street," Luther said. "I'll take Boulder back across the tracks and then take First. That way we'll be far away from the fighting—"

"Massacre is a better way to describe what's happening," Captain Townsend interrupted Luther.

"Okay, massacre," Luther conceded. "Now please put your head down so we can make it to my side of town and get Doctor Jackson taken care of."

Luther spun the car around and drove up Brady to Boulder. He turned left, drove across the railroad tracks to First Street. He made another left on First Street and stared directly ahead at a roadblock manned by the State National Guard.

"Oh shit," Luther exclaimed. "They're stopping cars up on Main."

Captain Townsend abruptly rose up in the passenger seat and sat erect.

"What are you doing?" Luther shrieked. "They're going to see you."

"That's exactly what I want them to do. I want them to see me sitting in this seat like I belong here. They'll probably think that I work for you and let you on through."

"Yeah, they'll figure I'm some rich white man driving his hired help out of the danger," Luther quipped. The car rolled up toward Main. "Here it goes." He glared at the State National Guardsman and kept driving. He and Captain Townsend looked straight ahead as the vehicle crossed over the intersection. The State National Guardsman also stared at Luther, then over at Captain Townsend, but did not raise his hand signaling for them to stop.

"We made it," Luther exclaimed. "That was a pretty smart move."

"More natural instincts than being smart. We know how the white man thinks," Captain Townsend explained. "That's the only way we've survived in this country by knowing how you all think."

Luther momentarily looked over at the Captain and then back at the road. "There's Mr. Rosewood's Funeral Parlor up there on the right. Let's pray he'll be thinking the right way." He pulled up along the side of the street right in front of the funeral parlor. "Come on, Captain, let's see if we can get this done." He climbed out of the car as did Captain Townsend, and the two men hurried to the front door.

Luther grabbed the doorknob and turned it. It didn't open. "Damn, they got it locked," Luther rasped. "Probably most businesses this close to the riot area are closed."

"Massacre." Captain reminded him.

"You're not going to let this go, are you Captain?"

"Not anytime soon. Your son lives; mine is dead."

"I'm doing my best." Luther's tone was contrite. "They're probably in the back in the living quarters." He briskly walked off the porch to the side and toward the back.

Captain strained to keep up with the young man. His legs were weak and tired. "You think it's safe to be going to the back of the house?" he asked. "Especially when they're not expecting anyone to show up at their back door."

"We don't have much of a choice," Luther rejoined. He reached the back door, momentarily looked at the Captain and knocked. Captain came up and stood next to him.

"I'd pray, but I don't believe God wants to get involved in this mess. He's probably angry with all of us," Captain Townsend lamented.

"Who is it and what do you want?" A voice sounded off from the other side of the door.

"We're here for Doctor Jackson," Luther answered. "He's been shot and killed in the riot. They've burned down the nig... Negro mortuary. We had to bring his body here; otherwise the mob would've dumped it in the Arkansas River."

367

"The surgeon, Doctor Jackson?"

"Yes, sir, the surgeon. His father, Captain Townsend Jackson is out here with me."

"Who are you?"

"Name is Luther. I'm a white man trying to make sure Doctor Jackson gets a decent burial. He saved my son's life, and I'm beholden to him."

The two men waited for someone to speak up or hopefully open the door. To Captain Townsend it was the most anxious moments he had experienced since the death of Sophorina.

"I don't think they're going to help us," Luther finally said. "Let's get out of here before they shoot us."

"No, they have to help us," Captain shouted. He raised his fist, intent to bang on the door, but before he did, the door swung open, and Harold Rosewood stood in the doorway with his rifle aimed at them.

"Hold up, Mr. Rosewood, don't shoot," Luther pleaded.

"Where's the doctor's body?" Rosewood asked.

"It's in the car out front," Captain Townsend said with anxiety in his words. The man was going to help, he thought.

"Captain Townsend Jackson, you come on inside," Rosewood instructed. "You go get the body," he continued looking directly at Luther. "My boy will meet you out front to help bring the doctor inside. I will not have a fine gentleman like the Captain carrying his son's body. He has suffered enough indignities as it is."

"Yes sir," Luther exclaimed with joy. "I'll meet him at the car." He took off running around the side of the house.

"Come on inside my home," Rosewood said. "This is a fine mess we have in this city. But you must know there are a lot of good white Tulsans who do not condone the actions of the riff raff."

"Thank you for accommodating an old man's wishes," Captain Townsend said as he walked through Rosewood's back entrance.

368

"You're not old; you're wise." Rosewood closed the door, and the two men walked toward the front of the house. "I promise you sir, I will take care of your son and keep him safe until this evil is over and you can dignify his life with a dignified burial."

"Thank you." Tears filled the Captain's eyes for the second time that evening.

"And I insist you accept the comfort of my home until it is safe for you to go back out. I understand they have been incarcerating all our fine Negro citizens just like they are prisoners in their own city. I will not let that happen to you."

"And the young man with me?"

"He'll be all right. After he gets the body inside, he can just leave the car out front and go on home. They're not bothering white people. Just your people."

"Isn't that always the case?"

"I'm afraid so. This is not a perfect world, Captain. But I'll do my best to make up for the inequities."

"Again, thank you. That's all a man can ask for."

They both watched as the two young men carried Doctor Jackson's body into the back area where he would be dignified with proper preparation for burial. And given the circumstances, that's all Captain Townsend Jackson could expect.

FORTY•SEVEN

"It's all over, sir," the lieutenant reported to General Barrett as they stood in the hotel suite set up as the command post.

The general walked over and looked out the window and was taken by the orange colored sky that penetrated the darkness of the night. The fires continued to burn while smoke and ashes blew into South Tulsa and covered the streets and trees.

"All the fighting has stopped?" he asked, then looked over at Mayor Evans and Chief Gustafson in the room with them

"Yes, sir, all the fighting has stopped. The prisoners have been taken to the convention hall and the ballpark. They are filled to capacity. Many of the Negroes escaped into the woods, and we didn't pursue them."

"Why not?" Gustafson asked.

"Because that was not part of my orders to them," General Barrett shot back with irritation. "How many prisoners you think you have?"

"I'd say a good four to five thousand. We got men, women and children."

"Good job, lieutenant," General Barrett said. "Any idea of the number of dead, both white and Negroes?"

"Don't know right now, but a hell of a lot more Negroes than whites."

"Good, that's the way it should be," Gustafson again interjected his opinion.

"Will you please shut up," Mayor Evans blurted.

"Thank you, Mayor," Barrett said. "You saved me from

having to say that." He then moved in closer to Gustafson. "Do you realize the mess you helped create in this town? Every major news outlet in this country is going to have reporters here covering this tragedy. You'd better come up with better answers than just to sound elated that more Negroes than whites died."

"What is wrong with you people?" Gustafson fired back. "You act like you're sorry we finally got rid of the hell hole in niggertown and run off or killed all them bad coons that rape, steal and sometimes kill white people."

"You idiot," General Barrett shouted. "You all didn't just kill the bad niggers You slaughtered good people, even some children from all accounts. My Jesus, you've burnt down the entire Negro section of the city. This was vigilante terrorism at its worst. And from what I understand, you deputized these maniacs. You tainted the good name of law enforcement, and if I have my way, you're going to pay. Now get your sorry ass out of my command post."

The lieutenant walked up next to Gustafson and grabbed his arm. "Let's go," he said. The two walked out of the room, closing the door behind them.

"There will undoubtedly be a Grand Jury hearing into the causes of this disaster," General Barrett snarled. "I plan to testify that Chief Gustafson was a co-conspirator in this riot because of his failure to squash it before it got out of hand. We have to make an example of him. You don't abuse law enforcement authority the way he has here in Tulsa."

"You get no argument from me," Mayor Evans said. "I'm sure the finger of guilt is going to be pointing at a whole lot of people, including the entire lot of people on the other side of the tracks."

372   "My orders from the governor is to keep the city under martial law, and for my men to guard the camps until we are absolutely certain that the violence has ended."

"The good citizens of Tulsa wouldn't want it any other way," Evans exclaimed. "However long it takes, we support your efforts and your work."

"As well as our orders," General Barrett added. "Now I think it's time for us to visit those camps and make sure the Negroes are at least being treated decently."

***

Gurley found shelter under the grandstand at McNulty Park as the rain poured down on the thousands of others stranded in the middle of the playing field. The morning was dark and dismal. But the reality of what had just happened a little over twenty-four hours ago made the darkness insignificant. They shot Emma for no apparent reason other than she was a Negro. They arrested him for the same weak reason. And they burnt down his hotel and all other businesses, again for the identical reason. He never realized that people's hatred for others could run that deep.

His eyes surveyed the field, concentrating on the many women who were trying to shelter their babies. White babies, he thought, were not suffering the same inconvenience. They were home under the protective roof and sheltered only by the color of their skin. All along, he'd believed the great leader, Booker T. Washington, when he preached to the race that hard work, obedience to the law, belief in the dignity of the country's values and trust in God is all the Negro needed to prosper in this country. But those babies out in the middle of the field, unprotected from rain and now homeless were proof that it was all a lie.

Gurley flinched as he felt a hand on his shoulder. He turned and stood directly in front of Barney Cleaver, dressed in his deputy sheriff uniform. He noticed the gun snugly tucked in the holster. Evidently, he hadn't been arrested like the rest of the Negroes.

"You must be the only free Negro in all of Tulsa County," Gurley chortled as the two men hugged.

"Not quite," Cleaver rejoined. "You're going to be free also. I came to get you out of here and take you to see Emma." 373

"Where is she?"

"At Booker T. Washington High School and doing quite well. The bullet only grazed her."

Gurley extended his arm and pointed out at the playing field. "What have we done?" he asked.

"We didn't do anything," Cleaver quickly responded. "It was the trouble makers, the men that followed Du Bois's guidance and believed they could actually fight back with guns."

"That day back in March, we predicted this would happen when they agreed to bring him here," Gurley said.

"And the worst part is that the trouble makers all got away. They're long gone."

"All of them are gone?"

"From what I understand. Smitherman and Stradford both left town, and the veteran O.B. Mann escaped out into the woods along with Peg Leg Taylor."

The rain continued to fall heavily. "You think we'll get enough rain to put out all the fires?" Gurley asked.

"That's the only way other than burning off over time, because the fire department has refused to get involved." Cleaver paused momentarily and then continued. "They killed Doctor Jackson yesterday in front of his home. His body disappeared, and nobody has seen or heard from his daddy."

Gurley smiled. "That old warrior is fine. He probably found a way to get his son's body and himself out of Tulsa. Probably on their way to Guthrie to bury his son up there next to Sophorina."

The two men stopped talking and gazed out on the field at the rain beating down on thousands of men, women, children and babies. "They are the real victims but nobody really cares," Gurley lamented.

"You don't have time for that, Mr. Gurley. Let me get you out of here and to your wife." Cleaver took the old man by his arm, and they walked toward the exit.

374　　　"And nobody really cares," Gurley mumbled as he walked out of the park and back into freedom.

Epilogue

April 20, 2000

She sat in her favorite old rocking chair staring at a repeat of *The Bill Cosby Show*. A smile covered her face as she watched the two daughters arguing over something relatively unimportant. It reminded her of years past when she and her two girl friends would fuss with each other. That was seventy-nine-years ago when she was only seventeen, full of life, young and without a worry in the world. She only wanted to attend her prom with her boyfriend, Verby. Of course, he couldn't come to the house and pick her up 'cause Poppa wouldn't have that. Veneice still felt the sting of disappointment that had gripped her body that morning when Ruth said the world was coming to an end, and Esther tried to run home to be with her parents, but Poppa wouldn't let her because it was too dangerous.

Usually by sunset Veneice would be in her old housecoat, preparing for bed. But this was to be a very special occasion, and instead of wearing the nightclothes, she felt alive and full of vigor in the blue dress, with a gold bracelet, gold earrings, and blue shoes. She was stepping out for the night with the young people. It was prom night at Booker T. Washington High School, and she had received a special invitation from the senior class to be their guest and experience what she was denied those seventy-nine-years ago. Veneice knew it wouldn't be the same; nothing could replace what she was denied, especially the chance to dance into the night with Verby. But at ninety-four, she appreciated the children thinking of a very old lady who experienced a lot of life and had been blessed with years beyond what she expected. Both Ruth and Esther had gone on to glory, as had her sister Olivia, momma and poppa. She had married once but divorced early, never married again and did not have any children. So whenever it was her time to leave this side of Jordan, all her memories would go with her.

375

Veneice still talked with Mabel Little, who was 103 and still bitter about the massacre of 1921. What hurt her most was not the loss of her businesses, but the loss of Pressley who died nine years later. Mabel sincerely believed that he died because white folks were so hateful, and that they owed a lot to the descendants of the Negroes who had lost everything they owned. Veneice didn't feel that way about white folks and didn't believe that money could make up for what she lost that day in 1921. Money or property could never replace the memories she was denied, memories of dancing in her blue dress with her boyfriend Verby.

Veneice always thought it interesting that back then she felt like a child in the presence of Mabel, but now the age difference didn't matter. They were equals in the spiritual, not physical journey of life. What mattered most to them was that spiritual trip they both knew wasn't far away.

Veneice glanced over at the clock. A little past seven, and the limousine would be there to pick her up at seven-thirty. She needed to pray before she left. Veneice turned off the television with the remote, closed her eyes and asked God to make this night as close as possible to what she would have experienced on June 1, 1921, in the ballroom at the Stradford Hotel.

Postscript

On June 9, 1921, Governor James Robertson ordered a grand jury investigation into the causes of the riot. After a week of hearings the grand jury returned fifty-seven indictments against Black Americans. Tulsa Police Chief John Gustafson was also indicted. Dick Rowland was charged with aggravated assault of a white woman, even though Sarah Page refused to cooperate with the hearing. Both John Stradford and Andrew Smitherman were listed as the main perpetrators of the riot and O.B. Mann was also indicted. Gustafson was the only person to be tried and convicted on a charge for failing to take necessary action to prevent the riot from escalating to violence. Over time, all the indictments against the Blacks were dropped.

Dick Rowland had been taken to Kansas City, Missouri, for safety reasons by Sheriff McCullough. He was one of the fifty-seven Blacks indicted by a grand jury He took up residence there, returning to Tulsa only one time to visit Aunt Damie. He told her that Sarah Page had also moved to Kansas City after the riot and that they saw a great deal of each other. He finally tired of her and moved to Portland, Oregon where he went to work on the docks. Sarah Page did not go with him. Sometime in the 1960's, Dick was accidentally killed while working on the docks.

John Stradford finally ended up in Chicago, Illinois where his son lived. He tried a number of businesses there but finally gave up when none of them were as successful as his businesses in Tulsa. He died in 1935 in Chicago. He never did return to Tulsa.

Andrew Smitherman made it all the way to Rochester, New York where he tried his hand at starting a newspaper, but was not as successful as he was in Tulsa. He never returned to Tulsa. He did write and publish a poem about the Tulsa Riot of 1921.

O. W. Gurley remained in Tulsa and became the state's star witness in the indictment of Stradford, Smitherman, and O. B. Mann. Because of his perceived treachery, he was labeled a traitor. He finally moved to Los Angeles, California where he died.

O. B. Mann went all the way to Toronto, Canada, but once the indictment was dropped against him and the others, he returned to Tulsa and helped run his brother's grocery store. He died of cancer in the 1940's. O. B. became somewhat of a legend in north Tulsa because of his strong stand against lynching.

Lloyd Jones continued operating the *Tulsa Tribune* until his death at ninety in 1963. The June 2, 1971 edition of the *Tribune* was dedicated to the Fiftieth Anniversary of the riot. Under the ownership of his two sons, the paper portrayed Jones as the one person who pleaded for peace and harmony before the riot. However, the editorial page of the May 31, 1921 edition of the paper had been removed and has never been recovered.

Sarah Page remained steadfast in her refusal to testify or press charges against Dick Rowland. She did move back to Kansas City and, according to Dick they spent a great deal of time together. However, he did not take her with him when he moved to Portland, Oregon. Her final whereabouts was not known.

Damie Rowland continued to live in the Greenwood section of Tulsa, Oklahoma. She managed to rebuild her boarding house right on Archer Street and lived there until her death sometime in the 1970's.

PLEASE FEEL FREE TO SHARE YOUR COMMENTS WITH THE
AUTHOR, FREDERICK WILLIAMS, REGARDING HIS FICTIONALIZED
VERSION OF THIS ACTUAL TRAGIC EVENT THAT OCCURRED IN AN
AMERICAN CITY IN 1921 AT THE FOLLOWING EMAIL ADDRESS;

fredwilliams@satx.rr.com

ALSO BY FREDERICK WILLIAMS

The Nomination

Beyond Redemption

Just Loving You

Black is the Color of Love

23.99

OCT 1 9 2018

CPSIA information can be obtained
at www.ICGtesting.com
Printed in the USA
BVOW03s0812091116
467333BV00001B/12/P

9 780970 995766